ENTER WILDTHYME

PAUL MAGRS

First edition

Proudly published in 2011 by
Snowbooks Ltd.
www.snowbooks.com

ISBN13 Library Hardback: 978-1907777-04-2
ISBN13 Paperback: 978-1907777-05-9
ISBN13 Digital edition: 978-1907777-46-2

A catalogue record for this book is available from the
British Library.

For Jamie Griffiths

PROLOGUE

The worlds and times visited by the old boiler were usually fully aware of the fact when the *Begins at Home* clanked and shuddered into their orbit. The ramshackle ship wasn't known for her subtlety or stealth. But then, why should she be? Ordinarily she had no reason to keep her ungainly green self out of sight. Her crew wasn't given to sneaking up on people and they had no enemies either. Or so they thought.

Earth was a different matter. Earth was known for being rather self-absorbed and inwardly-focused. When the *Begins at Home* heaved herself into the upper reaches of its atmosphere only a very few human beings were alert to her presence.

And most of those were in Darlington, which is a small market town in the North of England.

One of these on-the-ball individuals managed to sneak himself aboard the *Begins at Home*. This was something he shouldn't have been able to do.

Somehow, impossibly, the man with two plastic arms stole aboard the ship and started poking around. The ship's crew was quite unaware that any of this was going on. They were too busy staring at the soapy clouds wreathing the fabulous blue Earth and dreaming of all the loot down there.

This makes the crew sound rather like pirates, but they weren't – as the man with two plastic arms knew well. These people were simply collecting for charity.

It was a long time since he had been anywhere near a spacecraft and he dawdled a little, even though he knew time was short. He slipped into the shadows of the cluttered ship and peered into holds and storerooms. He picked over mounds of objects and art works from a hundred worlds. He pondered over bric-a-brac and rummaged through jumble.

Times were obviously hard out there in Space and Time, he mused. The *Begins at Home* had a rather shoddy supply of goods. Were people less generous these days? Was the universe rather poorer since he had last seen it?

He knew, however, that the object he sought was here, somewhere.

The Objet D'Oom – as it was called in some of the most melodramatic tales – had escaped from its home world, in the unfathomable reaches of Space and Time. And it was down to him – a man called Terrance – to retrieve it.

His plastic limbs trembled as he entered a certain room, deep inside the ship. Were his fingers tingling? They shouldn't be. They couldn't. He had no sensation in those rubber exiguities, naturally.

Yet they were. Just as they had, years ago, far from here. They had tingled like this, the *first* time he had stolen the Objet D'Oom.

And here it was. Perched on a metal counter with a whole heap of other worthless tat. In between statuettes and broken lamps and a cloak made from the hide of some unidentifiable creature. There was a thick-sided glass jar waiting for him. Its molten contents were dark and all he could see when he held it up into the light were tiny bubbles suspended within.

But he knew this was what he was after. He had it in his hands again. Being close to it, touching it, brought life into his artificial limbs. The sensation was wonderful and it made his old heart beat harder.

Because he believed in the idea of fair exchange, he produced from his burglar's sack three very expensive books from his collection on Earth. They were several hundred years old and of obvious worth. He laid them carefully on the bench where the glass jar had stood. Then he stowed the jar away in his bag and prepared to return home. The journey was quite arduous and hair-raising for one of his advanced years. It involved being quite literally discombobulated.

As he turned to go he felt a sudden violent impact and was almost knocked off his feet.

Immediately warning lights were going off and an outraged klaxon wailed throughout the *Begins at Home*. There were running feet pounding on metal walkways somewhere close at hand and voices were crying out in shock and dismay.

Terrance froze. He'd been rumbled! They'd caught him. He knew they were a peaceful people. Decent sorts. They wouldn't kill him out of hand. But he hadn't reckoned on being nabbed. He clutched his bag of loot closely to his chest.

The footsteps kept on thundering, the yelling grew closer and then further away. The noise increased in pitch. There was panic in the air and then – laser bolts being fired. The *Begins at Home* lurched like she'd been stabbed.

Someone or something was invading. They had broken into the ship and there was a battle going on, somewhere on the levels above his head. The whole place was ringing and pounding with sudden violence. He knew the peaceful crew didn't stand a chance.

There was nothing he could do to save them. He listened to their screams and wished he could be of more use. But he knew that the best thing he could do was simply to get the Objet D'Oom out of here. Obviously these invaders knew its secret too. They were after it as well, but had gone about getting it in a more forthright fashion.

He couldn't let this thing fall into the wrong hands. This slippery, precious thing and the life it contained.

As he stood there, listening to the sounds of death and mayhem, he had his finger on the button of the transmat device. It would whistle him away to safety. Back to his dusty shop in Darlington. He'd be in his familiar sitting room and in an instant all this would seem like a dream.

If he looked out of the dormer window through his telescope he might see something. The pinprick flashes and sparkles of a space battle up here, in Earth's junkyard. Aliens killing aliens and only a handful of humans knowing anything about it.

He was about to press the button when a younger member of the crew came tearing into the store room. He was a thin, blue-skinned boy, who stopped and stared in amazement at the man with two plastic hands.

'They're killing everyone,' said the boy. 'They're after something.'

The thief knew many languages and he nodded at the boy's words. 'I have to go. I'm sorry.'

'Who are you?' demanded the boy. He limped across the room towards him.

'That doesn't matter,' said Terrance. 'Look, you've got things here... it wouldn't do if they fell into the wrong hands.'

'I know,' said the crewman. 'I've come here to sort that. To get rid of this stuff...'

'Good.' The thief turned to go. 'Look, I can get you away from here. I can save just one of you, take you to Earth...'

The boy looked appalled. 'No! Why would I leave them? I won't go with you... I don't even know who you are...'

'You're right,' said the man. 'But they'll kill you. They'll kill the whole lot of you. They're looking for the same thing as I was. But they'll show no mercy.'

The boy's eyes were wide with shock and fear. 'What did we ever do to anyone? We were just collecting... just trying to do some good...'

'I know,' said Terrance.

There was more noise. Coming closer. Clanking and banging as doors were thrust open. The scrabbling of claws. The thudding footfalls. The hooting and barking of creatures who enjoyed dispensing violent death.

'Come with me,' Terrance told the boy again.

The alien shook his head. 'No. I must get rid of this stuff... despatch it into that world's atmosphere... before they come...'

'I've already taken what they're after,' said the man with two plastic arms. 'Are you sure you won't come with me?'

'No!' shouted the boy. 'I must stay here!'

He watched the man turn away and slowly disappear in a golden shimmer of noise.

What did he mean, he'd already taken what the intruders were after?

But there was no time to figure it out. The boy started to gather up the artefacts on the table before him. Everything in this room came from a certain planet, the name of which the invaders had barked at him and the rest of the crew. They wanted everything they had picked up from that world.

And here it all was. Busily, he bundled everything he saw together and made preparations for jettisoning the whole lot through waste disposal into the curdled atmosphere of the world below.

The dogs were coming closer with every passing second. He could hear them. Yelping and bellowing in the grimy confines of the old ship.

It made the boy feel perversely pleased in a way, that his final act in this life was to be dispensing gifts like this. Old, bizarre, unwanted rubbish perhaps – but gifts nonetheless.

Presents flung down to Earth with all his might from his place aboard the helpless and doomed *Begins at Home*.

CHAPTER ONE

The railway station was an old one, cavernous and noisy. Kelly stood self-consciously by the platform, hoping he wouldn't think she'd dressed up especially smart or anything in order to meet him. Her new hairdo was being blown all over the place by the air rushing through the sooty arches.

So Simon was coming back. He'd been away over four years, was it? Away at university, like he always said he would.

Would he be coming back home like a whole new person? Maybe she wouldn't even recognise him now. So much would have changed for him.

She had brought him a present. Something unusual. She was clutching it tightly as the train arrived and she felt herself getting even more anxious. Not just about recognising him or the awkwardness of meeting again, or even worrying that they would still get on.

Kelly was worried that Simon might have changed his mind. That could have happened, in just the time since their recent phone call and him making the journey back north.

He could have decided that it was all just a terrible idea.

And really, why had he even given agreed to the plan? He had nothing to tie him to this place anymore. Just fond memories, maybe. Nothing really palpable. His parents were dead and, in more recent years, the grandparents he had lived with in his teenage years had gone as well. He hardly had any friends here either – just Kelly – with whom he had enjoyed a sporadic email correspondence. She was his last link with the north, and maybe that wasn't enough to draw him back this way for good.

She had been so pleased (Admit it, she told herself) when he had said – impulsively – yes, he would come back.

He would come and take over running the shop. He would do his duty and hold the fort.

Now, all of a sudden, here he was. Just about the last one climbing off the train – looking up and down the platform. She felt a stab of affection for him – the slightly feckless way he was looking about – obviously wondering if he'd still recognise Kelly after all this time.

But then he saw her and grinned broadly. Same old Simon. His hair was shorter, tufted up as if he'd been sleeping on it. He was in a sloppy old T-shirt and an unspeakable purple cardigan too small for him, making him look more gangly than ever.

She hugged him and helped him with his bags. Swung one onto her shoulder and led him out of the station. He still smelled the same. The too-sharp cologne boys bought for themselves when they first started shaving. He hadn't changed at all.

'Can we sit down and have a coffee first?' he asked. He wanted to take stock of where he was. To realise properly that he was actually back home. Kelly smiled in agreement, feeling a bit shy as he studied her looks and the garish purple she'd dyed her hair.

'Yeah, it was a bit of a rash decision last night. Purple hair. Like I'm a teenager again.' She laughed at herself, keen for him to see that she could do so nowadays.

In the café they sat and she presented him straight away with his unusual present.

'Well, thanks…' He examined the object. It seemed to be some kind of glass jar. Cool to the touch and heavier than it should be. 'What's in it, jam?'

'It won't open, you needn't try! It could be anything. It's pretty old.'

'Where did you get it?'

'It was left for you. With the note.'

Ah yes. The note. The whole reason for his being here. Terrance's note, calling Simon back to the north. Calling for Simon to come and mind the shop. She had read it down the phone to him like it was a call to arms and Simon had complied. Here he was.

He held the jar up to the window so that it lit up a brilliant, jewel-like scarlet. On closer inspection the glass was bumpy and extra thick. Something about the object made him shiver.

'So, Terrance called me all the way back home, where I haven't been in years – in order to look after his business for him – and to give me a jar of jam?'

Kelly shrugged, stirring her cappuccino froth around. 'None of it makes any sense. But nothing ever did with Terrance, did it?' She smiled fondly at the thought of her old boss. For seven years – ever since her late teens – Kelly had helped out behind the counter at the Great Big Book Exchange on the insalubrious South Road here in Darlington. She could hardly remember a time when she hadn't spent a good portion of her week in the company of Terrance inside that labyrinthine and slightly musty shop.

Simon said, 'And there's still no word from him?'

She shook her head quickly. 'It's been over a fortnight.'

'What do the police say?'

'I haven't called them. This was deliberate on Terrance's part. He was getting out of town, away from here… He's never left the shop for years and maybe he thought it was about time he went somewhere else. I've never known him go anywhere else all the time I've worked for him.'

'And what do you think this is that he left for me? Some kind of heirloom? A paperweight?'

She looked at him and shrugged. Kelly had no idea what that jar was supposed to be for. 'All I know is that it's impossible to open. And something about it makes me feel you shouldn't even try.'

'So you've tried to open it, then?' he smiled at her.

She changed the subject brightly, and found she was taking on a patronising tone. 'So, the Exchange is yours, Simon. After all these years. Your favourite bookshop in the whole world. That's assuming it still *is* your favourite. Can you believe it? Could you ever have imagined it – back when you were a spotty sixteen year old and you first ventured inside…?'

He coughed. 'I was never a spotty sixteen year old..!'

She pictured him as he was then. A shy and quiet kid, coming in with his Grandma – both of them shopping for paperbacks on a Saturday afternoon. Sheltering from the rain on the sleazy South Road. They had been overawed by the musty confines of the Exchange and the endless cram-packed shelves. Kelly had been sitting at the cash desk – proud of her status there, at eighteen, as the owner's right hand girl.

'Now you're the prince in waiting,' she told Simon.

'But it should have been you,' he protested. 'Why couldn't Terrance have just given it over to you? You've run the place for years…'

She shrugged. She was keen to let him see that she wasn't bothered. And she wasn't. Possessions and status and stuff really didn't mean that much to her. If Terrance wanted to give Simon the shop – and leave her out of it – that was fine. It was his choice, after all.

'I don't want to be lumbered with a business,' she said. 'You know me, I'm a free spirit. I don't know what I want to do yet with my life – who knows where I'll be in a year's time, eh?'

He smiled – though he thought: she's still in the same place she's always been. She's in the same town, doing the same things. It's me who's been away and done something a bit different.

But now he was back. And about to have his own bookstore to run. The Great Big Book Exchange was his now.

*

As they walked into town together the sights and smells of the place were coming back to him full force. The brightness of the air in autumn seemed wonderfully familiar, as did the rows of shops, the old church and the Victorian indoor market. It was all inviting, and even quaint. Then he felt a bit panicked – was he coming back here to settle down? Was this him stuck here now?

He and Kelly chattered away inconsequentially past the shops. The main street was now pedestrianized, several shops had changed and he could see that in his absence the old town had changed quite a bit. They walked up South Road and the place looked dowdier and even more run-down than ever. As the cold breeze bowled them along Kelly was telling Simon about something else new: her poetry group at the Arts Centre on Vane Terrace.

'Poetry..?' he said. 'You never used to write poetry.'

'I just started recently. I've no idea where it all came from. But I suddenly got the urge. And I like going to the group, actually. It's a good crowd. Honestly. You'll like them.'

'Will I?' he pulled a face at her. The old Kelly used to go round saying nothing decent had been written by anyone since at least the death of Virginia Woolf.

'You'll come along tonight, won't you, to the Arts Centre?' she asked. 'For my… reading?'

He was surprised to be asked, in a way. He couldn't imagine the Kelly of old getting up on a stage in front of an audience to read out poems. The old Kelly had been self-protective and almost belligerently private about everything.

'Yes, yes of course…' he agreed.

She nodded, trying not to look too pleased.

But now he was keen to see the shop again. The Exchange. Only when he was there, breathing in that strange scent of compounded spices – nutmeg, cloves, cinnamon, mixed with tobacco and coffee grounds and whisky – only then would he really understand and start to believe that he really was back.

She let him become reacquainted with the place and watched as he moved from room to booklined room, soaking up that curiously unchanging atmosphere. She showed him to the flat upstairs, where he had never been before. This was his now, this two bedroomed flat where Terrance had eked out his solitary existence for all those years. Up here it was obvious to see that Terrance had left and had no intention of returning. Only the bare bones of his furniture and belongings remained: a faded green velour settee, a rack of chipped mugs.

'So where would he go to?'

'He didn't have any family, or anyone else…'

Simon was reminded of cats, going off alone to die somewhere. Taking their injured pride and retreating to where they wouldn't disturb anyone else with their passing.

Another part of Simon was thrilled at simply being given this shop and this flat. All at once he felt right here. As if this place had been the centre of his world all along and he just belonged here. He should have known that this shabby address on the South Road would be the place for him, after all.

Kelly watched him drift from room to room and she put the kettle on. She'd brought enough supplies for him to have some coffee. The machine up here was a sophisticated, futuristic one, just as in the Exchange below. Then she told Simon she would leave him for a while, to settle in.

His heart leapt a bit, at the thought of being alone inside the labyrinth of books. Now it really hit him that this was all his.

She smiled at him wryly, as if she knew exactly what he was thinking. She understood how incoherent his head was and how he was all over the place. She had known him since he was sixteen. Nearly ten years now. She just understood him.

They made arrangements for this evening. Really, he could have done with unpacking and trying to get his bearings. He could do with settling in. But the look on Kelly's face – a twinge of nervousness, was it? - told him that he really ought to be there tonight. To see her read at the Arts Centre with her group.

'I never thought you'd end up writing poetry…'

'I used to look at all the books in this building… and wonder how on Earth anyone could write any more. There seemed so many. How would you even start?' She shrugged lightly. 'I enjoy it. It's a good group of women. And we go to the bar afterwards. Friday nights. It's good.'

He understood. And he supposed that finding things to do here, fashioning a life in this town – they were things he would have to do, too. He had to settle into a routine and a life of his own.

There was no question in Simon's mind that he was staying here.

The Exchange was his.

For much of the afternoon he forgot about his unpacking and the desolate flat upstairs. He sat instead at the cash desk of the Exchange and imagined himself lord of all he surveyed. All these books. Every speck of dust. Every shining mote spinning through the lazy amber air of the late afternoon.

It was quite silent in the Exchange. There was a curious sense of calm. As if the whole place existed in a golden moment that went on forever. Or as if everything was holding its breath... in anticipation of something that was about to begin...

CHAPTER TWO

Anthony Marvelle came crashing into the shop, pinging the bell and grimacing. His sharp nose thrust ahead questingly as he stormed into the Exchange. He dragged behind him a cross-looking poodle. Dyed-pink pompoms jostled as its feet slid daintily on the bare wooden boards.

Simon jolted in his seat at the desk. He had been drifting off into sleep, sitting there, letting everything catch up with him. He frowned at the elegant, angular man in the dark suit and skinny black jeans. He stared at the haughty-looking dog, which appeared to be wearing some kind of bootees knitted out of spangly mohair.

The man with the flowing golden locks seemed vaguely familiar. When he spoke his voice was cultivated, raspy and tended to tail away at the end of sentences into a seductive murmur. He came up to the desk before talking and Simon found himself having to draw closer to listen to what he had to say.

'I know it says 'closed' on your sign outside but I thought I would try anyway, you see… murmur murmur.'

Simon frowned. He felt bleary. 'I beg your pardon?'

'Murmur murmur… some days in the north and I despaired of finding a decent bookshop of any kind and now I happen to stray upon… murmur murmur…'

It was no good. The man mumbled too much. It was like he was purring at Simon. He rumbled with words. Thrummed with them. Simon sat up straighter in his chair and gazed up at the craggy face, the yellowy locks. The man was attractive for an older bloke, sure. But there was something else. An aura. He was someone well-known, wasn't he? Someone Simon recognised.

The poodle had seated itself as far away as its leash would allow. It was gazing at the spines of books closest to the ground on the pine shelves.

'Murmur… pretty little object, hm? What might this little bauble be… murmur murmur…?'

Simon glanced sharply and saw that the dapper man had picked something up off the cash desk. He was holding it up to the light and examining it intently.

'Murmur?'

It was the jar Kelly had given him. Simon had lost track of it in all the excitement of returning to the shop. She must have left it on the desk for him, where it looked like something he might use as a paperweight. And perhaps that's what it was, just as he'd suspected. An exotic kind of paperweight. But now this stranger was staring at it and there was a glint of avarice in his grey eyes.

He was handsome, Simon thought. And that murmuring thing was pretty effective too, in the way it drew you in and made you hang onto his every word.

The man was looking at him with an eyebrow raised. He must have asked a question.

'I'm sorry?'

'How much… murmur murmur?'

'Oh! That's not for sale…'

The man frowned. 'Are you sure?'

'Very. It's a present. I've just been given it, today in fact.'

'It's very pretty. It's caught my eye. I'm used to getting things that catch my… mumble murmur.'

Simon swallowed. Oh, he was a right old charmer. What would he be prepared to pay, Simon wondered. By the look of that suit he was worth a bob or two... But, no. He shouldn't even think it. That jar thing was a present from Terrance and part of his strange inheritance. Kelly would be mortified if she found out he'd flogged it, as soon as her back was turned.

'I'm sorry,' Simon told the man steadfastly.

The poodle had stopped studying the shelves and was watching the humans now. It gave an interrogative whine.

The man sighed. His expression was rueful. Amused at his own defeat. He shrugged. 'All right. I know when I'm beaten... murmur murmur.'

Simon nodded and watched the man drift off to look at some shelves. He went to see the books that his dog had been looking at, closest to the floor. Obviously he was some rich kind of eccentric. Some loopy posh bloke. He smelled deliciously of lemon and verbena cologne. Simon breathed it in as he grappled with the chrome fixings of the coffee machine. He had his first customer in this new era at the Exchange! He had to get the coffee flowing! He had to do his job!

The man was murmuring to himself, drifting along the shelves. He had gone into that slow, delicious trance of the true book addict. Simon saw that he was falling for the ambience of the Exchange, as most new visitors tended to do.

Simon just wished he could remember who the bloke was and why he felt he recognised him. He was grinding coffee beans noisily when it came to him.

He turned around. 'Hey, you're Anthony Marvelle, aren't you? The poet fella?'

But the poet and his snooty poodle were both gone. The door was still closing gently on their heels.

Simon thought that was a bit rude. Whizzing off without saying goodbye, let alone buying anything.

Then he glanced at the cash desk and saw that the glass paperweight was gone as well.

*

Simon dressed up in his best shirt and least wrecked jeans for the evening. He had even hunted around in Terrance's flat for the iron. All the while he was stewing over the obvious, blatant theft of his precious glass jar. He mustn't tell Kelly he'd been so careless. It wouldn't be a good way to set off on this next phase of their friendship.

He left all the lights on in the Exchange and, as he went around securing and locking up the place, it hit him that he was responsible now, for maintaining this place and keeping it safe.

As he walked into town and across the corner of the park, towards the old Victorian terraces, he was thinking about Kelly and how, really, she'd had every right to presume that she herself might have been heir to the Exchange. And yet she was so sanguine about how things had worked out. She had seemed genuinely pleased about Simon's good fortune.

She had given him her new address. She had moved into a basement flat in one of the tall, pointed houses, not too far from the Arts Centre on Vane Terrace, their destination this evening. He knocked and came in for a bit, and saw that she'd gone a bit hippyish in her tastes. There were ethnic artefacts and wall-hangings about the place. It looked very much like a student flat, he thought, and realised that he didn't actually know if Kelly had ever managed to get into the college she had planned to. He hadn't kept abreast with all her plans, after all.

She was nervous. That surprised him. She was in an obviously new outfit – some kind of grannyish dress with a turban keeping her hair together – and she had the jitters.

'I've never read my work out in public before…'

Her work! He thought. She was taking it all dead seriously, then. Calling it 'her work.'

She had a folder tucked under her arm as she led them back into the hallway of the main house and locked her flat. She explained that the house was owned by one of her fellow group members, who was already at the venue, being in charge of it all. Then she took several deep breaths before they set off into the leafy street.

'Fancy you being a poet now,' he shook his head.

'Well, I'm not really. I like the group. And it's part of the bargain – we all read. We're all in a team together. We all get up there to celebrate the end of the literature festival that's been on this week…'

Now they were ducking through the traffic and into the small park, where the sycamores had turned colour and the ground was mulchy and springy with helicopters and orange leaves. Simon was about to ask another question about the workshop when he noticed a double decker bus parked at the kerb nearest them.

'What's that doing there?'

It was a bright red double decker. A Routemaster of the kind you once saw down in London, but not here. He squinted and moved to where he could see the front. Sure enough, its sign proclaimed that it was the Number 22 to Putney Common.

'That's a bit weird,' he said.

Kelly shrugged, her mind still on poetry and reading aloud in front of an audience. 'Maybe there's some loony collector…'

'There are curtains hanging up at most of the windows. Chintz.'

'New Age travellers,' Kelly said. 'That's what it'll be. They've clubbed together to buy a decommissioned bus.' She grinned. 'Can you imagine? Wouldn't that be great? You could set off and go anywhere in the world in your double decker bus…'

'Still seems a bit weird,' Simon said. 'Just sitting here in Darlington.'

He didn't know why, but that inscrutable bus was giving him a rather strange feeling. A bubbling sensation in his stomach. A tingle of apprehension all over his skin. What was that about? What was he sensing? He shivered and realised what it was he was feeling.

Excitement. Yes, it was a pleasurable feeling of excitement. Something was coming his way…

Then they were crossing the street again, Kelly looking absolutely terrified as they passed the water sculpture at the front of the Victorian building that housed the Arts Centre. She suggested a drink at the bar, before they went to meet the rest of her poetry workshop group.

The bar was at the very front of the building and Simon sidled up happily, noting all the fancy refurbishments since the last time he was here.

'I wouldn't be so worried,' Kelly was telling him. 'If it wasn't for the fact of Marvelle introducing us. Shall we have Martinis, eh?'

He gulped. 'Marvelle?'

'Oh yeah,' she said. 'This dead posh poet fella. Famous. He's been working with our group on this whole project here, while he's been poet-in-residence. He obviously hates us and our work. He clearly resents the harpies he's had to do all this stuff with. But tonight he's got to get up on that stage and praise us all to the skies!' Kelly laughed. 'He's just a posh git, really.'

Simon found himself saying, 'I met him. Just today.' He caught the barmaid's eye and asked for their drinks. There was a whole menu of different kinds of Martini's. Life in Darlington had certainly moved on.

'You've met him?' Kelly asked.

'He barged his way into the Exchange this afternoon,' Simon told her. 'He wouldn't listen when I said we were shut. He had this ridiculous, fancy looking dog with him.'

'That's Missy,' she tutted. 'He won't go anywhere without that poodle.'

'He was pretty rude,' Simon said. 'And weird, with all of his mumbling.'

'Oh, we have a good laugh about that. He thinks he's so charming… He's tried it on with at least three members of the women's poetry group during this literature festival.'

Simon almost told her that Marvelle had pocketed the paperweight. But he didn't. He bit his tongue.

And just then they were interrupted by a spate of shouting from the other end of the bar.

'What do you mean? That's perfectly good currency, that is!'

It was a raucous voice, verging on the shrill as it became more piqued. It went on…

'It's a Denobian slime dollar, of course! And it's definitely enough to pay my bar bill…!'

Simon glanced along the bar and at first couldn't see the source of all that noise. The queue for drinks was thick by now. People were shuffling and looking at each other, embarrassed by the crazy lady shouting at the other end.

'Poetry nights always bring in the loonies,' Kelly told him.

Just then the crowd cleared a little and Simon saw the most extraordinary woman waving her arms about furiously. She was bundled into a long coat trimmed with tufted green fur and she was jangling with beads and junk jewellery. A ludicrous hat with a floppy brim was perched on her head and her face was set into an expression of deadly pique. 'Just you listen, buster,' she shouted at the barman. 'I'm a special guest here tonight. You can't give me any hassle, you know! I've come a very long way indeed to be here! You've really no idea how far!'

CHAPTER THREE

Kelly was having a closer look at the woman. 'Oh! I think she's one of the other writers-in-residence here this week.'

Simon rolled his eyes. Another poet. And yet he was pleased when Kelly took it into her head to move down the bar and offer to pay for the woman's drink. She always had been impulsive, Kelly. And she was always interested in people who stood out from the crowd.

The bedraggled woman swayed tipsily and grinned at them. Her lipstick was purple and messy, Simon saw. And she had some kind of lilac streaks in her ash blond hair. But her eyes were the blue of faded denim and their gaze was steady and intent.

'Well, thank you, lovey,' she told Kelly, and picked up her gin and tonic as if it was a trophy she had won. 'That's very kind of you indeed. I've seen precious little kindness here in Darlington this week, I must say.'

Kelly introduced herself, and Simon, who found himself smiling awkwardly as the older woman led them back to her table. She had marked her spot by plonking an enormous, battered carpet bag on top of the polished surface. It was a huge thing, crammed with God knows what, and decorated with some strange kind of tapestry map.

'I'm Iris Wildthyme,' the woman grinned. 'Writer, scholar, bon vivant and transtemporal adventuress.' She sipped her drink. 'Though I'm supposed to keep quiet about the 'transtemporal' bit because it's meant to be a secret. I'm here incognito, you know.' She tapped her nose and stared at them beadily.

'Transtemporal?' Simon frowned.

'You *are* a writer!' Kelly said. 'I thought so! I thought I recognised you from the Festival brochure. You're one of the tutors, aren't you?'

'I've been teaching a group of hideous ne'er-do-wells how to write their ghastly novels,' Iris sniffed. 'What a dreadful bunch they gave me! All these funny men. Not a single looker in the bunch! And some of them were so rude to me, wanting to know what I'd published, and who I thought I was to give them advice, since they'd never heard of me. Oh, I've had the most awful week, lovey. I'll be glad to see the back of this place.'

Kelly and Simon exchanged a glance. She was smirking, Simon thought. Pleased with herself for finding another of her 'characters'. This old ratbag was right up Kelly's street, and now they'd be stuck with her all night.

'Oh, I wish I'd been with the poets' group,' Iris went on. 'They seemed like a much better bunch. Better than those stuffy pretentious men with their historical thrillers. Those poetry women looked like a proper laugh.'

Kelly jumped up in her seat. 'But that's me! That's us! I'm with the poetry group! We're reading tonight!'

Iris looked delighted. 'That's you, is it?' She gazed speculatively at Simon. 'And your friend?'

'That's just Simon. He's an old mate. He's just come back to town and he's here to show his support.'

Iris looked him up and down. 'Nice looking boy.'

Kelly burst out, 'Hey, we're having a do afterwards. One of the women in the group – Chelsea – she owns a big house near the park and rents me her basement flat. We're having an end-of-festival celebration. You'll have to come!'

Iris nodded. 'I think I will. Oh, heck – is it in honour of that whatsit? That posh fella? That long streak of foppish piddle, Anthony Marvelle?'

Kelly laughed. 'That's him!'

Iris shuddered. 'He's been mincing about all week like he's cock of the walk. I said to him, what am I? Chopped liver? But *he'd* never heard of me either.'

Simon narrowed his eyes. 'I thought you were meant to be here incognito?'

Iris frowned at him. 'I said incognito – not bloody invisible! Someone ought to teach that Marvelle fella some manners.'

Kelly nodded. 'He's been unbearable all week. A proper diva. You met him as well, didn't you, Simon? He went to Simon's shop this afternoon. But I think Simon thought he was charming, didn't you, pet?'

Simon blushed. Iris tutted. 'Well, maybe I'll come along to this party of yours. After the reading. Yes... hmm... I think that's maybe where I'm meant to be. Where I'm fated to be, if you see what I mean...'

Simon and Kelly didn't follow her at all, but the old woman didn't seem to mind one jot as she necked the rest of her gin.

Simon glanced at his watch. 'Isn't it almost time for the performance?' he asked Kelly, enjoying her sudden look of anguish.

*

Some hours later they were on the Tuscan patio in the back garden of Chelsea's house. Chelsea was the tall and glamorous longest-standing member of the poetry group. Every year she presided over the writing festival's final night party, and it was always at her house.

The house and garden were moodily lit with colourful lanterns. The music was a medley of Sixties tunes. Chelsea's several teenage children were moving about sulkily, acting as waiters and offering the assembled literature freaks profiteroles and wedges of oozing gateau.

Simon felt a little bit out of place, knowing hardly anyone, as he shuffled between the potted plants and the dressed-up guests in the garden. He checked the patio wall for spilled wine and sat where he could see all the goings-on, relaxing at last with a cigarette and a hefty glass of Merlot.

At least the poetry was over for the evening.

Two hours the readings had lasted. From Anthony Marvelle's earnest, hand-wringing, mumbling introduction right through the ten minute slots taken up by each woman in the group. The audience had listened patiently as they read a variety of pieces with a range of success...

Kelly had acquitted herself pretty well, Simon was pleased to discover. Her poems were complicated, somewhat phantasmagorical and utterly bewildering. He didn't have a clue what she had been writing about, which made praising it afterwards a surprisingly simple task. Kelly looked pleased by everything and the two of them had giggled all the way across the park to Chelsea's house. They got a bit hysterical laughing about the strange-looking poet called Carol, who had read out loud some smutty sonnets from her 'erotic sequence' in her 'forthcoming pamphlet.'

Iris was suddenly sitting beside him on the low wall. 'Well, I didn't think it was all that erotic, did you, chuck?' She was guzzling a large glass of pink wine and angling for a light. 'Don't these poets go on a bit, though?'

He laughed and found himself falling into conversation quite easily with her. Next thing he knew he was telling Iris all about his reasons for being back in this town, about the Book Exchange, and the way he had suddenly inherited it from its former owner.

'A man with two plastic arms, you say?' she smiled.

He nodded, wondering whether to down the last mouthful of wine and the gritty bits in the bottom of his glass. 'He was a proper man of mystery, Terrance. No one knew much about him, or why he had two false arms. I never even knew how he managed to cope with those arms of his. And now he's vanished without a trace.'

'And you've got a whole bookshop of your own. I'll have to come round and have a peruse.'

'It's more than a bookshop,' he told her. 'I must have spent hundreds of hours in there, all through my teens. Every Saturday I went. He had the strangest books on his shelves. Novels so long out of print that no-one has ever heard of them.'

'Ha!' Iris barked with laughter. 'Maybe they'll have mine, eh? The ones my so-called students this week had never heard of. To be fair, I suppose they *were* published quite a long time ago…'

She had that glint of mystery in her eye again. Almost teasing him. As if she wanted him to ask exactly how old she was. Instead he jumped up and took both their empty glasses. 'There's got to be some more booze about…'

Indoors he found that the hostess was holding court beside a chocolate fountain. It took some hunting to find a bottle of red that was still unopened. As he was passing through the crowded hallway, Simon clocked Kelly by the buffet in the narrow kitchen. Anthony Marvelle was all over her. When Simon approached Kelly's eyes flashed at him, but he was out of practice reading her non-verbal signals. She was either frantically waving him away or she was asking for help. He couldn't be sure.

'Kelly?' he said. 'We're out on the patio.'

Marvelle turned to look at Simon. He looked downright snotty, cross at being interrupted – and a bit tipsy. 'Do you want to leave me… murmur murmur?' he asked Kelly gently.

'Anthony was just telling me about his feelings to do with my work,' Kelly said. 'He's critiquing me.'

Simon rolled his eyes. 'Well, whatever. Iris and I are outside. It's much nicer out there.'

Marvelle's expression turned scornful. 'You're with that old witch, are you… murmur?'

'She seems very nice,' Kelly said.

'An old fraud… murmur murmur,' Marvelle frowned into his white wine. 'No-one's heard of her. No-one even knows why she was here at the festival. Her name was simply added onto all the paperwork. Everyone's too embarrassed to challenge her. And she's been completely drunk every day, at every event. And, apparently, she sleeps in a double decker bus. Awful… murmur murmur.' He shuddered fastidiously.

'Oh!' said Kelly. 'We saw the bus. With chintzy curtains at all the windows.'

It didn't come as a surprise to Simon, that the old lady he had been talking to lived in that bus. It seemed like exactly the kind of thing she'd hang out in. This detail only added to her bizarre allure.

Then he was aware of a whimpering, whining noise and realised that Marvelle's sinisterly coiffed poodle was there. It was angling for some attention. Simon and Kelly watched as Marvelle crouched and appeared to let the dog lick his ear. The poet's expression changed, as if he was truly listening to something the dog was telling him. Simon shook his head, feeling the alcohol fumes fogging his every thought.

'I'm okay here, Simon,' Kelly told him. 'I'll catch up with you on the patio, later.'

He was surprised. She actually wanted to spend more time with this creep Marvelle. As the poet straightened up – looking thoughtful – something flashed into Simon's head. 'Hey!' he burst out. 'When you were in the Exchange earlier today…!'

Marvelle stared at him. 'I beg your pardon? Oh, yes. Of course. So that was where we'd met before… murmur murmur.'

'Well, you slipped out pretty quick, didn't you?' said Simon accusingly. Kelly stared at him, alarmed by his accusing tone. 'And you whipped something off my desk, didn't you? You nicked something?'

Marvelle attempted a dismissive laugh. 'Don't be ridiculous. Why would I… murmur murmur?'

'I don't know,' said Simon sternly. He was feeling quite cross about it all now. How dare this bloke swan about, obviously feeling very pleased with himself, when he was some kind of thief? 'You swiped something off the cash desk. Something important.'

'Simon, what are you on about?' Kelly was looking at him as if he was sounding really drunk.

'It was your present, Kelly,' Simon snapped. 'The paperweight you gave me from poor old Terrance. Seriously. It was on the desk and, when my back was turned, your bloke here and his dog dashed out of the shop – and the glass jar was gone! He must have taken it!'

Anthony Marvelle stared at him. 'Look here, I'm not used to being accused of things like this. I'm rather offended… murmur murmur.'

'But it's true! What have you done with it?'

They were caught for a moment in dreadful silence, glaring at each other. By their feet, the dog Missy growled, low in its throat. Other party-goers and poets in the kitchen were listening in by now.

'Just let it go,' Kelly hissed. 'There must have been a mistake, Simon.'

Simon glanced at her. 'I don't think so.' But he could see he wasn't going to get any sense out of either her or Marvelle. Simon shrugged and took hold of the bottle of red he'd had his eye on. 'I'll be out on the patio,' he told Kelly. 'Come and find us when he's finished with you and your poems.'

*

When he brought Iris her drink she was talking quietly into an odd-looking mobile made out of polished cherry wood. Her vast carpet bag was open on her lap, and there was some kind of gadget with a sonar detector bleeping at her. When she saw Simon she started bundling everything away, and finished her phone call rapidly.

'Ta for the drink, lovey. I hear you had an altercation with that fancy poet bloke.'

'Not quite an altercation,' he said stiffly. 'But I really wanted to punch him.'

'Chatting up your girlfriend, is he?'

'Kelly's not my girlfriend. There's never been anything like that between us.'

She patted his knee. 'I know, lovey. So, what have you got against Marvelle, then?'

'He stole something from me. Something of great sentimental value.'

Suddenly Iris looked very serious. 'There is much more to Marvelle than meets the eye. And that dog of his. Just you watch out for them. And warn Kelly, too. Keep away from him.'

'I tried!'

'I mean it,' Iris said beadily. 'There's bad stuff going on around here. That's why I'm in town. This is where it all begins. Well, strictly speaking, it began a week or two ago, with the bogus meteor shower. But now I'm here and all the pieces are in place. I think... this whole escapade is about to kick off.'

'Escapade?'

'Didn't I tell you, lovey? I'm only a writer for some of the time. What I do most of the time is... have escapades. And adventures.'

'Oh. I see.' Though just then, Simon didn't see at all.

The evening became a little messy after that. More wine was drunk, and then a bottle of tequila appeared from somewhere. The hostess got a bit weepy and dramatic over a fireman she had just hooked up with. The writer of the erotic pamphlet attempted a rather clumsy striptease on the patio terrace, which prompted Simon to leave. It was past two am, he was surprised to see. And he had lost track of Kelly and Marvelle.

'I just hope she hasn't copped off with that creep,' Simon said, as he helped Iris totter down the hall and down the front steps of the tall house.

'Bye bye everybody!' Iris shouted to the still-noisy party, and Simon wasn't sure anyone was listening.

He tried knocking at Kelly's basement door, hoping to find her before he left. But there was no answer. She's left with Marvelle, he thought, with a shudder.

He staggered a bit, having to hold all of Iris's weight, as they reached the street. He was feeling rather gallant and gentlemanly. She was a dead weight, doubled by that huge carpet bag. 'Where can I help you to?'

'Just point me in the direction of my vehicle,' she hiccuped.

'You can't *drive* anywhere..!' He was scandalized by the idea.

'No, no, I sleep aboard my bus. That's where I live.' She winked at him. 'You must have heard the others gossiping about me back there? Eh? The batty old novelist. Sleeps aboard her Routemaster. A bag lady, eh?'

Simon denied he had heard any such thing. 'I saw it earlier. It looked like a very nice bus.'

'It is! It is! My pride and joy!'

They made fairly wobbly progress round the perimeter of the park. The leaves crunched beautifully underfoot and the stars swayed gently above their woozy heads. Iris fumbled with her keys for a while outside the bus and Simon looked up at its dark windows and its obviously recently-done paintjob. It struck him that it really was a splendid bus. And a wonderful vehicle to own and travel about in.

Iris went, 'Aha!' and produced her key. The concertinaed doors whooshed open wide enough to let her in, but no further. She flung herself aboard, turning back briefly to thank him for his help. 'I would ask you in for a nightcap, lovey, but the whole place is a bit disordered. Maybe another time.'

Simon smiled, and was about to say goodnight when he heard a low, gruff voice inside the bus addressing Iris. She shouted back grumpily, and evidently a row was starting up. She sighed and hurriedly shut the doors. Simon stood there for a moment longer, intrigued by the raised voices within. He wondered who Iris already had inside her bus. Her partner, perhaps? She hadn't mentioned any such person. Perhaps it was the voice at the other end of her mobile phone? And why am I so intrigued, Simon wondered.

He headed off, deciding to cut across the gloomy park, inhaling the night time aromas of mulchy fallen leaves and the curling mist. He shook his head to clear it of cigarette smoke and wine. Time to go home. To his new home. New, but so familiar of old.

It would make him feel weird and a bit spooky – like he was haunting the place – to creep into the Exchange tonight. He could still hardly believe that the whole place was his. The keys were in his jeans pockets. Striding across the park, it seemed like the whole town was his, somehow. He felt lucky. He had been given a fabulous gift.

And this was only his first day back in town. Quite a lot had happened in just one day.

There came a dog's shrill barking, then. Somewhere in the next street, perhaps. A nasty barking. Malevolent-sounding. He thought of Missy, that poodle in its mittens. He thought of the smarmy Marvelle and hoped again that he wasn't with Kelly right now. Simon hoped that Kelly had found her way home. Maybe I should go and check again, Simon thought. Maybe I'll text her…

Just then he emerged from the park, on the street that would take him through the town centre and towards the South Road. He was starting to text Kelly as he walked along and that's when he heard the revving engines behind him.

Powerful engines. Much bigger than a car. A shunting, steaming, snorting noise. The engines, surely, of a double decker bus.

He turned to see Iris's bus rumbling along the road adjacent to the one he was on. His heart jumped. The silly old woman *was* driving! Then he thought – maybe it was her companion at the wheel? The voice he'd heard. That gruff man's voice. Perhaps he was the one doing the driving.

Simon watched the bus until it vanished.

He blinked.

It literally vanished.

It didn't take a corner, it didn't swing round and head into town.

Instead, the bus had done something quite plainly impossible. A dark swirling space had opened up in front of it. A miniature black cyclone had rent the air for a second, and the bus had been swallowed in an instant. It was gone, and Iris with it. And the autumn night time was completely silent now. No engines, no dogs barking, all the birds asleep. Even the raucous party noise couldn't be heard over on this side of the park.

The double decker bus had driven straight into some kind of hole in the night air. And now it was gone.

Simon took a deep breath and found that the most shocking thing was that – somehow - he wasn't in the least bit surprised. It seemed like just the kind of thing that peculiar woman would do.

CHAPTER FOUR

'ALL RIGHT! OKAY!'

Simon stomped his way down the bare wooden staircase of the Exchange. The perfect stillness of the shop had been rudely broken at – what was it? He rubbed his eyes and stared at the old railway station clock above the cash desk. Twenty past eight a.m. Owwwww. That was his head... He hadn't drunk so much for a good long while.

Events of the previous night's shebang came creeping back to him as he fumbled with his cigarettes and lit one up. BANG BANG BANG went the front door again. 'All right..!' he cursed. Since when did the Exchange have over-eager customers at the crack of dawn?

Maybe it was Kelly. Come to berate him for not checking she was okay last night, stuck in the clutches of Andrew Marvelle.

He rolled the blind up and unbolted the door and stared at the unfamiliar silhouette waiting impatiently on the other side. Maybe not so unfamiliar after all...

Iris was beaming at him in the brilliant autumn sunshine. She grinned at his tousled, headachy appearance and his rumpled T shirt and boxer shorts.

'So this is how you welcome people to your new shop, is it, lovey?' Then she barged past him, gazing about with great interest. 'Oh, I must say, Simon. This place is like a treasure trove. It's like Aladdin's Cave. It's like the library at Alexandria...' She turned on her heel, surveying the shelves in

39

the first room of the Exchange. 'And I should know! Because I've been to both! I've been to all the greatest repositories of knowledge in the multiverse. That's one of the best things about my transdimensional bus, you know. Unlimited book shopping. Course, it helps if you're any good at stealing, too. So – how are you, chuck? You look terrible!'

Iris looked fresh as a daisy. It was galling. She had drunk way more than he had. She had chain-smoked throughout the entire evening. But she looked fresh-faced and gleaming as if she'd just returned from a week at a spa.

'Look, what are you doing here? What do you want?'

'You're going to help me,' she said. 'I have decided. You're just the kind of young man I want.'

He groaned and stumbled to the futuristic coffee machine. Oh god, this was his first proper day in the Exchange. This was the real start of his new life. Already it was rubbish. He slumped into Terrance's old chair, worn smooth by years of patient and modest bookselling.

'I'm serious,' Iris said suddenly. 'There's bad business going on, Simon. And I need your help. You are the one.'

'I am?'

'Oh yes. I can spot them a mile off.' She dropped her carpet bag heavily on the ground. 'I've been doing this stuff for a very long time, you know.'

He didn't have a clue what she was talking about. Turning back to the espresso maker in order to buy some befuddled thinking time, Simon suddenly hit upon an image from last night's dreams. Last night's troubled and incredibly disturbing dreams. So disturbing that he cried out involuntarily.

'Have you burned yourself, lovey?' she asked.

He turned to see that she was sitting in his chair, lighting up what looked like a black Sobranie with a gold filter. 'I've just remembered…' he said. 'I dreamed about the jar. The red jar that Kelly gave me. I was holding it up to the light… the light that comes through the door here at the Exchange… I was in this very room... and the golden light made the contents of the jar glow all… red like blood.'

'The jar,' mused Iris. 'Hmmm.' She popped her feet onto the beautifully polished desk. They were clad in knee high yellow vinyl boots.

'Yes, the jar… and there was something else inside it!' He caught his breath, hands frozen on the coffee machine as it warmed up. 'It was an eye! A livid scarlet eye… all veiny and furious. It was looking back at me… out of the glass. It blinked… and then it was gone. But there was a voice… a woman's voice in my head. She said… she said…' He looked at Iris, stricken. 'I don't know what she said. But it was the most vivid and horrible dream I've ever had in my life.'

Iris toyed with her cigarette. 'I thought as much. I was right. You definitely are the one I need. I recognised the sensitive type. The object has passed through your hands. And you've lost it, true enough. We need it back. We've got to get it back, Simon.'

'But that was my dream. It wasn't real… was it?'

She cracked out laughing. 'What, that there was a real eye in your jar of jam..? What do you think?'

'I don't know…' He fetched out the coffee cups. The delicious aroma was curling about him now, soothing his frazzled nerves somewhat. 'I don't know what's going on anymore, I don't think. Weird stuff. And you!' He stared accusingly at the old woman. 'You and your bus! You disappeared last night!'

She frowned. 'Did I?'

'I helped you to your vehicle. You were out of it. Zonked! Then, when I'd walked through the park… I saw the bus trundling along. And it disappeared… into thin air.' He looked confused. 'Or was that part of my dream too?'

'You *were* knocking back the Merlot last night, lovey,' she sighed. 'And then it was the tequila. But your big mistake was having some of that chocolate gateau on top. That can give you nasty dreams, that stuff.'

He squooshed their boiling coffee out of the fancy machine and brought it to the desk. 'I don't have the jar anymore,' he told her. 'It was stolen yesterday. That's how come I got into a fracas at that party last night.'

'With Andrew Marvelle,' said Iris. 'Hmm.'

'He came in here and just swiped it off my desk. I accused him last night, but he denied everything. He's such a smoothie. Kelly was right under his spell.'

'That poetical ponce,' Iris agreed, blowing on her java.

'But it's just a jar, isn't it? Just some kind of weird paperweight? Is it really that important?'

'Oh yes,' she said, quite seriously. 'I've got friends all over town, combing the streets and houses to find that seemingly innocuous *objet*. You see, it's very important indeed, Simon. It's probably one of the most vitally important bits of bric-a-brac on the Earth today.'

*

She convinced him somehow that he didn't need to open up the shop that morning and he had to accompany her around town. She had some obscure kind of mission to attend to, plus friends to meet, so his presence would be required. Simon went back up to the flat above, leaving Iris mooching in the book stacks, and he showered and dug around in his still-unpacked bags for something to wear.

He quickly tried Kelly's phone. There was no answer.

Iris nodded in approval at him when he reappeared. 'Come on then,' she said gruffly. 'I've told the others we'll rendezvous with them at lunch time.'

'Who are the others?'

She chuckled. 'Oh, you'll see. You'll be surprised, I bet!'

He locked the Exchange carefully. He noticed that there was a card in the window, in front of the spartan window display of children's books from the Fifties. 'Under new management' it said, in Terrance's painstakingly elaborate script. Simon hadn't noticed that yesterday, and it gave him a twinge of guilt to see it there. Terrance had such faith in him taking over his shop.

Iris was leading the way down South Road at a hurried pace.

'I wish you'd tell me more about what's going on,' he said.

'That's only fair,' she grimaced. 'Okay, here goes. You were right. You did see my bus vanish into thin air. It does that a lot. That's what it's supposed to do.'

'Right...' he said. 'Okay.'

'You weren't drunk or dreaming. You saw something you shouldn't have. Something very special indeed. Remember when I said I was a transtemporal adventuress?'

He nodded warily. It seemed so weird, to be having this conversation on the ordinary main road, with the traffic whizzing by, and all the dowdy furniture store rooms and kebab shops lining the streets.

'It's a transdimensional ship, you see,' she told him. 'And you've gone and witnessed my secret.'

She didn't look all that worried, if secret it was. She looked only too keen to divulge this stuff to Simon. He smiled and nodded pleasantly – and felt a bit sorry for her. She was obviously barking. He was starting to doubt what he had seen last night anyway. Double deckers didn't just disappear. He wondered if someone had spiked his drink – or his gateau - at the party last night.

'Oh, you'll see, lovey,' laughed Iris. 'I've had unbelievers for friends before, you know. And they always get a pleasant surprise!'

They were quiet until they hit the dank underpass, when Simon was struck by a thought. 'Who was the man, then? I heard a voice… welcoming you on board the bus last night. Then it sounded like you were having a row when I left you…'

'A man's voice?' She laughed gleefully. 'Oh yes! That's right! Oh, just wait till you meet *him!*' They emerged at street level outside a discount clothes store. 'Hmm. Don't let me go shopping while I'm here. There's nothing I really need. It's just shopping for the sake of it. And I need to stay focused on the task in hand. I'm very easily distracted, you see. You'll find that…'

The town centre was fairly empty, it being just after nine. 'We need to call off the search, that's what we need to do,' Iris was muttering. 'There's no use the others still scouring the whole town. Not now that we've found what we were looking for. Now that we know what the object was…'

In the market place stalls were being set up and they wandered through the noisy profusion of racks and vans and dirty great tarpaulins.

Iris had her strangely clunky wooden mobile phone out again. 'I've texted round the team. Told them we should meet earlier at headquarters. And they're very keen to meet you.'

'Team? Headquarters?'

She nodded solemnly. 'I'm afraid you're about to be drawn into something a bit surprising, chuck. Something that I only hope your human brain can cope with.'

'I'm sure it can,' he said, feeling vaguely miffed.

'The thing is... oh, how do I put this?' Iris took a deep breath. 'There are secret agencies at work, all over this world of yours. Working on behalf of mankind and protecting all of you lot against... well, nasty stuff. Stuff from elsewhere. Other worlds and dimensions and other times.'

'Okay,' he said. 'I'll buy that.'

She seemed pleased. She tottered ahead of him up the stone steps to the indoor market. 'I occasionally moonlight for one of these organisations. I'm not really a member, but I help them out now and then. When there's a crisis on, you know. I'm pretty good in a punch-up and I'm quite clever, you know.'

'What's the crisis?' Simon said. 'Is it really something to do with this stolen glass jar?'

'Bright boy!' she grinned. 'That's exactly it.' Then she paused. Her voice was carrying in the cavernous hall of the indoor market and she lowered it. 'Remember that meteor shower over Darlington a couple of weeks ago? A very freakish event.'

'I was still down south,' he said, watching her examine some spangly tights at a fancy dress stall. 'I missed it all, but Kelly said something about it. People were killed, weren't they? Hit by stuff falling out of the sky?'

'That's right,' she said, looking for the price on tights decorated with golden stars. 'Poor souls. Well, these weren't natural meteorites breaking through the atmosphere. They were sent here. To this particular place and time. Objects from outer space. Sent to Darlington. And mysteriously protected so that they didn't burn up in the atmosphere or smash when they eventually hit the ground.'

'My jar was one of them?'

She glanced from side to side, as if someone might be listening. She flipped the stallholder a coin for her tights and bundled

Simon away. 'Come on, lovey. It's time I took you to meet the others.'

Simon was starting to wonder whether he had let this go too far. He felt like he should phone Kelly again, just to check that she wasn't with Anthony Marvelle.

'Oh, leave her be, lovey,' Iris sighed, when he asked her. 'She's a big girl. She's older than you are and, if I'm not mistaken, she's a bit more au fait with the ways of the world, too.' A thought seemed to strike her. 'And it might be a good idea, too, to keep her close to Marvelle. Hmm…'

They headed straight for a little shop in the very corner of the market. *Magda's Mysteries* it was called and it was a remainder bookshop specializing, as far as Simon could see, in science fiction. Iris introduced him hurriedly to a woman with a thick central European accent – Magda herself, it turned out – who sat knitting at the counter. She was in a wheelchair with a tartan rug tucked carefully over her legs.

'Simon has just taken over the running of a bookshop too,' Iris told Magda. 'You're both in the same business.'

'The Exchange!' Magda sighed happily. 'Is this correct, Simon? You have taken over from Terrance?'

'You know him, then?'

'All book lovers know Terrance and his Exchange,' Magda said. 'At least, round here they do. It's a great, great shame. Isn't it? Isn't it a shame about Terrance?'

'What is?' Simon felt his heart lurch. 'Do you know what's happened to him?'

Magda looked alarmed. 'No, I don't know anything! I'm sorry! I shouldn't have…' Now she looked very flustered.

Iris broke in. 'The boy's coming with me. Downstairs. He's a part of this now.'

Magda nodded and pressed some kind of switch on her wheelchair. 'Very well. I am sorry. I didn't mean to imply I knew something about Terrance. I don't. I just meant… it is a shame he is no longer here.'

'But Simon is,' said Iris gruffly. 'And he'll do.'

A door appeared between the bookcases at the back of the shop.

'It's a lift,' Iris said. 'This is where we go downstairs.'

Simon frowned. 'What's underneath the indoor market? The sewers?'

Iris rolled her eyes. 'If you haven't guessed, lovey, it's a secret base. MIAOW.'

She was bustling into the lift and he felt he had no choice but to follow. Still at her counter, Magda was clacking away at her wool again.

'MIAOW?'

Iris explained, 'The Ministry for Incursions and Other Wonders.'

Then the door swished shut, taking them down what felt like several thousand feet, deep beneath the centre of Darlington.

*

His ears popped and his heart rate went crazy. At one point he thought he was going to pass out. He felt Iris patting his arm. As the elevator descended it became progressively shakier. It was jangling heavily on cables and chains that seemed as if they must have been in operation for a great many years.

At last the doors groaned open and Iris hustled them into a dank corridor.

'Hello? Helloooo?' she was shouting as they advanced into a cavernous space. Simon drew in his breath and held it for what felt like quite a long time.

'Erm,' he said at last. 'This really is a secret base, isn't it? With the... erm, computers and whatnot.'

Iris looked about at the empty control room as if noticing its details for the first time. The whirring banks of complicated controls. The vast screens hissing and buzzing with static. The damp black walls of rock. 'Do you like it?' she asked him.

'It's a bit unwelcoming,' he said.

'My thoughts exactly!' She tutted. 'It's all down to Jenny, who's the boss here. She's a bit butch in her decorating tastes. And everything else, as it happens.'

Then there was a tall woman in a leather jacket standing next to them, looking cross. Her dark hair was cropped short and she appeared to be sporting some kind of monocle. A black monocle.

'There you are, lovey,' Iris gabbled, nonplussed by the woman's abrupt arrival and forbidding demeanour. 'We can call the general search off now. We know what it is we're after.'

'Who is this?' barked the woman in the monocle and the leathers.

Iris flung herself down into a swivel chair and started fiddling with the controls. 'Oh, this is Simon. He's helping me with my investigations.'

'Another recruit,' said Jenny jeeringly. She didn't seem at all friendly, Simon thought.

'Simon, this is Jenny. An old, old friend of mine. Used to be a traffic warden. Then she was a traveller on the dear old transdimensional bus. Now she sits under Darlington trying to solve alien mysteries and defend the Earth and stuff. And pretty effective she is, aren't you, Jenny pet?'

Jenny scowled. 'What did you mean, you know what we're after?'

'She made a terrible time traveller!' Iris suddenly laughed. 'Poor thing. She used to get awful stomach upsets. You got the runs every time we went back into history, didn't you, Jenny chuck?'

Jenny took a menacing step forward and her leather trousers creaked ominously. Simon felt the hair on the back of his neck go up. This Jenny looked like she could do a lot of damage. 'Tell me, Iris. What have you found out?'

'Well, it's all thanks to this young man, here. I believe he's led me to just what we're looking for.'

Simon gasped. 'I have?'

Jenny said, 'The Objet D'Oom? He's got it?'

'Not now, but he did have. And he knows who's got it now. And do stop calling it by that silly name, Jenny. That's what the F'rrgelaaris called it, but they're a very silly people. Forever over-reacting. We don't even know what it really is... Though I've some nasty suspicions.' Then she cried out in triumph, peering close at one of the datascreens she'd been messing around with. 'There! I've been combing through the database of the literature festival administrator at the Arts Centre... and I've found out where a certain revered poet has been staying all week. That's a swanky hotel, I must say. I never got offered the same accommodation. They left me to sleep in my bus. Ah... he's due to check out today. By eleven. Hm. We don't have much time.'

'Marvelle?' Simon said. 'Are we going to get the glass jar back off him?' Simon was fiddling with a selection of strange objects, which were laid out on a bench beside him. It was an incongruous assemblage, here in the dimly-lit base. The table and its contents might have looked more at home at a church bring-and-buy sale. There was a broken jack-in-the-box, several old books, a china clown, a lamp made out of a Chianti bottle, some odd shoes and other items of dubious provenance. 'Having a clear-out are you?' he asked their surly hostess.

Jenny snatched a wooden antelope out of his hands. 'These were the objects that MIAOW operatives have been out hunting for all week, all over Darlington.'

Simon said, 'What would secret agents want with this old tat?'

Iris coughed. 'These are the things – some of the things – that fell out of the sky. In that so-called meteor shower.'

'And none of them are any use,' sighed Jenny. She picked up a hunk of bizarre, peach-coloured crystal and listened to it, as if it might be emitting a signal of some kind. 'They're just rubbish. What a waste of time.'

'Simon had the thing the whole time,' Iris said. 'Trust me, eh? Trust your old Aunty Iris to walk straight up to the heart of the problem!'

Simon frowned, 'I was only given the glass jar yesterday. Before that it had been with Kelly, and Terrance from the shop. He was keen that I was given it, though. Kelly even brought it to the train station when she met me. But then... I lost it. It was nicked.'

Iris made the screens before them flicker and spin with a bewildering set of displays. Then a muzzy black and white picture came up. It showed part of a corridor, two numbered doors, and a painting of a ship bobbing on the sea. Iris explained, 'That's a security camera on the third floor of the Duke's Legs Hotel. Room 319. That's where our objective is. He hasn't checked out yet.'

'Right,' said Jenny, and appeared to be fiddling with some kind of weapon that was strapped to her thigh. 'I'll go and see to this. What did you say this object looked like?'

'Like a jar of jam, more or less,' said Iris. 'According to Simon.'

'Raspberry jam,' he added. 'Hang on, you're going over there? To the hotel? In order to scrag Anthony Marvelle?'

Jenny nodded. 'And you're not coming, sunshine. I'm not having civilians with me.'

Iris pulled a face behind her back, as if to say, 'See what she's like?'

'My friend Kelly might be with him. I think… there's a chance she might be.' Though he hated even giving voice to the thought.

Jenny shrugged. 'I'll watch out for her. What does she look like?'

Simon tried his best to describe his friend and got as far as the purple hair. 'But I really don't know if she'll be there. Anyway, I think I should come along with you. It's my jar, after all…'

'No, it's not,' Jenny snapped. She was fiddling in a drawer for some other bits and pieces. Simon was startled to see her picking out a nasty-looking dagger. 'The Objet D'Oom doesn't belong to anyone on Earth. It doesn't belong here. It needs taking care of. It needs destroying or disposing of properly, by qualified people. By MIAOW operatives. That's what we're here for.'

She fixed both Simon and Iris with a grim look and then turned on her heel, hurrying out of the base on her mission.

'What, defending the Earth from bric-a-brac?' Simon asked, when she was safely gone.

Iris chuckled. 'She doesn't change. Actually, she does. She's even more butch and earnest that she ever was, poor love.'

'What will she do to Marvelle?'

'She'll probably just rough him up a bit. It's okay. She knows what she's doing.'

'And we're just going to sit here waiting for her? Doing nothing?'

'Hm?' she said. 'Goodness, no. I never do nothing, Simon. You'll find that out. It's just that I'm not doing the *obvious* things. The things that everyone is expecting. I'm usually off in the margins somewhere, doing something crucial but discreet. I let the likes of Jenny go stomping around with her guns and whatnot. Doing all the shouting.'

'So what are we going to do down here?'

'I'm going to use MIAOW's fabby computers while I've got the chance. And I'm going to get a fix on where these objects were coming from in the first place. If they were dropping out of the skies, then they must have been coming from somewhere, mustn't they? And now that stroppy old Jenny's out of the way, I can do a little snooping of my own...'

Simon was amazed by Iris's sudden, intent concentration as, cigarette clamped in mouth, she applied herself to the myriad controls before her.

'I'm making a few adaptations of my own,' he muttered, flinging off her floppy hat and producing a powder compact seemingly from underneath it. Inside the compact was a set of tiny controls. Iris stuck the device to the desk in front of her and it was as if she was using it to suck everything out of the MIAOW memory banks.

'That's interesting,' she said musingly, apparently reading the information that went whizzing by in a very quick and encrypted fashion. 'Panda?'

Then a huge booming voice filled the control room. It came crackling over the loudspeakers and made Simon jump.

'What is it?' the voice bellowed, urbanely.

'Ah, you're there, lovey. Good. I wasn't sure you would be.'

There came a sigh, hissing with static. 'Where the devil *would* I be at this time in the morning? I can hardly get out of the bus, can I? And go wandering around Darlington? Just imagine what kind of scenes might result! No – here I am! A prisoner!'

Iris shrugged apologetically at Simon. 'Don't mind him, chuck. He's always like this when he gets left behind.'

'But who is it?'

'That's Panda.'

'And he's on the bus?'

'I've rigged up a psychic link through the MIAOW hardware and so we can get all this lovely info to him – yes.'

'He's called Panda?'

Iris frowned at Simon's dimness. 'Yes, of course he is. Look, you'll meet him soon anyway. Just be a dear and shut up while I...'

Panda's voice boomed out again, echoing in the chamber. 'Who's that numpty you've got with you, Iris? He sounds a bit dopey to me.'

'That's Simon,' Iris said distractedly, jabbing more controls. 'Look, I'm sending you everything they've got on the subject of the object. And the coordinates that I've just managed to work out... Okay, lovey? Have you got them?'

Panda sounded cross. 'What? Now, you mean? Erm, hang on. I've got to hoist myself up into the driver's seat to see. Look, can't you put some steps or something in here?'

Iris sighed. 'He's always like this,' she told Simon.

'I heard that! Yes, look – all the lights are flashing. The coordinates are in there, I think. We're primed and ready, I believe.'

'Good!' Iris grinned, and started stuffing all of her belongings – tissues, tools, hipflask, compact, ciggies – back into her capacious carpet bag. 'Then I think our work in this gloomy old place is done, don't you, Simon?'

Simon wouldn't be sorry to get out of there. He was starting to feel a bit claustrophobic – and he could swear he'd heard a bat, skirling away in the upper ceiling like an evil set of bagpipes. 'Er, yes. Where now?'

'The bus,' said Iris, looking serious. 'Like I say, we don't always see eye to eye, me and the members of MIAOW. They're so intent on saving the world that they're pretty indiscriminate about who they go blowing up. Now, if they knew how to shake out these coordinates I've just procured they might be tempted to do something rather rash with who or what they find up there – at the end of the rainbow, as it were.'

Simon felt bewildered. 'End of the rainbow?'

'She means – in outer space – you bloody fool!' shouted Panda, making them both jump. They hadn't realised he was still listening in. 'Are you coming home or not, Iris?'

'We're on our way, Panda, lovey!' she laughed. 'Get the place ready to welcome this nice young man on board. And get the drinks ready!'

Panda sighed, loudly.

They turned to go.

But there was a large and squat vending machine blocking their way on the metal gantry.

Simon swore. 'Where did that thing come from? It wasn't there before!'

Iris elbowed him aside, seeing the problem at once. She hissed at him, 'Just play along with me. Be very polite.'

'It's a vending machine!'

'Exactly!' Iris said, and then flung open her arms. 'Barbra! It's me, sweetheart! Don't you recognise me?'

The vending machine gave a whirring thunk noise, as if it was thinking. Then it seemed to light up with inspiration. A very fruity and voluptuous voice said, 'Iris! They said you were back! I thought I'd heard your voice!'

'Barbra, dear. This is the latest recruit to my cause, Simon. Simon, this is Barbra. She's a recently established member of MIAOW. She's a spy. And quite deadly with her retractable fists, aren't you dear?'

'Oh, not really,' said Barbra. 'And I'm not really a spy. Mostly I *vend*. I do crisps and pop and chocolate bars. Do you fancy anything?'

'Er, no,' said Simon awkwardly.

He could tell at once that Barbra was disappointed.

'I'll have a can of, erm, orangeade,' said Iris. 'We were just heading out, back to the bus, Barbra. Things to do, you know.'

'You're leaving?' said the machine, as her inside lit up with a soft, rather becoming neon glow. She whirred and thunked once more and then a metal can dropped out of her front slot. 'There you are, Simon,' she said. 'But you can't leave, Iris,' she added earnestly. 'Won't Jenny be expecting you to be here when she gets back?'

'Oh no,' Iris said airily, popping the can with a less than fierce hiss. She remembered now: poor Barbara's pop was always flat, her crisps were almost always stale. 'Jenny won't mind if we just wander off.'

'But I thought she was wanting your help! With this strange business of the bric-a-brac falling out of the sky and randomly killing Darlington citizens! And this weird quest for the Objet D'Oom.' Barbra's voice had gone quavery and concerned. She was still resolutely blocking their exit.

'Oh, all that stuff,' said Iris. 'Well, that's all sorted out. Yes, that whole mystery and all that dangerous stuff. Done and dusted. I clear up that kind of thing in my lunch breaks. A doddle, oh yes! You see – I've found the Objet D'Oom for you. And that's just what old Jenny has gone to fetch. She's at the Duke's Legs Hotel right now, duffing up the bloke who nicked it. So you see, Barbra, we're all sorted!'

Simon gave a kind of hapless nod. He couldn't believe they were remonstrating with a robot that dispensed snacks.

'Is that all true?' said Barbra worriedly.

'Cross my heart!' said Iris. 'Would I lie to you?'

'And you're just going now? You're leaving us?'

'I've got a whole galaxy to show young Simon here!'

Simon's head felt a bit swimmy, momentarily, at the word 'galaxy.' Right now he had no idea how much the old coot was making up on the spot and how much might be true. But then… just look at this place. It was a real life secret base, with futuristic stuff in it. And they were talking to a robot. A real life robot. Who could talk and dispense snacks.

'Simon's joining you on the bus, is he?' Barbra said. 'Oh, dear. I see. How nice for him. I wish I could. I do love it on your bus.'

'I know,' said Iris sadly. 'But it was such a palaver, wasn't it, getting you through the doors and up and down the steps? You almost squashed poor Panda last time…'

'Still,' said the vending machine wistfully. 'It gets awfully lonely here in this base. It's not like they even let me out much to wander round Darlington. Jenny says I scare people. I mean, I'm grateful to MIAOW, for giving me a home here – so far from my own time and place – but it doesn't half get a bit lonely. Oh, I sound awful, don't I? A proper moaner.'

Iris patted her on the glass front. 'Look. Let us go now and we'll come back for you. Next time I go on a nice long voyage… we'll take you with us. As a special treat. What do you say eh, Babs?'

Barbra let out what Simon thought of as a hydraulic squeal of excitement. 'Do you mean it? Even though I'm so clunky and wonky and awkward and have to be helped around everywhere?'

'Of course!' Iris grinned. 'I'm a woman of my word, aren't I? Who was it convinced MIAOW not to dismantle you in the first place, eh? They were going to use you for spare parts! That night you first came to earth though the mysterious Dreadful Gap in time and space! Who was it saved your nelly then, eh, missus?'

'It was you,' said Barbra. 'Of course it was you, Iris. You and Panda. I owe you both a great deal.'

'Nonsense!' said Iris, surreptitiously sliding her unwanted can of orangeade onto a bank of controls. 'But really. Are you going to let us leave the base and go back to the bus? Please?'

Barbra looked as conflicted and torn, Simon thought, as it was possible for a vending machine to be.

CHAPTER FIVE

Iris and Simon hurried through the busy town centre, through a number of back streets and alleys. Iris seemed to know the town as well as he did, which seemed odd for the transdimensional traveller she claimed to be.

'Darlington?' she frowned, when he asked about this, as they swung past the junk shops of Skinnergate. 'Every transdimensional traveller knows Darlington like the back of his, her or its hand, Simon dear. You'll find that out, when you meet them. Darlington, you see, plays a similar function to the transdimensionally mobile as it did in the nineteenth century to posh people going to Scotland for their holidays. It was the start of their great journey north – a nexus point for adventurers and explorers. You know Scotch Corner on the motorway south of Darlington? That big hotel?'

He nodded dumbly, still trying to keep up with her. 'Well lovey, if you could see the Scotch Corner hotel in its full seven dimensions, you might be very surprised indeed. It's not just Scotland people are going to, you know. Darlington's the gateway to the entire multiverse, believe it or not.'

That statement proved to be one of the more challenging new things Simon had to swallow that day.

They reached the park and the bus with its drawn curtains. He tried Kelly's mobile once more as they ambled along. He texted her and hoped she was ok. He hoped she wasn't at the hotel when Jenny seized Marvelle. And he hoped she hadn't checked on the Exchange and found the whole place closed up for the day...

Then Iris was inviting him warmly aboard the bus.

'Your new home from home,' she said, as the doors whooshed open.

He stepped aboard hesitantly, wondering what on earth he was getting himself into.

But inside it was rather cosy, at first glance.

All the old seats had been torn out and replaced by a bizarre assortment of furniture and nick nacks. A chaise longue vied with a battered old couch for the greatest share of space. There was an Art Deco drinks cabinet and a bookcase crammed with paperbacks and star charts. The curtains and blinds were all drawn and the interior was glowing softly with shaded lamps. It felt like four o'clock in the morning... Simon's ears prickled as he stepped aboard and looked around – and it really felt as if he was stepping into another element or a different, timeless hour...

'What do you think?' Iris was smiling proudly, but with a hint of nerves. As if she thought he mightn't like what he saw.

'It's very nice,' he said stiffly.

'All a bit messy at the moment,' she sighed. 'But we've been up to our eyes in it, this last little while, me and Panda. We've had a number of investigations running in different zones simultaneously and it's easy to get behind with the washing and ironing and dusting...' She picked up a silvery cardigan that had been dropped onto the settee and hung it carefully on the back of a bar stool.

Simon gazed around. There appeared to be a little galley kitchen at the very back of the bus, where the entrance on a Routemaster usually was. It was clear that Iris had adapted and customised this battered old vehicle for her own eccentric uses. 'So how long have you lived aboard… a bus?'

'Decades! Centuries! I've no idea!' She stomped off down the gangway, picking up discarded bits of paper covered with vital notes, crisp packets and a slithery silk cravat as she went. 'It's really very hard to calculate, when you go *zig-zagging* like I do.'

'*Zig-zagging*?'

'That's the precise technical term I use for my peregrinations through space, time and the twisty corners of the multiverse,' she told him. 'We *zig-zag* through the galaxy. Me and Panda and the good old Number 22. That's our very favourite thing to do!'

She was heading for the cabin at the front of the bus, which had its own set of doors beside it. As she hoisted herself into the seat Simon studied the strange controls, which were nothing like any dashboard he had ever seen. They were all brass and wooden fittings, with additions such as an ancient flickering black and white television set hanging from the ceiling. It showed a snowy picture of the park and the words: 'Darlington - Human Era - Early 21st Century' which were just about visible. Iris was checking over a curious set of displays and readings, nodding with satisfaction as she lit herself another cigarette. She produced her powder compact again, and consulted the weirdly fluffy and fibrous display screen within.

'Panda's done a good job. He got everything we need from the MIAOW databanks. All right! Great! We can go!'

'Go?' Simon said. He sounded more nervous than he wanted to.

'Of course!' she said, and then raised her voice. 'Panda! Where are you? We're back! Have you fixed us those drinks?'

A gruff voice came from the stairwell just behind the driver's cab. There was a series of muffled, thudding footfalls as someone came down to join them. 'Not yet, you old harridan. Give me a chance! I was performing my toilette, as it happens.'

Iris tutted. 'Toilette indeed,' she said to Simon. 'He only puts on a new cravat and fluffs up his ears. He always makes such a fuss about it.' Then she stared past Simon, beaming with pleasure at the sight of her small friend, who had suddenly appeared before them. 'Panda, lovey. I'd like you to meet our new travelling companion, Simon.'

Simon turned to stare at the person whose voice he had heard resounding through the speakers in the MIAOW secret base. For a moment he had a problem putting that huge voice together with the figure before him, which was only about ten inches high.

Panda was frowning at him. 'This is him, is it, Iris? Oh *dear*.'

He really was a Panda. Plus, he was what Simon might have called a toy Panda, with glass eyes and coiffed black ears. Just the way he was standing there in the middle of the bus glaring at them gave Simon a sense of the formidable personality lurking within all that fake fur fabric and stuffing.

'Erm,' Simon said. 'Nice to meet you.'

Panda grumbled to himself and said, 'Likewise, I'm sure.' Then he turned swiftly on his stumpy feet and hurried to the drinks cabinet. 'Gin and tonic all right for everyone? We're out of lemons, I'm afraid.'

'I don't know if I could face a gin at this time in the morning,' Simon said.

'Oh, you'll have to, lovey,' Iris snapped, hurriedly setting the controls for immediate departure. Both sets of doors slammed shut. There came a powerful hum from the dashboard as it lit up like a Christmas tree. 'It's like a chemical thing, you see. We're about to journey into a strange, interdimensional zone. A kind of meta-reality. A corridor in the interstices of space and time, you know? We call it… *The Maelstrom!*'

'Oh, she loves saying all that to newbies,' Panda sighed, rootling around with ice cubes. They tended to stick to his paws.

'And…' said Simon, 'There's something in gin, is there? That makes the… journey possible?'

Iris rolled her eyes. 'No. The journey can be quite bumpy and hectic, though, and it sometimes helps to be a bit pissed. That's what I've found, in my not inconsiderable experience.'

'Oh, okay.'

Then Panda was beside them, with a fancy drinks tray and he was offering them what Simon discovered to be a fiendishly strong gin and tonic. 'Chin chin,' said Panda, slurping his. 'Have you ever been off-world before, Simon?'

Simon looked at his two hosts and took another sip of his drink. 'Never,' he said.

'Hang onto your hat, then, lovey,' Iris laughed, 'You're going to love this next bit! I just know it!'

*

'So… what kind of people would have been… on board this, um, ship?' Simon asked. He picked his way very carefully along the corridor. He was asking questions just to keep himself calm.

'People?' asked Iris. 'What makes you think they were people?' She and Panda were strolling ahead in the semi-darkness, quite unperturbed by their new environment.

Simon felt nauseous. The ground wasn't rocking beneath his feet, but it felt as if it should be. There was a heaviness to the air: a slight dragging sensation as he moved along.

Iris had a torch she'd plucked from her carpet bag. Its slim beam probed the darkness, revealing grimy metal fixtures and fittings.

'It's a rather unprepossessing first destination for the lad,' he heard Panda mumbling. 'It's a shame we couldn't show him somewhere nicer for his first trip aboard the bus.'

'You're not wrong there, Panda,' he heard Iris saying absently. 'This is a shonky old ship, isn't it? Old freight vessel by the looks of it. Mendavici Seven in origin, I'd guess, but bought and sold a few times over...' She read the name off a plate set into the oily wall. '*Begins at Home.*'

'And now used for hauling what seems to be a load of useless old gubbins about the cosmos,' Panda mused. Ahead, the two of them had paused and were peering into a dimly-lit store room. Inside was a riot of old junk. It looked like every charity shop Simon had ever wandered into – but this time the stock appeared to hark from a thousand different worlds. He could hardly identify what many of the objects were. He saw fabrics, ceramics, papery objects that might have been books. He stared and Iris dug him in the ribs.

'You can find out a lot about the universe by its second-hand tat,' she said wistfully. 'Welcome to outer space, Simon love. Has it sunk in yet?'

He gave her a smile that he just knew was bordering on the asinine. She grinned knowingly and produced her hipflask of gin. 'You look like you need a nip of this,' she said.

Had it sunk in yet?

He wasn't even sure. There hadn't even been time to strap himself in before Iris revved the bus's engines and the whole rackety vehicle started to shudder and shake down the road. It was a good deal noisier than any double decker he had ever travelled on. The bottles in the cabinet and the china on the shelves and in the galley kitchen had tinkled and chimed as the bus tore along the road – and one minute it was in Darlington, clear as day – and the next it was... elsewhere.

Panda had ambled over to him and patted his knee as the whole bus slid sideways in space and time. Simon only had eyes for the weird orange and verdant green pulsating beyond the bus's windows. The time winds came shrieking through the gaps and cracks in the bus's outer skin and Panda raised his voice to explain that they were now travelling through the Maelstrom – a kind of meta-dimension that offered the discerning traveller a shortcut between destinations.

Iris – clearly listening as she wrestled with the stiff steering wheel – yelled at them both: 'Otherwise known as the mysterious dimension in which space and time are *completely* buggered up!'

To Simon the strange effects outside looked rather like the murky water left by an artist washing his brushes. There was the same swirling effect, too - a kind of whirlpool of colour through which the bus was *zig-zagging…*

The journey had taken only a few minutes. About two tracks of the Shirley Bassey tape Iris was playing through every speaker on board. 'Never Never Never' was in full throttle when the bus reached the end of its short hop and they had found themselves here. In this maze of darkened metal corridors – a place that both Panda and Iris reckoned was somewhere in outer space.

It was only when they found the porthole that Simon started to believe them properly. And that was when it really sunk in.

It might have been a TV picture of some kind showing the Earth wreathed in its complicated cloud patterns. He supposed it might have been faked. But something told him that this was the real thing. That was the real planet Earth down there. Which puts me in orbit, he thought. Oh. Right. Good.

He was amazed to find himself pretty calm about that fact. And pleased, too. Iris peered over his shoulder and patted him heartily on the back.

'You're a cool one,' she laughed. 'I thought you might have had an attack of the ab-dabs! I can't abide screamers, you know. I like people who can take things in their stride.'

'So it's all true,' he said, feeling a little bit chilly now, he realised. He had goose flesh. 'You *do* gad about in space and time.'

She nodded eagerly. 'Righting wrongs and wronging rights and clattering about and sometimes causing a right old rumpus. Not bad, eh?'

They were interrupted by a gruff shout from Panda.

Iris was on the alert instantly. There was fear in the Panda's voice. She wasn't used to hearing that. She pelted in his direction, the torch beam swaying wildly. 'Where are you? I told you not to go wandering...'

'I'm here,' said Panda in a soft, sad voice.

He was in the doorway of a large flight deck. Simon followed Iris inside and stood bewildered before the infinitely complicated controls of the *Begins at Home*. Again there was that splendid view of the Earth – azure and brilliant with promise.

But the three visitors were more concerned, just then, by the two dead bodies slumped on the control deck. They were near-human creatures, leaking a dark, congealed blood all over the place. There were stark black burned patches on their coveralls.

'They've been blasted,' Iris said, examining them carefully. 'Vatrexiis, by the looks of them.' She glanced at Simon. 'The rag and bone men of this quadrant. They're known for shipping old rubbish about from world to world. Striking bargains. A bit of light thieving here and there. Nothing too outrageous.'

'Who'd have killed them?' Panda said, frowning. 'Who'd do this to the likes of them?'

'Someone not even interested in stealing their ship,' Iris mused.

'That store room looked like it had been turned upside down,' Simon said.

'You're right,' said Panda. 'It was a real mess, wasn't it?'

'They were looking for something,' Iris said. 'Whoever got on board and killed these two. They were after something in particular.'

Panda was peering closely at the female Vatrexii. He had noticed something stuck to the scorch marks on her arm. Carefully he tweezed it up – which was quite tricky with his clumsy paws. 'Aha,' he said. 'Look. A clue. Someone must have brushed against her. And left… *this*.'

Iris and Simon peered closer. The torchlight picked out a small bunch of long pink hairs.

'What is it..?'

'Dog hair,' Iris told him grimly. '*Poodle*.'

There came an almighty crash from further down the passage.

CHAPTER SIX

'They came out of nowhere. We never had a hope. Our ship – as you can see – was never any great shakes. Our sensors were rubbish. Our defences were kaput. And then… when they came out of the ether, snarling at our heels…'

'There, there,' Iris told the elderly Vatrexii. She made a kind of pillow by folding up her long coat. It was only when the injured man was lying on it she started hoping he wouldn't bleed all over it. He was in a pretty bad way.

Panda shuffled round till he was in the man's view. 'But what were they? Who were they?'

The Vatrexii stared at Panda, wondering if he was hallucinating from the shot of painkillers Iris had given him. He blinked and gawped and Panda grew impatient.

'Don't crowd him, lovey,' Iris said. 'Let him calm down. He's been through an awful ordeal.'

The man was blue-tinged and covered in the same burn marks as his dead colleagues. It was amazing he had survived this long, Simon thought.

'From the Dogworld,' the old trader said at last. 'Well, we haven't seen them in this quadrant for decades. They've kept to themselves, haven't they?' He became agitated, as waves of pain started beating at him again. They all knew the end was near.

'Is there nothing more you can do for him, Iris?' Simon asked.

She shook her head discreetly. 'Tell us your name. Tell us about the dogs.'

'My name is Harfolg. That doesn't matter now. I know I'm dying. But if I can pass on my warning... if you can tell the people down below... on Earth... tell them that the Dogs are searching... they are after a certain device. An object of some kind. They came surging aboard our ship – we were helpless. Firing their laser guns. Those horrible little hands they have. Swaggering and barking and making it plain that our lives meant nothing to them...'

'I've met those Dogs before,' Iris said.

'These were Dog Pirates,' Harfolg said. 'Renegades. Even worse than the usual sort. And they were after something... something infinitely precious and important to them. Something that we had foolishly picked up somewhere. In our idiocy... the crew of the *Begins at Home* simply wandered into this... We were so hapless... and now... now...'

'*Begins at Home,*' Panda said. 'I think that's a rather nice name for a vessel.'

'That was us,' smiled the man. He grimaced in pain and remorse. 'Swooping about the cosmos, picking up stuff no one wanted. Selling it on. We never caused anyone any harm... Why would we? But then... one day... we made a terrible mistake... and we picked up the wrong thing... and made off with it...'

Iris saw that he didn't have long left. Astounding, that he had lain here for two weeks, gradually fading away. She pushed her face closer to his. 'What was it? This thing? What did it look like?'

'I don't know. I never knew what it was. Only that they had detected it in our last shipment in the lower hold. There was a whole roomful of goods from a... certain, very distant world. Our youngest lad – Phelps – he ran down there. He knew the ship well and got away from our captors. That brave boy. He defied them. He jettisoned that last roomful of second-hand junk. He flung it all down into the atmosphere of your planet Earth. And then they ripped him apart with their bare teeth for what he had done.'

'It got there,' Iris said. 'Everything arrived intact. And we think we know what the object is.'

'They never got it?' he asked hopefully. 'That's g-good. I don't think the Dog Pirates should be allowed to get their hands on it...'

'It's a jar,' Iris said. 'A strange sort of jar.'

'Yes!' gasped Harfolg. 'They said something... about ancient glass... and how it contained something... something almost impossibly precious and rare...'

'We know where it is,' Iris said softly, patting him. 'You did a good job here. You and Phelps and the others.'

The old man's tortured expression relaxed a little at her words. Then he tried to say something further, but couldn't get it out. A startled look passed over his face and then he was still.

Simon gulped. First day in space, and the first death he'd witnessed. He swayed dizzily on the spot. He'd known other deaths before – he was an orphan, after all. But they had all happened some distance away from him. Behind closed doors. Discreetly. His parents had been killed in a plane crash when he was a young teen. That had been across the other side of the world. Though death was no stranger to him, he had never seen it this close.

Iris stood up next to him and he saw at once from her suddenly haggard expression that it was nothing new to her. Or to Panda either, who was suddenly tugging at the bundled up coat under the dead man's head. 'You can't leave this behind, Iris. It's your favourite.'

She led them away, back down the corridor, muttering to herself.

As he followed along Simon's mind was racing. Dogs had been responsible for this murder and mayhem? Space dogs with hands? It sounded too incredible to be true. And yet – having seen this much – he was prepared to take things on trust.

There were vicious, murderous space dogs with guns on the hunt for the jar.

And the jar was with Marvelle. Who had a poodle with him. And, the last time Simon had clapped eyes on him, he had had Kelly with him too. 'Oh my god!' he burst out, and gabbled all of this to Iris and Panda.

'I know,' Iris said testily. 'It's clear that phoney Marvelle is up to his armpits in all of this. He must be an agent of the Dog Pirates…! I suggest we tackle him pronto.'

The bus was wedged into the corridor. Luckily there had been enough space – just about – in the ship's interior for a dusty old Routemaster. Iris said it hardly mattered. Had the corridor been too small she'd simply have parked outside and gone to work with an atmospheric extrusion and a blow torch.

'I see,' Simon frowned, not really seeing at all, and following them aboard the suddenly even cosier and friendly-seeming bus. The shaded lamps clicked on automatically as they entered, and the music started up again, shockingly loud after the scene they had just witnessed. Panda flung himself down on the chaise longue, kicking aside a number of ancient film magazines. 'Those poor people,' he muttered.

'Can't we go back in time and prevent it all from happening?' Simon said. 'This *is* a time machine, isn't it?'

'It's a very wonky, wayward time machine,' Panda told him tersely, fixing him with a beady eye. 'If Iris started buggering about with fine adjustments to the time paradigm around us, heaven knows where we'd end up. Everyone would wind up being everyone else's grandfather, I shouldn't wonder.' He harrumphed loudly and turned back to the gin he'd left waiting on a coffee table. He picked up the glass with both paws. 'Rule Number One aboard the Celestial Omnibus, young Simon. We *never* give in to the temptation to improve things or tamper with things or otherwise arse about with Time. That sort of thing always, *always* goes tits up. Now, cheers.'

Iris was gunning the engine. 'Hold tight, boys,' she squawked, sounding cheerful all of a sudden. 'We're heading back home! We've got work to do!'

As Simon gripped a handy rail beside his chair, he was hoping that their work would involve finding out what had happened to Kelly…

*

His phone burst into life as soon as the bus was back on earth. Text from Kelly.

What do U mean did I spend the night with him? RU crazy? Why is the exchange shut, Simon?

He grinned ruefully – and with relief.

'It's all right, she says she's not with him.'

Iris came galumphing down the gangway. 'We'd best catch up with Jenny and the others, too. See how they got on…'

The bus had arrived back in its spot by the park. Panda was telling Iris to pop him in her carpet bag. He was coming to MIAOW HQ as back-up.

'I'm going back to my shop,' Simon told them.

Iris suddenly grabbed him by the elbow. Instantly he was reminded of the witch in *Hansel and Gretel* and her house made of gingerbread. He remembered how she would prod blindly at the boy she had taken captive. 'We can trust you, Simon, can't we?'

'O-of course.'

Suddenly she looked very sober. 'We've let you into our secrets now. Who we are. What we can do. Where we can go. You're on the bus now, Simon. You're one of us.'

'Yeah,' he said. 'I know. And I'm really pleased that you've... let me join.'

'What she means,' Panda broke in gruffly, 'is that we hope you won't go running off to the authorities and the papers now to sell us down the river. Or simply run away, never to be seen again.'

'Some people get freaked out by the whole transdimensional thing,' Iris said.

'Oh no,' shrugged Simon. 'Not me. I want to see more! All I've seen so far is a battered old spaceship! I'm up for this, guys. Really!'

Then he was waving them goodbye and dashing off the bus and down the street. At his back he heard Iris saying something to Panda. It sounded like, 'Nice to have a young person on board again.'

But Simon's mind was on his shop now, and Kelly. He texted her back. She was in the town centre. He'd meet her at the shop...

All the way there his mind was spinning. He could still smell the cold rust and blood and stale air from the *Begins at Home* on his clothes as he busied through the streets and underpasses. He'd really been up in the atmosphere, doing investigations with his new friends. He'd really been – where? Several miles directly above this very town...

What shocked him most was that he didn't feel too weird about it all. It felt like something that he'd been all ready and prepared for. Something had happened to him that he'd been waiting for all his life.

'It's hard to explain,' he said to Kelly, twenty minutes later, downstairs in the Exchange, which had opened its doors for the first time all day. Three browsers were in, so he kept his voice low.

'I don't believe a word of it,' Kelly tutted. She had greeted his whole reappearance with great scepticism and irritation. She had arrived with several large bags of shopping and a cross expression. 'And why did you simply assume that I'd spent the night with Anthony Marvelle at his hotel?'

Simon coloured. 'Well, he's such a smoothie. I thought you might have... I don't know. Been charmed or something...'

'What, and I'd fall right into bed with him?' She shuddered visibly. 'He's a horrible person, Simon. I thought I'd told you that. The way he rode roughshod over everyone at that festival and made them feel so silly and parochial.'

'You seemed to be getting on all right at the party last night.' Was it just last night they'd been to that party? Simon steadied himself against the cash desk. Something odd was happening to time, like it was turning soft and stretchy in his mind, like melted mozzarella on a pizza.

'I don't have to explain anything to you,' she snapped. 'We were just talking about my poems. He said they showed a primitive kind of promise. I thought a bit of flirting wouldn't hurt. He might get me into a small magazine or something. Anyway, you were the one running off with people. With that drunken floozy...'

'It's all true,' he said. 'There's a super secret base underneath the indoor market for these people. They're protecting the world from creatures out of other dimensions and stuff.'

'And her bus flies through space.'

'And time.'

'Uh-huh,' Kelly said. 'Make coffee, would you? You've ruined my day round the shops. And I suppose Iris has asked you to join her on her journeys and investigations all over the…'

'All over the galaxy, yes,' he nodded. 'Exactly. So I'm a bit worried about how I'll look after this place while I'm, you know.'

'Seeing the galaxy.' Kelly shook her head. 'Are you saying you want me to take on more hours?'

'Would you?'

'Terrance wouldn't be pleased. He left the shop to you. You're meant to be its new custodian.'

Simon had already thought about this. 'Yes, but he also – through you – left me the glass jar. The paperweight. The Objet D'Oom. Somehow Terrance is caught up in this. He knew what was going on, and what I'd get mixed up in. He could see all of this coming.'

Kelly studied him intently. 'The Objet D'Oom indeed. Who called it that?'

Simon explained all about Jenny, the head of MIAOW and how she'd gone to kick Marvelle's arse and retrieve the increasingly (it seemed) vital object. Kelly brightened at the mention of Marvelle getting his arse kicked. 'He was leaving for another gig in Cheltenham this evening. I hope she's got to him in time…'

As if on cue a rather shambolic figure came hurtling into the Exchange right at that moment. Iris had had a complete change of outfit and had found time for a hairdo. Her hair had been permed and teased into a weird conelike shape with a feathery fascinator stuck to it. She was out of breath and quite stricken.

'Ooh, Simon lovey. Get me a chair. Gimme a drink sweetheart. Am I all right smoking in here?'

Kelly looked scandalized. One of the customer's heads appeared round a bookcase, alarmed at the commotion. 'What is it, Iris?' Simon asked.

'Jenny's drawn a blank at the Duke's Legs. Marvelle had already checked out and nicked off. She found some brightly coloured dog hairs in his room and that was it. So - she's failed! She failed to get the jar off him!'

'That's bad, right?' Kelly said, pouring their coffee. She was determined to be the most level-headed person in the shop.

'It's terrible!' Iris burst out. 'That jar is terribly dangerous. You were fools for letting it out of your sight. You've done something incalculably silly!'

Kelly frowned. 'Why's your carpet bag moving about like that? What's inside?'

Iris liberated Panda. He burst free and boggled at Kelly. 'Hello, there! Who's this young lady, Iris?'

Kelly almost dropped the coffee cups.

'Never mind that, Panda,' snapped Iris. 'We're in deadly danger.'

Simon did the introductions. 'And this, Kelly, is Iris's friend, Panda.'

Kelly swore. 'You were telling the truth, weren't you? All of it. It's true, isn't it?'

They all looked at her. 'Is she a bit slow?' Panda asked Simon.

CHAPTER SEVEN

Simon decided to close up the Exchange early. They were all starving, it turned out, so he offered to cook something. Iris pulled a face.

'I'm a good cook!'

'I don't doubt it, lovey. But can you be bothered? We need to concentrate on our next move. We have to think about this properly.'

'Why don't we hook up with Jenny and MIAOW again? See what they think?' asked Simon.

Iris's expression went dark. 'I don't like their methods, as I said before. I don't think we should throw in our lot with them wholesale, as it were.'

'Iris is right,' commented Panda. 'We need to figure stuff out ourselves first.'

'Dinner, then,' said Iris breezily. 'Let's wander into town and eat somewhere fancy, eh? What about you, Kelly, will you join us?'

She nodded, not looking too sure about being seen with them, Simon guessed. She still seemed quite freaked out by the talking Panda – and by Iris's magnificent hairdo and her silver jacket and striped stockings. Somehow Iris looked a lot more gaudy than she had during the literary festival last week…

Iris barrelled up to Kelly. 'I must swear you to secrecy, same as I did Simon. You're in this with us now. Nefarious shenanigans.

Conspiracies from space. So just think on, lady. You're either with us on the bus or you're not.'

Kelly hesitated only for a moment. 'I'm with you. Iris. And Panda.' She looked at Simon and he almost smiled. Rarely had he seen Kelly so out of her depth.

*

Iris didn't find any restaurants to her liking on their wander through town. She frowned and huffed and bit and then turned on them in the middle of the street with a huge grin. 'What about my favourite place, eh? Why don't I show you that?'

There were some muffled noises from Panda in the bag, but they couldn't make them out.

'And where's that?' Kelly asked.

*

It turned out to be a balmy evening in Montmartre in June 1894.

'At least, I think that's the year,' Iris said, peering thoughtfully at a wall of peeling posters. They were advertising various cabaret nights at the Black Cat and the Moulin Rouge. Famous posters Simon recognised from art history books at school.

The whole place was so... *French*. Ludicrously French. Like a made-up set, with its cobbled winding streets, the higgledy-piggledy rooftops. Artists painting in the streets and accordionists wheezing melodically on street corners... and the street girls wandering in their shabby, brilliant finery...

Kelly walked a few paces behind them. She was flabbergasted.

The pale towers and domes of Sacre Coeur loomed above them all, against an inky night sky.

The most surprising thing was how sanguine Iris was about it all. She paused wearily to let Panda out of her carpet bag. 'No need to keep the poor mite hidden here,' she observed. 'This place is filled with all kind of freaks. No one will turn a hair.'

'Ah,' sighed Panda. 'La Belle Epoque! Well done, Iris! You got us here splendidly!'

Iris ambled alongside Simon as they headed for her favoured Bistro. 'So, this is what we do, Simon. This is our thing. We have deadly dangerous fun and adventures and so on, and it's great. Not everyone can cope with it all. (I don't think your pal Kelly is coping with it at all, do you? Just look at her face!) But we just love it, careering about from place to place. And I thought that you looked the type, too. Anyway, here we are! Paris in the good old days – lucky us! Just *smell!* That perfect combination of dance hall sweat and roasting garlic! Tangy red wine and filterless ciggies! Who else can do this, eh? Except those of us born to it. It's worth all the hassle...'

And Simon thought – Yes, it is! I love this..!

They had opened up a space in the air of another time zone. They were breezing through the past as if it was the easiest thing on Earth.

On a steep path under lit-up trees they stopped for a quick glass of cloudy pastis and to gather their breath. From here they could see all of Paris and its gaudy patchwork of gas-lit streets.

'What do you think then, Simon and Kelly?' Panda grinned, gripping his glass of liquorice-flavoured spirits with both paws. 'Are you enjoying yourselves? Better than staying in Darlington all evening?'

'This is my favourite month and year in Paris,' Iris told them. 'Right before everything changes forever. We're teetering on the brink, here. And I have to be very careful how many times I'm here on the same night. Very embarrassing, that can be, running into yourself. I always run out of things to say. But I think we're okay, though. I'm sure I heard someone say in the crowd that this is a Thursday. I've never been on a Thursday before. It's just as nice!' She knocked back her drink.

Simon was trying to take it all in. He wanted to be hyper-aware and conscious of every little thing, for his first journey into the past. The drink seemed to heighten his senses even more. He shivered pleasurably and looked at Kelly. She had a strange look about her. Almost disapproving.

'We can't be doing this,' she whispered to him. 'This just can't be happening. How can it be happening? What about... chaos theory? What about... if we change one little thing in a time we don't belong to... just by virtue of our presence surely we're moving air around, bits of dust... won't everything on Earth be knocked out of kilter..?'

Iris leaned forward and patted her hand. 'What's that, lovey? Are you getting all theoretical? Oh dear, I wouldn't bother about that. There's no point theorizing when you're actually *in* the blummin' past! All you can do is muck in and enjoy it all – and here we are!'

They sat quietly for a little bit. Panda's stomach rumbled loudly. Iris laughed. 'I've a table booked at Jean-Pierre's for eight o'clock!' she announced.

'I can taste those little froggy legs already,' sighed Panda.

As they sat for another drink and Simon gazed up at stars that weren't much different from how they were in his own time... (but seemed just different *enough* – brighter, somehow...) he was having an epiphany. About what it must be like to go from time to time and treat it all like a great big pub crawl... This could be my whole life now, he thought, with increasing excitement. I could be racketing about having fun – just like Iris and Panda do. With no worries...

Then they were walking up the steep hill again, under the shifting mass of leafy shadows, and Iris was clinging onto his arm for support. 'The marvellous thing about Parisians is they're so cool. That waiter didn't even blink when I paid by Denobian slime dollar, did he?'

Kelly was a few steps behind, and he could hear Panda bragging to her, about the places and times he had visited. Kelly was ominously quiet.

Iris lowered her voice, snuggling into Simon's arm, 'C'mon then, lovey. You can tell me. Kelly's surely not your girlfriend, is she? C'mon, have a heart to heart with your Aunty Iris. You can tell me… Gay, gay, gay, right?'

He laughed, and nodded happily, staring at the confusing network of yellow gas lamps sketching the shape of nineteenth century Paris at the foot of Montmartre.

Then they were in the Bistro, under an awning and studying huge hand-written menus. 'I could get to all the places I ever wanted to go,' he was gabbling. He was getting over-enthusiastic, he realised, and Iris was smiling at him indulgently. 'We could be in San Francisco 1976, or London when it's swinging in 1965… all those places I ever wished I was. Panda said something about Cleopatra's palace before, didn't you?'

'Oh yes,' said Panda, his eyes misting slightly. 'Incorrigible woman.'

'I always felt like I was missing out on something wonderful and grand,' Simon said. 'You know, coming from the north east in the era I do. But… that doesn't matter now, does it?'

Iris shrugged, divvying up the last of the wine. 'As I told you, Darlington in your time is a bit of a Nexus point. Specially for time travellers. There's more going on round your way than you even know about.'

He beamed. 'But now I'm part of it. Now I can take part in it all at last…'

Kelly thumped her wine glass down hard on the checkered table cloth. 'For god's sake, listen to yourselves!'

They all stared at her.

'This isn't some game!' she burst. 'This is serious! If it's all true… if all this is real…' Unconsciously she put her palms down on the table, as if she was steadying herself. 'Then we have to be careful. We can't mess about. This isn't an opportunity for playing about, Simon – you're going on like you can have some kind of gap year in space and time…!'

He grinned. 'Yes! That's a great way of putting it!'

'Look. If what she says is true,' Kelly nodded at Iris, who looked stung by her brusqueness. 'Then there are such things as… aliens. Other dimensions. Space and stuff.'

'Well, all that would seem pretty obviously true by now, Kel,' Simon said.

'Then we're in danger, aren't we? This lot at MIAOW – who are supposed to be defending us. Who are they? Can we trust them? And for that matter, can we trust *her*?'

Panda looked scandalized. 'Trust Iris! Why, she might be a flaky old moo at times, but I'm shocked at you Kelly! You seemed such a nice young lady…!'

Then Kelly said, through gritted teeth, in a voice that was turning slightly hysterical: 'And that… *stuffed bear IS TALKING TO ME!!*'

Panda rose up in his chair. He stood on the seat, his full ten inches in height and thundered: 'STUFFED?! *BEAR?!*'

Kelly looked beseechingly at Simon and Iris. 'This object… this glass jar that Terrance left behind… shouldn't we be finding a way of getting it back? If it's as dangerous and as important as all that, why are we wasting our time here..?'

Iris lit a cigarette savagely. 'If there's no time for a nice sit down dinner with friends and a couple of drinks, then what kind of adventure is that, eh, Kelly? You should calm down, lovey, you'll do yourself a mischief…'

They were interrupted then by a whistling, screeching noise overhead. The menus flapped and the awning cracked loudly in the sudden wind. Other diners and revellers in the Montmartre streets noticed the disturbance. A cry went up. There was some laughter, even a scream, as a weird green light passed overhead.

'What's *that?!*' Simon yelled, as the breeze died down and the green light faded.

'Ah,' said Iris.

There was a dull-sounding explosion – a hollow CRUMP – that came from the vicinity of the bottom of the hill.

'That was the graveyard, I think,' said Panda. 'That's where it landed.'

Kelly was on her feet. 'Landed? What's landed?'

Now there was more noise in the street. Montmartre was rousing from its drunken stupor.

Iris dabbed her lips on a napkin. 'I'm glad we managed to eat first,' she sighed. 'The Martian cylinder, lovey, that's what.'

Simon goggled at her. 'The *what?*'

'June 1894,' she snapped. 'Don't you know your history? Now I realise why I've never been here on this particular Thursday evening. It's the night the Martians arrive.'

*

There were crowds gathering on the roads and the pathways that led into the cemetery. The curious were flocking to see what had landed… and what lay at the heart of that greenish radiance.

Windows in the hotels were smashed, slates had fallen, a couple of chimney stacks had been knocked from rooftops. There was a curious suspension of festivities going on – even here, so close to the sails of the Moulin Rouge. People were shocked – in a part of town where no one was ever shocked.

There was a strange warmth in the air and a scent of burning…

As Iris, Panda, Simon and Kelly edged into the cemetery, following the crowds, they could see some of the damage wrought by the star that had fallen to Earth.

'Shouldn't we warn them all not to get too close…?' worried Kelly.

Graves and tombs had been ripped out of the ground. The dark earth had been ploughed up. Panda cried out when he saw the mouldering coffins that had been disinterred. He caught a glimpse of pale, withered flesh.

'Ooh, this is horrible,' said Iris.

And in the very centre of the graveyard there was churning smoke and hissing steam, mist wreathing around the smooth form of the cylinder's end. The silver craft had buried itself almost upright in the fresh crater.

'They're landing all over the world tonight,' Iris said. 'And for the next few days. This is where it all begins.'

Simon stared at her. 'But… how can that be? This didn't happen. The Martians never invaded in 1894!'

She frowned at him. 'How do you know? Were you there?'

'Well, no. Not until tonight, but…'

'It happened. In this dimension. Transdimensional, I said, remember? Alternate realities. That's what this is all about.'

'Erm, Iris,' Panda said, looking rather disturbed and muddy. 'Do you think we should hang about here? You know what comes next, don't you?'

'Ah yes,' nodded Iris. 'The old heat ray.'

Around them the Parisians were getting closer to the cylinder as it cooled noisily in the dark earth. They were overcoming their fear and were keen to examine the new arrival.

'We should warn them,' Kelly said.

'They won't listen,' Iris sighed. 'We can't do anything about helping this lot. Paris gets just about levelled between now and the turn of the century.'

'Can't we do anything?' Simon asked.

'It's already done,' Iris smiled sadly. 'Been there and done that, as it happens. I'm instrumental in the final battles with the Martians, in about seven years time. But I've no intention of getting caught up in all that palaver again!' She shivered inside her long silver coat. 'Who's for a drink and a bit of a bop at the Moulin Rouge, eh? It's just round the corner.'

Panda perked up at this. Kelly didn't look so sure.

'Oh, come on! Cheer up! It's just another alien invasion! You'll get used to them. You'll have to. Come on, let's go and dance, while we can...'

Which was what they did.

*

They danced more or less all night. At least, Iris and Simon did, in that portion of the gleaming sprung floor reserved for amateurs. Kelly sat with Panda in a booth mysteriously reserved for them by name, and they drank wine together. Kelly thought they should all have been more anxious to return home and to focus on the missing glass jar, but Panda reminded her gently that they could spend a fair amount of time away from the place they had left – and return to their starting point only moments later. Such were the mysteries of time travel. You just had to make sure you left good bookmarks behind you.

'Of course,' he added. 'That can turn into a bad habit. Iris has left bookmarks in times and places all over the galaxy... Half the time she forgets to go back, or it slips her mind what she was going back for anyway...'

Kelly pictured all of time as a book – fattened and thickened with pressed flowers, postcards, bank notes... scribbles in the margin that made no real sense.

Kelly watched the wiry woman cavorting with Simon. She had never seen Simon dancing with such abandon. Now he was improvising a kind of silly tango, which the two of them were playing out – Iris was the bull, he the matador – to the amusement of the other dancers. In their anachronistic clothing the visitors stood out a mile amongst the dandified gentlemen and the ladies in all their brilliant colours, their ruffles and silks.

Kelly was just telling Panda how she felt like she was in a painting by Lautrec, when Panda nudged her elbow and pointed out the small man sitting alone at a table near the stage area. He was scribbling busily on the table cloth and pausing now and then to swig green absinthe from a glass.

'There he is!' Kelly gasped. And it was as if it was really getting through to her, for the first time, that they had journeyed into the past.

'Simon seems to be a natural at this,' Panda observed. 'Taking it all in his stride. Flinging himself into enjoying it all.'

Kelly shrugged. 'I'm finding it harder to come to terms with. All this impossible stuff... I can't take it in...'

'Take your time,' said Panda. 'You're right. It should be impossible. It's absurd. That takes a little time, my dear.'

'I never can relax, even when I go on holiday,' sighed Kelly. 'My mind keeps working overtime. I'll be sitting on a beach and wondering if I really did turn off the toaster before I left the house at the start of the week. And now I'm here and I'm fretting about Anthony Marvelle and how we let him get his hands on that jar, when Terrance told us to look after it...'

Panda patted her arm. 'But as I explained, that doesn't matter. That whole world – your world – is on *pause* for now. Until we return to it and start time up again. We can re-gather our thoughts and take stock and figure it all out...'

'But that seems impossible too,' said Kelly. 'I guess I'm just a worrier.' She spent a little while explaining about how her dad had been a bit hapless and careless. The two of them had been alone during her childhood, and it had fallen to Kelly to see to practical tasks and concerns – to make sure the flat's rent and utility bills were paid, to lock up the doors and windows when they went out. She had been over-compensating like this throughout her life – for as long as she could remember.

Only half-listening and nodding now and then, Panda was turning over his own earlier words about time travel... and how time in their previous location was effectively standing still until their return. He wondered if it was quite true, and as straightforward as all that. Could time really be dammed up and put on pause? Anthony Marvelle was obviously in cahoots with those dreadful Dogs, and they had access to time travel technology. Couldn't they find some way around the safety features Panda had so blithely described? Why, even now they might be simply skipping away from the Earth in possession of the precious artefact...

'Drink up Kelly,' he said. 'It's three in the morning. If we don't get Iris back aboard the bus soon she'll dance herself dizzy. There'll be no stopping her. We'll be here all night. I've seen this kind of thing before. They had to scrape her off the floor at Studio 54.'

Iris was doing a strange kind of dance that involved strutting around like a chicken, thrusting out her neck and flapping her arms like wings. Simon was laughing and she had to explain it was a dance she'd learned on some world she'd visited a long time ago… And then Panda was with them and wanting to be picked up.

'I think we should go as soon as we can!' he bellowed at them. Iris sat him on her shoulder and swung him about a bit and he consented to dance to one number with them.

It took twenty minutes before they left that hot, noisy hall – and saw that Kelly had gone out ahead of them onto the busy street. Rue de Clinqcourt was rowdy, chilly, and brazen with squawking traffic noise and shouting. Simon remembered his phone and started snapping pictures of the red windmill and the crowds passing by.

Then they saw that Kelly was looking rather pale.

'What is it? What's the matter?' Iris hurried over to her, where she was standing on the pavement.

'I saw him!' Kelly gasped. 'While I was standing here, waiting for you to come out of there. I got a bit too warm and dizzy in there so I came here to wait for you. And he came breezing passed, bold as you like. In a top hat and dressed as if he belonged right here. But it was him! It was him!'

'Who, love?' Iris gripped her arm. 'Who are you talking about?'

'And he had his dog with him. He had that poodle on a lead. They were bustling along with the same snooty looks on their faces.'

'Marvelle?' Simon gasped. 'You saw Marvelle here in Paris?'

Kelly nodded.

'Where did they go? Which direction?' Iris demanded.

Panda was horrified. 'They've got time travel! And they're following us..!'

CHAPTER EIGHT

What did Simon tell her in those first few days and nights aboard the bus?

They were doing so many things and it was all quite hectic – but he felt impelled to say stuff, to explain his life – to confide in her. Something about the avid old ratbag invited his confessions and he found himself mouthing off and wondering aloud.

He couldn't stop himself. Kelly gave him a few funny looks – as if she thought he was out of control – that wayward tongue of his was giving too much away.

They sat up late that night in Montmartre – with some delicious hot chocolate Panda had whipped up on a small pan on the galley stove, and watched the pretty lights falling out of the sky. The sputter and green fizz looked like Alka Seltzer from outer space. Kelly had to remind herself what these soft, bright flares really represented – an actual invasion force from the planet Mars…

Right then, bleary-eyed and still in a state of shock from all they had seen in the last twelve hours – she was listening to Simon coming out with all this stuff about his family. About his Gran and Grandad, who he'd lived with from the age of sixteen. And the death of his parents in a plane crash. As Kelly well knew, they'd been heading off on a holiday of a lifetime – which they had won on a TV game show. The video tape of the particular episode which recorded their triumph had been in Simon's possession ever since – the ten years since. He had never had the heart to watch it - to see his young, jubilant, doomed parents on that gaudy studio set as the credits rolled and the tinsel rained down. And now he didn't even have a video player anyway.

'Oh chuck,' Iris said, blowing on her hot chocolate. 'What a terrible story.'

'My condolences, young man,' Panda added gruffly. They were sitting at the formica breakfast bar. Spilled hot chocolate stood in rings and pools. It looked almost lilac in the dusky light.

Kelly still couldn't believe Simon was opening up like this to these bizarre people. He had always been so reserved – even clammed up – with her and she was supposed to be his closest friend. And yet he'd been away, hadn't he? Away in his university town across the other side of the Pennines and the craggy moors. Maybe over there, in recent years, he had learned to be another person. More open and more confident and able to take weirdo shit like this – like this night, this bus, this old bag and her talking Panda. He could take it all in his stride.

He's gone past me, Kelly thought gloomily. I can't handle any of this as well as he can. Not at all. This drinking chocolate in Paris aboard a London bus – with Martians dropping out of the sky all around us. And Toulouse Lautrec sitting there with his tin of crayons just a few yards away from me, giving me the glad-eye over his glasses. Kelly didn't think she'd ever get used to things like that.

'You're on the bus now,' said Iris, wiping her mouth daintily with a hanky. 'This is where your real education begins. Isn't it, Panda?'

'Oh yes,' grinned Panda. 'You'd better believe it. We can show you a thing or two aboard the Celestial Omnibus…'

Suddenly Simon had the feeling that he'd been at an audition. This was the final stage, this deceptively casual suppertime chat.

He could sense that Kelly was agitated beside him. She wasn't happy with any of this.

Then Iris was pulling down a paper blind over the window closest to them. It lit up as if by magic, showing a bewildering display of geometric shapes – spirals and whorls and intersecting bodies in motion. 'Star charts?' Simon asked.

'Good!' Iris patted him on the hand. 'But – even better than that. This is an atlas of all time, space and myriad possibility. At least, it's a fragment of one. A good portion of one. Each window aboard the bus shows a different bit of the jigsaw. It's like the atlas of all time is written on the insides of her eyelids. Groovy, eh? I shouldn't have any of this stuff at all, you know.'

Kelly looked frankly sceptical. 'But how? How can you have such a thing? Where did you get it from? And this bus – why is it a bus? And who are you anyway, really? Where do you come from?'

Iris regarded the girl as if she'd only just noticed her, perched there on a bar stool. The older woman's face darkened with irritation. 'None of that stuff's interesting,' she snapped, batting her black painted lashes haughtily. 'I prefer to remain mysterious. An enigma. That's the way I like to be. You join me on the bus knowing only what you need to know – that I am a traveller, a diarist, a great thinker, a good friend – and a being of complete fabulousness. Is that okay, lovey? Can you handle that?' She thrust her face close to Kelly, making the girl recoil at the whiff of gin. Tension bristled between the two women, until Simon broke in.

'Yes, yes, we understand! You're an enigma. We get it. We won't ask too much.'

'And I'm an enigma too,' put in Panda, popping their empty mugs on a tray and wiping round quickly with a dishcloth. 'So don't you go asking me any silly questions about how come I can talk and walk and be such a towering intellectual when, to all intents and purposes I look – from the outside, to the untrained eye – very like a (*ahem*) stuffed toy.' He boggled at them warningly and Simon agreed that he wouldn't ask silly questions of his new friends.

'Right,' said Iris, snapping into action. 'We've got a short side-step trip to make before this night's out. A quick whiz across the rooftops of Paris and over the churning grey of the Channel… to London in just under a hundred years' time. There's something I have to do in South Kensington in the middle of the night and then we can head back to Darlington and pick up on the trail of Mr. Anthony Marvelle…'

'But he was here in Paris tonight,' Kelly burst out. 'I saw him here. He must have come after us. Didn't you believe me?'

Bustling up the gangway, Iris never spared her a backward glance. 'Of course I believed you, lovey. But this is time travel, yes? We have to wonder, don't we – was Marvelle following us, or were we following Marvelle? We don't want to be chasing round after chimeras, you know. We have to go about these things in the correct order. We can't go *zig-zagging* about willy-nilly. And there's something I really must check before we do anything else…'

'Back at the office?' Panda asked.

'That's right, chuck. Back at our office in South Ken in July 1973. We won't be long! Back in your precious Darlington for breakfast time!'

The engines started up with a bronchial chatter and Jimi Hendrix came crashing out of the speakers in glorious multi-coloured loops of noise. Kelly experienced a wave of sickly tiredness. She noticed Simon staring at her, concerned.

'I'm okay,' she murmured. 'I just wish I knew what the old bat was on about half the time. I mean, how can we nab Marvelle by chasing forward in time to 1973? We should just go after him here, surely? Doesn't that make more sense? This is like being in some horrible dream...'

Just as she spoke the smoky lemony spill of lamplight outside smeared and obscured the pinprick lights of Montmartre. Together all their surroundings rushed away and the bus was suddenly elsewhere again. They caught a glimpse of woolly banks of polluted cloud cover and the slanting rooftops and gables and labyrinths of streets and then it all swept into an indecipherable scrawl beneath them.

Kelly and Simon clung to the breakfast bar as the bus caromed into the Maelstrom, plunging deeper into time itself.

'It might not seem logical or sensible,' Simon was shouting. 'But I guess Iris must know what she's doing. There'll be some method in her madness, I'm sure. And she knows it's important, getting the jar back from Marvelle. She'll know what to do. We just... just have to trust her!'

He knew right then, as he said it, that trusting Iris was something he was utterly prepared to do. He already trusted the old woman with every jot of his being. He didn't question that. As the whole bus juddered and thumped and swerved madly from side to side he looked across the breakfast bar as Kelly shielded herself from falling nick nacks and geegaws. She looked incredulous. Trust Iris? Kelly just wanted the bus to stop somewhere familiar and safe. She wanted it all to stop so she could get off.

*

Iris did in fact keep an office in London, which seemed an extraordinary thing to do, for a woman who claimed that her double decker bus contained all and everything she would ever need.

The bus shimmered into existence – a mite more subtly than usual – in South Kensington, the middle of one summer's night in 1973. Somewhere near the Victoria and Albert Museum. It was midnight and her crew were yawning as she led them across the road into a maze of quiet back streets.

'It's an office where I keep certain documents and objects under lock and key. Artefacts and papers too dangerous to keep about your person or on board your bus for very long…'

Simon liked the sound of mysteriously powerful objects and documents.

She led them to a small boutique called *The Gilded Lily*. Its darkened windows displayed a whole load of velvet shoes – pointy and platformed, bowed and strappy. Iris sighed at them all and tried to interest Kelly, who couldn't disguise her pleasure at the sight.

'The office is upstairs,' Panda told them, watching Iris hunt around in her bag for a splendidly large jangle of keys. 'It's Friday night,' he said. 'On Saturday night this whole building - shop, glamorous shoes and office upstairs - is utterly vaporized. Everything vanishes or is destroyed.'

'Really?' gasped Kelly. 'How do you know?'

'Uh, time travel?' Iris laughed, as the black door before them sprang open, revealing a dimly lit stairwell and a whiff of patchouli.

Panda ushered them up the stairs. 'The office only exists for three days in total,' he explained.

'But who vaporized it – I mean, who *will* vaporize it?'

'We will, or rather, *did*,' said Iris, as if the answer was obvious. 'That's how we keep the secret and special stuff safe, you see. Just allowing it three days' existence in our care. Then we can go back and back to it, and no one will ever know the three days we were ever here.'

This sounded not exactly foolproof to Simon.

But then they were standing at a doorway with pebbled glass. There was actually a sign that read, 'Iris Wildthyme – Transtemporal Adventuress', like a 1940s consulting detective. Underneath, in a far less assured hand it read, 'And Panda – Art Critic.'

When the door creaked open the wood-panelled room within smelled less musty and unused than they expected. There was a feeling of someone having just departed – a swirl of golden dust in the air, the lamps left burning – and a bottle of gin standing open on the incredibly messy desk.

'Probably one of your future or earlier selves popping in,' Panda said to Iris. 'I wonder if I was with you.'

She was flipping through the papers on the desk. 'Sometimes we leave notes for each other. Hm. Nothing today.'

'I still think you should have a little soiree for everyone,' said Panda, 'For the evening when everything goes *whoosh* in flames. It'd be nice to see some of the others.'

Iris shrugged. 'Maybe one day.'

'We're really in 1973?' asked Simon. He was peering at a calendar on the dirty, mouldy plaster. It showed a picture of a sexy traffic warden and seemed to consist of three days in July only. Notes were scribbled in many hands and coloured inks in the too-small squares. 'Hey,' he said. 'I knew that date was familiar! Saturday night!' He turned on them all grinning. There was a shunting noise and a grunt from Iris as she levered open filing cabinet drawers.

'What was that, lovey?' she asked absently, flipping through files.

'The Saturday night! When it all goes *whoosh*! It's a famous date!'

'Is it?'

'It's the night of a famous concert at the Hammersmith Odeon,' he said. 'The retirement show of my favourite ever rock star. An all-time classic live album came out of it. I was too young to have been there, of course. But I always dreamed about it.'

'Oh, really,' scowled Panda, as if he found all this pop music stuff very trivial indeed. 'Who was it? Petula Clark?'

Simon shook his head, looking very shivery and excited all of a sudden, as he realised what time travel was really like. He could be there! He could actually go there tomorrow night! He could be in the stalls at the Hammersmith Odeon – and get his screams recorded for posterity on that live LP he had treasured all of his life! 'Vince Cosmos,' he told them. 'The greatest glam rocker of all time. He retires on stage tomorrow night and plays his best gig ever. Amazing! And the Tomorrow Twins played support to him. Oh god, can we go, Iris? Can we be there?'

'Can we *have been* there'?' Kelly corrected him jokingly and, for some reason, this earned her a sharp glance from Iris, who was now wearing a pince-nez.

'No, we can't,' Iris said shortly. 'I'm afraid we're too busy, chuck. Sorry to disappoint you. But maybe we can go next time we're in this neck of the woods.'

'Oh, okay,' said Simon, looking thoroughly disappointed.

'Chin up, dearie,' Iris added. 'That concert will still be there in a hundred years, you know.'

'Vince Cosmos!' Panda chuckled. 'There are some funny rumours and tales about him, you know.'

'There are?'

'Well, you know how he pretends to be an alien?'

'Ye-e-es..'

'I'll say no more!' Panda tapped his black furry nose.

'No time for all that now, lovey,' Iris said. 'We're in trouble.'

'What is it?'

'Well, I've hunted all the way through this cabinet of mine. There was something very particular locked away in here. And it's not here. And the fact that it's not here is very, very disturbing.'

'What is it?'

'Someone's been and let themselves in and taken away a certain pair of scissors.'

'Scissors?'

'Pinking shears, to be exact. And look. They left a note.'

It didn't say much. It was on fancy pink paper with a queer watermark. There was a scrawled note in an elaborate hand.

'Read it!' Panda said.

Tough luck, ducky. Kiss kiss kiss – Marvelle.

Iris was pale. 'I thought as much. That's how he and his poodle are mucking about with time. They've nicked the magic pinking shears! They can go *anywhere* now! We'll never catch up with them!'

CHAPTER NINE

There wasn't much of an opportunity to ask Iris about anything much the rest of that night. She went into a kind of sulk. 'It's not a sulk,' she snapped, as she locked up the office and their small group traipsed back through the streets to the bus. 'I'm just pondering the awful disasters that are likely to befall us. And when I say 'us' I don't just mean us four – I'm talking about the whole flaming galaxy, as it happens.'

Back on the bus, Panda started mixing a pitcher of Margueritas and Iris went onto the top deck for a while (library, observation deck, bathroom, wardrobe and guest bedroom). She was going to consult her diaries, she said, to see what she might find. Her friends were allowed to doze for a bit in the company of Panda, who decided to make them omelettes as an early breakfast ('I make magnificent omlettes! Killer omelettes!') And soon the bus was filled with choking fumes and the reek of charred egg.

Kelly sat with Simon on the chaise longue. 'I wish they'd just take us home,' she sighed. 'I'm knackered. I can't keep up with all of this.'

He smiled at her. He could. He knew he could keep up with it all. Despite the talk of disaster and danger he was loving every minute of this. He couldn't wait for Iris to come stomping crossly down that spiral staircase and to see where she would whisk them to next.

When she did come down however, she looked even gloomier. 'I must talk to Jenny and MIAOW again. If Marvelle has the pinking shears, then they need to be warned.'

Simon followed her to the driver's cab, where a mug of black coffee was waiting for her – and a Dusty Springfield tape – both left there helpfully by Panda.

'These scissors,' Simon began.

Iris fussed with the intricate controls of her bus. She combed her hair out with her fingers, clamped a ludicrous hat onto her head and lit herself a black cigarette with a golden filter. She wasn't in a talkative mood so she just said: 'Ancient object. Most deadly. Shears through the Very Fabric of Space and Time. Heinous in the wrong hands. Which it currently is.' She dinged the bell. 'All aboard! Good! We're off!'

And that was the end of her explanations for now.

Next thing, the double decker was lurching into the Maelstrom once more, where the time storms raged and, when he looked, Simon could glimpse strange figures and faces in the ethereal green and orange mist. Or was he imagining it through fatigue? They were like ghosts out there, flaunting themselves and jeering at the lit up windows of the bus. Panda – having given up his omelette attempt – noticed what Simon was staring at and prodded his shoulder.

'Don't even look at them, Simon. They are the Roadkill. The spectres and victims of millennia of time travel. Those who came a cropper as they tried to harness the mysteries of time. If they latch onto you they will transfix you with their basilisk stare… they will command you to open our doors and to let them aboard…' Panda shuddered visibly. 'Nasty old things. Like Time Zombies. Best avoided, really. We seem to have hit a nasty patch of the fiends, on our way back to Darlington…'

Simon tried to do as he was told, and not to look too closely at those soundlessly shrieking faces, those tattered, beckoning limbs…

And then the next thing he and Kelly knew, it was morning. The bus was pulling into the kerbside in the blue dawn, just outside the old indoor market building in his home town. It was market day in the main square outside and already vans and lorries were turning up and burly men were erecting stalls, unrolling awnings that flapped in the morning breeze and unloading miscellaneous goods. Robert peered round the bus's chintz curtains and it was good to see ordinary stuff like carpets and crates of oranges and racks of jeans.

'Thank god,' Kelly muttered. She looked dark-eyed and dishevelled after their night out.

'Okay,' Iris said. 'I've brought us back to the exact next morning after we left! How's about that for navigation, eh lovies?' She seemed brighter now than she had ever since leaving South Ken.

'The next day?' Kelly said. 'I should think so.'

Iris frowned at her. 'It's rather tricky, you know, getting this time stuff right. You should be more grateful for my amazing prowess.'

'I never wanted to go anyway,' Kelly said. 'I had no idea that it was so tricky. Or that we should feel lucky you could even return us home.' Kelly shook her head blearily. 'Anyway. Cheers. But I've got work to do.'

Simon was biting his lip. He could see how much Kelly was aggravating Iris. Was she going to blow both their chances for being invited back aboard the bus?

'We've all got work to do!' Iris snapped. 'Come on, Panda chuck. We've got to tell MIAOW some of what we've found out. And Simon?'

He gulped, almost jumping to attention. 'Uh, yes, Iris?'

'You get yourself back to your bookshop.'

His heart sank a little. 'Yes, I've got to open up. I've neglected it already…' He was mumbling dolefully, earning a savage look from Kelly.

Iris waved her hands. 'No, no, *no*. Get back to your shop and pack a bag or two. Grab everything you might need for a good long while in space and time. We're going on a bit of a yomp this time, I think! No more of this pussy-footing around Earth and its environs for us! We're about to head off into the galaxy at large! So – go and get on with it! I absolutely refuse to leave this world without you. You're on the bus now, boy, and you'll feel better if you have a few of your own things with you.'

'Er,' said Kelly. 'And me?'

Iris tutted. 'You're staying here and looking after the bookshop. That's where you're needed most.'

Panda watched his two new human friends leave shortly after this – marching into the market – Simon hardly able to contain his delighted excitement. 'You were too hard on the girl, Iris,' he said. 'She's all right, really.'

'Something about her rubs me up the wrong way,' Iris said. 'She's a right moody little madam. I can't be doing with that sort on board. Remember – it's my bus, and what I say goes! Now, come on, chum. Best pick up your furry little feet and hop into my carpet bag. I've stuff to do and a rest to take, as my old auntie used to say!'

*

Kelly went back to her landlady's house and was surprised to find it still in disarray from the party. Chelsea was in rubber gloves and apron, hunting for cans and plastic plates and wines bottles and dumping everything in one bin bag. She looked messy but still impossibly glamorous.

'Oh! So there you are,' she said, raising both eyebrows as her lodger made her appearance. 'That's got to be the longest stop out ever! Not that I'm checking up on you of course. It's none of my business.'

Kelly joined her in the kitchen, where Chelsea set about making coffee – her eyebrows still up and avid for gossip. She shucked her rubber gloves and cleared a space at the kitchen table for them both. 'So it was Marvelle then, eh?'

Kelly gasped. For a moment she thought Chelsea must know something about the missing jar from space and all the weird stuff happening.

'You needn't look so shifty,' her landlady laughed. 'All the poetry ladies saw how you and him were thick as thieves during the party. You went off with him, didn't you? You've been away for over twenty four hours!'

'I never went off with him!'

'Oh yes, of course!' Chelsea shook her head. 'We could all see what was going on. He's a notorious old rake. He made passes at at least four of the lady poets during the festival, and succeeded with at least two. No one will talk about it, just veiled hints and allusions. So come on, what's he like? What did I pass up on?'

Kelly was starting to feel a bit got at and cross. 'I never slept with that slimeball. I wouldn't!'

Chelsea looked incredulous. She teased for a bit as they had their coffee, but she could see that Kelly wasn't going to tell her any more. Eventually she put the tin lid back on the chocolate biscuits, re-donned her rubber gloves and announced she was going back to her housework. 'By the way, did you see anything more of that Wildthyme woman?'

Kelly silently shook her head. This time she was lying and she knew she looked it.

'Well, someone did some checks on her, and it turns out that she doesn't really exist. All those books she was meant to have written – all bogus. She was here under false pretences. And she took all the spirits from the party. Nesta saw her filling her carpet bag with bottles. What an awful woman! I knew there was something dodgy about her.' Then Chelsea picked up a pile of post from the Welsh dresser. 'These came for you, by the way.'

On her way to her rather gloomy basement flat Kelly flipped through the sheaf of bank things and rubbish.

It seemed hardly any time at all since she'd moved in here. A few weeks after joining the Arts Centre poetry group she found herself becoming good friends with some of the women. Women much older than she was were taking her under their wing for the first time in her life. They felt sorry for her motherless state and were wary of her rackety, biker father, going off on his endless road trips and leaving his daughter alone in that terrible flat of his. Chelsea had been careful not to express her fretting over Kelly's terrible life, because she could see the girl was a bit prickly and independent. But Chelsea's teenage kids were both forever on the point of moving out and she needed to lavish her care on someone. So Kelly was it. Chelsea had the basement done up as a tiny bedsit and offered it at a peppercorn rent to her new friend. Kelly – wary of charity – had agreed and already she'd been here almost a year.

It was her sanctuary in the heart of town. The mouldy, tatty tower block flat of her childhood was just something she dreamed about now and then. After her father had gone off on his last trip – his longest trip, revving off into the sunset, never to be heard from or seen again – she had let the council take back the rotten flat and decided to concentrate on her own life.

She loved this couple of small rooms below street level, with their Indian prints, band posters, shelves stocked with slim volumes of poetry and spiky, healthy yukka plants.

What was it today, though, as she put on the lights, flung her jacket and mail down on the bed – what was it made it feel a bit hollow and dim? She even felt slightly shut in and claustrophobic. The small window, high up on one wall, showing stone steps to the street and occasionally some passing feet… all of a sudden it felt a bit prisonlike. And Chelsea's tone – so mocking and insinuating at the kitchen table. So what if Kelly had been a dirty stop out and slept with someone Chelsea didn't approve of? It was hardly any of her business. She hadn't really been concerned, either. She'd just been amused, scandalized and keen for details…

It was then that Kelly noticed the lavender envelope with the handwritten address. It had been stuck to the back of a flyer from a DVD rental company. It was a private letter addressed to her, and it had the flowery handwriting of Anthony Marvelle all over it. She grabbed it up and ripped it open. The paper inside was delicate, tissue-thin. It even had a delicate fragrance she couldn't identify.

Dearest Kelly,

I imagine that by now you have heard the most dreadful things about me, your having spent some time in the company of the woman known as Iris Wildthyme. I really cannot impress upon you too much the fact that she is not to be trusted. She is a dangerous lunatic, given to the oddest kinds of invention. Now, I will not lie to you – I respect you far too much for that – as a student, a poet and a woman. I will not claim that everything Iris Wildthyme says is false. She is, in part, exactly what she claims to be, and some of her powers and abilities are astounding. Seemingly impossible, perhaps. I think by now that you will have experienced some things that you never thought would be possible. She has taken you places in order to prove she can do what she claims and you are now home – in a fever and tumult of incredulity. Perhaps you want to shut it all out and deny it.

But I think not. You are a clever, creative woman. You can cope with the truth, I believe. You will be home now, reading my letter, having been shown a little of what Wildthyme is capable of.

You have seen a tiny corner of space and time. She has proved to you that it is out there – not as an abstract quality. Not as something distant. But as something we can touch and taste and feel. Time and space is something we can travel into, Kelly. We can be there. Not just here. We don't belong just here. Not the likes of us. We deserve far, far more. We should be free to roam… in the way that Wildthyme takes for granted. Don't you feel like me? Like a butterfly, pinned and wriggling to a collector's board. Pinioned to history and planet Earth. Longing for freedom. Don't you long for freedom?

I imagine that's how you feel. And so … you have a certain number of choices.

Wildthyme will attempt to bring her onto your side. I believe she will succeed easily with your friend – the gullible Simon. I am sure that will be the case. He is an easy target for that old crone's blandishments. But you, Kelly. I am convinced you will see through her.

She is thoroughly wicked, Kelly. Utterly devoid of human feeling. Under that camp, ludicrous exterior, all that flim flam and silliness there beats a heart of molten silver. Livid mercury courses through her veins. She is cold, unfeeling, ruthless. She will stop at nothing to get her hands on the Hysperon glass.

I must exert every fibre of my being in order to keep it away from her. I fear for my life, though. I am almost alone in this endeavour. No one understands what will happen if this jar falls into her talons.

Will you? Will you understand? I think you will. I felt… I felt a kind of kindred spirit in you when we talked that week and that last night, at the party, in Chelsea's kitchen. And afterwards, of course.

I wanted to explain to you – about Iris Wildthyme and what she intends to do with the jar. I wanted to tell you about Hyspero – the world on the brink. About the Empress and the Ringpull… the Dark Magic and the Clockworks…

I can't do all of that in a letter.

Will you meet me? Will you, Kelly? And give me one more chance?

Soon?

Your friend,

Anthony Marvelle

CHAPTER TEN

So here was Barbra – who had travelled the length and breadth of the universe. Quite against her own will for much of the time. As a mere Servo-furnishing she'd never had much choice about where her clunky old body was transported to. Where she could be of use, was the obvious answer. Wherever anyone needed a supply of cheap comestibles. Wherever you went in Space and Time, she would remind herself proudly, people would still be wanting snacks. Whoever or whatever they were, all type of beings still became peckish between meals.

Whether they really ever wanted Barbra's standard supply of warm, flat orangeade and wilting potato crisps was beside the point. That wasn't something she gave much thought to. Everyone loves pop and crisps! And Barbra was indispensable! Of course she was! Wherever in the cosmos she happened to pitch up.

For the last little while she had been underneath Darlington. A town believed by most of its inhabitants to be rather mundane, even commonplace. Barbra knew different, of course. She knew it as the nexus point - a miraculous cat's cradle of interdimensional strings and holes that it truly was. It was down one of those holes that she had once fallen – tottering helplessly into one end, in her native far future aboard the space station Antelope Slash Zebra Nitelite – and winding up here, with stunning alacrity.

She emerged screaming into the waiting arms of the MIAOW operatives who had foreseen her coming through the aperture known to them as the Deadly Flap. Using all their very complicated instruments and other geegaws Barbra barely understood, they had calculated that she would break through into their quotidian reality right above their base and inside the indoor market itself.

The MIAOW operatives hadn't been all that kind to her at first. It hadn't taken long for Barbra to realise that their interest in her advent wasn't wholly altruistic. Rather, they were keen to cannibalise her precious and futuristic parts. Her feelings were quite hurt to find that it wasn't for her own sake they had been so glad to see her.

She was mulling this over one afternoon in the gloomy, cavernous MIAOW base and trying to engage Magda in conversation.

'Well, we didn't know that you were *you* then,' said Magda. She was knitting some complicated kind of garment in sea green wool. For some reason, when she was knitting, her Eastern European accent would grow thicker and sometimes Barbra found it difficult to follow her full meaning. On the banks of controls around her several important-looking lights were blinking busily and Barbra wasn't at all sure that Magda had taken note of them. Magda continued, 'If we had known then that you were *you*, then we'd never have thought about breaking you up and using you for spares. Really.'

Barbra didn't know whether she found that comforting or not. She wondered how many other beings had been thrust through the Dreadful Flap, into the waiting clutches of MIAOW, and what fates had befallen them in their turn. She knew there were cells underneath the main control room. She heard funny noises sometimes – night and day – cries and shouts, threats and murmurs. Jenny and Magda and the other MIAOW girls pretended not to hear these disquieting, often chilling sounds.

Or, if they did, they made some excuse. Barbra was perhaps hearing warped echoes of past events or shadow happenings, refracted through alternate dimensions. Yet Barbra knew that she was actually hearing the inconvenient noise of alien prisoners. Right beneath her feet and castors there was a zoo full of hullabaloo.

She was fearful of asking too many questions. Really, she was fearful of the MIAOW people full stop. They could shut her down, no bother, at any given moment. Her usefulness could be over in a flash. Quick as a human could inflate an empty crisp packet and make it go pop.

She shuddered at the very thought, setting her cans quaking inside her.

Magda was watching her over her knitting. Magda was suspicious and slightly scared too. No one in MIAOW was very comfortable. All were a bit paranoid. All of them knew that nothing was quite what it seemed here at the nexus point, where the fractures ran through the quotidian like cracks in shattered glass.

The MIAOW ladies would spend all their time watching their backs, waiting for a moment when Jenny's attention slipped and they could nip away from this secret base. When they might abscond from the dangerous business of belonging to MIAOW.

'Of course, it was Iris who ensured your safety,' Magda pointed out thoughtfully. 'She begged and pleaded with Jenny to spare your life. You should be grateful to the old bag.'

'I am, I am,' said Barbra hurriedly. She had never stopped being grateful to Iris Wildthyme. Without her intervention – and that of her Panda companion – Barbra would have been reduced to spare parts in a thrice.

'She is sentimental, that woman,' said Madga, stirring in her wheelchair, shifting her tartan blanket on her single knee. 'She is soft-hearted. Very dangerous, that. She should look after herself better. She should beware who she allies herself with. And be more careful who she lets aboard that bus with her…'

Barbra wasn't sure what Magda meant by all of this, as her muttering grew darker and more doomy. Barbra's innards were lighting up with the soft glow of hope. She was remembering what Iris had promised her, not so long ago – the last time she was here, just passing through.

She promised that this time they would take me away, thought Barbra. They promised me that there would be room for me on their magical bus..!

At last Magda noticed all the flashing lights on the console beside her. She cursed at their urgency and insistence, flipping a few switches angrily, and scowling at the results. 'Well, well. That's very interesting, isn't it?'

*

Jenny came breezing through the MIAOW base less than an hour later. She frowned at the placid scene in the control room.

'You don't look like you've been doing very much.'

Magda grimaced at her. 'What are we supposed to be doing? You know how little I understand all of these displays, these Christmas lights.'

Jenny gritted her teeth. 'You're supposed to keep me appraised of what's going on out there. When you're on watch you're meant to be, you know, alert.'

Magda bit through a strand of wool with her pointed teeth and examined her handiwork critically. The lighting down here was so sombre, she thought she might be getting a migraine. 'It's been a very quiet afternoon, as it happens.'

Jenny explained brusquely that she was going straight back out. Operative Wildthyme had rematerialised in town, somewhere on the South Road, and Jenny needed to see her. Magda smiled to herself, thinking of how Iris would hate being called 'Operative Wildthyme.' 'Yes, we already know the bus is back,' Magda said. 'We saw it on the scanners earlier, Barbra and I.'

'Where is Barbra? Isn't she supposed to be on duty with you?'

Magda shrugged sulkily. 'Look, can I go back to my shop now? I'm wasting precious time down here.'

Jenny dismissed her, feeling exasperated. Why were the MIAOW staff so truculent? Why didn't they just do what she said? Look at Barbara, for instance. Nice enough, even pleasantly chatty and still grateful for being given a place to live in the twenty-first century. But the vending machine couldn't be relied upon. Where was she now? Probably skulking about in the lower levels, somewhere in the catacombs. The machine had a creepy fondness for the darkest corners of the base.

Right now Jenny had to focus on Iris Wildthyme and the tasks ahead. She hated to admit it, but her own efforts had produced very little in the way of results. Iris had come blundering in and within minutes had seemingly discovered more about Marvelle, the Objet D'Oom and the circumstances of its arrival than MIAOW would ever have been able to. And that particular brand of productive blundering was precisely why Iris was still valuable to the organisation. Hapless and drunken she might be – but somehow she always got stuff done. Somehow. Even after all these years and several months spent travelling with her, Jenny still didn't understand how it worked. Jenny was conscientious. She was assiduous. And she was dismayed each time Iris galumphed past her, in the rackety course of her investigations.

Now the message had reached Jenny that Iris had had a bit of a tentative poke about and discovered a few alarming facts about Marvelle and what he might be up to. Iris had been necessarily vague in her phone call, which Jenny appreciated. Iris had a nasty tendency to blurt things out.

Jenny hurried out of the base, nodding hellos to the operatives who were replacing the scowling Magda at the control desk. Nice women from the old stationers shop on High Row. Jenny didn't know them well, but knew they were more reliable than Magda, who looked relieved as she rode up in the elevator back to the indoor market with Jenny. Sometimes Jenny wondered why MIAOW bothered with Magda at all.

'Funny, the way Barbra wandered off,' Magda said. 'She's been in a funny mood all afternoon.'

Jenny didn't have time to think about the vending machine right now. Barbra was very low on her list of priorities. She emerged with Magda into *Magda's Mysteries*, helping the woman over the step with her wheelchair, and then she was off, zipping into the indoor market, her mind set on the task in hand: getting information out of Iris.

Magda set about opening her shop. Might as well see if she could get some customers in for the afternoon. She sighed heavily at the dusty stacks of books. Business was awful lately. Sometimes she wondered if the weird emanations and the bad karma from the secret base downstairs somehow put her prospective customers off… No one ever really spent very long browsing in her shop.

'Magda,' said a very familiar voice. It was whispering tinnily and made her jump.

'Barbra! What are you doing up here?'

The vending machine was hiding behind one of the bookstacks. There was a faint mist on the inside of her glass front. 'Jenny's gone, hasn't she?'

'Why, yes, but you shouldn't be up here, Barbra. You're not supposed to leave the base...'

'I know, I know,' she fretted. 'But I had to get out. Just for a while.'

Magda was concerned. The thing was, Barbra wasn't much use as a secret operative. A few months ago Jenny had given in to her plaintive request for something interesting to do, to help out and pay her way. She had been assigned a small job, just a bit of surveillance on the railway platforms in Darlington, Newcastle and Edinburgh. There was some kind of creature causing havoc on the East Coast Line – a supernatural mystery that MIAOW (come to think of it) had never really satisfactorily sorted out. The job had seemed tailor-made for Barbra, who could – after all – impersonate a vending machine better than anyone. Still, she had messed up by insisting on talking to people, freaking them out and drawing attention to herself. Ever since, she had been confined to the MIAOW base. The question of her getting out and about had not been raised since.

Magda watched, alarmed, as Barbra eased herself forward on her castors and her clunky front feet. Her cans were rattling and she hissed pneumatically as she headed for the door.

'But, you can't...! Barbra! Where are you...?'

But Barbra was grimly determined. She didn't say another word to Magda as she left the shop. She put all of her strength and coordination into moving along, slowly, cautiously. She was terribly out of practice at covering long distances.

In the market place people looked alarmed. Some laughed and pointed. Some were scared. Others thought it was a publicity stunt of some kind and looked for hidden cameras. But Barbra

117

was mostly left to her own devices as she found her way to the most level, access-friendly exit to the market and got herself onto High Row, the mainly pedestrianised shopping street. She had memorized the street maps quite efficiently, and had sussed out where the Exchange was. Only a mile or so to where the bus was parked. She just had to keep her head down and bustle along, down the high street and through the subways. No one would bother her, no one would stop her… If she just minded her own business…

CHAPTER ELEVEN

Everything she saw on the way interested her a great deal. The darkened cavern of the cinema with its double set of glass doors; the service station with its rigid petrol pumps like sentries, and the furniture display rooms with those strange, squashy chairs that humans in this era favoured. Barbra had to keep reminding herself how far back into time she had been propelled. This was, in fact, a time she knew very little about. She was shocked by the number of cars on the South Road, belching their fumes everywhere. The air itself seemed like a terrible soup, compounded of all this muck and the myriad spicy scents from the kebab shops and fried chicken bars. She paused to peer into a kebab shop window and watched a young man slicing ribbons of meat from a pale, glistening torso which, for one horrible second, she thought was human.

They are barbarians back here, she thought, moving on. Her innards were wheezing and panting by now. She had come less than a mile. It was much further than she was used to. But she had to press on.

No one tried to stop her. She got some very strange looks from fellow pedestrians, but mostly they hurried on. She kept ploughing onwards in a straight line, praying there wouldn't be any trouble. She had no way of defending herself. If some rough lot seized her and demanded all of her comestibles, she would simply have to do as they said.

But no one stopped her. She was so impossible, so bizarre, perhaps the few people who noticed her were scared to acknowledge her. They hurried on, using the oncoming, spitting rain as an excuse to put their heads down and scurry past.

And at last Barbra found herself at her destination. According to MIAOW's records this dusty shop had been here under the same name for forty years. The Great Big Book Exchange was painted in bright letters of pink and lime green above its front window. Some kind of yellow, crinkly polythene clung to the inside of the window, protecting the paperbacks on display from the harshness of the sun. Though there was precious little sun in the rainy canyon of South Road.

Barbra shunted herself up to the front door and examined the opening times. The 'closed' sign was turned outwards, but there was a warm orange glow deep within, beyond the frosted glass, so she knew people were home. This was where she was supposed to be. The bus was near here somewhere. Her new friends were close by. She lurched forward and crashed into the wooden door, rather more heavily than she had intended.

'What the..?' Kelly was at the cash desk. As Barbra tottered into the shop, dismayed at smashing the glass and causing a fuss, Kelly dropped her coffee onto the book she was reading and the keyboard of her laptop. She jumped up and was about to launch into a volley of abuse when she realised what it was exactly that had come falling into the Exchange.

Barbra was holding up both skinny retractable arms. 'I'm sorry! Oh dear! I'm here to see Iris. Is she here? The machines said she was here. With her bus. Please, have I come to the right place? I've run away, you see. Oh, look, I'm sorry…'

Kelly was mopping the worst of the spills off the computer, but she knew it was hopeless. The thing was fizzing at her. She could only stare helplessly back at the vending machine.

'Is she here?' Barbra asked again. 'And Panda?'

'T-they're upstairs,' Kelly said. 'With Simon.'

'I've broken the glass door,' Barbra said. The grey wind and spots of rain were following her in, lifting loose papers and sending a chill through the Exchange.

'I'll… sort it out,' Kelly said. She really didn't know how to handle this. She had thought she was back in normality, sitting at the desk in the Exchange. Happy to be in her usual place at home. Able to forget some of the recent weird stuff. But now… *this*. 'Erm, who are you?'

'I'm Barbra. I'll never make it up those stairs.' Barbra indicated to the narrow staircase behind the Kelly's desk. 'Is that where they are?'

Kelly went to shout down Simon and his new friends. 'You've got company!'

'It's not anyone awful, is it?' came Iris's voice, cawing down the back stairs, all gin and cigarettes.

'It's me, Iris!' Barbra warbled back. 'I've come to join you on the bus! I've run away from MIAOW!'

*

They decided that the easiest place to convene was aboard the bus, which was parked in the narrow alley at the back of the terraced row of shops. Then they could leave Kelly to get someone in to see to the damage to the front door. As she got on with that, Simon mouthed apologies and thanks to her, and then he was helping Iris to help Barbra into the alley at the back.

'What a lovely bookshop!' Barbra was exclaiming. 'And it's all yours, did you say, young man?'

Panda followed on behind, grumbling to himself. No one had really expected Barbra to run away and join them on the bus. The offer had only really been made because no one really expected her to be able to get herself away at all. It had seemed quite impossible that she could have got her square bulk out of that base. Let alone all the way through Darlington town centre alone. But here she was.

In the back alley Panda stood shaking his head as Iris jumped into the cab and lowered a ramp from the double doors. Then Simon had to help Barbra struggle inside. There came the tinkling of china and the grinding of furniture as items were thrust aside to make room for the flustered runaway.

This is going to be a disaster, Panda thought. We've hardly any room aboard, as it is, what with Iris adding Simon to our gang and the bus being ever so slightly smaller on the inside than it is on the outside. It's just typical of Iris to go out handing invitations willy-nilly and land us with this silly robot woman.

'Aren't we lucky, Panda?' Iris shouted at him, noticing his scowling face as he crossly tied and retied his cravat. 'Isn't Barbra a marvel, coming all this way to be with us?'

'Humph,' said Panda. 'Yes, indeed. I'm sure she'll be a positive boon to us on our travels, Iris.'

Inside the bus, hearing this, Barbra beamed. 'Thank you! Thank you so much for welcoming me like this. I promise I'll be no trouble. I'll sit quietly in a corner and occasionally dispense delicious refreshments!'

Then they were all aboard the bus. Panda was mixing the drinks.

There was a moment of awkward politeness before Barbra remembered something. She produced a memory crystal and carefully passed it over to Iris. 'This is everything MIAOW has on file about Marvelle. They've been tracking him through the multiverse for some time, it turns out. He's been all over the place with that poodle of his. I thought you could do with the info.'

Iris cackled. 'Brilliant, Barbra! Well done, lovey!' She patted what she imagined was the vending machine's head. 'See? You're not a burden at all! You've done something fantastic already!' Iris was peering into the purple depths of the crystal menacingly, as if she could see a tiny Marvelle running around inside it. 'So we can get after him now, with this. And get back on the trail of the Objet D'Oom.'

'And not to mention the pinking shears!' added Panda, jauntily. He took a swig of his gin.

'Marvelle's got the pinking shears?' Barbra gasped. Even as a very lowly MIAOW operative she had heard of the magical properties of the pinking shears. To MIAOW members they were legendary.

'I'm afraid so,' said Iris. 'He whipped them away from under my nose.'

'So that's how he's flitting about through time and space,' said Barbra. 'Jenny was driving herself mad, wondering how he did it. Now we know. And he can go anywhere, can't he? He's probably tootled off already with that glass jar.'

'But we can get after him,' said Iris, weighing the crystal in her hand. 'Thanks to MIAOW, and you, Barbra. We aren't beaten yet.'

CHAPTER TWELVE

So what had happened to Jenny on the way to the Exchange?

By rights she should have been there, catching up with Iris's news and adventures, well before Barbra had crashed into the shop. And she would have been, had she not been nobbled en route.

In broad daylight. The dogs had caught Jenny as she cut through the park. She cursed softly under her breath as she realised what she had walked into. An ambush. That scampering and panting. The crackling of leaves under manicured claws. The soft, thunderous footfalls of fastidious, intelligent hunters.

These weren't just any old pets out for a walk.

There came a menacing growl at her back.

She turned. There were three of them. Suddenly surrounding her. Orange, hot pink, ice blue. Fancy collars, bootees, pompoms. Hackles raised, teeth bared.

Marvelle stepped lightly from behind the trunk of a tree. 'I am so sorry murmur,' he smiled and Jenny gasped at the suddenness of him.

'Call them off, Marvelle,' she snapped.

'I can't tell them what to do. The dogs aren't my pets murmur,' he said solemnly. 'But then you already know that, don't you, Jenny mumur? You know more about them – and about me – than is ideal, actually murmur murmur.' The fair-haired poet squeezed his distinguished features into an expression of genuine regret. He wore a charcoal suit of exquisite cut. He looked immaculate, standing there and wincing at her. She found him galling in every aspect. She was clammy, hot and cross in her long coat. She felt stupid and trapped and useless.

'I don't know anything about you,' she told him.

'You came after me. Stalking me in the corridors of the hotel where I was staying. What were you after, Jenny? I'd like to know murmur murmur.'

'Coincidence.'

The dogs growled again. The orange one snickered at her.

'You're after something from me,' Marvelle mused. 'What is it? And who are you working for murmur? MIAOW, I suppose murmur?'

Jenny could see there was no point in denying it. Marvelle was clearly bright. He might write doggerel, but he seemed to be informed. 'You shouldn't know about MIAOW.'

He laughed. 'I know plenty. You bitches have kept tabs on me for years. Wherever I've got to in time murmur murmur.'

'Time?'

'Don't play dumb, Jenny. You needn't pretend with me. You've a file on me wide as... as a double decker bus, haven't you murmur?'

She shrugged. Then her eyes widened as he produced something from his jacket's inside pocket. Something astonishing. A green glittering pair of scissors. Long scissors with jagged teeth that fascinated her as he waved them playfully in the air, swishing the blades.

Just then a strange hush fell over the leaf-strewn corner of the park. The air became somehow thicker, rippling like jelly. All sound grew muffled, the traffic noise more distant, the dogs silent, birdsong muting to nothing.

Jenny's mouth was dry. 'The Blithe Pinking Shears.' Her voice sounded hollow to her own ears. Like a recording played back on a broken machine. Just watching Marvelle scissoring the air made her feel like she was coming unstuck from their shared moment in time. The Very Fabric... of Space and Time... the phrase dropped lightly into Jenny's mind. It was fraying all around them... coming away at the seams... and now Marvelle was chuckling at her.

'Are you surprised to see them in my possession murmur?'

'I know they're dangerous. No one should be let loose with them...'

'Indeed,' he agreed. 'They are an astounding creation. Ridiculously dangerous and wonderfully powerful murmur murmur. But do you know even half of what they can do, eh Jenny?'

She was finding it hard even to look at the swishing, slashing shears for very long. The daylight was blurring and refracting, surrounding the blades in a nimbus of kaleidoscopic colour.

'I'm going to do so many wonderful things with these,' Marvelle sighed happily. 'I'm such a lucky fellow. You really can't imagine murmur murmur. That's two impossibly precious objects I've purloined recently. Would you like to be my third, Jenny? Whisked away from under Wildthyme's nose?'

Now he was plucking at a strange glitch in the air. It looked like a scratch on a screen, or a loose silver thread poking out in mid-air. One poodle yapped and another was slobbering eagerly. Marvelle tugged at the thread and a hole started to open up in daylight.

There was a space of pulsating darkness beyond.

Another dimension, Jenny thought. Another time.

Right then she made a decision. She had to keep close to this man. Wherever he went, whatever happened. It was her duty. It was the only thing to do.

'Where did you get the shears?'

'That old coot had them murmur murmur. Your friend. Iris Wildthyme.'

Jenny was surprised. Marvelle saw that it was her genuine reaction. 'Iris had them all this time?'

'She thought she could put them somewhere safe. Somewhere no one could get their eager mitts on them. But she never banked on running into me murmur murmur. She doesn't stand a chance against me, Jenny. You know that, don't you? And she'll be horrified when she discovers exactly what I'm up to. The big picture, and all that murmur murmur. That dreadful hag will be mortified. And she'll set herself against me with every fibre of her nasty, raddled being murmur murmur.'

Jenny was still transfixed by the widening gash in the air. She stared into the sparkling ripples and currents of the dimension beyond…

'Tell me what you are planning,' she said.

'To find out, you must come with me murmur.' He smiled at her warmly, brandishing the scissors invitingly. 'You can find out everything before Iris does. You know it's your duty to come murmur. Your duty to MIAOW and your whole world.'

'I-I…' Jenny hesitated. She hated how vulnerable that made her look. What was he doing to her? It was like mesmerism. Or *murmurism*. She had to harden herself up again.

'I know there's no love lost between you and the Wildthyme woman murmur,' Marvelle purred lightly.

'What?'

'I know all about it murmur murmur. I know she once betrayed you.'

'How do you..?' Jenny shook her head, frowning. 'It wasn't betrayal. It wasn't like that. We just stopped seeing eye to eye. I stopped travelling with her through the galaxy. It was all a long time ago, anyway…'

'No wonder you never got on,' said Marvelle. He took a cautious step towards Jenny. 'I think you're more my sort than you are Iris Wildthyme's murmur. You're a much classier person altogether. Just like me murmur murmur. So… come with me, Jenny. Come and explore. Come on a voyage with me murmur. You really won't believe where I'm going, or what I'm up to murmur.'

Jenny simply nodded and stepped up to the swaying gap in the Very Fabric. By now it was conveniently large enough for both him and her and then the three dogs to slip through.

When they had done so it sealed itself up again.

Though not quite tightly. Not completely.

As Iris would say: one of the reasons the Blithe Pinking Shears were so dangerous was that once they cut into the Fabric of Space and Time, nothing would mend it perfectly again. The damage was permanent and the darkness would always be plain to anyone looking for it.

That darkness from beyond would always show up through the tatters of lace.

CHAPTER THIRTEEN

They were all sleeping in. Barbra couldn't believe it. She didn't understand how sleeping worked, and she knew it wasn't the same as her switching herself off for a few hours. She knew they needed to rest, but she couldn't believe that the others weren't as excited as she was. Even Simon, who had done hardly any travelling yet. He was curled up on the chaise longue on the lower deck, snoring away.

Barbra was humming with expectation and suppressed excitement.

They were in a new place. After a year or more in Darlington Barbra had succeeded in getting a lift to somewhere else.

An alien world. She just knew it. She hadn't been told yet. She had no idea where or when they might be. The bus had eased gently out of the Maelstrom in the middle of the night and no one else had been awake to witness it. Only Barbra. And she knew that they were somewhere alien and intriguing and wholly new.

The early morning light shone through the chintz curtains and the drawn blinds, streaming through any gaps it could find. It shifted and stirred, as if looking for nooks and crannies to probe and illuminate.

I'm here, world, Barbra thought to herself. Come and find me, she told the fresh sunlight. I've been too long underground in that awful secret base. I know my comestibles have been mouldering inside of me. I know I've been seizing up and getting old before my time…

She ambled gently up the gangway, careful not to knock into and break anything. China and glass tinkled at her stealthy tread. She knew how ungainly she was, and that she took up more than her share of space aboard the bus and was determined not to get in the way.

She extruded her mechanical arms and fiddled with the tape deck in the cab of the bus. Something gentle and baroque, she thought. During her Terran sojourn she'd become quite fond of Classic FM and some of that soothing, plinky-plonk music they played was just the right thing for easing her new chums into consciousness. The harpsichord seemed a perfect accompaniment to the golden sunlight as it grew stronger aboard the confined and messy bus.

Barbra set off back down the gangway, determined to grapple with the mysteries of the steam kettle and the Baby Belling. She knew people liked something hot to drink in the morning, and her cans of pop just wouldn't do.

'Barbra?' Simon propped himself up on one elbow, rubbing his tousled head as she squashed past. 'What time is it? Where are we?'

'I've no idea!' she burst out. 'I don't even know how to find out!'

'We're not in the Maelstrom anymore,' he said. 'We're not rocking about.'

'We've landed,' Barbra said, and then her attention was taking up by trying to squeeze herself into the galley kitchen. She found she had to stand in the doorway and stretch her concertinaed arms as far as she could. 'Tea?'

'Please.' Simon was up and about now, folding his sheets and duvet and cramming them into an overhead locker. Already he had found that space was of a premium aboard the bus, and the two new crew members would have to be careful not to crowd the place out too much. It seemed a small price to pay for his ticket to adventure.

As Barbra ran the tap she wondered aloud, 'Where does the water supply come from, do you suppose?'

Delegated to tea-making the night before, Simon had already asked for and received an answer from Panda. A staggering answer to do with transdimensional plumbing. 'Apparently there's a direct link to a Canadian lake somewhere in 1924. A kind of invisible, time-travelling pipeline. That's why the water's so cold and fresh.'

'Amazing!' said Barbra. 'This technology… everything that Iris has… it's way in advance of anything I've ever seen. No species I've ever heard of has mastered the things that she does so easily, so calmly. She's incredible! Where's she from, do you think?'

Simon pulled on yesterday's jeans and t-shirt, feeling a bit grubby as he did so, and hoping Iris would let him use her en suite bathroom later. 'I don't think she likes to be asked about her past, and all that,' he warned Barbra. 'Best not to ask too much and just enjoy it.'

Barbra nodded thoughtfully. 'It's none of anyone's business, is it?' she said, setting the kettle on the hob. 'Everyone's history is their own. And we're all on board the bus as new friends. Everything starts anew from here. Right now. The past doesn't matter one tiny bit!'

There was something about her tone that Simon found a bit strange. As if she was over-keen to forget the past. But he was too sleep-dozy and excited to think about that too much.

He started fiddling with one of the parchment blinds. 'Let's see what's out there. I can't wait, can you?'

As Barbra came to join him there was an awful, abrupt ripping noise. Simon cried out in horror and tried to shush himself.

'What have you done?'

He swore. He'd been too rough with the blind. Or pulled it the wrong way. Now it had a rip in it about ten centimetres long. He swore again and found the string he should have been pulling in order to raise the blind. 'That's a good start,' he cursed. 'Iris is going to kill me.'

'Don't tell her yet,' said Barbra. 'Not straight away. Look, if it's rolled up, you can't tell it's been damaged…'

Simon tried to conceal the harm his habitual clumsiness had caused, and he felt terrible about it. Unlike Barbra he knew these weren't just any old canvas blinds to shield the bus from the solar rays and the time winds. They were fragments of the Atlas of All Time – and on one of his first mornings on the bus he had gone and put a bloody hole in it.

'Oh my!' sighed Barbra, squinting as the sunlight reflected off her glass frontage. 'Just look at it out there! It's beautiful!'

*

Iris and Panda came clattering down the spiral staircase dressed and ready for action. Iris was wearing an extraordinary set of jungle fatigues in lilac and midnight blue. Her hair was crammed under a pith helmet and both she and Panda had a heavy duty set of goggles dangling round their necks. Panda had even changed his cravat into a more durable one.

'Are we ready to explore?' grinned Iris, accepting the huge mug of tea Simon passed to her.

'It's a jungle out there,' he told her.

'I know! I looked out of the top window.'

'But a weird jungle. Like nothing on Earth.'

'Of course!' She tutted at him. 'Anyone fancy a bacon sandwich before we head off?'

'Head off to where?' quavered Barbra. 'I mean, it's very pretty and all out there, Iris. But is this a random destination, or…?'

'Random destination!' chortled Panda. 'Of course not! This is all because of you, this is, Barbra dear.'

'M-me?'

'Of course,' said Iris, moving to the windows and staring out at the frosty woods beyond. 'That crystal you gave us. Somehow it brought us here.'

Simon frowned. 'But how would MIAOW's databases know about… other worlds like this?'

'They shouldn't,' said Iris. 'They're a strictly Earth-based operation. Oh, over the years they've tried to get their hot little hands on my bus. They're ever so keen to explore space and time to their own nefarious ends. What secret society wouldn't? But really, they know nothing. They shouldn't know anything about this planet. Wherever it is.'

'What's it called?' shouted Panda from the kitchen, where he was rootling about in the miniature fridge. 'We're out of eggs, by the way.'

'We shall have to ask the locals what it's called,' Iris said, peering intently into the frosty depths. 'There's a settling a couple of miles north-west, according to the bus's instruments…'

Simon caught his breath. 'An alien settlement!'

'They aren't alien to themselves,' she reminded him. 'You're the odd one out, here. The only human on this new world.'

He looked at her and was keen to ask: well, what are you then, lady? If you're not human? But this morning she looked as if she might take offence at that.

Iris swept into action. 'I'm going to fix up some supplies, hip flasks and so on. Panda's making breakfast. I suggest the rest of you dress up in something warm enough to brave the elements out there. It's a tad nippy.'

Simon clambered upstairs to examine the wardrobes on the top deck. He hadn't been up here yet. Iris gave him quick instructions on using the sonic shower (using which turned out to be quite a surprising, not unpleasant experience, as it happened) and then he went hunting through the racks of miscellaneous clothing, feeling as if he was at some very eccentric kind of jumble sale. There seemed to be male and female garments from a vast array of times and places: robes, gowns, boas, hats, bikinis and togas. He fetched out a duffel coat and a woolly hat with a pompom. And that's when the bookcase containing Iris's journals caught his eye.

When he picked out the first leather-bound volume, he wasn't even sure what it was. His incurable nosiness and bookishness led him to examine the books before he even consciously decided to. Then the book's heavy, creamy pages fell open to reveal handwriting in watery blue ink. Paragraphs slanted and scratched their way across hundreds of pages. And there were about fifty-odd volumes in the rickety bookcase. Iris's life-story. Her journals. Her *secrets*.

Simon felt ashamed of prying into an old woman's secret papers. He slammed the book shut but, before he knew it, had slipped it into the deep pocket of his new coat. He didn't experience the slightest twinge of guilt as he responded to Panda's shouts from down below and the tinging of the bell, telling him breakfast was ready.

After demolishing the bacon sandwiches – doorsteps of fried bread oozing with ketchup and somewhat singed and crispy rashers – it was time to fling open the hydraulic doors and to help Barbra amble down the ramp.

'I do hope I don't hold you people up too much,' she worried.

Iris and Simon both had her by one arm as they guided her down onto the ground. Both were keen to assure the Servo-furnishing that she was no bother to them at all. What was more, her refrigerated interior was ideal for storing their food supplies. Panda had put some buns and bananas and Iris's flask of gin inside Barbra for safekeeping. Barbra was pleased to be able to help.

Simon was very conscious of his first few steps on the brittle undergrowth. My first moments in an alien land, he thought. He didn't say them out loud, in case his widely-travelled companions thought him too gauche. But to him, everything felt novel and weird. The air was even nippier than he was expecting. The silvery blue bark of the trees and the dark leaves were lurid and shimmering, as if colour itself was more intense here than at home.

As they stood around examining their new environment – Panda with his goggles on, changing the settings and peering intently at everything around him – Simon could hold it in no longer. 'You really can do it! You can travel to other planets!'

The icicles on the branches and vines shivered at his words. Iris shushed him. 'Don't get carried away, lovey. I know it's exciting and everything. But we don't want to be too noisy and draw unwanted attention, do we?'

Says the woman who's landed a double decker bus in the middle of the jungle, he thought. He turned back to look at the scarlet bus, vivid in the clearing. Kelly should be here, he thought. She'd soon get used to it. She'd be all right.

But Iris didn't trust her, did she? She had taken against his friend pretty quickly, which Simon still felt was a bit unfair. Iris had said that some travellers worked out okay on the bus. Others not so. He remembered what she had said about Jenny, and how she had had the runs every time they travelled through the Maelstrom. He had seen that Iris's ribald laughter had covered over a more serious truth: that Jenny and Iris had fallen out, somehow, during their time together on the bus.

He was learning that Iris's laughter and panache often covered up darker truths. Even sinister truths.

Then Panda cried out. 'I've probed the vicinity,' he announced.

Iris yelped with laughter. 'Oh yes, lovey?'

He scowled. 'Using my new goggles and my tracking device, yes. And if you could get yours to work, Iris, you could have scanned the locale for yourself. Anyway, it turns out that this settlement is less than two miles in...' He held out his paw decisively. 'That direction. And also according to my plans, we have less than an hour's daylight and this wooded area is absolutely thick with wildlife inimical to life.'

'What kind of wildlife?' Barbra asked him.

'Never mind that now,' Iris snapped, locking up the bus. 'Get those castors of yours extruded, Barbra. We've got to get a move on, I reckon.'

'What will the people in this settlement be like?' Simon wondered. 'They might not be all that pleased to see strangers.'

'There's only one way to find out stuff like that,' said Iris, getting exasperated. 'And that's by going there and introducing ourselves. We have to. This is where Marvelle went, according to the crystal. This is the first place it's leading us. So – we have to get after him.'

CHAPTER FOURTEEN

Of course Panda couldn't be of any help manhandling Barbra through the undergrowth. His job was to scurry on ahead, peering with his goggles into the verdant darkness, and keeping them on the right track. Iris and Simon were left to make sure their vending machine friend didn't get wedged between the tree trunks or tangled up in vines. Simon was sure that he was doing the bulk of the work and, after about half an hour, he was exhausted.

They rested in a clearing of wafting grasses and strange transparent flowers, something like daffodils. An eerie breeze reached down from the empty skies, which were visible here at last, in a gap in the canopy overhead. The flowers were jangling and Simon distracted himself by listening to their soothing noise, blocking out Barbra's babbling apologies.

'Look, it's all right, Barbra,' said Iris, and Simon could tell she was getting impatient with the robot. 'We don't mind if you slow us down... Though it *is* getting a little bit dark now...'

Panda was rummaging through Iris's carpet bag, and fiddling with a scanning device that seemed to be made out of polished cherrywood. 'There's a little bit further to go, I'm afraid. Down a hill, into a wide valley – and that's where this little town is. But at least it's all downhill!'

The small bear seemed indefatigable to Simon. He wondered if he ever experienced tiredness in those plump, stuffing-filled limbs. At that moment Panda caught Simon staring at his legs and returned his look crossly.

As they rested, the sounds of their new environment became more apparent. They had stopped thrashing at the branches and crashing through the fallen leaves, and now, in the stillness, they heard the distant cries of birds and the muttering and chattering of alien beasts.

Simon wondered about the air and whether it was safe to breathe. And about inoculations and radiation levels and any number of things that Iris hadn't bothered to consider when they left the bus.

He looked at her and saw that her face was suddenly alert and pinched. Her ears were cocked under that garish pith helmet.

'What is it?'

She frowned. 'Something's coming.'

Panda looked alarmed. 'What? But my scanner doesn't say anything...!'

She glared at him witheringly. 'Bugger what your scanner says. Jump in my bag!' She held open her carpet bag and Panda clambered in. 'He's not very good in these situations,' Iris told the others.

'What situations?' cried Barbra, rocking on her castors and looking worried.

Simon could hear the noise quite plainly now. Something large and angry was thundering through the woods, smashing everything in its way. It was making as much noise as Iris's bus would have done, had she chosen to plunge it straight into the undergrowth.

They stared wildly about at the trees around them and tried to pinpoint where the noise was coming from. Closer and closer it came, shattering the quiet of the frozen glade. All of the leaves and branches and the vegetation underfoot was trembling and tinkling, almost fearfully.

'It's coming for us,' Simon whispered.

And then the creature burst through out of the darkness and into plain sight.

It roared with triumph and reared up on its back legs. Its livid green eyes shone with satisfaction at the sight of these strangers in the woods.

Simon almost choked in shock at his first sight of the thing.

'Don't make any sudden moves, lovey,' Iris warned him. 'It's watching us very, very closely. Its eyesight isn't good because it lives in the depths of the jungle. It's too bright here... but he knows we're here.'

'W-will it attack?' Barbra hissed.

The creature was rather like a cross between a bull elephant and a rhino, with immense, savage tusks and a nasty habit of pawing the ground, as if readying itself to charge. Its nostrils quivered wetly as it sniffed out its prey, obviously relishing their scent and proximity.

'It's going to eat us, isn't it?' said Simon. 'The bloody thing looks hungry.'

The strangest thing of all about the creature was that its body was translucent. It took a few moments for them to realise that its hide wasn't simply camouflaged to blend brilliantly with the vegetation: it was actually see-through. When they stared they could see the intricate, pulsating organs at work inside the powerful body. They could see his heart pounding with excitement, like a great hunk of green crystal.

'It's a transparent rhino,' Simon gasped, just as the beast decided to charge.

Iris flung herself at Simon and barrelled into him, knocking them both flat on the ground. All the air was squashed out of his lungs as he fell under the surprisingly heavy form of Iris Wildthyme. He heard the creature roar past them, snorting with pleasure, playing a game with them. It tore around the glade as if it was taking part in a jousting competition.

Iris rolled off Simon and jumped to her feet, bundling her carpet bag protectively under her arms. 'We've got to get away from that thing,' she panted. Panda's muffled shouts from inside her bag succinctly underlined that point.

Simon got up and started to back away towards the trees, as the creature turned again and was preparing to charge them once more. He thought frantically. What if they ran into the trees? Even if that didn't stop the monster, it might slow it down a little...

Then he noticed that Barbra was standing by herself in the middle of the glade.

Perhaps the creature hadn't even realised that she was a living being. It had ignored her completely.

But now Barbra took it upon herself to draw its attention. She was raising her extendable arms in the air and calling out to the beast.

'Barbra, don't..!' Simon yelled.

'She's buying us time,' Iris said. 'Oh, the brave thing. Come on, lovey. While she's distracting him...'

Now the creature had noticed her. Its eyes blazed at the temerity of the vending machine. It snorted and pawed the ground. It hunched its massive shoulders and prepared to charge...

'Get yourselves away!' Barbra shouted at them. 'Run!'

Iris grabbed Simon's arm and hauled him bodily into the undergrowth, and the relative safety of the shadows beyond the trees. 'But *Barbra*...!'

Seconds later they heard the noise of a tremendous impact. They heard the clatter of hooves and an almighty roar. The two of them jumped at the crunching and splintering of glass…

'It's killed her..!' Simon hissed.

'Strictly speaking,' whispered Iris dolefully, 'She was never truly alive.'

He wrenched himself out of her grasp. 'Yes, she was! She was Barbra!'

Then he hoisted himself out of the glittering, silvery undergrowth. He braced himself for new danger and whatever dreadful sight might face him in the clearing.

But what he saw made him let out his breath in one explosive rush. 'Babs!' he called.

'Y-yes, dear?' she said, with pretend nonchalance. Even at this distance, as he emerged from the bushes, he could see that the robot was shaking all over.

'What have you done?'

The beast lay at her feet, obviously dead.

Iris scrambled across the glade, swearing in her amazement. 'She's killed him! She's gone and killed that magnificent specimen of… of… whatever he was!'

Panda wrenched open the carpet bag and poked his head out. 'Let me see! Let me see what's going on! What's she done?'

They all stared at Barbra and the large corpse before them. It had been hewn into a tremendous number of ragged portions. It was as if something far bigger than she had ripped it carelessly apart. Green blood leaked everywhere, coating the translucent grass like a vile emulsion. The creature's flesh was hardening, vitrifying and crazing over with tiny cracks as they stood there and watched with awe.

'I-I just held my ground, that's all I did,' Barbra stammered. 'I wasn't going to let that bullying behemoth harm my new friends.' She seemed dismayed at the destruction all around her. 'I-I really don't know my own strength, do I?'

They all looked at her with alarm in their eyes. There was a curious smell in the air, above the coppery tang of the monster's blood. It was like the ozone crackle of electricity. It made them wary of even touching Barbra, in order to give her a congratulatory pat or a hug. Simon thought she might electrocute them on the spot, or even lash out again and tear them all limb from limb…

Iris recovered her composure first. 'Er well, thank you, Barbra, for rescuing us quite so… erm, effectively, lovey. I'm sure your talents for, ah, hand-to-hand combat will come in very useful during our travels together…'

And then it was time to resume their journey as dusk set in with a vengeance. Now Panda was leading the way again, with goggles perched firmly above his black nose and his wooden tracking device held before him.

Barbra went on a bit about her fight as they walked. They felt less irritated at helping her along. In truth, none of them had actually seen her battle the beast, since they'd been face down in the stinking mulch of the forest floor during the crucial seconds. They had just seen the bizarre evidence, moments later.

After a while Barbra started to sound remorseful. 'You were right, Iris. He was a magnificent beast indeed. But I had to do it. He would have killed us all. He'd have stomped us to bits and devoured our remains. I had no choice, did I? I had to do… what I did.'

Iris nodded grimly and agreed with her. 'You did right, lovey. It's a harsh world out there. Sometimes we have to defend ourselves the only way we can. That's what these adventures are like…'

'But,' Barbra sighed. 'I had no idea! I've never been in a fight before! I never knew I could do such things..!'

*

'Poor Jenny. So, it was all true. Wildthyme wasn't joking murmur murmur. You really don't travel well.' Marvelle chuckled and poured her a tot of absinthe. 'This will settle your delicate tummy, I'm sure.'

Jenny scowled at the vivid green of the drink, severely doubting that Marvelle was right. She cursed her constitution. She'd forgotten quite how uncomfortable time travel was for her. She'd had to queue for the toilets here, too, and everyone had been staring at the tall dark woman from the future, in her leather jacket and her black monocle. She had stood out a mile and this irked her as well, as did the rudimentary lavatorial arrangements.

Jenny liked to blend in. To seep into the background and weigh up situations from a safe vantage point.

'There were a couple of aliens in the queue for the facilities,' she told her languid companion. 'One of them didn't look at all human. They were making no effort to mix in. Disgusting.'

'This is another of those nexus points for travellers such as ourselves, Jenny,' he shrugged. 'You'd be surprised who and what turns up here, and hardly anyone bats an eyelid murmur…'

'It's wrong,' she said abruptly. 'Interlopers, time boffins, extra terrestrials. They should keep themselves more… discreet. They carry on like a bunch of tourists.'

He laughed. 'But can't you see why they all flock here? Isn't this just marvellous murmur murmur,' the poet grinned, taking in the whole of the dance hall in a sweeping gesture. Jenny had to concentrate to hear him. The music was very fierce by now and the whole of the Moulin Rouge resounded with the stamping of feet and the sawing of out-of-tune strings. As she watched, the dancing girls whirled past in their layers of frothy petticoats, legs flashing out like blades. They moved in strict machinelike formation, shrieking provocatively at the enthralled crowds. To Jenny they were like some kind of sexy combined harvester, ploughing their way down the shining dance floor, but then, her mind always ran on rather prosaic, mechanical lines like this.

She was so irritated by Marvelle and having to sit here with him and his favourite poodle, Missy, that she wasn't even enjoying fin-de-siecle Paris and the sight of all those lovely girls. The heady atmosphere had touched her not one whit and the absinthe hadn't even made her tipsy. Marvelle's smarmy simpering and murmuring were driving her nuts.

'We should be away,' he mused. 'Murmur murmur.'

Jenny swigged the last of her drink. 'Okay. Let's go.'

They knew Iris and her friends had been and gone. They knew they were close behind – or ahead – of them, but luckily no collision had occurred yet. Marvelle was quite happy to keep a safe distance between him and the Wildthyme woman. He knew how she could scupper his plans, especially if she really set her mind to wresting the glass jar out of his possession. As he moved through the bustling, raucous crowd he wondered whether Iris had discovered his other theft yet, and whether she knew he was flitting about in time using the pinking shears. Surely it wouldn't take her long to realise that?

But she had been here this night. He knew that much and he was lucky to have missed her. On their circuit round the room they had observed the diminutive form of Toulouse Lautrec at a prominent table, scratching at one of his drawings obsessively. Jenny had – despite herself – been rather intrigued to see him at work, though really the fine arts meant very little to her. She was thinking about the value of an original sketch by the dwarfish master.

As she and Marvelle and Missy the poodle had leaned in to see what Lautrec was drawing, the small man became alert and defensive. He glared at them drunkenly and spat out a few choice Gallic insults. Missy had growled at him warningly, nudging him with her cold wet nose.

That was when Jenny had spotted the tablecloth and its sketches from earlier that night. It wasn't hard to pick out the figures of Iris wildly, anachronistically jitterbugging, rendered in lilac pastels – and the gawky form of Simon strutting his stuff beside her. Somewhere in the lightly-sketched background sat a Panda with a glass in both paws.

Marvelle tried to ask Lautrec – in atrocious French – whether these strangers were still in the building. How long ago was this? But Lautrec was belligerent and stinking of drink. Even though the dog growled at him and removed her mittens to display those pale, cruel-looking hands and her golden blaster – the tiny artist would not be drawn.

They had left him in disgust. Though not before Missy had whisked away his precious tablecloth and rolled it up. Lautrec shrugged. If that was the price of being left alone – then so be it. All he wanted was peace and quiet in which to drink, and to concentrate on his drawings of the dancing girls. He was glad to see the back of these two and their freakish dog. And maybe he had imagined the whole thing. Poodles with hands and guns, indeed. It was all some nightmare, no..?

The three travellers emerged from the nightclub and found night-time Paris in an uproar. The streets were lined with confused citizens, hurrying to and fro. The air was shrill with blasts of police whistles and the honking of horns and clattering of hooves.

147

'Oh yes,' nodded Marvelle thoughtfully. 'All this kerfuffle out here reminds me that I have another little job to do this evening, before we leave 1894 murmur murmur.'

He led them through the dark, dripping alleys up the hill behind the Moulin Rouge. Here there were more people than Jenny would expect to see at this hour of the night. They were moving in two directions: some were hurrying away from the graveyard. They each had a strange look about them. They were pale and shaking, some of them, as if they had witnessed something that had uprooted their sense of the world entirely. They had to be away. They had sensed great danger, perhaps. Some of them were remonstrating with others who were streaming up the hill and the winding streets, towards the cemetery. With a sense of dread building in her, Jenny wanted to turn back as well. Where was Marvelle taking her this time?

She knew he didn't really think anything of her. She knew he would risk her life and regret its loss about as much as he might regret breaking a nail. Less, maybe.

The graveyard was sonorous with human chatter and a strange, thrumming bassline of background noise. An alien vibration that Jenny knew couldn't belong to this time and place.

They advanced into the middle of the cemetery, with Missy pulling eagerly towards the mysterious source of heat and noise. Eventually they joined the frightened crowd that thronged about the fallen space craft. Jenny held her breath at the sight of that smooth, pearlescent extrusion.

'It landed here tonight,' Marvelle explained. 'Murmur murmur. Big deal for them. Paris has never seen the like murmur.'

Jenny stared at the crater around the ship and now she could see the blackened corpses strewn about the place, still lightly steaming in the predawn air. At first she thought they might have been bodies disinterred by the force of the capsule's landing. But then she realised. 'Heat ray. They've been showing off their heat ray.'

He nodded. 'The people here don't realise yet what's about to hit them murmur murmur.'

'They're Martians?' Jenny asked.

'Hmm, murmur,' he said. 'Do you have them in your history, Jenny? Did Martians invade Paris in the summer of 1894 murmur?'

She boggled at him. 'Of course they didn't! You know they didn't!'

He smiled wryly. 'I thought I knew that, yes. You're right murmur. Of course they didn't. So… we've stepped sideways into alternate time. Very interesting murmur. Anyway. I've got a little job to do here, if you don't mind.' He snapped his fingers. 'Missy? Will you come with me murmur murur?' He smiled at Jenny. 'You could wait here if you like, dear. Missy's coming in because my Martian's terrible. Hers is much better murmur. She spent a little time there once, on a mission for the Dogworld.'

Jenny tried to make out what he was on about. 'You're going down there? To talk to them?'

'Of course! That's why we're here. I've something to pass on to them murmur murmur.' Now he was slipping a hand inside his immaculate suit jacket (uncrumpled, Jenny noted, by any of the evening's exertions.) To her surprise he produced a colourful flyer and a number of tickets for some kind of pop concert.

'What are you going to do? Tell them to stop invading the Earth..?'

He laughed at her, with just a bit of a sneering expression. 'Hardly! I don't think they'll listen to me, do you? I say, dears, would you mind just tootling back off into space? We'd really rather you didn't invade today murmur murmur.' He rolled his eyes. 'No, I've just got to pass on a few details to them, to give to the Martian Time Agents.'

Jenny gasped. 'They travel in time as well?'

He ignored her. Her questions were starting to get him down. 'Anyway. You wait here while Missy and I give them a knock murmur murmur.'

'You can't leave me here! And you can't go knocking on their capsule. They'll use their death ray thingy on you!'

'I doubt it, murmur,' he said. 'And I'll come back for you Jenny. I give you my word of honour. Don't you believe me murmur murmur?'

She frowned at him, and watched as he and Missy sprang lightly into the crater. A few cries went up from others in the crowd, warning him and the dog to stay back. Marvelle ignored them all and approached the space craft.

Jenny could hardly look. What if he got zapped and blasted into hell? Right now, before her very eyes, and the pinking shears with him? She should have insisted he left them here with her, just in case anything untoward happened. Though she doubted she could ever wield them herself with any degree of accuracy...

I'm going to be stuck here, she thought. Stuck in the nineteenth century, in an alternate world ravaged by Martians.

What on earth was Marvelle playing at? And what were those papers he was so dead set on passing over to the invaders? She had managed to get a quick glimpse of the writing on the tickets, but could hardly believe what she saw. They appeared to be a pair of tickets for seats in the front row at a concert given by Vince Cosmos in 1973.

Jenny could remember Vince Cosmos. He was of her era. She had never owned any of his records. Music had never really been her thing. But she knew who he was.

She sat in the graveyard and waited for Marvelle to come back. She had absolutely no idea what he was up to or what Vince Cosmos might have to do with it. Why would Martians want to go to a pop concert at Hammersmith Odeon?

In all the crazy noise and panic of Paris and the inky shadows of that night, Jenny was feeling very alone and out of it. Where's my secret base? Where are my operatives? She was used to feeling a whole lot more secure than this.

CHAPTER FIFTEEN

Panda was very proud of himself, navigating through the dark with his

makeshift device. 'I told you I'd find civilisation for you!' he laughed, setting off at a run. Between the trees and the lights of the small settlement, there were low, flat fields. They found that they were running through some kind of vegetable crop; stumbling in the channels between tangled vines and plump gourds. Here, where the soil was tilled, even Barbra could make quicker progress towards the smoky, welcoming lights of town.

Simon hoped they looked presentable enough. He glanced round at his companions, wondering how out of place they were going to seem to the locals. Perhaps they should be more careful, and subtle in their approach... But Iris – who was surely more used to this kind of thing – was striding ahead in her purple jungle fatigues, face shining in the moonlight and shouting something about gasping for a drink. Simon realised how hungry he was. They had been walking for hours, it seemed, fighting for every step of the way through the forest. What if there was nothing they could eat in this village? What kind of creatures would live there anyway? And what if they weren't even friendly, or willing to play host to these outlandish visitors?

Iris jabbed him in the ribs as they approached the first of the wooden buildings, which seemed little more than shacks. 'Oh, don't look so worried, lovey. What's the matter with you? If you go round fretting all the time, then the life of a wanderer isn't for you. That's where that Jenny went wrong, you know. Always looking over her shoulder and panicking about what was coming next…'

Simon made a conscious effort to appear less worried.

They were suddenly standing in the middle of a main street in the little town. Tall wooden buildings rose on either side and seemed to continue all the way across the span of town, perhaps up to a mile away. Each window glowed softly with candlelight and there was a gentle susurration of life about the place. It was peaceful.

'Right,' said Iris sharply, rubbing her hands together. 'Pub.'

'Good plan,' said Panda, setting off briskly in what he felt was the right direction.

'I wonder if the people here have ever met a Servo-furnishing before,' Barbra wondered. 'I hope they won't be frightened of me.' She was still thinking about her fight with the beast in the forest, they all realised. Barbra was struggling to get used to the idea of herself as a potentially lethal weapon.

Simon brought up the rear as they ambled down the main street. He was aware of eyes at windows, marking their progress. Out of the corner of his own eye he caught a few flitting movements in the side streets. The locals were aware of them. They were cautiously monitoring the visitors.

To his slight surprise, Panda's instincts were unerring and he led them straight to a colourful-looking inn called *The Winged God*, from which all the noise in town seemed to emanate. They entered into a cheery atmosphere of chatter and clinking glasses. Some peculiar kind of music was playing and they stopped for a moment to bask in the welcoming warmth of the place.

Simon was very pleased that all noise didn't cease at once and all eyes turn to glare at the strangers with hostile intensity. There was a brief, polite lull in the buzz of conversation, nothing more.

It was a low-ceilinged, smoky place, with rooms branching off in all directions. It was cosy, decorated with rugs and wall hangings of brilliant colours and design. The people looked more or less human to Simon's eyes. Perhaps shaggier, perhaps shorter than the people he was used to. Neanderthal might have been an accurate – if unflattering – way of describing them.

He held his breath as Iris pushed and shoved her way to the bar.

Panda observed drily, 'Funny, really. The constant and universal things in the galaxy. Pubs. Bars. Iris being pushy in queues. The funny looks she gets.' He patted Simon on the knee. 'You'll get used to it, young fellow.'

Barbra was getting more attention than the others, but even that consisted of only sidelong glances and raised Neanderthal monobrows. 'They seem quite civilised, really,' she whispered to Simon. 'I wonder if any of them are peckish?'

'Yes, you might pick up some extra cash,' Simon said. 'Taking light snacks and pop to distant outposts.'

Panda found them a quiet nook, where they could sit together and watch the rest of the clientele. Iris followed them there with a tray of drinks.

'What are you doing hiding away in the corner? No one can see us over here.'

'You always like to stand out,' Panda groaned.

'Of course! What's the point of going to all the trouble of turning up, if you hide yourself in the background?'

'She's got a point,' said Simon. 'We're the new faces in town. People will be interested.'

'What did the bar-being say, Iris?' asked Barbra. 'Did you quiz him about where we are? Did you find anything out?'

'This is the world of Valcea,' Iris said, hunkering down over her glass. She had ordered some rough, local approximation of a gin and tonic. Each glass was fizzing rather busily, emitting steam and smelling of kiwi fruit, for some reason.

'Valcea?' echoed Panda thoughtfully.

Iris nodded and slurped her drink. 'Yes, well. I've been here before. A long time ago. That glass monstrosity we came up against back in the bush set my mind racing and rang a few bells. Valcea was the world of the Glass Men. Back in time immemorial, when I was last here. And a fearsome bunch they were, too. Up in their City of Glass...'

Simon drank and felt his weird gin bubbling and steaming all the way down. 'Urgh. So, do you have any sense of why we are here this time? And why Anthony Marvelle might have been here?'

'I could hardly go wading in and asking all that, could I?' she scoffed. 'Excuse me, but have you seen any poodles with hands and guns hereabouts, eh? And what about foppish poets with pinking shears? No, Simon. You have to box more cleverly than that, on investigations like these...'

'But you think he's been here?'

'Or will be,' said Iris. 'Quite soon. At least, according to the crystal that Barbra nicked from MIAOW.'

Barbra winced. 'Don't say 'nicked', please, Iris. That makes me feel awful.'

There was a disturbance then, at the front of the bar. A few shouts went up and ripples of consternation went through the room.

'What is it?' Iris was up on her feet as the other drinkers got up and hurried to see what all the fuss was.

'Pick me up!' Panda demanded. 'Carry me!' He hated to be left out.

The crowd was so thick they couldn't get back to the main doors of *The Winged God*. They ended up staring at the street through a bay window, and squinting through the distorted glass at the darkness outside.

'There's some sort of struggle going on out there,' said Simon.

A carriage pulled by horses had come to a halt outside the pub. The wagon and the horses themselves were bedecked with thousands of tiny mirrors, stitched like chain mail. The effect was uncanny. It made the driverless carriage seem ghostly as it stood, apparently waiting, at the door.

Women were moaning and wailing. One older woman seemed to be drunk, and she was pulling at the arm of a strapping young lad. He and three others, plus two young girls, were clambering aboard the glittering wagon. The older woman and several others didn't seem at all happy about this. Arguments and protests were breaking out.

The silver horses merely stamped and waited, their breath misting the air before them. Now that he looked more closely, Simon saw that they looked less like earth horses than he had at first thought. They had elephantine trunks and sharp claws instead of hooves, as if they needed to maintain a tight grip on the frosty terrain.

'This is very interesting,' Iris said. 'It's as if these youngsters are setting off somewhere. Or they've been sent for… by whoever owns the carriage. And their families aren't too chuffed.'

'Obviously some sort of ritual,' Panda said. 'Sacrificial, maybe.' His expression darkened. 'We're best off leaving well alone. It doesn't do to get too mixed up in local rituals.'

'Too right,' said Iris. 'Are we ready for another at the bar?'

Outside the weeping family members were fighting a losing battle. The sacrificial victims (if that's what they were) were dead set on going. Soon all six of the grim, expressionless youngsters were aboard the carriage. The doors slammed shut of their own accord. A general cry of despair went up from the gathered crowd and then the horse-like beings bolted back into action. With a great clatter of claws and jangle of mirrored shards, the carriage was off again. It slid swiftly into the darkness and away.

'I'll go to the bar,' said Simon. 'Same again?'

Iris gave him a handful of the local currency. She never explained how she had come by it.

The barman was the first of the locals that had spoken to Simon. He fiddled with bottles and glasses and kept his beady eyes on his customer until Simon felt quite uncomfortable.

'Do you get many, erm, strangers in these parts?' Simon felt he had to break the tense silence at last.

'Not many.' said the barman. 'Every few years we get a ship landing. Usually someone on the way to somewhere else. No one really comes to Valcea for its own sake. You lot after rooms tonight?'

Simon agreed readily, deciding that someone ought to make arrangements. He glanced back at the others and saw that Iris had broken into song. She was declaiming rather raucously, kicking up her legs and drawing attention to their party in the corner.

'I've only one room left,' said the barman. 'You'll all have to share. That woman.'

'Iris?' he winced. 'I'm sorry she's being so noisy.'

The barman shrugged. 'She's singing one of the old songs. Tell her to watch out. Not everyone round here is glad to remember the old times on Valcea. How does she know our songs, anyway?'

'I don't know her all that well,' said Simon. 'I've only just started travelling with her.'

The man shoved the glasses across the rough bar and pushed his snout-like nose closer to Simon. 'You just warn her to watch out. She looks like the sort who could easily come a cropper. Know what I mean? You just tell Grandma to keep her trap shut, otherwise she's out on the street. And you don't want to be outside on nights like these, do you?'

'I guess not,' said Simon, and shuffled away with the drinks, to tell the others he had made arrangements for their lodgings – and to warn Iris to pipe down.

*

It seemed unfathomable to Simon that he had somehow come away on this journey without packing anything to read. Putting aside the fact that he hadn't packed a proper caseful of clothes or any of the other vital items he might need in order to explore the cosmos, leaving without a bag of books seemed to him the worst thing of all.

Late that night in the dark, musty room above the inn, this thought sank in at last. Iris's fluting snores rose melodically from the shapeless mass of blankets on the room's single bed. The more querulous sound of Panda's sleeping played noisy counterpoint. He appeared to be snuggled into Iris's arms.

Barbra was quite still, standing guard at the door. Her neon tubes and numeral displays were dimmed. Simon wasn't sure if that meant she had closed herself down, or whether the oddly sophisticated machine really could fall asleep and conserve her energies that way.

Simon had always been an insomniac. Just like his gran and just like his mam. They too had been familiar with the hot, vexed feeling of sitting up in an armchair like this in the middle of the night, and looking with envy at others to whom sleep came naturally and easily. Perhaps this was the reason they became readers in the first place. Maybe one caused the other. Or perhaps it was the other way round, and excessive reading brought on insomnia. Simon often had those nights when the words kept jiggling and his brain was too active, buzzing along in the dark.

Either way, he was quite used to sitting up like this in the early hours.

Downstairs the inn was quiet at last. It had stayed fairly raucous even after Iris's eventual and rather drunken exit. She had stumbled on the rough wooden staircase, cut her hand, and finished off the day feeling rather cross – and hoarse, from all the singing.

It was now, in the quietest watch of the night that Simon realised he did, in fact, have a book with him. There was a small, dense volume stowed away in his coat pocket. It thunked against his thigh as he hefted the coat over his lap for warmth. He remembered what it was – the book he had purloined from the top deck of the bus. It was one of the volumes of Iris's diary.

Maybe it was wrong of him. He was sure she would mind. She was rather secretive, wasn't she? She was furtive when it came to questions about her past.

This just made him more curious. He flipped through the pages and peered frowning at the dates scrawled on the gorgeous, marbled endpapers and could make neither head nor tail of them. Iris clearly worked on some calendar system he had never come across before.

Her handwriting was cramped and impatient, marching slantwise over page after page. The entries seemed to have been written in the midst of whatever action was going on, in quiet moments and odd lulls. There was a breathless urgency about the bits and pieces he could decipher.

He flipped backwards and forward, dipping in here and there. Sometimes the writing became a bit dense and senseless, as Iris lost the thread of her thoughts or became too involved wrangling with herself, or complaining about someone. Other times there were sudden flashes of clarity and those moments would ring out in the night, sometimes rather startlingly. Here was an account of Panda and Iris hobnobbing at Hampton Court and swishing about in the corridors of power. Then, skipping ahead four hundred years to escape beheading, and arriving slap-bang in the middle of a Shirley Bassey concert on the very same spot.

As he read on he realised there were scribbled accounts here of lives and times on other planets and in other dimensions. There were references to beings and places that he would never recognise or understand in a million years, without journeying there himself. Iris's rough drawings of some of those creatures didn't really help him either. Things that he assumed were doodles in the margins of her notes were actually detailed sketches of the creatures she had sometimes encountered.

The universe was spinning around him in that pokey and dark bedroom. He leaned towards the window and the moonlight spilling onto the page, straining his eyes to keep on drinking all these details in. What a treasure trove her journals were, he realised. On the bus she had dozens of these volumes, detailing her *zig-zagging* progress through the dimensions.

How many years had she and Panda been travelling together? How difficult it must be, to keep track of time when you lived it like this. Perhaps her diaries were the only way of maintaining some kind of link with her own personal time paradigm, and measuring how far she had come. At that thought, Simon felt a little stab of guilt for slipping this unique book into his pocket.

It was as if he had taken one of Iris's most precious belongings. She had trusted him to rummage about anywhere on the bus, and he had betrayed her, sort of.

He read on. Once or twice he laughed out loud at some of the observations she made, or the escapades she got up to. She never made excuses for herself or her mistakes. She was quite frank on the page about her blind spots and her blackouts – and the times when she made dicey situations even worse with her loud mouth and meddling ways. Even though she often set out with the best of intentions, she often caused more damage than good, but she was refreshingly honest about that as well.

It all seemed like an appallingly dangerous way to live, though, Simon thought.

He jumped then, as there came a loud crash from the street outside.

The window was open slightly, letting in a cool night breeze. It wasn't windy enough to bang shutters, which is what the crash had sounded like.

He was jumpy. He was being silly and jumpy. Why shouldn't there be noise out on the street?

But he kept on looking.

And he had the weirdest sense that something down there was looking back at him. Something in one of the side streets. It had eased into a hiding place and was staring back at him as he studied the quiet town. He didn't know what should give him that feeling. Perhaps it was Iris's book. He was starting to share her sense that the universe was full of enemies and ne'er-do-wells, lurking round the corners and plotting to do you down. Her tales of her own ramshackle adventures were acting on his already pretty healthy paranoia gland.

He let the blind drop and settled himself determinedly in the chair, putting the book away and deciding to ignore any more noises, and to sleep properly, for a couple of hours at least.

To his surprise, he did.

CHAPTER SIXTEEN

Time in Darlington had moved on. Unbeknownst to the others.

Kelly returned to work at the Exchange. She did it automatically, with something approaching relief. She was used to the routine of it, and the soothing boredom of it. She was used to dusting the glossy shelves and fetching out the library steps to denude the corners of cobwebs. She looked forward to seeing the faces of the regular customers and taking their Exchange membership cards, the cardboard gone soft with age, and adding on their new credit with each new choice they made.

Autumn deepened and darkened. It came sweeping into town, stirring all kinds of detritus on the rooftops and roadsides. The breezes were like long, stuttering gasps and sharp indrawn breaths. The mornings became sharper, nippier and still she waited for Simon to come back.

She went back to the Arts Centre for the weekly meetings with her poetry group. At first she wasn't keen but, as usual, her landlady Chelsea jollied her along and bullied her out of her basement. Kelly pulled on her heaviest coat and yanked a snood over her head for the short walk across the park. It was as if she was going in disguise for these evenings out, talking about poems and drinking alcopops in the bar afterwards. Some of the women gossiped about how the poet they all knew – the sophisticated Anthony Marvelle – had seemingly disappeared without a trace. It had been in the papers, even on the telly. They thrilled to the thought that his last public engagement had been with them, at their festival. They hoped he wasn't dead.

But Marvelle was a man who had often left mild scandals in his wake, by all accounts. Probably he had run off with someone's wife. He'd turn up again in Malaysia or Australia or somewhere, after a suitable period. Perhaps it was even a publicity stunt.

Some of the poetry group members even nudged each other and whispered that the last person Marvelle had been seen with was Kelly. Hadn't she been enjoying his undivided attention that last night of the festival, at Chelsea's party. Did she know anything, perhaps, about the mystery?

When Kelly heard this she scowled. She hated the fact they'd even noticed her and Marvelle conferring in the kitchen. She didn't see why she should be gossiped about, let alone linked with the man's disappearance. There was nothing she could say. She couldn't engage with any of the discussion. The only information she had was outlandish, unbelievable – and certainly none of their business.

The gossip rolled over and blew away. The season went on. The weeks went by.

Kelly found that the only people she really spoke to were her customers at the Exchange, and even those, not too enthusiastically. At home she was quiet around Chelsea – and Chelsea was quiet too, going through a new relationship and – as far as Kelly could make out – making another hash at it. The postman, this time.

Kelly did think that Marvelle might have dropped her another line. She was miffed that, having sent that first, rather odd letter, his communications had abruptly dried up. She hadn't known where or when he wanted to meet her. She'd have been happy to. She didn't trust Iris either and she thought he had a point.

But he had never written to her again. It was as if he had given up on her, all too easily.

And then she thought – maybe something has happened to him. That's why he never followed his letter up. Maybe Marvelle had come a cropper. They lived in such a dangerous, uncertain world, he and Iris – or so it seemed.

These were Kelly's thoughts, turning round and round and she realised there was no one she could talk to about them.

She cursed Simon again for not being there.

She felt daft for believing what Iris had promised. She had believed that she really could bookmark the very day or the very hour that they had left. She had been convinced that they would be back by now. She felt silly for hoping for them to pull up at the kerbside in their bus. Each day she kept an eye open for them.

She felt forgotten by them, and rejected. They hadn't wanted her as a fellow traveller. She knew she hadn't been keen enough, or impressed enough. I should have tried harder, she thought. I should have enthused more over those places Iris took us. I hadn't realised all of my reactions were under scrutiny.

Here came the first glimmerings of winter. The frozen mornings. The shop decorations.

She'd hear a banging at the door of her basement flat or at the front of the Exchange and she'd get excited, momentarily. It was Simon standing there, surely, all tanned and foreign-looking. He'd come back from who-knew-where with presents and stories and amazing things to tell.

But he never turned up.

Books came and went, in and out of the Exchange. They came and went with their customers, changing like the tides, blowing around like the leaves.

Then one day, something happened.

Kelly was visited by a lady who said she belonged to an organisation called MIAOW.

At first Kelly didn't let on that she knew about a body with just that name. She played it cool. She helped the woman into the Exchange. She was in a wheelchair, with a rug covering her lap. She had dyed jet black hair, dark glasses, and a pale complexion.

'I am Magda,' said the woman. 'I've been here before. On bookish business. Perhaps you remember?'

The woman had a German or a Dutch accent and, all of a sudden, Kelly *did* remember her. She remembered Magda coming here to talk books with Terrance. Not recently. But Kelly could see her sitting there with a bagful of remaindered science fiction hardbacks, trying to barter with Terrance. Trying to gain Exchange membership. Kelly frowned. Hadn't there been some kind of row? Hadn't this Magda wheeled out of here in high dudgeon?

The woman in the wheelchair was studying her keenly. 'I know about the bus. I know you have been aboard the Celestial Omnibus with Iris Wildthyme.'

Kelly blinked. 'You do?' She was in a kind of spell, staring into the woman's eyes. They were heavily made-up and mesmerizing.

'I've known many people who have disappeared aboard that bus with Iris,' Magda chuckled. 'I've never been lucky enough to be invited, myself. But never mind. I'm not bitter. We just get our kicks where we can, eh? Some of us weren't built for travels in Space and Time, eh?'

Kelly tried to play dumb. 'Travels in t-time?'

Magda rolled those eyes at her. 'A lot of people have disappeared lately. At MIAOW we've lost our leader, Jenny. And the vending machine, Barbra, she's gone too. Though she was neither use nor ornament, to be honest. But they've gone.

Whistled off into time and space. MIAOW is in chaos without Jenny. And I think you've lost people here, too, haven't you?'

Kelly nodded. 'Simon. And Terrance, who you know. The man who used to own this place.'

'The man with two plastic arms,' Magda nodded. 'Yes, I know him. Though he never had any liking for me. I always thought we should have got on better. Him with his arms, and me with… you know, legs.' She shrugged listlessly. 'And it's Iris right behind all these disappearances. The mistress of the magical bus.'

'Is it?' Kelly said. She didn't want to give away anything more. She was experiencing a stirring of deep unease. She was imagining that everyone who was gone was dead. Or as good as dead. They had vanished into the past, or been swallowed up in some other dimension. She started to feel panicked.

'I think we should join forces, no?' Magda said. 'Tell me what you know. Tell me at once.'

*

This dislocated feeling was familiar. Jenny remembered it from before. Turning up somewhere new and having to ask someone. Being put in that pretty humiliating position of having to admit that she didn't really know when and where she was.

Now she was in a hotel foyer. Pretty plush. Somewhere teetering on the edge of the Golden Chasm, the Miramar was one of the super-hotels of the first human expansion beyond their own solar system. She'd been here once with Iris, a long time ago. Travellers from Earth often used this particular spot to wet their whistles before embarking on the longer trips.

We're leaving our system and our millennium, Jenny mused. Anthony's trips are sending us further and further afield, like he's stretching his wings. Flexing them. Preparing to make a bolt for it, into the wide blue yonder. Those pinking shears went slash, flash, swish through the Very Fabric with each trip they took, and Marvelle seemed to be getting more expert. It was as if he was hacking his way mercilessly through vast stretches of time.

To what end, she wondered. Where is he taking us, ultimately?

It was the evening after their day in Montmartre. They were well away from the Earth and that century now. Paris had fallen under the Martian onslaught, as had all the other cities of the Earth – at least, for a little while. Anthony, Missy and Jenny hadn't stuck around long enough to see.

She nodded tersely as an ancient waitress brought her tea things on a wobbling hostess trolley. She eyed the name badge and asked, 'How long have you worked here, Jessie?'

'Me, ma'am? Over a hundred years, here at the Golden Chasm. Before that, when the Miramar was perched on the Spiral Wing, I did about twenty years there.'

Jenny wasn't really all that interested in the old woman. She was just passing the time, while Anthony was off doing whatever he was doing, elsewhere in the hotel. Probably preening himself in the spa. 'You must have seen some changes here, then, I guess?'

The waitress pulled a face. 'Hardly any, ma'am. That's the point of this place. Hardly anything changes. Hardly anything at all. And that's how the guests like it, you see. All around us the universe is getting up to its usual kerfuffle and everything changes before you can catch your breath. But here, you see. Here… we are timeless.'

Jenny had to smile at her earnestness. The almost simian smile she received in return made her feel a little less bristly. She found herself relaxing slightly. Unwinding, perhaps, for the first time in what seemed like weeks. She enjoyed the Edwardian splendour of the place – the brass and wood fittings and the aspidistras and antimacassars.

'You look a bit fraught, ma'am, if you don't mind me saying,' said the waitress. 'It'll be that Mr Marvelle. He been running you ragged?'

Jenny took out her monocle and rubbed her tired eyes. 'You know him?'

'Regular here at the Miramar, isn't he? One of his usual stop-off points, this is. Has been for, I'd say, a couple of decades. We're quite used to him coming through with his... er, young companions.'

'Women?' Jenny laughed. 'This is where he brings his women? For mucky weekends at the edge of the universe?'

'I wouldn't like to say. Er, I'm sorry, ma'am...'

'Oh, you needn't apologise to me. I'm not one of his women. I'm just a... fellow traveller. I wouldn't have anything to do with that slimy old git, seriously.'

Jessie the waitress was nodding slowly, with a very serious expression on her kindly, wrinkled face. She bent forward, speaking up a bit over the noise of an excitable and loud party at a nearby cluster of settees. 'Yes, I'm glad about that. You see, I don't think Mr Marvelle is that kind a man, or that reliable a fancy man, to be honest. I've heard some brutal things about him. And him looking like such a gent, too. I think he's a bit of a seducer. All that mumbling and murmuring! Ha! I'd give him what-for, if he tried it on with me.'

Jenny poured her tea. 'I bet you would. Will you have a cup with me, Jessie?'

'Oh no, ma'am. I couldn't possibly. The manager would have my guts for garters if he saw me hob-nobbing even this much. I just thought I should warn you, ma'am. Beware of Mr Marvelle.

He's always up to no good and he looks out only for himself. Wonderful poet, mind. Lovely wordsmith!'

And then the ancient Jessie was off, rumbling along arthritically with her hostess trolley on the luxurious carpet.

Jenny drank her tea, lost in contemplation, half-observing the raucous lot at the next coffee table. She understood that they belonged to some kind of literary convention that was happening somewhere in the Miramar that weekend. They were a set of weirdly composed beings: creatures of rock, small insect-like beings, and someone elaborately coiffed from head to foot in purple fur.

The tinkling of the muzak lulled her, and the chuckling of the water feature that dominated the large reception. Jenny found herself drifting almost into sleep. And then she felt a cold wet nose brushing her arm.

'Missy.'

The dog glared at her with open dislike. 'Anthony has booked you into a room of your own.' Missy bared her teeth horribly, showing lots of pink gum and yellowed fangs. 'Personally I wouldn't have run to the expense. But whatever.' She flung off her bootees – having no need to disguise her hands here. She tossed Jenny a large key ring. 'We'll be in the next room. Don't even think about whizzing off anywhere.'

'I won't,' Jenny said. 'Where would I go?'

The poodle narrowed its wicked eyes. 'I don't know. For all we know, you might have some secret method of calling up that Wildthyme bitch. You could still be in cahoots with her.'

Jenny rolled her eyes. 'Cahoots? No thank you.'

A few minutes later the ex-traffic warden and reluctant time traveller was showing herself into a single room that wasn't too shabby, she was pleased to see. It looked a bit spartan and she felt suddenly sad and bereft that she was arriving with no luggage of any kind. She'd been wearing these clothes for three days and felt just dreadful in them. So this was a good time to relax, replenish and refurbish herself.

She sat heavily on the weirdly shaped and squashy bed.

And that's when she saw what Marvelle had left sitting on her bedside table. At first she thought it was some kind of innocuous ornament. But no. It had been put there by Marvelle. Into her safe-keeping. For some inscrutable reason of his.

It was a glass jar. Ancient glass. Bulky and blobby and filled with hard, bright bubbles. A jar containing a gruesomely red viscous jam.

It was the Objet D'Oom. The Hysperon Jar.

And for some reason Marvelle had placed it right beside her hotel bed.

CHAPTER SEVENTEEN

The next morning Simon was surprised to find that Iris was up and about bright and early. By the time he had negotiated the primitive plumbing arrangements upstairs at the inn, she was already down in the bar swigging on a vast mug of what smelled reassuringly like very strong tea.

'Ah, there you are…' She spared him the quickest of glances. She was wrestling with a range of intricate tools and using them – now that he came closer he could see – to mess around with that memory crystal that Barbra had given her. Somehow she had opened the thing up and was peering at the innards through a jeweller's magnifying glass. Simon was surprised to see that the insides of the crystal were liquid. Something like mercury ran through tiny veins.

'What's this all about?' he asked blearily. 'How can you tell anything from that?'

'Aha!' she said, wielding a fork with her free hand and spearing a large chunk of a messy-looking omelette. Simon wasn't sure but it was almost lavender in hue. 'You'd be surprised, lovey, at my very many and abstruse areas of expertise. And believe it or not, I'm getting quite a lot of interesting stuff out of this little bauble.'

'Oh yes?' He came to sit on the bench with her. He glanced around at the empty bar hungrily. 'Er, where did you get your breakfast?'

'That barman's took a shine to me,' she grinned. 'He was a bit off with me last night, what with all my singing and carousing and so on. But this morning he's been nice as pie.'

It was true. When Iris returned to her work the barman appeared, smiling a bit smarmily and listening to what Simon wanted. He even enquired after the other members of their party. Simon told him, 'Well, Barbra never really eats anything, and Panda's woken up in an awful mood, so I guess we won't see them for a while yet. But I'd love what Iris has got, please.'

The barman nodded graciously and backed away into the kitchen. There was something about him that Simon just didn't trust.

'So what's on the cards today then?' he said. 'Are we still on the lookout for Marvelle?'

'Yes, of course,' she said. 'And that's what I'm trying to glean from this little gem. The information is in here... about his movements. If I can just trigger it right, we'll find out exactly where it is on this world he'll manifest himself. Or maybe he already has. Maybe he's here already. The bus tries to be as accurate as it can... but there might be a little leeway...'

She went back wordlessly to her work. Simon's breakfast appeared – and the ragged-looking omelette was very good, though he hesitated to ask what kind of creature the eggs had come from. After some time there was a great thunking and clattering from the hallway and it was Barbra, coming down the wooden stairs unaided. She was followed by a scowling Panda.

'I've had the most appalling dreams all night,' he announced, hauling himself up to sit at their table. Irritably he tried to tie his own cravat. It was looking rather frayed at the ends, Simon saw.

'Rubbish, Panda,' Iris murmured. 'You slept like a babe-in-arms all night. You hardly stirred.'

'Babe-in-arms,' he grunted. 'I should know, shouldn't I? I should know what kind of dreams I had.'

Barbra – as was becoming her habit – tried to mollify him. 'What did you dream about, Panda? Oh, and by the way, would anyone like any crisps or pop for breakfast?'

They all shook their heads and Panda coughed. He said, 'It was a very confusing and horrible dream. And you were all in it.'

'Cheers, lovely!' Iris laughed. 'Confusing and horrible, indeed!'

Panda's expression was dark. He looked troubled as he thought himself back into his nightmare. 'We were in some horrible, draughty throne room. Yes, that's right. A vast kind of palace and everything was icy to the touch. Harsh, icy and very dark red. We could hardly see each other in the gloom. We were stuck there. We were being held there against our wills. And there was some sort of malign presence in the room... An evil creature...'

'It sounds awful, Panda,' Barbra said. 'Luckily, I don't get many nightmares. When my lights go out, mercifully, that's it. And I don't have much of a subconscious to speak of...'

'It was much more like a premonition,' said Panda. 'I felt like I was dreaming about somewhere that we were going to go. I've had them before, haven't I, Iris? I've seen into the future.'

'That's true,' Iris said, fiddling deftly with the crystal's workings. 'He's seen some very funny things in that furry old head of his. He's been a prescient old Panda in his time.'

Simon chuckled and Panda stilled him with a single boggle of his glass eyes. 'I haven't told you the worst. As we came face to face with this... malign being in her throne room... others were there. Others whom we know. There was that Anthony

Marvelle, and... Jenny. And your friend, Simon. Kelly. And Kelly was lying there on the floor. Dead, I thought.'

Simon gawped at him. 'What? Kelly?'

'I'm afraid so,' said Panda.

'But it was just a horrible dream,' said Simon. 'You're not really psychic, are you?' He felt Barbra extrude one of her thin, mechanical limbs and rub his back.

Iris gave them a worried look. 'Actually, Panda really *is* a bit psychic. It's something to do with where he comes from and his true nature. But we're not sure about that, are we chuck? We're not at all sure about these peculiar gifts of yours.'

'No,' said Panda thickly. 'We don't know much about all of that. All I know is this. We've got to get to Marvelle and Jenny. And they will have Kelly with them. When we see them, they'll have taken Kelly away from her home and the Exchange. They need her for some reason. We were foolish to leave her, Iris. They were saying – in my dream – that she is the key, somehow. She is the... what was the word?'

'Oh come on, Panda, think!' Iris said suddenly. 'If it's important you must remember it!'

'There was a word, yes...' Panda said. 'The malign presence in the room. She spoke up suddenly. There were pink eyes glowing in the darkness. The most horrible eyes I have ever seen and they were looking at all of us. And the word... the word she used about Kelly... it sounded like... it sounded like '*Ringpull*.''

They all stared at him.

'*Ringpull?*' Barbra said. 'Like on a can of pop?'

'It can't have been that,' Simon said. 'Maybe it was 'riddle'? Or 'wrinkle'? Or 'wormhole'?'

'I don't know...' Panda sighed. 'That's what it sounded like. And then it was morning all of a sudden, and you bloody well woke me up.'

Iris looked at them all appraisingly. 'Well, let's bear it all in mind and not get too het up about it. Panda has dreamed some pretty rum things in his time. Not everything has come true, has it, chuck? Kelly might not wind up lying there dead. It could all just be a.. whatsitcalled. A metaphor.'

Barbra and Simon still looked very worried by all of this.

Then suddenly – as if on cue – the memory crystal lit up brilliantly. Iris set it down on the scarred wooden table and they all watched it open out.

No one noticed the barman approaching them with another trayful of tea mugs. He was as fascinated as they were by the unfolding crystal petals and the spinning globe of light that hovered before them.

'Wow,' said Simon. 'A picture's forming…'

'It's showing us where he is,' Iris whispered. 'That's where Marvelle is. That's where we'll find him.'

It was a hologram of a city. A ruined City of Glass, high atop a wintry plateau. It was a marvellous place. Even partly destroyed it looked magnificent with its snapped spires and fallen domes.

'The old city of Valcea,' said the barman. His rough voice broke into their still, silent moment, making them all jump.

'It looks like it's been abandoned,' Iris said.

'It was,' said the landlord, setting down the tray and rubbing his beard. He looked terribly perturbed. 'No one would go there for many years. Not since all the trouble in the Old Days. It was a cursed city. A place of decadence. But now…'

'Now?' said Simon.

'That's where they take the sacrifices. That's where they take our young people to. Up to the old city. To meet the New Gods. That's who live there now.'

'Crikey,' said Iris.

It surprised Kelly that she and Magda became something like friends during that autumn. Like many of the connections Kelly made with people, it happened first of all through books. She visited Magda in her remainder shop at the indoor market and oohed and aahed at some of the stock. Kelly was going through a Paranormal Mystery and Gothic phase in her reading, and was excited by the stacks of US import paperbacks, all glossy and brand new on the table in the centre of Magda's tiny shop. Together they enthused over their favourites in the genre.

Every few days Kelly would pop by the shop, buying a number of incredibly cheap books and taking a couple of iced buns from the bakery on the high street. Magda found it hard to leave the shop and to nip out for lunch. With the wheelchair it seemed more hassle than it was worth, and she was glad that her new young friend visited with treats like this.

In return she would regale Kelly with top secret information from the MIAOW archives. Despite herself, and knowing it was quite the wrong thing to do, Magda would show off about the various strange investigations and impossible affairs she had been a party to, as one of the ladies of MIAOW.

Kelly sat listening, still not sure whether to take it all for gospel truth. By now she had seen enough of their impossible things to believe these outlandish claims to do with creatures under the earth and from outer space. Visitations and possessions. People, objects and buildings that were haunted by intelligences from beyond.

Sometimes after work Magda would make the long trip up the South Road in her chair and come to visit the Exchange. Kelly flexed her rudimentary cooking skills and made her Welsh Rarebit and let her roam the endless stacks of books. Those sharp eyes missed nothing as she peered around, sending Kelly up the stepladders to fetch down strange old volumes and dusty, ancient paperbacks that even Kelly hadn't noticed before. Here, for example, was a fat little calf-bound volume that looked as if it had been there for a hundred years.

'The *Aja'ib*,' Magda gasped, breathing in its strange, spicy scent. 'How funny. How strange that Terrance should have such a thing in his possession. May I buy it?'

Kelly explained that this wasn't how it worked. At the Exchange you didn't buy books that then became yours. It was all about bringing books back when you were finished with them, and then leaving with something else next time.

'Ahh,' said Magda in her raspy, foreign accent. 'If what they say about the *Aja'ib* is true, it is not a book that you can *ever* be finished with. It's an endless sequence of tales and puzzles from another world. Legends and myths that go spiralling on forever.'

'Another world?' Kelly said.

'Another planet,' Magda nodded. 'Yes. A world called Hyspero. So… May I take it?'

Kelly felt uneasy as she made out the little grey card and filled in the slip to say which book Magda was taking away from the Exchange. Even though she hadn't been aware of the volume's existence until now, it suddenly seemed – now that Magda was stowing it away in her handbag with her knitting – that something was shifting in the dusty, amber atmosphere of the shop. Dust was trickling out of a hole in the world… It was as if a cornerstone of the building had been dislodged. But this was nonsense. It was just an old book. Some old science fiction thing, right up Magda's street.

The following Friday Kelly took a local bus out into the wilds of the countryside. Using a scrawled page of directions, she went to a village somewhere beyond Scotch Corner on a dark and breezy night. When she stepped onto the village square there was still a mile or two to walk through narrow country lanes, up and down rolling hills, through puddles clogged with fallen leaves. The bare branches above clattered against each other in the rising wind and she wondered how Magda got herself home each night from the town. It seemed like such a long, inconvenient way to come.

At last she was at Magda's house. A farmhouse standing alone on the bleak brow of a hill. Magda welcomed her warmly and showed her into a low-ceilinged, cramped little place, every room lined with books of all kinds. A gloopy sauce redolent of tomato and oregano was bubbling away on the hob and Kelly found herself relaxing at the kitchen table with red wine and the deliciousness of being cooked for. Magda thumped away energetically at the pizza dough she was making, and told Kelly all she knew about Iris Wildthyme.

'Then you think Simon is in danger?'

'Of course!' Magda wheezed, as the air filled up with puffs of white flour. 'But everyone who goes off with Iris knows what the risk is. You must have felt that yourself.'

Ruefully Kelly admitted it was true. 'I really couldn't handle it at all. I would hate to live like that. All over the place. Never knowing where you're going to be next.'

Magda sympathised. 'I like a steady life too. I like living in one place only. My early life… I came from somewhere quite different to this, you see.'

Oh no, Kelly groaned inwardly. This is where Madga tells me that she's from space too. She must have given away this feeling in her expression because Magda laughed then.

'Oh, my dear. Don't be so worried-looking. You mustn't live in dread and worry, you know. You must embrace the next new thing that comes into your life. The next new and outrageous thing. You should be grateful that new things are still coming your way. That's what it means to be young. Now. Help me with getting these pizza bases rolled out…'

Kelly smiled and her chair scraped loudly on the kitchen flags as she stood to help. Then there came an unearthly howling from outside the farmhouse. It shook them both and they stared at each other. The howling rang out three times, then died away into a softer keening.

'Do you have a dog?' Kelly asked.

Magda looked as alarmed as she did. 'I've often thought it was a good idea. Living out here alone… but, no…'

The howling had become a less terrifying barking. It was closer. Beyond the dark bay window of the kitchen.

Then there was a knock at the back door. A steady, confident knock.

Madga frowned. 'W-will you get that?' she asked Kelly. All of a sudden she looked very helpless and old, sitting there with her mohair sleeves rolled up and bits of dough stuck in her hair.

Kelly took a deep breath and marched to the back door, flinging it open abruptly.

And there, with his smug-looking poodle squatting beside him, was the immaculately-turned out figure of Anthony Marvelle. 'Kelly, dear. I said I'd come, didn't I? Didn't I say that I would meet you once more? Murmur murmur. May I come in murmur..?'

CHAPTER EIGHTEEN

Jenny slept deeply that night in her sumptuous room at the Super Hotel Miramar, high atop the endless cascading of the Golden Chasm. Even so, she couldn't help turning over in her mind, the question of why Marvelle would leave the glass jar in her possession. He was aware of her work with MIAOW, and he knew that she had been searching for it. And now he had left it by the side of her bed, plain as anything. Was it some kind of test? Was he seeing if he could trust her?

She didn't trust him. He knew that she didn't trust him. She could barely abide him. So why was he playing games like this with her?

Leaving the softest lights in the room glowing, she lay down and, before she drifted into that deep sleep she stared into the crimson depths of the jar. Jenny felt the slow turning of the Miramar and it was a comforting sensation, rather than a startling one. She pictured the whole hotel on its fragment of rock spinning idly above the abyss. She wished she'd had a chance to observe it. There was some kind of deck at the top of the hotel, she thought she remembered Iris once telling her. Tomorrow. Perhaps tomorrow she would go up there to see…

Then all of a sudden, she was elsewhere.

She looked around thoughtfully. Jenny wasn't a fanciful person. She hardly ever dreamed and, when she did, her dreams were often of rather practical things. She solved problems in her sleep and it was all a bit abstract. She rarely found herself in the illusion of somewhere real and solid, like this.

She recognised it as a wine bar in Darlington. She had been here before. Oh god, that disastrous date. When her fellow MIAOW operatives forced her to go and meet someone. They thought she was too dedicated to the job. She needed to get out and mingle with normal people. Those who had never heard of MIAOW, or even suspected that Darlington was a hotspot for interstitial activity. And so she'd spent a dim evening in a lesbian bar off Skinnergate with a woman called Ella.

And now she was back there, on an uncomfortable sofa at the back of the club, but luckily there was no sign of that Ella, who had run her own gallery and talked about nothing but herself.

There was someone else sitting with Jenny tonight. A very small woman in a red dress, with masses of auburn hair. Her face was squinched up in a moue of pleasure as she sucked a cocktail through a straw and smacked her lips.

She really was tiny. The squashy sofa just about swallowed her up and she had to sit perched right at its edge, dangling her dainty feet perilously over the side. 'Hello there,' she told Jenny. 'You're the traffic warden, aren't you? The one in charge of MIAOW? And they're the ones who came looking for me.'

Jenny was too startled to do anything but nod dumbly.

'You seem a little slow,' the woman observed. 'Have a sip of your drink. It can be quite steadying in situations like this. By the way, this *isn't* a dream.' She glanced around at the lesbian bar and its meagre Wednesday night clientele. 'Well, all of *this* is. I've plucked the setting from your memories, of course. But I'm coming in from the outside. I'm real, as it were, and transmitting directly into your cerebral cortex. And what's more I got the drinks in. Cheers!'

Jenny found her voice at last. 'W-who are you? What do you mean, transmitting into my cerebral...'

'Hm,' said the woman. 'I'd heard you were rather literal-minded, but no one told me you were slow. I'm visiting you. In your mind. Hello!'

'But who are you?' Jenny growled. She hated stuff like this.

'My name is Euphemia, as it happens,' said the woman grandly. 'And it's nice to be back in a normal body again, as I used to be. Before they shoved me away. Before I turned into something ghastly... into the form you know me as...'

'I'm sorry, but that's not clearer...' said Jenny, shaking her head. She stared at this little apparition, in her scarlet frock with a slit rather high on one leg.

'I'm the very first Empress,' sighed the lady. 'The one they deposed. The first one they got rid of. They put me away. Bottled me up like summer fruits and shoved me on a shelf, deep underground.'

'What?' Jenny was startled.

'Don't interrupt, dear,' snapped Euphemia. Her outlines were shimmering as she warmed to her theme. She was surrounded by a kind of glamour. 'This is what they do to their Empresses on that world. It seems such a civilised land in so many ways. So advanced. Such an ancient civilisation. But underneath all that sophistication and grandness there lurks some barbaric practises... And I was a victim of them. So long ago...'

'Where is this?' Jenny asked. 'Where are we talking about?'

'Hyspero, dearest,' said the little woman. 'The world of Hyspero, at the very edge of the known universe. The ancient, perplexing, curious world of Hyspero.'

'And you were... Empress there?'

The pounding dance music had faded into a distant succession of hollow beats, Jenny noticed. There was a bubble of quiet surrounding the two women now, as if they had slipped into some other space. Euphemia's voice filled Jenny's mind, mellifluous and tinged with regret.

'I was Empress for a hundred years. The first they ever had. And they betrayed me. They sealed me up in a jar. They stopped me up in a glass jar filled with nutrients and all this horrible gunk, to keep me alive in endless torture. All this beautiful flesh of mine rotted and bloated and fell away... And it was only my fierce will to survive that kept me going.'

'That's horrible...'

'And I'm alive all this time later. For generations I've watched Empresses come and go. They've had the same nasty trick played on them, each of them, when they've ruled for long enough. Some go willingly to join their ancestors – the fools. Others are dragged screaming into the catacombs beneath the Scarlet Palace. Miles and miles those tunnels unwind. And on shelves millennia deep there are jars and jars and jars. Each containing a tiny Empress, still alive, preserved in those horrible juices.'

Jenny stared at her. 'But... you've got out. Somehow.'

The Empress nodded. 'I escaped, yes. Or rather, I was stolen.'

'Who by?'

'That, I don't know. Not yet. They took me away from Hyspero, though. And they thought I'd never return. That was the idea, you see. But I have to get back. If I don't... the most horrible thing will happen. They don't understand. They've all forgotten. Even the present Empress doesn't understand...'

Jenny watched Euphemia's face twist in anguish. Impulsively the MIAOW operative said, 'Let me help you.'

'You trust me?'

'Yes.'

'You're with Marvelle,' Euphemia said.

'I'm sticking with him for the sake of the Objet D'Oom,' said Jenny. 'I'm not letting it out of my sight.'

'I do love that name they gave my little jar,' chuckled the Empress. 'It's rather like being a genie in a bottle. As if my appearance portends some dreadful cosmic calamity.'

'And does it?' Noise was returning to the lesbian bar, now. The music was getting louder. A rowdy crowd had entered from the snowy street.

'Oh yes,' said Euphemia, suddenly serious. 'I think something awfully calamitous will happen. And it already *is* happening, so long as I am away from Hyspero. Whoever ran off with me never knew what they were doing. It seems no one understands the truth about Hyspero and its long line of Empresses...'

Suddenly Jenny was awake.

The phone in her hotel room was bleeping insistently.

'It's your early morning call, murmur murmur,' said Marvelle from the room next door. 'We've got to get going. There's someone else we've got to pick up before we go any deeper murmur murmur.'

Jenny rubbed her eyes and tried to sort out her thoughts. 'What time is it?'

'Come on. Get ready. Have you got the jar there? I left it in your safe-keeping murmur.'

Her eyes moved to the bedside cabinet, where the jar still stood. It looked rather innocuous, if vivid. Images and phrases came jolting back into her head, leaking out of her dreams. She stared into the red murky depths of the glass. Was there really a tiny body in there? An ancient and wizened Empress?

'Why did you leave the jar with me? You know MIAOW was trying to get it out of your grasp.'

'Were you?' Marvelle said. She could picture the smug smile on his handsome face. 'Well, now I know I can trust you, don't I,

Jenny dear? We're on the same side, aren't we murmur murmur? Now, do hurry. We'll have breakfast on the observation deck, I think and we'll take a little look at space and everything, murmur murmur. You'd like that, wouldn't you? And Missy is very fond of a vista. And then we must get on murmur. We've a great distance to cross, you know...'

'We're going to Hyspero, aren't we?' Jenny said, impulsively. It was out before she knew it.

There was a tiny pause. She wanted to hear his amazement. She wanted to surprise him by knowing the truth. But Marvelle put the phone down and all she got was a series of distinct clicks on the line.

*

Simon volunteered to return with Iris back through the forest to fetch the bus. Panda was content to remain with Barbra at the inn for the morning. He still felt dreadful from his so-called night's rest and he could spend the time studying the maps that the helpful barman and innkeeper had provided. With a bit of luck, he might be able to plot out the journey they were to take to the City of Glass.

'I'm not at all keen on us splitting up like this, though,' Iris moaned to Simon as they set off, waving to their companions. 'Nothing good ever comes of splitting up.'

'It's too much for Barbra,' he said. 'She didn't say anything. But I could tell she was dreading hauling herself through the woods again.'

Iris grunted. Now they were going at a brisk pace through the cultivated fields beyond the town. 'I wonder if it was a mistake, agreeing to let her come along with us,' she mused.

Simon didn't like to answer that. He knew that Barbra – nervous as she was – was having the time of her life. But it was

Iris's bus and it was down to her who came along on these rides. 'She'll be okay,' he said.

Iris nodded. Then she was thinking about getting to her bus and having a change of outfit and making herself feel a little bit glamorous again. She couldn't wait to be back aboard the good old Number 22. When she was away too long she started to feel unsure and peculiar. It was as if the presence of her interstellar vehicle somehow did more than reassure her. It replenished her and topped up her vital energies, as if there was some strange mystical link between mistress and omnibus…

They struggled through the crisp, frosty woods in relative quiet for much of the morning. Iris led the way, unwavering in her sense of direction.

Now that they were alone, Simon was bursting with questions for her. There were all sorts of things about her life and history he suddenly wanted to ask. But he held his tongue, mostly. There was something determined and almost cross about her demeanour today. He knew if he went on too much to her he'd get short shrift. At one point, however, they stopped for a breather and to chew on the bizarre sandwiches the innkeeper had provided them with, and as they sat on a fallen log Iris became more talkative.

'I've been a bit morose today, lovey. Sorry about that.'

'It's all right,' he said. 'It looks like you've got things on your mind.'

'I have indeed!' she chuckled, producing her hipflask and swigging back a mouthful of gin. 'Usually I'm a lot more carefree than this, you know. But… there's just something… ominous going on here. You know, like background noise? You know that feeling when all the hairs stand up on the back of your neck? And you know you're caught up in something… something really bad?'

Simon felt suddenly alarmed. 'And that's what you think, then? That something really bad is going on?'

She nodded quickly. 'It's down to that Marvelle. I just know it. I didn't like to believe it at first. I thought he was just some silly vain fop, messing around with cosmic things he didn't even understand. But then... when I saw that he'd whipped off with the Pinking Shears... Well. That was a very bad moment for me, Simon. He shouldn't have known about them. He shouldn't have been able to get his lily-white hands on them. They're too important to fall into the grasp of a fella like him...'

'Why do you think he wants them?'

She looked very gloomy. 'There could be any number of reasons. They're a very powerful tool. I'm hoping he doesn't know the half of it. But... putting their loss together with the theft of the Objet D'Oom... that places some very strange suspicions in my head. As I've said before, I've a nasty feeling I know what's inside that glass jar...'

He waited for her to explain further. She had clammed up, though. Her expression was bleak. 'Ah, well. There's no use speculating and making ourselves feel bad. It might all just be a silly mistake.'

He knew she was fobbing him off. But he didn't push her any further as they pressed on and advanced into the woods. They were careful to keep as quiet as possible, fearful of another attack from the indigenous beasts. This time they didn't have the surprisingly agile vending machine to save them.

At last they came unharmed to the clearing where the bus was parked.

Simon could see at once that something was very wrong.

'Oh no...' Iris moaned, setting off at a stumbling run towards her beloved vehicle.

In the gloom of the silvery glade all the bus's welcoming lights were on. A gentle, golden radiance surrounded it. But Simon saw that the hydraulic doors had been wrenched open. One of the windows had been smashed. The jagged broken glass looked shocking.

Iris was crying out, 'Who could do this? How could they..?' She sounded indignant and scared at the same time. She examined the locks and the doors carefully and rapidly, seeing at once that they had been cut through expertly. 'One swish of the Pinking Shears,' she gasped. 'That's how he got aboard.'

Simon gasped. 'Anthony Marvelle did this? He tried to steal your bus?'

She cried out in rage. 'Be careful. He might still be around. Him and that vicious dog of his.'

But they found the bus empty. Simon sighed with relief as Iris thudded back down the spiral stairs and declared the bus abandoned.

'We're lucky he didn't nick it,' Simon said.

'He doesn't need it,' Iris spat. 'Not with the shears in his possession. He's proved himself a dab hand at using them, hasn't he?' Then her eyes widened as she peered past Simon at the broken window. 'He's yanked out the window blind, look!'

One whole piece of the Atlas of All Time had been torn roughly away from the window and taken away.

'That's very bad news,' Iris said. 'How did he even know they're not just ordinary blinds? And why did he take this particular piece..?'

Simon made her a fresh drink, commiserating with her. 'It must feel awful. My grandparents were broken into once. Their bungalow. While we were all away on holiday. It felt really nasty, getting back and finding everything turned upside down...'

Iris was ashen-faced, slumped on the violet chaise longue. 'He's taken other stuff as well. Upstairs on the top deck. My diaries. All the shelves have been cleared. He's taken every single volume of my flamin' journals.'

Simon felt his heart leap at this bit of news. It thudded loudly in his ears, throbbing guiltily as he thought about his own theft from her bookcase...

'Those diaries really shouldn't fall into the wrong hands,' Iris said. 'Without my diaries... I feel like my past has been robbed. I feel like only half a woman, somehow...'

'We'll get them back,' Simon said. 'All of your stuff.'

'He shouldn't have been able to get aboard...' Iris moaned. 'See? He's worse and more dangerous than we even thought... And I was right. About where he's going. I was right about where all of this is leading. That fragment of the Atlas he took... it's the Penumbra of the Galaxy's Ultimate Portion, as the folk who live there call it. So! That's where he wants to be.'

'And where's that..?'

'Hyspero,' Iris said thickly. 'The world on the Brink. That's where he's leading us. And I've got the nastiest suspicion why...'

CHAPTER NINETEEN

Magda asked, 'Where is she, Marvelle? Where have you taken Jenny?'

He smiled winningly and issued smoothly into the farmhouse kitchen. As he pulled up a chair he glanced round appreciatively at the room. 'What a lovely, remote place you have here, Magda. Isn't it rather worrying, though? To be so far from town? In the middle of nowhere?'

She scowled at him through her thick eye make-up. 'I like the peace and quiet.'

'It could be dangerous, though,' smiled Marvelle. 'If you were to be broken into and, say, bludgeoned to death murmur murmur? Wouldn't that be a pity? And no one would hear what was going on, murmur murmur.'

Missy the poodle was sitting at his feet, resting her pointed chin on the table top and growling under her breath at both Magda and Kelly.

'Are you threatening me, Marvelle?' Magda snapped.

'Oh no, not me, murmur,' he simpered. 'But I must say, it surely isn't very wise for a MIAOW operative to live out in the open like this, far from help. Especially when she has – shall we say – limited mobility. You ladies have enemies everywhere, don't you? All across Space and Time murmur murmur.'

Magda shrugged. 'No one knows I'm here.'

'I do,' said Marvelle. There was a touch of ice in his voice. 'And if I know, then all sorts of people could get to know, couldn't they?' He turned his attention to Kelly. 'So! You've thrown in your lot with MIAOW then?' A theatrical look of dismay crossed his face. 'And I thought we were friends, Kelly? I thought you could see my side of this whole affair murmur murmur.'

She was extremely wary of him, and his dog. 'I don't know anything about sides,' she said. 'Not any more. You wrote me that letter, claiming all sorts of stuff about Iris…'

'Yes, and I offered to come back to see you, murmur murmur,' he said. 'I'm sorry if I'm a little later than planned. Which month are we in now?'

'November.'

'Ah, really? Well, I've had a lot on, murmur murmur. Preparations to make. Plans to put together. Supremely powerful cosmic contraband to look after…'

Magda broke in. 'You've got the Objet D'Oom! But you need to give it to MIAOW. You don't know what you're messing with.'

He laughed. 'I know a good deal more than you, Magda. What are you? Just some stooge. Just one of the silly women in the secret base. You haven't got a clue about what's really at stake murmur murmur.'

'Haven't I?'

'Nuh-uh,' he grinned. 'And I know that for a fact because old Jenny knows nothing, too. And I've quizzed her quite thoroughly. She's as in the dark as all of you here. No one but I know what that jar contains murmur murmur.'

'Iris knows,' Kelly said impulsively. 'I'm sure that Iris knows what's in there, too.'

'She'll be no problem,' said Marevlle. 'She'll be out of all our hair pretty soon murmur.'

Kelly gasped. 'Why? What are you planning? You… won't hurt her, will you? And Simon..?'

Marvelle was helping himself to a glass of the Merlot Kelly had brought for her hostess. He slopped some on the colourful tablecloth and immediately started sketching out planets and stars and loops connecting them, lazily and contentedly. 'Wildthyme will get what she deserves. Simon, I will try my best to rescue him. He's an innocent caught up in these machinations. I can save him, Kelly. I can bring him home murmur murmur.'

'Good,' she said, and was aware of Magda's eyes, fierce on her.

'Kelly, you mustn't believe in this awful man. You don't know half the things he's done…'

'If he can bring Simon back, and keep him from getting hurt, that's enough for me.'

'But he's got another agenda, Kelly. He doesn't really care about Simon. He'll do away with Iris if he can…'

Kelly looked at Magda, wrenching her glance away from Marvelle, who was grinning throughout this exchange. 'Magda, you don't trust Iris either. You said that she and MIAOW never quite saw eye to eye. Even Jenny doesn't think much of Iris these days.'

Marvelle was on his feet in one smooth motion. 'Will you come with me, Kelly? We've got rather a lot to do. There's quite a distance to cover tonight murmur murmur.'

Kelly was on her feet before she knew it, drawn by his seductive murmur… and something in his eyes… a compelling light she couldn't stop seeking out from across the room.

'He's hypnotising you, Kelly…' Magda warned.

'Rubbish,' snapped Marvelle. 'Murmur murmur.'

But Kelly followed him across the room, almost against her will. She felt the poodle moving alongside her, brushing its body against her, chivvying her to the door. 'We have to go after Simon,' Kelly felt herself iterating. 'We must save him from Wildthyme.'

'He's on another planet, murmur murmur,' said Marvelle. 'He's so far away now, and he hasn't got a clue where he is. I think he's scared, Kelly. He's been led away by that terrible woman murmur murmur…'

'Yes,' said Kelly. 'She *is* terrible. I saw… I saw the life she leads. It frightened me… It was so random… So confusing…'

Marvelle unlatched the kitchen door and let Kelly stumble out into the darkness without a backward glance. With Missy trotting at her heels, Kelly wasn't even aware that she hadn't said goodbye to Magda.

Magda was aghast. 'That's how you led Kelly away. You mesmerize them, these girls and take them away to god knows where.'

He cackled. 'Don't worry, old woman. I won't be taking you anywhere murmur murmur.'

Her eyes blazed at him. 'I knew you were up to something wicked. But you will be stopped, Marvelle. Gloat while you can.'

His bland smile seized up in a rictus of fury. He launched himself at Magda and before she could even cry out he had kicked her wheelchair over. She gave a great screech and disappeared under its spinning wheels in the corner of the kitchen. Marvelle stood there watching her sobbing and panting, trapped under the heavy chair.

'Don't mess with me, murmur murmur,' he warned, and then whirled out of the farmhouse, slamming the door behind him.

Kelly and Missy were waiting out there. The girl tried to blink away her confusion. 'Did I hear someone shouting?'

'No one, sweetheart,' he murmured, kissing the top of her auburn head. 'No one you need worry about murmur murmur.'

'Can we go now?' Missy growled. 'That wind is freezing.'

The clouds were moving faster across the wide skies south of Darlington. They curdled around the moon, yellow like cream on the turn. Marvelle took a long, appreciative sniff of the evening air, and then set off, leading his tamed ladies towards the rip in the Very Fabric he had cut with his shears less than an hour before. 'Back to the Hotel Miramar, I think, high above the Golden Cascade,' he told them. 'I believe we're meeting the delectable Jenny for breakfast murmur murmur.'

*

It seemed as if they waited all day long in that grimy inn for Iris and Simon to return.

Panda wasn't the most patient being at the best of times. As he explained to Barbra, 'I like to be up and at 'em. I like to know what I'm doing and getting on with it. Otherwise, if there's nothing to do, I like to relax utterly. I can't stand all this sitting about on tenterhooks.'

'Hmm,' mused Barbra. They were in the bar, tucked away in a corner, keeping a cautious distance from the other clientele passing through that afternoon. 'Well, as a vending machine – a mere Servo-furnishing, my whole life is based on hanging around, waiting to be of use. I'm quite used to the tenterhooks, as you put it.'

'How awful for you,' Panda sighed.

'Still, it does seem like a good long while that our friends have been gone, into those woods. I do hope they've had no trouble with any of the creatures out there…'

'Iris will be all right,' said Panda, looking more worried than Barbra had so far seen him.

As the afternoon wore on and the light outside started to fade Panda pored over some maps of Valcea the innkeeper brought him. 'They're very old,' the barkeeper said gruffly, unrolling the crackling charts and filling the air with golden dust. Panda sneezed repeatedly and swore.

'You're not joking!'

'It's a long time since anyone here went on any kind of journey of their own,' the man sighed. 'We like to keep to our own parts of the forest, these days. There was too much upheaval, in the old days. Now, when anyone goes to the city of Valcea it is not of their own accord. They are taken there. To the New Gods…'

'Yes, yes,' said Panda brusquely. 'Well, if you wouldn't mind letting me concentrate on these rather complicated-looking things, thank you very much…'

Barbra was ashamed of Panda's rudeness. She let the innkeeper lead her off into the dark, low-ceilinged kitchen in order to have a private word. She had thought of a way she could be of tremendous use to her fellow travellers on the next phase of their journey, and was pretty excited about the idea. 'I want you to put a supply of food and drink into my interior,' Barbra said.

The innkeeper drew back – in seeming superstitious dread – as she unlocked her front cabinet door and it swung open. 'You… are you one of the New Gods?' the man cried, falling back against a work bench.

'Hardly!' laughed Barbra. 'I'm just an outmoded refrigerated unit! Whatever gave you the idea I was like your gods?'

'Y-you share something in common with them…'

'Really?' But Barbra wasn't very interested in the local theology. She was more interested in surprising her friends with the things she managed to coax the innkeeper to place inside her. There was a haunch of some kind of roasted meat, a flagon of chilled rough wine, a wheel of yellow cheese and some oddly-shaped fruits. 'Wonderful!' Barbra clapped her extendable hands. 'Now, is that enough, do you think, for our journey to the city of Valcea?'

He shrugged. 'Should be. But... are you really going there? Into those haunted ruins? It is madness, Barbra. You might find anything there... It is the place we all fear most of all...'

Barbra refused to allow herself to feel frightened. 'Iris is our leader,' she said. 'For whatever reason, she says that we have to go to the ruins of this city, and so we will.'

'And face the wrath of the New Gods..?' whispered the innkeeper. 'They show no mercy. Terrible things are said about what they do to the sacrifices that are taken to the city. They say they draw out their living energies and feast on them... leaving our young people just living, deathly husks...'

'We'll simply have to watch out for ourselves then, won't we?' Barbra said cheerily. She started to offload the cans of pop and packets of crisps that the innkeeper was accepting in exchange for his supplies of food and drink. Just as she was about to seal her glass front up again, the man seemed to think of something else, and dashed off. 'Wait!' he said.

Barbra wished he wouldn't bother. She was embarrassed by his sudden solicitude, as he returned with a carton of some very strange-smelling eggs. 'These are a great delicacy here in Valcea,' he said softly, as if his breath could shatter the eggs. 'You must be very careful with them. We consume them on quite rare occasions. Valceans believe these eggs bring us good fortune.'

Barbra sighed to herself as she accepted the eggs and stowed them away. She didn't like to hurt the innkeeper's feelings, but a sense of foreboding overtook her just then.

The innkeeper beamed at her broadly.

Barbra should have trusted her instincts at that point. It was only much later, when one of the eggs started ticking quietly to itself, deep within her innards, that she realised what her feeling of dread had portended.

But that was all later. Right now they were interrupted by a small hullabaloo, which had started up in the bar. Panda was up on the bar itself, crashing a metal tankard repeatedly against the solid wood and crying out excitedly.

'Panda, whatever is the matter?' Barbra shuffled out of the kitchen as quickly as she could.

'They're here!' he cried jubilantly. 'They've made it back!'

'Iris and Simon?'

'And the bus! They've just pulled up outside in the bus!'

Other patrons of *The Winged Man* were peering out of the inn's windows now, craning to see the source of all the groaning engine noise. They looked fearfully at first, thinking it was another carriage, come to take further sacrificial victims to the city. But it was something more friendly and more bizarre. It was the Number 22 to Putney Common in all its crimson glory.

'Iris!' cried Panda, dashing outside, still clutching the ancient charts and running into her arms as she came hurrying out of her bus.

'What's the matter with you?' she laughed. 'Did you think we'd come a cropper?' She laughed and hugged her friend to her. Simon emerged blinking in the evening light behind her and he looked worried, Barbra thought. It was then that she noticed the smashed window at the back of the bus.

'Oh, we've had a bit of an adventure,' Iris sighed. 'We tried to make a short hop through the Maelstrom to get here. To save us driving through the woods, you know. But there's something wrong with the bus. Nothing bad. Nothing serious!'

Panda looked alarmed.

'I'll get it fixed,' Iris told him. 'But it's set us back a bit. The old lady's outer defences are a bit messed up. It means we'll have to travel in the normal way, using wheels, for a while.'

She was being too cheery. Barbra realised why. It was because, as long as the bus was crippled like this, there would be no leaving this world of Valcea. They were stuck here for the duration. Barbra felt a terrible pang somewhere deep inside her coolling unit. No wonder Simon looked worried.

Panda took the news in his tiny stride, however. 'Oh, you'll sort that out in a jiffy, won't you?' he laughed. 'Come and have a drink, Iris! Before we set off into the wide blue yonder, eh? Let's have a little snifter. A bit of splashy splashy, what? And I can show you these marvellous maps and charts of where we have to go! Just as well I've been studying them, eh?' He led them all back into *The Winged Man* as if he owned the place. 'I know all about the lay of the land! And now it's just as well, eh?'

CHAPTER TWENTY

MAGDA'S STORY

I wasn't always in a wheelchair. I wasn't always down here in the depths beneath Darlington, either. These are just the circumstances in which I find myself during my twilight years.

Oh, I call them the twilight years of my life – though really I've no idea how long I will live. Cut off from my kind, I'm ignorant about my life expectancy. None of us – none of the ladies of MIAOW have any inkling of how old I might get to be.

I don't really need this wheelchair all the time. Only on dry land, though I guess that's where I spend most of my time these days. I've seen some people glance at my knees under this tartan rug when it's slipped a bit and I've had to give it a yank. I've had to cover up my beautifully scaled lap and my thick, curling tale. I don't like people looking too hard.

Whhssshht – it's out of sight again before anyone can look twice. It doesn't pay to advertise and you don't want everyone knowing your business. Not when the society you're working for prefers to be secret and you're essentially amphibious, as I am.

Whatever happens, and whatever they're really like as an organisation, I will always be grateful to MIAOW. To the girls here in the team under Darlington, and to our mysterious superiors down south. They took me in and looked after me and made sure I had a place in the world; a job of work to do; a roof over my head and even a bijou heated pool in the basement.

That's what MIAOW does, you see. All of its agents and operatives are freaks of nature, of one kind or another. Broadly speaking. We find them and give them succour and sanctuary, and some of them come to work for us – for a while at least. Who best to help out with the supernatural, the monstrous and the dispossessed than more of the same? It's a lovely job. I feel like I'm really helping out when I'm in the control room and manning the switchboard in our hidden base. It's only intermittently dangerous, the work we do.

As it is now, for instance.

With our beloved Jenny gone – off in the clutches of that smarmy Anthony Marvelle – the day-to-day running of MIAOW Darlington has dropped into my lissom lap. It's a role I never anticipated taking on. I am awful at admin, it turns out, and I can't keep a clear head in a crisis. I feel somewhat adrift and at a loss. Alone at the helm – and other nautical metaphors. I even feel tempted to simply walk away. Or rather, roll away in my motorized chair, with all due haste. I could switch off all the computers, unplug them, turn off the lights and leave the base, sealing it up behind me. And never mention the secret MIAOW again.

But I know I couldn't do it. There was a reason – a vital reason – that Jenny went off into the embrace of our nemesis. That jar he took away – the Objet D'Oom we were all scrabbling around for – it will unleash unholy havoc. We all know it. Iris knows it. I could see it in her eyes – even under all that silver mascara and her mint green eyeshadow – I could see that the old dame knew the power stoppered up in that jar.

Unlike many in MIAOW I actually trust the occasional operative known as Wildthyme. It was she who brought me into the fold, as it were. So long ago now, it seems. Back in the Eighties. She found me living rough in a damp little cave on the shore in the shadow of a nasty old nuclear power plant. I blame the pollutants in the water supply but I was well nigh feral in those days. Also, I was forced to subsist on a lousy diet. The result was that I had gone a bit loopy. I am afraid I took to singing my siren song at full belt in and around that nuclear power plant. I lullabyed key members of staff. I seduced the main man and ultimately got him to trigger a dreadful disaster that almost resulted in the whole place going up in a puff of blue smoke and tinselly fall-out.

Luckily Iris was called in by her old pals in MIAOW. She soon got to the bottom of it all. She prevented the station's meltdown, the top man's breakdown and went on to unmask moi as the irresistibly erotic magnetic force behind it all. In short, she made me see sense and brought me into MIAOW and its protective arms. So I'll always be grateful to the old ratbag, I really will.

Iris has a good heart. Not everyone can see that. Jenny can't see that. Not anymore. She won't trust Iris because, as she says, 'Wildthyme knows more about the workings of the cosmos than she'll ever let on. She's deliberately obfuscating things and playing innocent when really she understands big, important things. Things we have a right to know. When I travelled with her she let some of her secrets slip... and she's not from our universe at all, Magda. That much was plain. She's from elsewhere. At times it's like she's spying on us... or is amused by the littleness of us all...' Jenny shuddered and stopped talking for a bit. She'd spooked herself. We were sitting in some grotty bar, both a bit pie-eyed, if truth be told.

She went on to explain to me that Iris only ever pretended to be a daft old bag and that her exterior actually covered up something... rather terrible. Something that she really didn't want people to know about.

'Have you ever heard her talk about the Obverse?' Jenny asked me earnestly.

I had to admit that I had never heard of any such thing. But then Iris had never confided in me at all during her sporadic visits to Darlington. Nor had I ever been close enough to her to pick up an unguarded word… or a cryptic slip of the tongue.

'What's the Obverse?' I asked, feeling a bit warm in that busy bar with the blanket pulled over my lap. How I longed to fling it off and to flex my gorgeous tail where everyone might see it and hang it all. I imagine how my scales would shimmer under the mirror ball… and all those Darlington fellas would ooh and ahh!

Jenny didn't know what the Obverse was. It was just something Iris had drunkenly alluded to on a couple of occasions. She had muttered darkly. Jenny thought it referred to a place…

'All the answers are – I think – in her journals,' Jenny told me. 'Upstairs on her bus. We must try to get hold of them if ever we can. Next time she returns to Earth, perhaps. Imagine, Magda… all of the secrets of Iris Wildthyme…'

But in the event none of us had ever succeeded in getting upstairs aboard that bus. What would I do, anyway? Slither up there, up that spiral staircase? I had never even been invited aboard the old Number 22, though sometimes I longed to be asked. For all her devil-may-care bluster, Iris is shrewd and ultra-careful.

And anyway – she's far from here right now, it seems. There is no point in hankering after her fabulous secrets or her diaries or adventures by her side. We can't even be sure we'll ever see her again. Or Barbra. Or Jenny.

And now – even Kelly has gone. Whisked away by Marvelle.

Soon there'll be no one left in Darlington. Everyone will be in Space and Time. That's how it's starting to seem.

CHAPTER TWENTY ONE

'Can't we get any more heat in here?' Panda complained. He was shivering on the chaise longue as the bus thundered through the Valcean countryside and the broken window panes rattled.

'I'm trying, lovey!' Iris shouted back from the cab. 'We've been through the wars, though, and we don't have time to effect the necessary repairs.'

Panda scowled and pulled the heavy rug more tightly around his shoulders. For all of his complaints however, Simon could tell that he was relieved and happy to be back aboard the bus again. 'I didn't like that inn or that innkeeper very much,' he muttered darkly. 'It seemed a very nasty little town to me.'

'Oh, I thought it was quite charming,' Barbra burbled. 'Quite rustic, in its way.'

'You don't get out much, dear, do you?' said Panda. 'What about the way they happily gave their young people away to be sacrificed, eh? That was awful!'

Barbra shrugged. 'You forget, Panda. I am a machine. I may look and sound more lifelike than most machines, but in the end I am quite logical and expedient in my thinking. Obviously the people in that town were doing what needed to be done, in order to survive.'

'How heartless!' Panda cried, boggling at her.

'Well, that's what I'm saying,' Barbra said. 'I have different emotional responses to things. I'm a vending machine. You're a Panda. We're both going to feel differently about some issues.'

Iris was earwigging from the driving seat. 'And it all contributes to life's rich tapestry!' she called out.

Simon was listening to them, content not to say much. He was fretting once more about the diary of Iris's he had stolen from upstairs. It was still stowed away in his pocket. He would find the right time, he thought. There would be a perfect moment, he was sure, for telling her he had managed to rescue one single volume from her past...

The landscape spooled past them in a blur of icy silver. They had hit a stretch of mostly featureless plains. Blond mountains stood jaggedly on the horizon in every direction and something of the bleakness of the place was starting to affect their mood. Iris cranked up the heating and put her favourite mix tape on the stereo. Panda called out various complicated directions from the chaise longue.

It had been a long time since the bus had undergone such a rigorous road-testing. In recent months Iris had taken it on short hops back and forth through the Maelstrom and they had travelled hardly anywhere by wheels, in real time. She was hoping fervently that the old vehicle would be up to it.

There was a very good reason for travelling in real time. Everyone aboard knew it. With the windows smashed they were asking for trouble by slipping into the Maelstrom. Simon recalled those Time Zombies swishing about in the dark ether very clearly indeed. The very thought of them being able to steal aboard the bus through exposed nooks and crannies gave him the horrors.

No, before they could ever leave Valcea they had to get these repairs done. Simple as.

And where better to get the windows fixed than in some fabled City of Glass?

Panda sloped off to make a cheese soufflé for lunch.

'It didn't come out quite as planned,' he sighed, as they gathered around the breakfast bar.

'Ha! Never mind, lovey,' Iris grinned, tucking in. 'Doesn't matter, does it? I'm just glad that we're all here together. Back on the bus again, travelling off to some fantastic destination.'

'Have you given any thought to what we might find when we get there?' Simon asked. He hated that serious, pragmatic note in his voice. Why couldn't he return some of Iris's enthusiasm?

'The New Gods,' Barbra said, in a quavering voice. 'That's what people said, back in that town. That's who was demanding their children. Some kind of Gods!'

'I wonder who or what they are,' said Panda. 'When people claim to be gods and so on, it's usually aliens of a more advanced stripe mucking about, isn't it, Iris? Dreadful colonial types lording about the place and cracking the whip.'

'Oh yes,' she said, peering at a forkful of very strange-tasting soufflé. 'We've had to overturn some nasty regimes in our time, haven't we chuck?' She sighed happily. 'Sometimes there's nothing nicer than stirring up a bloody good revolution.'

Panda winced, as if her words brought back some uncomfortable memories.

The rest of that day proved to be pretty uneventful. The land turned more gentle and lush with pale grass. The mountains receded into the far distance, into a hazy miasma as the light started to fade from the day.

In the early evening Iris declared herself boss-eyed and tired from driving. 'And my legs are going all bandy from sitting up in the cab.' She cursed herself for choosing travelling companions who couldn't share the driving duties with her, and then cheerily stomped off to build a camp fire outside.

They sat in the roaring blaze for several hours, until the darkness encroached and tucked itself in all around them, narrowing their horizons to just a few yards. They sang songs and swapped fragments of improbable stories. The air swarmed with their words and laughter: it was as if there was hardly enough time for them to relate and explain to each other everything they wanted to. Suddenly, in the midst of all their chatter, Simon realised that he was enjoying himself. He was happier than he had been for months. In the freezing back of beyond, eating meat that had been charred on the camp fire. Meat that Barbra the vending machine had produced triumphantly from her refrigerated recesses. Simon was happy. Sitting here with no idea how or when or if he would ever get home. Happy with a garrulous old bag, a small, stuffed Panda and a somewhat insecure vending machine.

'I think we're safe enough sleeping under the stars, tonight,' Iris declared, emptying the last of the wine into Simon's glass. 'Don't you think? The fire will burn away till dawn and we can drag out some old blankets.'

'Excellent idea,' Panda slurred. 'According to the maps we're up in the mountains tomorrow. We'll be cooped up in the bus together for a while. We should take advantage of the open prairies while we can.'

There had been neither sight nor sound of dangerous life forms. If any arrived, the fire would hold them back, they were sure.

They heaped blankets and rugs and made themselves comfortable. Iris turned down the clockwork-powered stereo (which, to Simon's surprise was playing an episode of the John Peel show from Christmas 1987.)

Soon it was time to get settled down and to watch alien star patterns in a sky the deep purple of hoi-sin sauce.

'Tell me, Iris,' Simon called out sleepily across the camp fire, 'What's that constellation called? That one there, that looks like a rearing horse?'

'What?' she said, sleep-fuddled. 'What are you on about?'

'The names of the constellations,' Simon said. 'Where in space are we?'

'How should I know?' she snapped. 'I don't go in for all that astrology jazz.'

Then her snoring started up and Simon suspected her of faking it. Panda's snores were loud and genuine enough. Simon watched Barbra take up a defensive position a little further away from the fire, and her lights dimmed slightly in the night.

Everything went very quiet on the grassy plain, in the middle of nowhere.

Until several hours later, when Simon was woken by a strange creaking noise.

He lifted himself up on one elbow and looked at the others. No one else had been disturbed by the sound. But it was still there. The aggravating noise of unoiled hinges. It reminded him of wardrobe doors inching open in the night.

This was extremely perceptive of him, but in a way he would never have guessed. Not in a million years.

For this was the night that the Closets came out.

*

Simon woke before dawn.

The squealing noise sent his heart racing. He sat up and threw back the covers. He pulled on his jacket and laced up his trainers. His pulse thudded loudly, threatening to drown out that noise.

Had he imagined it?

But no, that squealing noise was still there. Wheeling above his head. Some kind of flying creature, perhaps. A predatory bird, or a bat, maybe. Or something worse. He had no way of knowing what kind of creatures lived here.

He stirred the embers of the fire back into life. The flames flickered into renewed life, but they looked a bit pathetic. We've got nothing to defend ourselves with, he thought.

Squuueaaaaakkk.

The others were still asleep. Barbra's lights had dimmed almost to nothing. The Number 22 was a bulky oblong on the horizon. Only a faint glow from its instrument panels in the front cab could be seen.

He wondered whether he should wake the others. Get them to board the bus. They were too vulnerable out here…

Squueeeeeaaaakk.

But was it all that safe aboard the bus anyway? With its dented sides and its broken windows. What good would cowering aboard do them if they came face to face with some horrible flying nocturnal beast?

Simon made himself a flaming torch from dried grasses and hurried down the hill. He wasn't quite sure what it was he was trying to achieve. Perhaps he wanted to get into an open space away from his friends, to draw the source of the noise out into the open… He wanted to see what it was… to assess the danger.

The noise reminded him of police helicopters, whirring and droning over city centres at night. Yes, that was exactly what it was like. But these beasts moved without the constant whir of engines and blades. There was just a swift shushing of something that sounded like wings and that awful squealing noise.

He glanced sharply to the left and then the right. Something at the corner of his eye. A squarish block of darkness, blotting out the purple skies and the unfamiliar stars. Then it was gone.

A winged beast of some kind. Coming close and then rearing up into the higher realms. Taunting him. Watching him from above.

'Come out!' he called. 'Come on out and show yourself!'

Sqquuueeaaaak.

The noise was drawing him on. Leading him further across the prairie.

The long, lush grass rippled in the stiff breeze. Dawn was on its way. He could feel the whole landscape tensing up in expectation.

'Simon! What is it?'

He whirled round to see that Panda had awoken and pursued him across the grass. The small bear could be quite nippy when he chose to.

'Some kind of creature. I've tried to draw it away.'

Panda looked alarmed. 'We should wake Barbra. She made mincemeat of that other thing, in the woods.'

SQUUEAAAAK

Suddenly the thing was right above them. Simon had to duck quickly to avoid getting his head smashed in. Then it was gone again.

'There's a strange smell,' mused Panda, in the sudden stillness. 'Camphor. Mothballs!'

'It's a giant moth?'

'Only if moths smell of mothballs,' tutted Panda. 'Which they don't.'

'Then what the hell is it?'

Luckily Panda had brought his goggles with him. He fumbled with the night vision setting. 'I've been looking forward to having a go with this,' he grinned, looking like a tiny fighter pilot, consulting the skies. 'Ah!'

'What is it?' Simon said, crouching by him.

'They're going away,' said Panda. 'They know that we're watching them. There's about seven of them... How curious!'

'What were they?' Simon asked.

Panda pulled down his goggles and his eyes were wide. 'They were... wardrobes..!'

CHAPTER TWENTY TWO

Back at the camp they wasted no time in waking Iris and coaxing Barbra back into life. Naturally neither lady had any problem imagining flying adversaries such as the ones Panda had glimpsed.

'I wonder why they were spying on us asleep,' Iris mused, stirring scrambled eggs in a pan over the camp fire. 'I hate the thought of anyone watching me sleeping.'

'I *thought* I was getting some strange remarks back in that town,' Barbra said. 'Obviously, on this world, living furniture is something they're quite used to.' Inwardly, her mind was spinning. The very idea of living wardrobes was very exciting to her. It was as if she had arrived somewhere and found herself in the midst of living ancestors. From what Panda had said, these creatures were made of wood and flew about flapping their open doors. Their hinges squeaked eerily. For some reason that picture gave Barbra a frisson of pleasure that she herself could hardly understand as yet.

Perhaps this is the world all my kind evolved from, she thought wildly. Perhaps I have discovered some long lost *spiritual homeworld…!* But she kept these rather exciting thoughts to herself for now.

'They gave me a very strange feeling,' said Panda. 'I'm not sure why.'

'Surely they can't be all that dangerous?' Simon said. 'What could they do to you?'

Iris gave him a solemn look. 'Never underestimate what an alien being can do to you. We don't know their capabilities as yet. Now – come along, everyone!' With that she made them all strike camp. It was time to be moving on.

Iris was quiet for the rest of that morning, guiding the bus into the foothills of the sandy mountains. She had to concentrate on her driving as the track grew rougher and the gradients steeper. The road started to zigzag quite perilously and Simon found that he had to stop himself looking out of the windows at the sheer drop first on one side, then the other.

Panda tried to reassure him, 'She is a marvellous driver, you know. Do you know how many years she's driven this bus?' Then he spoiled it by adding, 'And of course, *if* she drove over the edge into the chasm, we'd have little to worry about.'

'You mean the bus has defences that would save us?'

Panda frowned. 'No, I mean we'd all be dead well before we hit the bottom. Look how high up we are now!'

Simon felt himself turning green. He made a pot of tea and took a cup to Iris, trying not to disturb her concentration too much as she grappled with the wheel. He, in turn, tried not to look out of the front windscreen at the scree-littered road.

He sat with Panda on the chaise longue. Panda was blowing on the tea in his own miniature cup.

'So how long has Iris been driving the bus, then?' Simon asked him. 'The way you said that, it sounded like you knew.'

'Oh, she was gallivanting about the galaxy well before I knew her,' he shrugged.

'But where did she get a bus like this, in the first place?' Simon persisted. 'She must have said. You're her best friend, Panda. She must have told you *something* over the years…'

'I never pry,' said Panda, quite primly.

'Do all the people where she comes from have buses that move through Space and Time?' Simon said. 'And if they did, what would be the point of that? They'd never be in the same place at the same time. Do none of them get on with each other?'

Panda merely gave him an inscrutable look.

'You're not going to tell me anything, are you?'

'I don't know a great deal,' said Panda. 'And Iris isn't one for looking backwards, you know. What you'll find, being aboard the Celestial Omnibus with us – is that it's all onwards and upwards with us. We're always moving forwards, and hardly ever looking back…'

*

PANDA'S STORY

When I say I don't know where I'm from, I'm not being simply obtuse. Though I'd never rule that out, of course. Being simply obtuse is to me one of the finest pleasures life has to offer. Alongside fine wines, marvellous theatre, beautiful women and doing lots of shouting when the need arises.

So – I don't know where I hail from. Iris – the old harridan – puts that down to my 'most unusual physical make-up, lovey'. And she says it in that very patronising way – all elongated vowels and pitying simper. I reply hotly – that there's *nothing* unusual about my make-up! Not where I come from! I bet that there, *everyone* is ten inches high with small black ears and piercingly intelligent button-bright eyes.

'Oh dear,' she sighed, during our most recent fracas over my genesis. 'That's just the point, Panda lovey. How do you even know that? Who's to say there's a whole planet of Pandas out there somewhere? I think you'd better prepare yourself to face the fact that… well, you might be… the only one.'

Really? I boggled at her. She really thought that in her infinite wisdom and kindness she was introducing me to a thought that had never before passed through this cultivated noggin of mine. I bellowed at her – something cutting about existential crises – and she started yelling back and soon we were having a bloody good barney. The type we really like – sitting up front in the cab of the bus as it thundered its merry way through the Maelstrom. It was the kind of row that the old fishwife and I relish best – the no-holds barred kind, when we even forget what we're arguing about. We're both secure in the knowledge that it doesn't really matter – no one will get hurt. We're just shouting for the sheer fun of it.

It's one of those things that keep us together, Ms Wildthyme and I.

On the subject of memory, I can't even tell you how long we've been travelling together. With all the flitting about we do – backwards, forwards and diagonally through the alternate paradigms – it's well nigh impossible to pin down anything at all. Some events we've done, done again, gone back to with gusto, then with ennui, erased from history, reinstated, improved upon – and then lived through once more for good measure.

I think I've relied over the years on the thought that Iris is scrupulous about keeping her journals up to date. Oh yes – a pretty explosive set of memoirs she had stowed up there, on the top deck. Even in the most hair-raising of circumstances I sometimes spy her scribbling away in some fat notebook she can pop away into her carpet bag. I've had a peek and they're full of wild exaggerations and embellishments, of course. And her prose is rather gung-ho at times. When she totes me about in her bag I get a little look at her innermost soul. Hot stuff indeed

– scandalous, libellous, seditious, and sometimes obscene. And she beefs up her own part in our shared adventures no end.

I suppose a stylist of my calibre ought to keep his own record of the marvellous times we have shared. I shouldn't deprive future historians of the chance to harken to this Panda's distinguished voice. I had a little manual typewriter once. I was rather fond of all that clattery noise. But my elegant paws were a mite too thick and I kept bunching up all the keys and jamming them.

And maybe it's best just to live in the moment, no? To let others do all the chronicling and fussing about what happened when and after what? Chronology, continuity – pah! I prefer to live and run about!

I *do* remember that once I lived in London, in the home of a man who had travelled with Iris in his youth. He was rather keen on remembering and writing down all the adventures he had shared with her. Well, when I helped him to edit the manuscripts he wrote, I used to think Tom made all that silly sci-fi stuff up, to be honest. I'd go along to his book launches and signings and I was amazed at the people who turned up. They were actually reading these nonsensical books he wrote! I – being a very pragmatic and down-to-Earth Panda in those days – used to laugh.

That was, until the day Iris herself turned up. She caused quite a fuss in the middle of one of Tom's bookshop readings. She swept back into his life – complaining that his surreal Roman-a-clefs were giving her publicity she really didn't want. Tom wasn't at all glad to see her. Rather like the surly Jenny in that regard – an ex fellow traveller who would rather stay at home in their own lives, thank you very much. Another one who wasn't tempted to clamber back aboard the bus.

For me, though – that first time I saw Iris Wildthyme – protesting about her erroneous fictionalisation – it was love at first sight.

Silly old cloth-eared bat. Horrible dress sense. Foul-mouthed old besom. Can't sing for toffee. Lies through her teeth. Burps in her sleep. I do love her, though. And she knows it.

CHAPTER TWENTY THREE

Iris was indefatigable, once she got going.

It was as if there was some symbiotic relationship between woman and machine. For over twenty four hours (two and a half days on Valcea, it turned out) she sat in the cab of the bus, with her hat clamped on her head, smoking her way through an entire package of cocktail cigarettes.

As the mountains grew loftier the passes became narrower and her silent concentration grew more intense. She even stopped playing her old mix tapes.

The bus veered and wobbled around corners, teetering madly at fathomless crevasses. Everyone aboard sat quite still during the roughest parts of the journey. They perched silently and listened to the cocktail cabinet jingling and the cracked glass in the windows rattling.

Simon tried hard to keep his nerve.

He even tried to sleep, but it was hopeless. Knowing that Iris was up front in the cab, eyes fixed firmly on the perilous road ahead. How could he sleep? He just wished he could drive a bus and help out.

'Go and ask her if she wants a cup of tea,' Panda whispered to him, in the middle of one dark night.

Simon nodded. As he made his way up the slanting gangway he was entertaining himself with the horrible image of Iris falling asleep at the wheel. Couldn't she just succumb to exhaustion, like anyone else? Why was she so stubborn? Why couldn't she simply rest?

'She won't be told,' said Panda, following on his heels, kicking aside debris dislodged by their bumpy ride. 'Surely you know that much about her already?'

Simon was just about to retort when he slipped sideways through a gap in the Very Fabric of Space and Time.

'Oh, bugger,' wailed Panda, seeing what had happened.

Simon had gone. Then his head reappeared. 'What? What was that? Where am I?'

Panda sighed dramatically. 'You see? That's what Iris meant, about the Blithe Pinking Shears falling into the hands of amateurs. Little creeps like Anthony Marvelle don't know how to restitch the holes that they leave in the warp and weft of the universe.'

Simon stepped back into the bus's gangway with some alacrity. 'I was in some kind of a public toilet!'

'Really?' said Panda, not greatly interested. 'Well, thanks to Marvelle, we've got a link across the galaxy to where he came from when he boarded Iris's bus behind her back.'

'So he's leaving holes all over Space and Time?' said Simon.

'He's leaving holes like Iris gets ladders in her tights,' said Panda.

'But doesn't this make it easier to find him?' Simon said urgently. 'Can't we just… follow him through the gaps?'

'That's a mug's game,' said Panda. 'It's like an endless series of tunnels from one random spot to another.'

But Simon thought they could at least try. He was intrigued by this gap in the fabric. It seemed to lead back to somewhere on Earth, if the signs in the gents' toilets were anything to go by. He cajoled Panda a little and, after they had taken the bleary-eyed Iris her tea, they slipped quietly through the gap.

'Where are you two going?' cried Barbra, waking up. 'Wait! Don't leave me!'

But they already had.

*

The toilets were nondescript, but the building in which they were housed gave Simon a sudden rush of excitement.

'Oh my god! The Hammersmith Odeon!'

The lobby was seething with teenage girls, and a smaller number of boys. They were in a frenzy of excited hormones and glitter. All of them were clutching tickets, banners, and fragments of outrageous fancy dress cobbled out of pvc, cardboard and stuck-on feathers. Everything was wilting in the heat.

Panda demanded to be lifted into Simon's arms. 'I don't want trampling underfoot.'

Simon was aghast with pleasure. 'We're here! It's July – 1973!'

Panda affected ignorance. 'So? It's a bit rough and noisy, if you ask me.'

'It's the final concert given by Vince Cosmos. Remember? We were talking about it when we visited your headquarters in South Ken.'

'Ah yes,' mused Panda. 'Where Marvelle robbed us blind. Hmm… so he's been here as well, for some reason.'

A loud voice on the tannoy cut through the piped music and instructed the hectic crowd to take their seats in the main auditorium.

'Help!' cried Panda, as they were drawn along in the adolescent crush. The vast darkness of the concert hall drew them in. 'We don't want to go in there, do we?'

Oh, but we do, thought Simon. This was better than toiling up the perilous sides of some ancient mountain. His mind boggled as they hurried into the gig and the lilac and crimson lights flashed about on the drapes that covered the stage. So Iris has a transdimensional rip on the lower deck of her bus that leads straight into the last concert that Vince Cosmos ever gave.

It was one of the locations in history that Simon most wanted to visit.

I'll be on the live LP screaming my guts out, after all, he thought happily, as the house lights dipped and they were drawn right to the front of the standing crowd.

Panda grumbled his way through the warm-up act, a duo called The Tomorrow Twins whom he found very superficial. He shouted loudly about the noise of screaming girls and the horrible smell of sweat and dry ice.

When Vince Cosmos himself appeared – in moon boots, cat suit and purple fedora – Panda quietened down a bit. He realised that his companion was behaving as if he was present at some kind of miraculous religious occasion. To Simon this was like using Iris's bus to visit the resurrection of Christ. Rather pleased with this comparison, Panda made a special note to mention it to Iris – and as a possible future destination, too. The Biblical event, that was, rather than the pop concert.

Actually, Iris would love it here as well. Panda seemed to remember that she had some Vince Cosmos tapes. She liked the retro futuristic sound of that trashy glam rock. She liked its witty blending with Twenties cabaret music and its hint of vaudeville.

They stamped and screamed and hollered for more. Even Panda. There were wafting clouds of illegal substances being smoked all around them and Panda felt his eyes growing glassier. Holding him tightly in his arms, Simon was gazing raptly up at Vince Cosmos – who was only a matter of yards away.

Panda was content to let the boy have his moments of fanboy adoration. Everyone embarking on this ramshackle life of time travel had to have at least *one* of those moments in the early days. For Panda it had been a trip to London Zoo in the Sixties, where he had visited the famous Chi-Chi, the lady Panda. Iris had been startled by some of the things her new friend had yelled at the elderly lady in the bear pit, but she figured it was something he simply had to do. Travel in time brought out these needs and urges in people, as they realised that they could go anywhere and meet anyone – within reason.

This was Simon's moment. After just a few days with Iris and Panda, Panda figured the boy could do with a treat.

Then, turning away from Simon's deliriously happy and sweaty face, Panda noticed the two Martian agents standing either side of them.

They had wormed their way to the front of the crowd, silver-eyed and behatted, but with those tell-tale vestigial tentacles masquerading as sideburns. In a flash Panda saw that they were carrying energy weapons, which they were aiming straight at the androgyne currently warbling a Jacques Brel number on the stage.

'HOLY FLAMING NORA!' Panda bellowed, dragging Simon to the ground as hard as he could. 'MARTIAN ASSASSINS! *WATCH OUT!!*'

CHAPTER TWENTY FOUR

Everything happened rather quickly after that.

Simon was startled by Panda's quick-thinking shove, as were a number of shrieking girls. The Martian Agents were on the alert in an instant as their cover was dramatically blown, and they set off their energy weapons, hissing and crackling uselessly into the audience. Sudden screams cut through the acoustic number Vince Cosmos was playing.

The effect on Vince was the most startling of all. He leapt off the stool where he had been strumming his twelve string guitar and now his skinny body was tensed and ready for action. He was brandishing his instrument like he was going to brain someone with it.

Later that hectic evening Panda would have to tell the tale again and again, about how he darted forward and bit one of the Martian assassins on the face.

'Martians are very superstitious indeed about Pandas, it turns out,' he explained each time he told the story. 'It's all to do with some ancient legend they've got from the dawn of their history, about a certain Panda deity who visited them in a scarlet chariot that came from the stars… And, so anyway, by startling our two would-be killers quite thoroughly, I managed to save Vince here from a grisly end.'

This was at the after show party at the Café de Paris, where Panda and a rather bemused Simon were guests of honour.

Vince's record company people and his personal staff clustered around the strange duo, plying them with drink and attention, and keeping an eye on them. They didn't want the newspaper people getting to the heroes of the hour.

'I wish we could have seen the end of the concert though,' said Simon sadly. He was rather perturbed about that. In his world Vince had announced his retirement from pop music at the end of that very Jacques Brel number. But now, with all the kerfuffle and sizzling laser bolts and Panda bellowing at Martians, things hadn't gone quite according to otherwise established pop history. Certainly, Simon's live LP and DVD of the show didn't go like that.

Suddenly he had a feeling that between them, he and Panda and the Martians had rather profoundly buggered up history.

The Martians had vanished. In all the confusion and the stampede that left Hammersmith Odeon like a warzone, with police, fire brigade and ambulance people swooping into action to succour terrified teenagers, the aliens had flown the coop.

'So why are the Martians so keen on seeing you dead, Mr Cosmos?' Panda asked, peering darkly over the rim of his Martini.

Vince was looking pale but glamorous in a sky blue satin suit, cut forties style. His personal staff – a rather mulish-looking girl and a furious dwarf – were sitting protectively at his side as he shrugged and looked helpless. 'I've really no idea, Panda,' he said in his characteristic South London drawl, 'Until tonight I had no idea there were such things as real Martians. I just sang songs about made-up space stuff…' Vince's staff glanced at each other wordlessly at this, and Panda knew immediately that they all knew more than they were saying.

'Hmm,' Panda said. 'Well, let me warn you. There are all sorts of bloody aliens and whatnots whizzing about our heads all the time. So, you have to watch out. It's 1973, right? Well, that's when it all gets a bit bally messy. Simon and myself here, we come from a different dimension, you know. And we came here on the bus.'

Simon frowned at Panda. The Martini was going straight to his head, it seemed.

'There really are aliens and other dimensions?' Vince was wide-eyed, sipping champagne.

'Millions of the buggers,' sighed Panda happily.

Simon left them to it for a while, mingling round the party on his own and snapping a few covert and priceless photos on his phone. He saw famous and familiar faces, young again and enjoying themselves in the opulent surroundings. All of them were gabbling excitedly about weird assassination attempt. Panda was the hero of the hour and Simon found himself basking a little in the reflected glory.

Then he found himself standing by some potted palms with the warm-up act from tonight's show – the teenage duo, The Tomorrow Twins – who seemed feverishly excited by the whole thing.

'We sing about aliens, too!' Tommy Tomorrow burst out.

'I know!' said Simon. They exchanged hasty introductions and Simon listened to the kids babbling happily about their first show to a live audience. Then he noticed a rather elegant woman in a slinky black dress propped up nearby against a plaster pillar. She was wearing a large hat that shaded half her face. She was holding a black, gold-tipped cigarette and was waiting for a light. Simon leaned forward to oblige her. Feeling that she must be someone very famous, he wanted to get a proper look at her. She was familiar somehow…

'You pair of skiving bastards!' she hissed in his ear.

Simon jumped.

'How dare you? Nipping off here to enjoy yourselves! And all the while there's me, labouring away up that bloody mountain!'

'What?!' He stared into her face. She was older. She was a good few years older and a bit more elegant in her dress than he was used to, but there was no mistaking the dulcet tones of Iris Wildthyme bellowing down his ears.

'What are you doing here?' he gasped. He'd dropped his drink on the stone tiles.

'I'm just here incidentally, lovey, on a different investigation. But I've caught you out, haven't I? You and that bloody show-off, Panda! Getting up to transdimensional shenanigans behind my flamin' back! I knew there was something you two were up to that night I drove the bus up that mountain on Valcea. Oh, but you were so cagey about it! So secretive! Well, now I know why, don't I?'

Simon stared at her. 'You're from our future time, erm, paradigm, then?'

'Oh yes,' she said, snatching his zippo lighter off him. 'A good long way afterwards. And let me tell you, you've got some exciting times ahead of you, my young fella me lad!'

Tommy Tomorrow touched Simon on the elbow. 'Is there something the matter, Simon?' He had a soft, lilting accent and when Simon turned to look at him it was straight into his huge, brown, puppy dog eyes. He suddenly remembered keeping a poster of Tommy Tomorrow in his sock drawer. A poster filched out of *Look-Out!* Magazine. 'Erm, no, it's nothing. Just an old friend.'

'Pah! Friend!' Iris squawked. 'You just watch out, Simon. You and Panda, the two of you. You've got to keep your eye on the ball, you know. You can't go mucking about in Space and Time like it's all a great big laugh, you know.'

Suddenly Iris looked deadly serious. He saw how much older she was in this later aspect of hers. Her voice was cracked and ragged. Her face looked ravaged.

'But… *you* were the one who said that it's all a game, really. It's all about having fun… at least, that's what you always imply…'

She grunted and slurped the last of her gin, crunching hard on an ice cube. 'Well, maybe I was wrong back then. Maybe the stakes were higher than I ever knew. Things are going to get scary for you. So just you think on, Simon lovey. And you tell Panda, too. Get back aboard the bus and try harder. You make sure you pull your weight and help your old Auntie Iris. Hmm?'

Then she was off, abruptly, slipping into the packed crowd of partiers at the Café de Paris.

'What was she on about?' Tommy's twin, Trisha asked. 'Was she out of it on something?'

'She's gone…' Simon said. 'Did you see which way she went?'

Tommy hadn't. 'Hey, look,' he said. 'There's a party on, at our manager's house in Maida Vale after this. He wants to get everyone round there. It's all about promoting me and Trish, really, and sucking up to Vince Cosmos's people. But it should be a good do, man. And you're more than welcome.'

Simon was getting the glad-eye from Tommy Tomorrow. If he'd had another drink he'd have dropped that one on the floor as well. But then he reminded himself of what the older, sadder Iris had just told him. He had to wise up. Get with the program. And stop larking about.

'I'm sorry,' he told Tommy. 'Maybe next time I come through this way, huh?' And then he kissed him, making Trisha gasp. Was that a faux-pas? Simon hardly knew.

Then he went off to fetch Panda, who was still bragging about saving Vince from the Martians. 'They're lucky I only bit them,'

Panda was declaring. 'If they'd hung around I would have done a bit of my ju-jitsu on them.'

Simon dragged Panda away from the crowd for a quiet word.

'What is it?' Panda snapped, looking vexed.

'I've just bumped into Iris, over by the potted palms.'

'Don't be ridiculous!' said Panda hotly. 'We left her aboard the bus, driving up that hill!'

'It was a *future* Iris!' Simon said. 'And she gave me a kind of warning. She said things are going to get scary for us. We've got to stop messing about.'

Panda swore bitterly. 'Typical! Just when you're having fun, you get some bloody apparition from the future telling you off. Come on. We'll get a cab back to Hammersmith right now.' He swore again. 'I was really enjoying myself! They all think I'm a hero!'

'I know, I know,' Simon sighed, following him out of the most glamorous party he'd ever been invited to. He stole a quick backward glance at Vince Cosmos before he left, all shiny-faced with glitter, and promised himself that one day he'd revisit 1973 if he could.

*

They slipped back through the rip in the Very Fabric and found themselves back aboard the bus. Under the heaving, groaning engine noise Barbra almost gave them away. 'Where have you two been? You've been away for an age!'

Panda shushed her. 'We had some very important business to attend to, didn't we, Simon? That gap there, hanging in mid-air is extremely dangerous.'

'But you didn't seal it up?'

'Er, no,' said Panda.

Simon wondered what would happen to that rip in the air. Presumably now that they had that link with 1973, time would march in tandem with time on the bus, with the Nineteen Seventies moving forwards at a rate of one second per second just as they themselves were ageing now… in whatever they called their own personal time stream.

'I've got some safety pins somewhere,' Panda said. 'Do you think that will hold it? Probably not.'

'I hate the thought that Anthony Marvelle is just swinging about all over the universe, opening up these holes,' said Simon. 'He could unleash all kinds of chaos.'

'He's going to do much worse than that,' said Panda. 'If what Iris suspects is true about that Objet D'Oom.'

'What does she suspect?'

'Best not say yet,' said Panda. 'She might just be doom and gloom mongering. But the old bat is usually right. Anyway, it's imperative that we catch up with Marvelle when he arrives in the Glass City. That's the best we can do for now.'

With that Panda hurried down the gangway to check on how Iris was doing.

Simon turned to see Barbra opening up her glass door. 'Crisps and pop, Simon?'

He nodded, though he wasn't at all hungry, after the wonderful canapés at the Vince Cosmos aftershow party. Once more he was trying not to hurt Barbra's feelings, but he couldn't help blurting out, 'Are your insides bleeping?'

'What?' she cried. 'I don't think so, are they?' They both listened hard. 'I think it's the signal for more coolant. That's what it is.' She hurriedly passed him his crisps and pop and closed her door, seeming rather flustered.

Then Iris was yelling from the front of the bus. 'We've made it! We've done it, fellas! It's plain sailing now! Hurray!'

Simon darted to the window and saw that the road had widened and levelled off. At last they were away from the perilous edges and onto some kind of plateau. He let out a breath that he hadn't even known he was holding.

In celebration Iris put on her music again. Cilla Black came crashing through the speakers as dawn broke over the distant mountaintops, golden and yolky.

'There's a little town here,' she yelled at them all. 'Perfect place to stop and get breakfast and have a bit of a rest!'

*

Iris parked the bus in a village square in the early morning when there were very few locals about. As they clambered onto the cracked and parched earth and helped Barbra, they caught a glimpse of a few early risers. They were tall, stringy beings with translucent hides. Their eyes were a shining gold, turning to stare at the newcomers with alarm.

'Oh dear,' said Iris, wrapping a pashmina tightly about her neck against the early morning chill. 'I hope we won't frighten them too much.'

Panda was examining the cracks in the ground. 'Watch where you're standing, everybody. Look, these cracks widen as we get closer to the dwellings. Some of them are several feet across. And they're very deep indeed.'

'Oh!' cried Barbra, not liking the sound of that at all.

'We won't stay here for long,' Iris said. 'Long enough to get our bearings. According to the crystal, we've got a day at most to get ourselves to the city to meet Marvelle. If we miss that opportunity, we've missed him completely and wasted our time, I'm afraid.'

They ambled across the open square towards the squat, roughly-built houses and none of them liked the way the earth crumbled underfoot. Gravel and dust became dislodged at every step, tumbling into the dark cracks. It made a very unsettling noise.

'It doesn't feel very safe,' said Barbra, clinging onto Simon.

'Perhaps we'd better go back to the bus,' said Simon.

'I wanted to see what it was like, though,' said Iris. 'I'm an explorer, remember?'

'Well, we've seen,' snapped Panda. 'And it's horrible. I feel like I'm going to fall down one of these bloody holes any second.'

And then, all of sudden, they saw that they were surrounded.

The townspeople had assembled silently around them in a circle.

'They must be very light on their feet,' Iris frowned.

'They must be, to live here,' Simon said.

Each of the glass people wore flowing robes, which seemed to be more substantial than the bodies within. The brightness of the morning sun rendered their actual flesh almost invisible. Just those golden eyes stared out implacably from under their protective hoods.

'The Glass Men of Valcea,' Iris said under her breath. 'I met them many years ago, when they still inhabited their city. But they've been ousted by the New Gods, by all accounts. And this is where they're hiding out. Up in this mountainous nether region. Clinging to life by the skin of their teeth…'

Simon felt as if they were being watched by silent ghosts. 'Are they dangerous?'

'I suppose they are,' said Iris. 'But I've no idea how they feel about strangers. I expect they've been pretty isolated up here for some time…'

'Oh, you nightmarish woman,' Panda groaned. 'You've placed us in dreadful danger yet again, haven't you?'

As if on cue a great cry went up from the Glass Men, all at once. There was a curious chiming noise as they moaned together. Simon realised that they were singing, or humming. It sounded rather like when you run your finger round and round the rim of a crystal goblet.

'I think… they're *praying*…' Iris whispered.

Panda perked up. 'Are they worshipping us?'

The song of the Glass Men went up in pitch and fervency as Barbra moved forward, shuffling on the crumbling earth. 'I think… I think it's *me*…!' she gasped tinnily.

'You're right,' Iris said, watching how the townsfolk responded to the vending machine's every move. 'Barbra… they're singing to *you!*'

CHAPTER TWENTY FIVE

BARBRA'S STORY.

It was much later on that foreshortened day in the town at the top of the mountain that Barbra unburdened her soul to Simon.

Well, not completely. She knew better than to tell someone all of her secrets. At heart she was a naïve and trusting, credulous person, but her experience in recent years had taught her to toughen up. It didn't do to make yourself vulnerable to people – even if they seemed like they were going to be your firm friends. You had to watch out for yourself – especially when your whole front was made out of glass and your insides lit up like a fridge.

That night she told Simon a little about her life, as they relaxed in the most commodious of the buildings in the Valcean town.

The glass people had been charm itself. They couldn't communicate with the strangers very effectively, and they were the shyest creatures Barbra had ever encountered – but they had done their best to make their visitors comfortable. They made it plain – through a combination of mime and hymn-humming – that Barbra was their idea of a goddess of some kind, and that they were more than happy to revere her.

'But in a very polite and non-invasive way,' Barbra had commented, very pleased with their reception.

Now Panda and Iris had trolled off to some kind of spa that involved submersing themselves in bubbling oleaginous mud, which Simon hadn't liked the look of at all.

Their absence gave him a chance to talk a bit more to Barbra who, despite her nervousness, was opening up more than usual.

Simon sat near her in a room decorated rather like he imagined a harem looked, with rugs and tapestries and cushions flung everywhere. Barbra was sitting proudly in the centre, like the best piece of furniture that the Glass Men possessed.

'Furniture,' Barbra chuckled. 'That's very fitting because, you see, that's what I am, essentially. A Servo-Furnishing, created by a brilliant man in a distant Earth outpost. I come from a much later period in history than you, Simon. From the 59th Century. I believe you can't fathom that, can you? Yes, when I was living in Darlington, in your 21st, I'd tell people about the 59th and they would give me some very strange looks. Even Magda – whose background isn't the most straightforward and everyday – even she couldn't empathise with such a distant era.

'Not that I saw much of the 59th Century, to be honest. I was put together by this brilliant scientist who specialised in creating mechanical servants. He invented this wonderful, fully automated house he called *Showo'm*. It ran like clockwork, tending to its few inhabitants. We were state of the art, we were. All we Sevro-furnishings of the first generation knew it. I suppose we were a little too pleased with ourselves. I was particular friends with a super-advanced and rather gentlemanly sunbed and he thought he was a god amongst appliances, he really did.

'Of course, fads and fashions come and go. New devices get invented and some of us stop working as efficiently as we used to. And both my sunbed friend and I were soon relegated to the storage rooms deep below *Showo'm*. We weren't wanted anymore. You see, there's some kind of fault with my motor. I don't think I keep comestibles as cool and as fresh as I ought to. Besides being creaky and a bit clunky, of course.

'I watched them bring in this very zippy model with a transdimensional insta-kool interior – and I knew my days were numbered. I knew I wasn't so great a vending machine. I mean, people are very nice, and they don't like to offend – but I know that my pop is often a bit flat and my crisps are quite stale at times.' She sighed deeply and Simon heard the gurgling of her inefficient cooling systems.

'I was put out to pasture. Our creator wanted to dismantle us and cannibalise us. A few of us were lucky to get away with our lives from *Showo'm* on that remote world. We stole an escape pod called Helen one day and flung ourselves into the void. Which was terribly exciting, actually.

'I had a few months in various space stations and ports. There are some pretty insalubrious places for an old vending machine to hang out, let me tell you. But I thought I could be safe by pretending not to be sentient. I could dim my lights and retract my limbs and simply play dumb. But people still won't let you alone. They bang on your sides and smash in your glass and rob you blind. They try to get their fingers and tentacles into your money box.'

'Tell me about it,' said Simon, and then felt sorry for interrupting.

'And then one day I fell down a hole in the Very Fabric of Time and Space,' said Barbra. 'A completely random gap in the air. I was in this dreadful shopping mall on a station called Antelope-slash-Zebra-Nitelite. I was knocking around with a bad crowd. I was desperate by then. My systems were running down and I was half-crazy, I think. I had hooked into a collective of decommissioned Servo-furnishings – a kind of pirate gang, really. A band of robbers – mostly pay-and-display meters, condom machines and hand-driers. A real crew of roughnecks. I was glad to find this portal into another time and place – it

241

seemed like providence had placed the frayed aperture right in my path – and so I pitched myself through it…

'You see? That's why I was so interested in this business of Anthony Marvelle cutting open gaps in space-time with the Pinking Shears. Because I've already experienced the phenomenon. I've been down one of those holes already. And that's how I wound up in Darlington, tens of thousands of years before I'd even been built. Prehistory, really. And I was so grateful to Iris for not letting MIAOW dismantle me. She championed me and made them take me on in a junior capacity as a trainee operative.'

'Wow,' Simon said. 'That's some story.'

'You'd never think, to look at me, would you?' she smiled. 'That my life's been such a Space Opera?'

'And now you're a goddess,' Simon added.

'I think they just like the way my glass lights up,' she said. 'It isn't really about me, as such.'

Iris and Panda came back wearing towelling dressing gowns, looking fresh and glowing from their mud baths.

'Ooh, we've had the most heavenly-smelling unguents plastered *all* over us, haven't we, Panda, chuck? And I feel *marvellous*.'

Panda tutted. 'They've tufted up my fur something awful,' he growled, and flomped down on cushions next to Simon.

'Do you think you can get some of your worshippers to bring us a drink, lovey?' Iris asked Barbra. 'I'm gagging and I can't traipse back to the bus dressed like this.'

'I'm not sure they have alcohol here,' said Barbra. 'But I do have a flagon of rough ale that the innkeeper gave us.'

'Rough ale?' frowned Iris. 'Well, I suppose it will do.'

Just as Barbra was opening up her front to let Iris help herself, several Glass Men were issuing silently into the opulent room.

They were coming in to do a little late night worshipping, at a discreet distance. But when they saw Iris grasping the weighty flagon and hefting it out of Barbra's interior their gasps rang out loudly.

And then next thing was, Iris was seized and dragged to her feet, still clutching her rough ale to her chest. She spluttered and cried out, but there was no reasoning with the outraged Valceans.

'Oh dear,' said Barbra. 'I think they think you've violated their goddess, Iris.'

Simon was shocked to see that the Glass Men's hearts were burning orange in their chests as they took firm hold of the heretic.

'They look absolutely livid!' Barbra said, unnecessarily.

*

It all turned out for the best, that Iris was manhandled away and taken to endure a bizarre form of torture. She later explained that the device the Glass Men took her to was called something like 'The Transparency Review', and it involved lying on a comfortable couch with electrodes stuck to her head.

'I suppose all they were doing was looking into my mind,' she told her chums afterwards. 'It's a bit frustrating for all of us, not sharing a common language, and that's one of the nicer things about their mind-reading device, it allows me to crack the secrets of the Valcean tongue, and now I can communicate with these lovely fellas no bother.'

'What are they saying, then?' asked Simon impatiently. 'What do they want with us?' He was impatient because he, Panda and now Iris had been banged up in a thick-walled cell, while Barbra was off still being Queen for a Day.

'Even more important and interesting than the language business,' Iris went on, 'is the fact that the process of making my hugely complicated mind transparent to them allowed them to learn than Iris Wildthyme is no stranger to the men of Valcea and vice versa! Oh dear me, no. Though it turns out that my previous – rather dramatic – adventure on this world was something like thirty thousand years ago, though they do have some records of the events of those fatal days. Well, they showed me some murals and they had a few epic poems but I couldn't make much sense of it all. This was back in my drinking days, so my recall of what transpired on Valcea isn't the best. I remember something about being seduced by their king, and that's about it. And I do remember that the palace in the Glass City was a fabulously opulent place. And that their king was a right dab hand at the old seduction lark.'

She sank into the corner of the dusty cell, looking rather sorry for herself. 'You see? This is what's so terrible about the loss of my journals. Oh, I'll give that Anthony Marvelle a right good scragging when I get my paws on him.'

'Yes, me too,' put in Panda, looking piqued. 'How dare he nab your diaries! Several lifetimes' worth of interstellar adventures and expeditions! All that immensely valuable knowledge! Completely unique in the Multiverse, that repository of arcane lore and terrible old gossip!'

She reached out at patted his tufted ears. 'Thank you, Panda, lovey. I think I'm quite inconsolable, actually, about the loss of my diaries. Oh, dear. It's all gone wrong, hasn't it? There's Marvelle gallivanting around with the Blithe Pinking Shears, my journals and the Objet D'Oom in his possession. And with them he can accomplish all sorts of terrible things, especially if it's true, what I suspect about his ultimate destination...'

'Where?' Panda asked eagerly. 'Where is that? What is the dreadful man trying to accomplish?'

But Iris was too busy waxing mournfully to give him a proper answer. 'And what have we managed to do? Bugger all, that's what. We've racketed about with some clues as to where Marvelle might turn up... but have we found him? Have we put a stop to him? No! We've just made it worse!'

Iris sat sulking for a moment or two. She looked as if she was furious with herself. She patted her tigerskin-patterned coat pockets and produced a packet of Gitanes. 'Anyone?'

'I'm trying to give up,' said Panda solemnly.

Simon took one and choked a little on the heady blue smoke. He came to a swift decision. He would own up to his own small – if significant - misdemeanour. 'Iris, I have to tell you...'

'What's that, lovey?'

'I-I took one of your books.'

Her eyes narrowed. 'What did you say, Simon?'

He quailed before her piercing stare. 'When I was using your upstairs. I saw the bookcase. I was intrigued, of course. But I should never have touched them.'

She gasped. 'My journals?'

'This was before Anthony Marvelle snuck aboard,' he said. 'Before he stole all the rest of them. I... I took one to have a look at. I opened it up and next thing I knew, I'd stowed it away in my pocket...'

Panda was boggling at him. 'You're another thief!' he exploded. 'And we trusted you! We let you aboard the Number 22 as a trusted new friend!'

'I know,' said Simon miserably. 'I don't know what I was thinking of. It's just me and books... I can't seem to help myself...'

Iris shook her head wildly. 'No, no! Don't apologise! It's *wonderful!* You're saying that you managed to rescue one of my diaries before that slimeball poet stole the rest of them? One of them survived his wicked theft?'

Simon reached over for his duffel coat and rummaged around in the deep pockets. Snuggled into the silk lining he found the palm-sized leather-bound book. He held it up and the meagre light glimmered wonderfully on the marbled edging of the pages and the worn calfskin of its binding.

Iris gasped. 'Volume Ninety Seven,' she grinned, seizing it from his grasp. 'You know what this means, don't you? What luck! What amazing good fortune! That's incredible! You're amazing, Simon! You're wonderful!'

'I am?'

'Yes!' she cried, and reached over to kiss him on the nose. 'This volume! This very one! Look Panda! Maps, charts, detailed notes. Passwords, magic words, spells of invocations.'

'What?' said Panda gruffly. 'What are you talking about?'

Iris said, 'Somehow, spookily, Simon laid his precious little hands on Volume Ninety Seven of my journals. From donkeys' years ago.'

'And that's relevant to now, is it?' said Panda. 'And our present predicament and our long-distance tussle with Anthony Marvelle?'

'Oh yes,' sighed Iris happily, 'You see, Volume Ninety Seven is all about my first visit to the world of Hyspero, on the very Brink of this universe.'

Panda frowned. 'I've heard of that place before.'

'In legends, perhaps,' smiled Iris. 'It's a beguiling world, wrapped up in fabulous mystery. I've been there several times and only just managed to survive to tell the tale.' She waggled her sole-surviving journal in the air before them. 'And this little booky-wook of mine gives us all the information we need to survive on that weird and dangerous planet.'

Simon was frowning too. 'But... I've heard of Hyspero too. I think. Something I've read perhaps...'

Iris told him solemnly, 'Legends have got as far as your planet too, it seems. Very interesting.' She suddenly laughed. 'Simon, you're a genius! Don't you see? This book is what Marvelle was ransacking my bookshelves for. He took off all my diaries in order to get his mitts on the info in this particular tome. Number Ninety Seven! But unbeknownst to him – unbeknownst to us all – Simon here had already wilfed it away!'

Simon looked embarrassed again.

'Why does Marvelle want to know about Hyspero?' Panda asked.

Now Iris jumped to her feet and paced around their cell. Her triumphant grin had faded and she looked immensely troubled once more. 'That's because I was dead right in what I suspected, chuck. It's because the Objet D'Oom originally hails from Hyspero. It is perhaps the most precious single artefact from that entire world. Somehow it ended up on Earth. And Marvelle is intent on taking that jar and its potent contents all the way back to Hyspero for some wicked purpose of his own. I hardly like to imagine what that is, but I think I know.'

Simon and Panda were about to press her further rather firmly, but then they saw that Barbra had joined them. She wore some kind of jewelled headdress and she was flanked by semi-transparent flunkeys in robes. She coughed discreetly.

'My dears,' she told them, 'I've explained to them what we want. And they've agreed to help us. They'll let us go to the Glass City, even though they fear the place dreadfully. They live up here in this mountain eyrie in order to avoid the beings they call the New Gods. But because they worship me and because you appear in their ancient legends, Iris, they are willing to lay down their lives for us. We can progress to the city. But on one condition.'

The glass bars of their prison cell melted away and Barbra stepped forward, extending her arms, beckoning them to freedom.

'What's their condition?' Simon asked.

'That, after our visit to the City, I must return to remain here,' said Barbra. She kept her tone quite neutral and mechanical, though they could all hear the nervousness and doubt in her voice. 'They want me to stay here forever as their goddess and never go home with you people again...'

CHAPTER TWENTY SIX

It was in the nature of a man like Anthony Marvelle to take everything pretty easily.

'You've never had to struggle for anything in your life, have you?' asked Jenny the ex-traffic warden bitterly. This was over breakfast on the observation deck of the Super Hotel Miramar. They were in the midst of what might comfortably be called a superb vista. The Golden Chasm. Coronas on fire. Distant nebulae going haywire in the multi-hued depths of deep space. Comets and stars doing the dance of the Sugar Plum Fairy as if simply to entertain the breakfasters at the Super Hotel Miramar as they lingered, awestruck, over their full English breakfasts.

'*Struggle* murmur murmur?' Marvelle pondered. He tossed back his mane of golden hair and paused with his patrician profile superbly outlined against the fizzing effervescence of outer space. 'No, I wouldn't say *struggle*, exactly. I have worked relatively hard to achieve my goals, I think, murmur murmur. However poisonously privileged an ex-traffic warden from Darlington might find me, I don't think even *you* could deny that I have worked hard, Jenny murmur murmur.'

'Huh,' she said. By now she thoroughly despised the man and his easy charm. The way he glided through life getting just what he wanted made her want to throw up. She wished she had never consented to this mission and to spending so much time with him. Unusually, she found that she was wishing she was with Iris on the bus instead. That was something she hadn't wished for in an awful long time.

'Aha murmur,' Marvelle grinned wolfishly. 'Here comes the most recent addition to my harem. Good morning my dear murmur murmur.' He beamed up at Kelly as the girl made her way between tables and came to sit with them.

'Everyone's so… alien,' she said.

'Yes, you'll find that in outer space,' snapped Jenny, and then realised how nasty she sounded. Why couldn't she be nicer to Kelly? The poor girl would be terrified and disorientated. She had been well-nigh kidnapped by Marvelle, at least that was how she told the tale.

'Best get a hearty breakfast,' Marvelle told them both. 'I think we've rested long enough in this delightful spa. It's time we moved on to our next destination. A rather chilly little world, so you'd better get something nice and hot inside you murmur murmur *murmur*.' He raised both eyebrows waggishly.

'What are you eating?' Kelly asked Jenny. 'What's that?'

Jenny sighed. 'It's what they call full English breakfast. I didn't want to hurt the waitress's feelings.' On her plate she had several scones, heaped with cream and jam, some chips and beans and a poached egg. And what looked like an onion bhaji surmounting the lot. 'He's right though, Kelly. You're best filling up when you can, when you're travelling in this hectic manner. You don't know where your next meal is coming from.'

'As you can tell, Jenny is an old hand at the interstellar commute murmur murmur,' chuckled Marvelle. He plucked an overdone rasher from his plate and tossed it to Missy the poodle.

Kelly still looked as furious as she did the moment he kidnapped her from Magda's house. 'I still don't understand why you need me. I don't see what any of it has got to do with me.'

'Why, you're very special murmur murmur,' said Marvelle. 'I knew that from the first, my dear. Those poems of yours you showed me, during our festival of literature with your nice group of lady poets. I knew then that here was a *voice* murmur… a *special* voice murmur murmur… and a special girl I would be a fool to let slip beyond my grasp. What was that first poem of yours you showed me..? It fair took my breath away murmur murmur…'

To Kelly and Jenny's astonishment Marvelle closed his eyes and, going into a kind of winsome reverie, recited one of Kelly's stanzas aloud:

'Through Dii h'anno Doors murmur
Night of the very Brink
Take our fragments of murmur – faint one day – the murmur
murmur
Over the magic breach
Misty murmur aperture
Where swords of murmur murmur and
Clockworks sorcery
Though ceaseless murmur cannot obey
The Ringpullworld murmur murmur
Dark murmured logic …'

'You memorized my poems?' Kelly looked alarmed and embarrassed.

'That was one of your poems?' Jenny laughed. 'That was dreadful!'

'I can't believe you memorized it!' Kelly said.

Marvelle's bright eyes snapped open. 'Oh, how could I not know it off by heart? It is music to my ears murmur murmur.'

'It is?' said Jenny.

'Oh yes,' said the poet. 'I knew it as soon as I read it. As soon as I heard those amazing words falling from Kelly's wonderful lips murmur murmur. Don't you think those lips are wonderful, Jenny? Don't you think she's a beauty murmur murmur?'

Jenny looked discomfited. 'Whether I think she's a beauty or not is completely irrelevant, Marvelle. What's going on? Why is that poem so important?'

'It's a prophecy murmur,' he said simply. 'Or rather, a set of instructions murmur murmur.'

'What?' said Kelly. 'But… I just made it up. It just came out of my head like that…'

His eyes narrowed and his voice went very solemn. 'It's the truest example I have ever heard… of the universe speaking through someone, murmur murmur.'

'W-what?'

'It's a message,' he said. 'A message for me. You are the key, Kelly. The key to something marvellous and impossible murmur.'

He sat back and patted his poodle and smiled happily at his assembled harem. He looked very smug, Jenny thought. As if some great cosmic gift had just landed in his lap. And perhaps it had.

Across the table from her Kelly looked scared and well out of her depth.

Then Jenny became aware of a dry rustling in the back of her own mind. A polite, delicate cough. She listened hard. '*Jenny…?*'

The voice was in her head. It was the tiny woman. The Empress. Talking to her again. 'Excuse me,' she told the others, and hurried away from the table.

She paused by some kind of bizarre fruit tree beside the kitchen doorway and pretended to be polishing her monocle on a napkin. 'Hello?' she said inside her mind. 'Are you there?'

'I'm here,' said the tiny Empress. The jar was back in her hotel room, but the voice was as clear and bell-like as it had been when she had lain in bed with the Objet D'Oom on her bedside table. This time the voice sounded panicked and shrill. 'Did I hear correctly?' The Empress Euphemia cried. 'That… prophecy that Marvelle recited. That is terrible news for us, Jenny.'

'Really? Why?' But Jenny already knew it was bad news. She had seen it in Marvelle's smug grinning. The triumphant light in his eyes. He knew he couldn't fail. He had everything he needed to fulfil his mysterious plans.

'That girl Kelly,' said the Empress. 'Somehow… he knows what she *is*. What she represents. The power she has.'

'Power?' gasped Jenny. 'But she's nothing. She just works in a bookshop…'

'She is more than that. She is the aperture, the key… The weakest point in the whole universe. She… she…' The Empress was becoming incoherent now, thrashing around inside Kelly's mind as if she didn't know where to turn. 'She must not be allowed to get to Hyspero. Do you understand, Kelly? If Marvelle manages to take this Kelly girl to Hyspero, then all is lost. The tide cannot be turned back. There will be dreadful disaster. He doesn't even realise, the fool…'

'But…' Jenny said. 'How can I… I mean… What can…'

'She must be stopped at all costs. She must not get to Hyspero. She must not be taken to the Scarlet Empress. Do you hear me, Jenny? Do you promise?'

'I don't understand…'

'You don't have to understand. Just promise me, woman. For the sake of this dimension and many others. Promise me you will prevent Marvelle taking that girl to Hyspero. Destroy her if necessary. Yes, yes. That would be the best thing all round. It's cruel but I can see no other way. She is the gateway, the aperture, the key. I can see the coming chaos through her. She is tiny, a mere pinprick of life in the whole of creation. You must kill her, Jenny. As soon as you can.'

'I can't!'

'You must,' whispered the Empress, and then she was gone from Jenny's mind, as swiftly as she had come.

Jenny swayed a bit on the spot, reeling with the magnitude and madness of the voice in her head. She felt an arm reach out to steady her and opened her eyes to see the waitress she had talked to earlier.

'Are you all right, dear?'

Jenny just stared at her. 'No, I don't think I am…'

'Oh dear. What seems to be the upset?'

But Jenny couldn't say. Murder, she thought wildly. That's why I've been brought on this mission, after all. The forces of chaos have contrived and connived things so that here I am, a million parsecs from home and in my own future and my destiny is entangled in the murder of a civilian. A girl who lives in the same town as me. A girl who's never done me any harm. But now I'm being told that my duty is to kill her.

Somehow she never doubted the voice in her head. The tiny wizened Empress from the jar spoke the truth, Jenny knew. She accepted that, just as, bit by bit, she came to accept her grisly mission.

'Where have you been?' laughed Marvelle. 'We're leaving soon. Off into the wide blue yonder. Pinking Shears at the ready!'

Kelly scowled at her and Jenny gave a sickly smile. I'm a MIAOW operative, she reminded herself. Sometimes we need to do messy, unfortunate things. I have to be strong, don't I?

*

With their usual quietness and grace the Glass Men led their exalted visitors back into the parched outdoors.

'Someone's given the bus a bit of a clean,' Panda pointed out. 'And they've repaired the broken window, look!'

Iris cheered up slightly at that. 'They're skilled with glass, I suppose,' she conceded. 'That's very kind of them. I was worried about that broken pane.'

Barbra addressed her new people in rather a grand fashion, promising them that, following their mission to the ancient city, she would return to be their queen.

'Hm,' Simon said, observing their reactions. 'They look well cheesed off that Barbra's coming with us.'

'Who can blame them?' said Iris, unlocking the doors of the bus. 'She's the most precious person they've ever seen. And they're having to watch her set off to this place they dread. This city that lurks in all their nightmares and legends. They're letting her face off against the New Gods…'

'Goodness,' said Panda, hopping aboard the bus ahead of them. 'Barbra's really become a kind of mythic figure, hasn't she? Going to fight the gods for her people – hurrah! I thought she was just some old vending machine.'

With a great deal of arthritic clanking awkwardness Barbra hoisted herself on board the Number 22. 'I still *am* an old vending machine, Panda,' she said. 'But it's like my old colleague, the sun bed Toaster used to say – that sexy old reprobate – one day everyone finds their natural place in the universe. Everyone finds the ones who love them.'

Iris turned round in the gangway, frowning deeply. 'Do they? Is that true?'

Barbra shrugged happily, adjusting the tiara she'd recently been given. 'I like to think so. I like to think there's a reason and a goal for all the chaos and mess and nastiness in life.'

'Pah,' said Panda. 'There's no rhyme or reason. It's all just a big bloody mess. There's no guarantee of happiness for anyone, I'm afraid.'

'Oh,' said Barbra. 'That's a bit nihilistic of you, Panda, isn't it?'

He scowled at her and got Simon to help him close the doors on the bus.

Iris was in the driver's cab, consulting a map with which the Glass Men had presented them. It wasn't very clear at all, but she got the gist of the location of the city. 'Thank goodness they fixed the window,' she said. 'If we had to drive through these mountains it'd take us a few more days. And according to the crystal from MIAOW, we don't have that long.'

'You mean Marvelle is imminent?' Panda said. 'He's due to arrive in the city very soon?'

Iris double-checked by peering into the MIAOW crystal that Barbra had nicked. She was shocked by how finely they had cut it. 'We've been messing around too much and enjoying ourselves. These little detours and mud-baths and spa treatments. We've got to catch up with that meddlesome dandy.'

'And punch him up the hooter,' said Panda darkly. All of a sudden Simon could see that their diminutive companion was spoiling for a fight.

Iris told Barbra to give her subjects a wave and then plunged the bus abruptly into the Maelstrom.

The ornaments and glasses and windows rattled and shook. The world about them swept into a tooth-aching miasma of spearmint and tangerine.

'We're on our way!' Iris screeched, and for good measure cranked up Abba's 'The Visitors' album to full volume so that no one could hear themselves think.

CHAPTER TWENTY SEVEN

Snip snip snip

Murmur

Jenny was starting to hate the meticulous way Marvelle used those pinking shears. His mouth would purse up with concentration and it was like he was doing surgery or something as he sliced and snipped through the Very Fabric.

They were in the grounds of the Super Hotel Miramar, a discreet distance from the building itself. They had crossed several lawns of short grey grass and a maze built from fallen, pitted asteroids. The air here was thin and there was an unpleasant smell. Marvelle muttered something about the hotel's famously leaky force shielding and how, in a matter of years, something terrible was due to happen to it. 'The whole atmosphere gets ripped off in a solar storm. Yanked off like cellophane. Terrible disaster murmur murmur. That eggy smell isn't your breakfast repeating, my dears, it's the first signs that the Miramar's shielding is dodgy murmur murmur.'

Kelly wanted to know how Marvelle knew so much about places that weren't Earth. He sighed. 'Because I'm not *from* Earth? Will that do you? Haven't you got that *yet*? Murmur murmur.' He sighed. 'Golly, Kelly, you may have the universe pumping the chiming poetry of the spheres out of your wazoo, but you're rather slow on the uptake sometimes murmur murmur.'

'You're like Iris, then?' Kelly said. 'Do you come from the same place as her?'

'*Certainly* not,' he said, with a shudder, and then he applied himself to finding a solitary spot and started cutting away at the Very Fabric with his magical scissors. His poodle Missy was wearing shades now and looked highly irritated by the two human female companions.

'Now ladies,' said Marvelle. 'We're going somewhere very special indeed murmur. Valcea is an alien world populated by people built from molten glass. How or why they came to be like that, no one knows. What's amazing about them is that you can see their hearts glowing in their chests like burning coals. I've never actually met them before, but by all accounts they're quite fascinating murmur murmur.'

'So why are we going there?' asked Jenny peevishly. 'Presumably they've got something you want or need?'

'Very good, Jenny,' he smiled. 'You're learning. And yes, indeed. Valcea has a rather special connection to our ultimate destination. It has access to a kind of... corridor, or wormhole that spans the universes and will take us where we want to be murmur murmur.'

'Can't you just use your scissors?' Kelly asked.

'Unfortunately not,' said Marvelle. 'With the kinds of distances involved I couldn't be accurate enough. No. This is the best way. The Corridors of the Glass Men are the best we can do. They're rather famous in their own way, you know. It should be something of a special experience for us. I've always wanted to try them out.'

'Corridors don't sound very exciting,' said Kelly. 'And what's at the end of the Corridor then? What's the big deal there?'

'Hyspero,' said Marvelle, almost under his breath, like a whisper. As if he hardly dare say the name out loud. As he said it the hole he had made in the universe gaped invitingly open

258

and it was ready for them to step through. 'Okay. We're ready. Come on, ladies murmur murmur. After you.'

*

For several days Magda couldn't get the picture out of her head. Whenever she closed her eyes she could see the snarling face of Anthony Marvelle. He who was usually so smooth and debonair. He had snarled in her face and upended her wheelchair, sending her sprawling onto the floor of her kitchen.

She knew he was a nasty bastard. He was too smooth, too charming. Well, he had shown his true colours.

She could still see Kelly walking after him, too. All entranced, all mesmerized up by him. Walking off into who knew what kind of danger after him.

Rarely had Magda felt more alone than she did in the days following this dreadful scene. Even when she had lived alone in a cave, half mad with bad fish and radiation poisoning, she had still felt less bereft and desolate than this.

MIAOW in London were on her back. They kept calling and representatives were threatening to make a personal appearance. The Darlington branch were in trouble, rudderless and swimming helplessly against the tide of the oncoming workload. Incursions were going unremarked, occurrences were going uninvestigated. Reports of strange and impossible events weren't getting logged properly or efficiently and MIAOW central HQ were wanting to know why Darlington was failing to deliver.

Magda floundered. She tried to explain that her colleagues were absent – or rather, off investigating. She was sure they would be back before long. She couldn't even explain where they had gone or what they were doing.

The face of Mida Slike from MIAOW central appeared on the giant viewscreen deep under the indoor market and grimaced hatefully. The scar down her cheek was glistening in the chilly light. She threatened and bullied Magda and told her that Darlington had better raise their game and step up to the plate and various other sporting metaphors than Magda inwardly groaned at.

'You can't let us down,' Mida said. 'You're one of the most crucial centres of MIAOW operations. There at the Dreadful Flap – that terrible nexus point for multi-dimensional exploration.'

Magda tutted and nodded her head. She knew all this. She knew they had an important job to do and it was fatal to let any of it slip and get behind. But what was she supposed to do about it? She had called in all the relief workers and the sleeper agents. But they weren't trained up enough. They could barely cope. She knew she could never explain this to Mida Slike at Central Command.

'We'd be happy to send one of our lot to help you out…?' said the commander, with a cruelly suggestive look on her face.

'Er, no, thanks,' said Magda.

'This is all Iris Wildthyme's fault, I just know it,' growled Mida Slike. 'Every time she appears! This always happens! Chaos! Mess!'

Magda let her boss rave, glad that she was out of the firing line for a while.

Later, when the screen was blank and Magda turned her attention to the afternoon's work, a great wave of despair came over her. The map of the North was suddenly blinking and ablaze with reports that needed investigating and she knew they would never catch up. She watched the ladies arrive for the afternoon shift – a couple of trainees who worked the rest of the time in Greggs the bakers. They took up their positions at the main desk and Magda sighed. It seemed useless suddenly. What could they really do to stem the tide of weirdness that was constantly assailing Darlington? Honestly, a bunch of women who worked in a bakery, a fey librarian called Alan and a gloomy mermaid in a wheelchair?

She went upstairs and sat in her remainder bookshop all that afternoon and served her few customers in a very unfriendly way.

And then she took out the book in her handbag that she had started reading last night. It would distract her. Soothe her. It was bound to.

It was an ancient thing. Queer-smelling. Very tactile with its thick pages and ragged edges. Its maroon leather binding. The *Aja'ib*. An ancient book she had come across at the Great Big Book Exchange. Had she bought it? She couldn't remember. Somehow it was in her handbag. Surely it would be expensive, an old thing like this..? Surely she'd remember haggling over and paying a decent price for a book of this ilk..?

It was a compendium of strange old stories. That much she had discovered last night, sitting up in bed with a tot of sherry and feeling glum. The strange stories had lifted her out of herself and given her a restful night's sleep for once. But the stories had no real beginnings or ends and scarcely made any sense at all. Locations shifted, characters entered and exited with hardly any rhyme or reason. Nothing quite added up in the *Aja'ib*... but Magda found that she was happy to return to it this afternoon... She found its lack of logic somehow soothing.

The book fell open at a page seemingly of its own choosing.

And straight away it was telling her about a race of men built out of glass. Soft, molten glass that felt warm to the touch and yielded easily to pressure. Their feelings were quite plain to each other. Their hearts glowed and their pulses raced all in plain view of each other. Their brains lit up with ideas or dimmed with tiredness.

Their enemies envied them their beauty and found them easy to kill. You just had to catch them unawares... and push them over roughly. They fell very badly and crashed into a million deadly splinters. If you killed a glass man you had to be careful that a shard didn't fly back at you and pierce your eye. That way the soul of your victim would enter your own and take you over.

So precious and vulnerable they were, they lived in a vast City of Glass. They called it Valcea, the crowning achievement of their whole world of Valcea. No one had seen a city like it. The Glass Men were safe in their icy palace where there was no secrecy, no subterfuge, no opacity at all.

They lived there for more than a thousand years and defended themselves against many enemies who came to see what they were being so precious about. Some people suspected that the Glass Men of Valcea were actually hiding something infinitely precious. Something even more precious than themselves.

Many years went by and no one discovered what their secret was. Until the time of the New Gods, who came to Valcea in a great swarm. They ousted the Glass Men and destroyed most of them. They shattered and smashed them and took their city off them. And the remaining Glass Men went to live in the mountains, hiding themselves away in the shadows where no one might find them again.

And so the New Gods found out what the secret was that had been hidden at the very heart of the City of Glass.

Dii h'anno Doors.

CHAPTER TWENTY EIGHT

'Now, *this* is what I call an alien city,' said Simon approvingly as they all stepped off the bus and assembled on the smooth jade glass outside.

'Do you, lovey?' said Iris. She gave a sniff of disdain. 'Well, I've seen better if I'm honest. And I've been here before. They've let the old place go to rack and ruin.'

Panda slid about experimentally on the sheer floor while Barbra looked perturbed by their new surroundings.

The Glass City was like a vast iceberg carved by time into a million beautiful, grotesque towers and minarets. Buildings as tall as the mountains they had travelled to rose up about them, sheer and featureless and blandly reflecting the open skies. There were no lights and no windows. All was stark and bleakly impressive.

'It's gone a bit green since I was last here,' Iris mused. 'Some kind of bacteria or mouldy stuff coating everything. They've obviously let their window cleaner go.'

She led them away from the bus and Simon felt a momentary jab of panic as he watched her wander blithely into the city. Would they ever find their way back in the labyrinth of glass? But he was learning to trust in her instincts, in the fact that she would always be able to lead them back to the bus.

Iris wandered through canyons and corridors of glass. It was hard to see which way to turn because the whole place teemed with slanting reflections. It was like navigating their way through a murky hall of mirrors.

'If we move about enough they're bound to realise we're here, sooner or later,' Iris told them. 'Most of the city is high up. Right at the top of these spindly pinnacles, and we need them to let us in.'

'Can't we shout? Stomp around? Smash some things up?' said Panda.

'They'll see us, chuck,' Iris told him.

'So this is where Marvelle is coming,' Simon said. 'This is where it all ends up. I wonder what he's after?'

Barbra said, 'The crystal never explained that. It just told us that he'll be here. Right about now.'

'Hmm,' said Iris. 'I'll give him such a thumping when I see him. Giving us the runaround. Stealing stuff he's got no right to even know about.'

'How did he even know about things like the Objet D'Oom and the Pinking Shears?' Simon asked her. 'For a poet he seems remarkably well-informed.'

'That's what worries me,' Iris said. 'I suspect he isn't human at all. He couldn't have plans like he has and just be some bloke from Earth…'

'Over here, everybody!' Barbra called. 'I've found a door!'

And so she had. A dark oblong had opened up in a wall of glass Simon knew they had already passed. The opening hadn't been there before.

'They know we're here,' Iris said.

'Are they watching us?' asked Panda.

'I'll go first,' Iris said and produced a hot pink laser blaster from inside her boot. She set it to 'pen torch' and led the way into the city.

Inside it was very cool and dark. The pink light of her laser gun picked out a blank path ahead of them. A featureless corridor. To Simon it felt like they were walking into some kind of mausoleum. Their voices echoed sharply when they whispered to each other. The four friends kept very close together and moved rather slowly, owing to Barbra's keen sense of caution.

'Listen,' said Panda sharply.

Squueaaakk.

Simon knew that noise. He recognised it instantly from down on the plains and their night by the camp fire.

It came again. Oily, harsh. Very close by.

'W-what is it?' warbled Barbra.

'We've got company,' said Iris. 'I think they have come to get us.'

Sqqquuueeeal.

Panda bravely led the way. He was clearly spoiling for a fight, Simon thought. But then what could a small Panda *do* in a fight?

'I smell mothballs,' he said.

'I should go first,' said Barbra, obviously thinking the same thing as Simon.

They rounded the corner and were immediately set upon.

They barely had time to blink or collect their thoughts.

A tall black shape swept round the corner and fell upon them. Its heavy doors were open and squealing nastily. Its deep, dark recesses opened up like the tomb itself.

Iris swore loudly. So did Panda.

Barbra thrust herself forward bravely and flew at the wardrobe, even though it stood over a metre taller than her. Its castors screeched horribly on the glass floor and there was a wrenching, splintering noise of antique wood.

Simon grabbed Iris as she was flung backwards and just about cracked her head against the wall. Panda had disappeared somewhere in the melee as the torch skittered away. A terrible fight broke out between Barbra and their assailant, lit only by the lambent glare from her interior.

'I can't hold him!' Barbra cried at last. 'H-he's too strong!'

Panda spat. 'Bloody wardrobe!'

Iris led a desperate charge and, between them, they almost had the piece of furniture over on its side. But then they were joined by another one, and another. All of them swung and clashed their doors menacingly.

There was no use fighting it. They could see now. They were prisoners.

'It's all right,' said Iris, rubbing her bruises. She managed to retrieve her torch as they were bundled away and marched deeper into the city by their captors. 'This is what we wanted, isn't it?' she told her friends. 'We wanted to get into the place somehow. Now they're taking us. And – what's more – I've still got my laser gun. We can get out any time we like. What can a bunch of old furniture do to us, eh?'

Simon didn't like to dwell on that fact too much. These were the New Gods of the city, he knew that much. The Glass Men were terrified of them, as were the more human inhabitants of the town they had visited. The New Gods could command sacrificial victims and seemingly rule the whole world of Valcea from up here on their vitreous palace. Not bad for a bunch of wardrobes, he thought.

Iris and her friends were going to have to box clever.

*

The first thing their captors did was separate them. Simon and Barbra were led into a cell and shut in there alone.

'We'll find you again!' Iris called out. 'Don't worry! We'll... *Glurrrrkk!*' And then someone shut her up and dragged her away.

Simon looked gloomily at Barbra. 'It's just us then.'

'I wish they'd left Panda with us,' Barbra sighed heavily. 'He makes me feel better, somehow. That little fellow.'

Simon frowned. Fond as he was of Panda, he didn't find him exactly reassuring. 'Where do you suppose they've taken them?'

Barbra shrugged and winched in her hydraulic limbs. She thought she might as well conserve strength as they sat here waiting. Simon started banging at the misty glass of the walls.

'It's so thick you can't even see through it,' he said despondently, and slid to the ground. 'We'll never break out.'

'I'm not strong enough just now, I'm afraid,' said Barbra. 'Otherwise I'd give them a good battering. But I think we'd better just wait.' She sprang open her main door. 'Can I get you something to eat?'

Simon passed his eye over the rather untempting supplies she had picked up what felt like months ago. There was a box of lilac eggs given to her by the barkeeper at *The Winged God*. 'Er, no. You're still bleeping inside, by the way.'

She seemed to listen hard. 'You're right. Indeed you are.' Then her door slammed shut. 'If and when we get out of here I shall have to get it seen to.'

Simon wondered if there wasn't something a bit shifty in the way she had reacted.

Several hours seemed to pass drearily in the cell. They became rather depressed in attempting to cheer each other up, and eventually fell into a companionable silence.

Until the heavy doors slid open again.

'Iris!' cried Simon, jumping to his feet. But it wasn't Iris.

Two rather tall cedarwood closets were standing at the door, leaving no chance for him to push past to freedom.

'What do you want?' snapped Simon firmly. 'Have you brought our friends back?'

The wardrobes said nothing, but slid back on their castors to reveal three human figures, plus a pink dog.

'Oh my goodness!' shrilled Barbra, flushing suddenly.

The wardrobes silently shoved forward Kelly and Jenny.

'Kelly!' Simon cried out, and gathered her in a hug. She looked just as pleased to see him, thought Jenny and the poodle known as Missy didn't look at all glad.

'I never expected to see you again!' Kelly burst out, pummelling him in her excitement. 'What is this place? Where are we supposed to be?'

Barbra broke through their reunion by yelling out in a surprisingly loud voice: 'Anthony Marvelle! You've got a lot to answer for, sir. You are the cause of all of this. We've been looking for you, Mr Marvelle!'

Marvelle stood between the tall wardrobes and sneered at the noisome vending machine. He shrugged and simply murmured deprecatingly at her. He looked just as immaculate as ever, which was rather galling to the somewhat dishevelled occupants of the cell. Jenny looked supremely miffed with her hair awry and her monocle missing. She rolled her eyes when she saw that it was Barbra making all the noise.

'So you've survived, then?' she asked them. 'Even after spending some time with Iris. 'But I see she's abandoned you. Dumped you here on an alien world with the savage and frankly bizarre natives. Same old Iris.' Jenny slumped to the ground, almost vanishing into the folds of her battered leather coat. Simon thought she looked rather depressed and wondered if her old digestive complaint was playing up, due to all the time travel.

'She hasn't abandoned us,' he burst out. 'She was hauled away by those... wardrobe things.'

This was precisely what they were doing with Anthony Marvelle and his poodle just then.

'Ha!' jeered Kelly, as the doors slid shut. 'Some old prison cell is no good for the likes of him, then!'

'I'm so glad to see you!' Simon told her as they were sealed in once more, inside the slightly more crowded cell. 'But what were you doing with that preening poet fella?'

'He kidnapped me! I was round at Magda's place and he came in waving these scissors about and next thing I know... I'm in outer blummin' space.'

Jenny snorted. 'Happens to the best of us.'

'Where have you been, then?' Kelly asked Simon in turn.

'We've been chasing after Marvelle. Barbra got us that crystal, remember, to track him down – and it did – to here, in this city, right now! And it's taken us all our time just to get here. To rendezvous with you!'

Jenny groaned. 'We'll never stop him, you know. He's got everything he wants now. All the pieces are lined up. Nothing can stop him now.'

'It's been horrible, Simon,' said Kelly. 'First you lot never came back with the bus, and then I was taken off by Marvelle... and now he's coming out with all this stuff about why we're here on this planet. And something about me. Something about why I'm integral to all of this.'

'You?' he asked.

'That's what he was saying,' said Kelly glumly. 'I thought it was all about you and Iris and that I was just incidental. But... it seems like there's something he needs from me. And it's not like a sex thing or anything I suspected. I mean, he's a dirty old man, but there's a like… science fiction reason he needs me here.'

'Right…' said Simon. 'I wonder what.'

'Believe it or not,' sighed Jenny. 'But Kelly's the only one who can give Marvelle what he wants. He's known all along. The Objet D'Oom, the Pinking Shears, the charts from Iris's bus and even her diaries. All these things were smaller prizes. Important, perhaps – but not as important as precious Kelly here.'

Kelly felt very self-conscious all of a sudden. They were all looking at her.

'We won't let him use you,' Simon told her firmly.

'We might be too late,' snapped Jenny. She was hoiking in her long coat pockets and produced a familiar-looking glass jar.

'The Objet D'Oom,' said Barbra in reverent tones. 'That's it! The thing that set all of these peculiar events in motion.'

'It is indeed,' said Jenny grimly. She gripped the impossibly tight lid of the jar. 'It's been placed in my safe-keeping by Marvelle. But what even he doesn't know is that the tiny occupant of this jar has been speaking to me for several days…'

'Speaking to you…!' said Barbra, quaveringly.

'Oh yes,' said Jenny. Her face contorted as she wrestled with the jar. 'And she's been giving me dire warnings. She's telling me what we have to do. And what we must *not* let happen.' With a sudden cry of effort she wrenched the lid off the jar.

They all looked, transfixed, as a wisp of crimson vapour rose out of the neck of the glass jar.

'Good grief…' whispered Barbra tinnily as they all backed away.

Jenny set the opened jar down on the ground.

Even she was amazed by what happened next.

CHAPTER TWENTY NINE

Iris and Panda were shuffled and cajoled into a rather pokey room that was too full of Victorian furniture. 'Ghastly furnishings,' cursed Panda, as the wardrobes closed in on them.

'Cheer up, chuck,' Iris grinned. 'We've faced worse together, haven't we?'

'Oh, indubitably,' he said, as they were led before a large table affair. 'I'm not afraid of a city inhabited by shonky old furniture.'

'I wonder how they got here,' Iris mused. 'And why they chose to adopt this particular form…'

Next thing she knew Panda was up on the table somehow and the table itself was extruding vines and branches of living wood. Her best friend was wailing and thrashing about as the supple, leafy twigs lashed him to the varnished surface. 'What's happening to me?'

'I-I don't know…!' she cried, tugging at whiplike fronds of vegetation. 'I'll get you free, though! I'll..!'

'Leave the creature be!' boomed a huge voice, shocking Iris so much that she ceased her rescue attempt at once.

'What? Who was that?'

'It was me!' came the huge voice once more.

She blinked and saw that the voice was coming from the tallest and most elaborate of the ancient pieces of furniture. Its doors were slightly ajar, revealing a terrible blackness within.

'So you can talk, can you?' she said, looking piqued.

'Iris, tell him to set me free from this thing,' Panda shouted. 'These twigs and things… they're getting into my head!'

She was shocked to see that he was right. The fast-growing branches were extruding filaments that had surrounded Panda's vulnerable noggin. He gasped and cried out as they pierced his plush fur.

'Leave him alone!' she shrieked.

'They're reading my mind…!' Panda howled. 'They're getting inside my brain…!'

Iris turned on the talking wardrobe in fury. 'Hey, you lot! Leave my little chum alone! What's he ever done to you?'

'He is a time traveller,' boomed the wardrobe.

'So am I!' Iris gasped. 'And I've been at it longer than Panda has. So why don't you tie *me* down to your dinner table and try to read my thoughts, eh? Why don't you pick on someone more your own size, lovey?'

'You are too guarded and subtle,' said the wardrobe. 'Your mind would be closed to us.'

'Subtle?' jeered Iris. 'Ecky thump. Are you sure, chuck?'

'Yes,' said the wardrobe. 'We found it hard to believe, too. But we have reached out to your mind and it's a closed book to us. You are giving very few of your true secrets away, Iris Wildthyme.'

For a moment she looked wily and triumphant. 'I've always been a deep 'un,' she said, and then became aware once more of Panda's frantic wriggling and affronted bellowing. 'Oh, look, do leave him alone. Don't harm him. He's my best friend. And there's nothing he can tell you about how to travel in time. He doesn't understand any of it really. He's just my little pal who comes along on the bus with me. He doesn't have any secrets, really…'

The wardrobe growled. 'There are vast depths to the mind of the Panda…' it said, in a very dark voice indeed.

'Ha!' cried Panda. 'Did you hear that, eh? Vast depths, eh?'

'Shurrup, Panda, man,' Iris said. 'I'm trying to save you here.' She rounded on their enemy. 'Look, let him go and I'll tell you some of my secrets, I promise. I'll tell you people anything you want to know.'

The wardrobe seemed to mull this over. Panda's cries subsided somewhat as the leafy tendrils withdrew from his brain.

Iris stared as the talking wardrobe opened its heavy doors wider. She felt drawn to peer within.

'You must help us, Iris Wildthyme,' said the voice from inside that musty, mothbally darkness. 'We don't understand who or what we are. We have powers… strange powers… very unlikely powers for pieces of furniture, which is what we know we truly are. But… here on Valcea they fear us. They call us the New Gods. But we don't even know why.'

Iris frowned. 'But you carry on as if you're their gods, don't you? You demand sacrifices. You make them give up their strongest young people and you bring them here to your city…'

The wardrobe replied guiltily, 'We are driven by dark forces that we do not understand. All we know is that we contain… such furious energy and power. It must be appeased and fed… It requires life forces… more than we can ever provide…'

The wardrobe's doors creaked open even further. Iris inched nearer. Was that a glimmering light in there? A kind of coruscating flame…? Surely not… She was drawn closer towards the doors.

'Look inside, Iris Wildthyme,' said the reverberant voice. 'Can you see that fragment of fire within me? The light that shines in the void?'

'I… I can…' she said, and found herself right on the wooden threshold of the giant wardrobe. Her yellow vinyl boot slipped on the shiny varnish and for a second she teetered there. But she was held still, transfixed, by the image of golden flames, dancing in the darkness, in the depths of the wardrobe.

'Iris!' Panda screeched from the table. 'Get back from there! He's tricking you..! He's...!'

Panda's voice was suddenly silenced and Iris felt something nudge heavily at her back. She lost her grip on the doors and her skinny arms windmilled frantically in thin air. She whooped with dismay and felt herself tottering into the wardrobe itself.

The doors slammed shut on her.

The talking wardrobe looked very pleased with itself, in as much as a wardrobe could.

Panda was sitting up on the table by now, wrenching the branches off himself. 'What have you done to her?' he thundered. 'Where have you put her?'

'She has been swallowed,' said the wardrobe. 'I've taken her off to the spaces within. She'll be very interested in what she finds there, don't you worry, Panda. She'll find plenty to keep her stimulated.'

Panda boggled at him. 'Keeping her stimulated *isn't* a problem,' he growled furiously. 'I demand that you bring her back at once!'

'She is investigating the mystery of the *Dii h'anno Doors*,' said the wardrobe. 'She will be able to explain to the New Gods the mystery of our nature. She will divine the truth for us.'

'And when she does,' added another voice, 'What wonders we will see murmur murmur.'

Panda looked in horror to see Anthony Marvelle issuing suavely into the already overcrowded room. 'You devil!' he spat. 'You're behind all this! You made us come here. You nicked all of those... cosmic gubbins things. The pinking shears and so on. What is it you want, eh? Will you stop at nothing?'

'No,' said, Marvelle. 'Generally, I'm quite determined. And I'm rather pleased to see my somewhat convoluted plans coming to fruition murmur murmur. Iris is safely locked away in the collective unconscious of the wardrobes of Valcea – tick. Kelly is safely packed away, ready to wield her unguessed-at powers in aid of my terrible cause – tick. Those useless saps Jenny, Simon and Barbra are locked away in a glass cell where they can quite happily rot for all I care. Oh, and MIAOW Darlington is about to be disbanded by its superiors for failing to hit its annual targets. All in all, a good few days' work, I think murmur murmur *murmur.*'

'Pah!' cried Panda, whose eloquence was eluding him in the face of Marvelle's triumph.

'Oh, and me?' grinned the dapper poet. 'I'm about to come by the magical means to span the entire multiverse, and take us all to a world on the very Brink of the impossible.'

'Hoo-flaming-ray,' snapped Panda, deciding that he had nothing to lose anymore. He launched himself in that instant at the silk cravat loosely knotted around Marvelle's throat in a last ditch attempt at throttling him.

*

The prisoners in the glass cell drew back in amazement.

There was a tiny woman standing beside the glass jar. She had appeared out of the Objet D'Oom in a shower of glittering gold and now she was standing before them – very small, very glamorous, flickering in crimson flames.

'Hey, how are you all doing?' she said, wiggling her hips like Mae West. She was in a 1930's style sheath frock and her hair was all golden bubbles. 'I am Euphemia, the first Empress of the world of Hyspero. I'm *very* pleased to meet you all.'

Barbra, Simon and Kelly were just staring at her, unable to reply for some moments. Jenny looked equally aghast, even though she had met the woman in her dreams of Darlington lesbian bars. Here was the miniature monarch in the flesh, getting all sassy and diva-ish on them.

Simon couldn't quite believe what he was seeing. He remembered when he had first taken possession of that ancient jar and he had stared into its murky depths. That night he had had a very troubling dream, about holding the glass close to his face, and an eye opening up and staring back at him. Was that this woman, back then? Calling out to him telepathically and letting him know she was there?

He had expected there to be some kind of shrivelled, raw-headed, bloody-boned monstrosity inside the jar. Something hideously preserved well beyond its sell-by date. And yet here was this Empress Euphemia with the hourglass figure and the gleaming curls.

'Is no one gonna talk to me?' she piped up, looking worried.

'We're sorry, your highness,' stammered Jenny at last. 'You've taken everyone aback.'

'Ah,' said Euphemia. 'Of course. Well, here I am – I'm really here – standing before you. The delectable, morsel-sized Empress of Hyspero. Wrongly kidnapped and held prisoner against her will all these years...'

'Who kidnapped you?' Simon said. 'How did you get to be in Darlington? And where is Hyspero anyway?'

She looked at him and beamed. 'Hello, young man. You should have looked after me a bit better, shouldn't you?' She laughed, as if to reassure him that there were no hard feelings. 'I've no concept of time or distance, I'm afraid. I just know that my world is a long way from yours, and it stands at the very Brink of your universe. It is the gateway to somewhere else –

somewhere much stranger and nastier that no one really wants to get to. Except for that fool Anthony Marvelle, of course. That's what this is all about. His wanting to go into… the Obverse.'

'And he needs you, does he?' asked Kelly. 'And the shears, and all the other things, in order to get there?'

'Yes, sort of, Kelly honey,' said the Empress kindly. 'And if he succeeds in getting to the Obverse and stealing their legendary Dark Magic, there will be horrible repercussions. Great big, nasty, endless, *cosmic* repercussions. So we have to stop him at all costs, all right, everyone?'

They found themselves nodding firmly.

'That's good,' said the Empress. 'Because we've got to work together.'

'What do we do?' asked Kelly.

The Empress eyed her sharply. 'We do everything we can in order to keep *you* away from Marvelle,' she said. 'It's you he wants, Kelly.'

'I knew it,' said Kelly.

Barbra said, 'But what is it about Kelly? I mean, nothing against her, and I don't mean to be rude… but what's so special about Kelly?'

'That's right,' Kelly readily agreed. 'Any of the others, I could imagine. But me, what have I got going for me? I can't do magic or any of the techno stuff. I've never been out in Space and Time before. All I've ever done is work in the Great Big Book Exchange…'

'Exactly,' said the Empress Euphemia sagely, rubbing her palms together as if she was suddenly chilly. Or as if a shiver was going right through her.

'I don't understand,' said Kelly.

'There's something… *more* to that bookshop, isn't there, Empress?' said Simon impulsively. 'I knew it! I always knew it!'

'Simon's quite correct,' said the Empress. 'And, during the years you have sat there, so patiently at the cash desk in that quiet and dusty place, you have absorbed some of the special reverberations...'

'What?' gasped Kelly.

'There is a book there, hidden amongst the many books. The *Aja'ib*.' Euphemia lowered her voice when she said the name, as if it wasn't quite safe to say it out loud. 'A sacred book of tales that comes from Hyspero itself. It is our great repository of folk stories. Our magical history.'

'How did an alien book get into the Exchange?' asked Simon. He noticed that Kelly was looking extra thoughtful and he realised that she must once have seen this strange and precious volume.

'Terrance put it there,' said the Empress. 'The former owner of the Exchange. He knew every single book in that shop. He knew the value of what he had hidden away.'

'Terrance!' gasped Kelly. 'Are you saying--?'

'Let me explain something,' said the Empress. 'Under the palace of the Scarlet Empresses on the world of Hyspero, there are catacombs hidden miles beneath the arid earth. Here are where the Empresses are stowed away when they abdicate. Tens of thousands of years' worth of us, preserved in these jars. Oh, we don't die, we just feel the need to take a nice long rest. I was the first in my long line to have myself put away like that, following on traditions I had learned about from earlier dynasties that had existed on our world.'

'Sounds horrible,' Simon breathed. 'You were entombed...'

'Kind of, honey,' said the Empress. 'But you've never witnessed life on Hyspero. Such a hectic, dangerous place. It exists in a permanent state of magical anarchy and evolution. Like living in a madhouse or a fairy tale. Being Empress of that lot can be pretty exhausting, let me tell you. So, it can come as something of a relief to be retired and taken down into the cooler catacombs and to adopt a more advisory role...'

'You're conscious the whole time?' asked Barbra. She remembered, with a shudder, her own years of retirement, after her inventor deemed her no longer worthy of use. She had been consigned to dark storage rooms deep underground and so perhaps could empathise with the doughty Empress.

'We fade in and out of sleep. The slightest word or mention of our names can jar us awake again. Just as, one day, I became suddenly aware that there was an intruder in the catacombs. A non-Hysperon native. A human being. An impossible creature. He wore a dark cloak and was disguised as a vizier to the current Empress and he was stealing about like a villain. Looking for something. A prize. He was looking for me.

'He crept along, mile after mile of sandy-floored tunnel. He examined the ornately-labelled jars on the shelves that lined the walls. And at last he came to the final jar of all and read my name on the more modest name-plate below me.

'I saw him grin with pleasure when he saw that he had unearthed his treasure. He reached out to grasp my jar. He muttered something about the Objet D'Oom, which I later learned was the rather insulting name invented for me by some silly, alien races I'd never even heard of. And I braced myself, horrified at the sacrilege of being lifted down from the shelf against my will. I heard his fingers rubbing against my glass sides. They... squeaked like rubber gloves. His hands were insensate, almost clumsy as he reached for me and I was scared that he was going to drop me and dash me to splintery bits on the floor...'

'He had rubber fingers..?' Kelly burst out.

'He had plastic arms,' said the Empress solemnly. 'The man who picked me up and stowed me away in his big black sack was a man with two plastic arms.'

She paused and stared at their expressions of amazed horror.

Then Jenny cried out, 'Someone's coming!'

They had only a split second before the heavy glass doors slid open. The Empress shivered into smoke and vanished, back inside her jar.

There was a wardrobe in the doorway. It growled at them eerily and surprised them all by lumbering forward, towards Kelly.

'*Me?* It wants me?'

'We won't let you take her,' said Simon, interposing himself.

The wardrobe shoved him away and he fell heavily against the wall.

'It's okay, it's all right,' Kelly said. 'I'm coming.'

Jenny flung herself at them. 'No! Remember what the Empress said! We have to keep you away from them... It's vital that...!'

But it was hopeless. The wardrobe knew what it was doing. Its doors lashed out on unoiled hinges and just about broke Jenny's arm. She leapt after the glass jar of the Empress, to prevent it from being smashed under the creature's heavy castors.

And then, all of a sudden, it was gone. And it had taken Kelly with it.

'That's exactly what we *didn't* want to happen,' said Barbra dully, earning herself a furious look from her colleague from MIAOW.

CHAPTER THIRTY

Iris felt like she was floating for quite some time. Tumbling and twirling through swathes of violet mist, she surrendered herself to the sensation since she knew there was no way she could go back the other way. The force propelling her was too strong. It was a kind of gravity that forced her through the dark hole of the wardrobe and out the other side.

Or maybe the very opposite of gravity – frivolity. Could that be true?

It was rather like driving through the Maelstrom aboard her dependable omnibus. Except here there was nothing familiar. No silly ornaments and gee-gaws hanging around the windscreen, no mascots on the dashboard and no favourite mix tape blasting out on the stereo. Here she was alone. Just her, coasting and careening through layers of cloud that were icy blue and Milk Tray purple. Stars were going off in her head and she hoped to goodness it was because of dimensional pressure rather than anything permanent happening inside her old noggin.

She held up her hands before her eyes and she couldn't see them. I'm disembodied here, she thought. At one with the universe at last, perhaps. Had it killed her, being shut up in that old wardrobe? And shouldn't I be in Narnia yet, by now?

Imagine touching down in some ancient land of fauns and lions and wicked witches. Battles on the plains and everyone waving medieval pennants. Armies of heterogenous monsters trotting out to do each other a mischief. Iris could be queen and tell them all what to do. She could watch Empires and Kingdoms rise and fall in a little land all of her own making.

But there wasn't anything like that at the back of *this* wardrobe. Just these endless skies, shot through with silver threads and golden pathways leading who knew where.

Feeling lonely and nebulously urgent, she tried to remind herself where she ought to be. Not investigating the interiority of these mysterious beings known as the New Gods, but outside, in Valcea, helping her friends – who must be in terrible danger by now. She tried to recall exactly who her friends were… Panda, of course, who hardly ever left her side… and the new boy, erm, Simon, was it? And… *what* was it they had to do? The clock was ticking, wasn't it? And they had to get on… They had to prevent something… Something terrible from happening…

There was another wardrobe in front of her then. Painted in a violent shade of apple green. She trotted across the void quite nimbly and threw open both its doors. The whole interior was filled up by the laughing face of Anthony Marvelle. He was sweating and feverish with excitement and Iris recoiled from that giant, saturnine face.

'There's nothing you can do about it, Iris murmur murmur,' he chortled, guffawed, whinnied and gurgled. Mirthful tears squeezed out of his eyes and ran down his golden complexion. 'I've got everything now. All the elements I need to affect my journey to the Farthest Brink murmur murmur. I'll get there with all my goodies – and Kelly, too – the New Gods will show me the mysteries of *Dii h'anno Doors* and I'll get us to Hyspero and it'll be too late for you to stop us murmur murmur!'

She didn't bother replying to him. When her various enemies started yelling about their triumphs like this it was, in her vast experience, way too late to start reasoning with them. Perhaps being in possession of the Blithe Pinking Shears and the Objet

D'Oom had blown his mind? He had a very finely balanced mind, as she knew – more used to turning stanzas on the tiny lathe of his poetical sensibility. He should really be at home fretting about enjambments and line breaks – but here he was, howling with mirth, his head in a box against a cosmic kind of backdrop. Well, that's where poetry could get you sometimes, she thought grimly, and started doing the backstroke in quite a stately, determined fashion, in order to get away from the manic fop.

He came following, paddling a kayak. 'I mean it, my dear murmur murmur. I'm going to break through the Ringpull into the Obverse. And there's diddly-squat and bugger-all you or your daft friends can do about it murmur murmur.'

She sighed and stopped doing her strenuous arm strokes, and found that she moved quite nicely ahead of him down the celestial river, even so. 'Now, why would you want to go into the Obverse, Anthony? A nice boy like you? Do you even know what's through there? You wouldn't like it at all, you know. You should listen to one who happens to know.'

'I know enough, murmur murmur,' he said, looking displeased by her calm. 'I know that it's where *you* hail from. You and your fabled ancestors murmur murmur.'

She croaked with laughter. 'Fabled ancestors, my arse! I had a number of peculiar aunts and we lived in a decrepit old house in the mountains. Nothing special about us. Nothing grand or mysterious. Nothing to see! Move on, Anthony Marvelle. Stop prying into secrets not your own. Go home, you silly boy!'

Then she gave a kind of backflip and was dazzled suddenly by her own skill. She felt like a kingfisher, bolting out in a flash of sapphire and orange, from a bank across the stream. She jolted away from her nemesis and his canoe and next thing she knew, she was standing alone in a shopping mall.

She didn't recognise it. It was grander than any she had ever seen on Earth. Arcades stretched into infinity. Terraces rose in endless layers up to a crystal ceiling that drenched the place in bogus sunlight. There was no one about and the mall was eerily quiet – just the muzak and the tinkling of perfumed fountains.

Then she saw the Servo-Furnishings running amok.

Robots suddenly surrounded her as they thundered on castors, cartwheels and pneumatic legs, clacking and jiggering along the tiled concourse. Iris squealed and cried out as she got thoroughly jostled by them. Metal elbows nudged and rubber hands shoved her roughly out of the way. She received a confused impression of being stampeded by hand-driers and condom dispensers and slushy-makers. They callously ignored her distress as she ended arse-over-tit in the fake shrubbery. From their curses and catcalls she could tell they were embittered and very anti-human, lugging their swag bags with them. She heard them smashing in the window of a sportswear shop and grunting with mechanical laughter as they clambered inside through the window display to loot the place.

'Oh dear,' said a warbling, familiar voice. 'I'm so sorry, madam.'

Iris looked up to find skinny arms extending, helping her out of the ferns.

'Barbra?'

'You know me?'

It was Barbra some years before she had first met her in Darlington. The vending machine looked a bit more battered and scuffed, here in the mall, where she was a quietly reluctant member of the shopping mall pirate crew.

'We'll be friends in the future,' Iris told her. 'I promise. Thank you for helping me. I wonder if I've somehow drifted into your past or your subconscious, or mine? Am I really here, do you know?'

Barbra nodded. 'This is space station Antelope-Slash-Zebra-Nitelite. It's after hours and no humans should be here, I'm afraid.'

'I wonder what brought me,' said Iris. 'I was shoved in a wardrobe, you see. On the world of Valcea.'

'Who shoved you in a wardrobe?'

'The wardrobe himself. He wanted me to understand him and his race a bit better. They've been made gods of their world, you see. And they just didn't want it and they don't understand why.'

'Being made into Gods!' Barbra sighed. 'That must be nice for them. You mean… there's a world where living furniture is venerated and worshipped?'

'Oh yes,' Iris said. 'You'll see it someday.'

'I can't see myself ever leaving this ghastly mall,' Barbra said sadly. Then she perked up and all of her insides lit up. 'Can I interest you in some pop, maybe? Some crisps?'

'Er, no thanks,' Iris began. Then she relented. 'All right, lovey. Why not? I'm a bit peckish, actually.'

Barbra beamed and opened up her glass front. 'I'll let you have these for nothing. On the house!'

When she opened herself up there came a strange, insistent bleeping from deep within her. 'I'm not sure what that is…' she frowned. 'I wonder if my coolant is running low…'

Iris looked aghast. 'I know what it is. It's a bomb! There's a bomb inside you, Barbra!'

Barbra had a split second in which to look dismayed before the whole mall went up in a flash of emerald green fire. The terraces came tinselling down, along with the hundred thousand Christmas trees that generally stayed up all year round. The plaster monuments and porticos came crashing around Iris's ears as she turned to flee…

And then she was standing in an incredibly loud place, crammed into a crowd of young people. Her eardrums were bursting. Was that skirling electric guitar? Pounding drums? Tinsel and streamers in the dark air? That lingering scent of patchouli and pot?

I've been blown into hell by the force of Barbra's exploding body, she thought wildly. She started to dance, jerkily, as if she had no choice. I'm in a… what do they call them? A mosh pit in hell?

But she wasn't. She was in the audience at the Hammersmith Odeon on a certain evening in 1973. She looked up and saw Vince Cosmos, the greatest glam rocker of them all, finish off a number and then, amid the screams of his fans, take up a tall stool and an acoustic guitar and come to the front of the stage for a quieter song. The long green feather on his hat nodded moodily in time to his strumming.

At that moment Iris saw Panda and Simon standing right at the front of the audience, looking excited and very pleased with themselves. They were flanked by what were surely Martian agents in strange hats. Iris started yelling in order to warn them. Everyone looked at her in irritation. Vince Cosmos frowned and peered down, his silver eyes shaded by his fedora. 'Hey lady, what's up down there?' he asked.

The Martian agents were drawing their laser pistols from under their long coats.

'HOLY FLAMING NORA!!' Iris heard Panda shout out.

*

At the end of the day Magda was still reading the ancient book at the cash desk of her shop. Night had dropped lightly over the market place in Darlington and everyone was dashing home. A fine frost had started to lace the windows and the pavements when a sleek, anonymous car pulled up outside *Magda's Mysteries*.

But Magda was reading about the iridescent and caustic woman warrior who went spinning through multifarious dimensions, head over heels. About how she fell through the doors into other lands, visiting moments that were of vital importance to her, to her friends, and the mission she was on.

Magda frowned, recognising names and faces here and there, realising that this book had fallen into her scaly lap at just the right moment somehow, surely in order to tell her something.

She read about Iris and the men with tentacle sideburns and their ship that came from the red planet. She read about the averted assassination of the rock star at somewhere called The Hammersmith Odeon. And then she read about Iris finding herself aboard a roughly-patched together space craft. A salvage machine, hovering on the furthest fringes of Earth's atmosphere. Iris recognised it at once, of course, as a ship she had already visited, not long in the future. She kept to the shadows and watched its blue-skinned owners going about their harmless business. They were bric-a-brac collectors, magpies in space. When the killer dogs attacked – intent on finding something or other in the supplies of old rubbish that filled the ship's hold – the crew were helpless.

Iris tried to intervene. Knowing she shouldn't, still she tried. She was chased by the savage dogs and almost bitten. She ran shrieking, deeper into the mucky ship, poodles snapping at her heels. The slavering, howling dogs unnerved her. She knew they'd rip her to pieces, given the chance. But she eluded them

– set as they were upon their task of finding the Objet D'Oom and murdering the peaceful crew. Iris could slink away to the darkest corners – and there she noticed something very odd. A man with two plastic arms, skulking about. Taking something from amongst the stuff on board. A glass jar. He was choosing a glass jar from amongst all the teapots and figurines and stuffed toys. Stealing it for a second time.

And then she was gone again, fleet as thought. And she was in an opulent throne room, sheer across the other side of the galaxy. There was another smooth-sided glass jar, though this one was a full ten feet tall. It housed a malign presence and she was thrashing about inside, sloshing life-preserving nutrients against her glass walls.

'I'm not coming back here,' Iris said. 'I've been to this ghastly world before, and I'm not coming back.'

'Yes, you will,' said the Empress, angrily.

'It's too dangerous. It's too close… to the Brink,' said Iris.

'We will see you here,' said the Empress. 'You and your gang of misfits. I can't stop him alone, Iris. You have to come here. Otherwise… Otherwise we will have something far more terrible to face.'

Iris was in despair. 'It's always me. It's always *me* who has to sort it out!'

And then she was soaring, plummeting upwards above the spiked towers of the Scarlet Palace on Hyspero. Somehow she shot through its rafters and rooftops and was plunging into the boiling, turbulent skies of this far-distant world. She glanced down to see the palace and whole city of Central Hyspero growing smaller below her. Like a blotch, like a dirty stain on the immaculate, rugged white face of the ancient deserts.

I'll never go back there, Iris told herself, as she flew into space.

What's this? I can't fly. How am I doing this?

She was doing the backstroke again, ploughing into the darkness. Ahead there was a kind of gigantic ringpull in space. She knew it was there. She knew what it was all about. The light of the Hysperon sun glinted off it quite prettily, all silvery gold and inviting. Iris knew why she was seeing it, why she was being shown this weird cosmic feature. It was a reminder – from the Empress, from all of the Empresses, of the danger they were facing. They were telling her she had work to do here, at the Brink of the Obverse.

She sighed, turning lazily in the vacuum, breathing easily and swirling her long, zebra-skin coat tails about her. She hovered thoughtfully, snuggling the lush green fur of her collar. She lit a Black Sobranie and wasn't even pleased that she found she could smoke easily in outer space. Of course she could. She could do *anything*, couldn't she?

Even sort out this business right across the galaxy.

Magda paused at this point, with the old woman smoking a cigarette in space.

Weird.

Then she became aware that the last customer of the day was marching towards her cash desk. She wasn't buying books.

It was a tall woman with a neat black bob. She wore a beret and a silver mackintosh. Magda gasped when she looked up at that stern face and saw a gleaming scar running down the woman's cheek. There was only one person this could be. Magda had read the files, seen some of the footage, been shouted at from a viewscreen. This had to be Mida Slike.

'MIAOW,' said Mida Slike.

Magda cringed. 'Can I help you?'

'We're closing you down,' Mida Slike said curtly. 'We're very unhappy with the Darlington branch. You're not performing as well as you should.'

Magda gasped. 'We're doing our best! But everyone's been… kidnapped! Or they're otherwise busy.'

Magda shushed her harshly. 'Be silent! How dare you discuss MIAOW business so openly, in public.'

'There's only us here.'

'I can see things have gone very slack and slipshod round here,' Mida Slike said. 'I suggest you take me down to your base at once and explain to me fully what's been going on.'

Magda sighed. It was time to shut her shop for the evening, anyway. She closed the *Aja'ib* reluctantly and thought about her plans for going home and having a nice long soak in her specially adapted bath. She yearned for a gin and tonic and *Midwinter Murders* on the box. But here was one of her mysterious superiors from down in the smoke. Demanding answers and, of all things, competence from her.

'We've been doing our best,' said Magda stiffly.

'I should hope so, too!' said Mida Slike shrilly.

'It was all going fine… until Iris reappeared.' Magda felt disloyal saying this, wheeling herself over to open up the secret elevator.

'That's usually true,' sighed Mida Slike. 'But this time it's gone too far. You've left Darlington and the Dreadful Flap too open and vulnerable, while you've all been messing about with Ms Wildthyme. And we at MIAOW are going to have to relieve you of your duties.'

Magda gasped. She felt just *terrible* as she accompanied Mida to the secret base.

CHAPTER THIRTY ONE

Far across the universe and several thousand years in the future, events were moving towards their climax in the ancient city of Valcea.

While Barbra sat quietly thinking about the strange sounds emanating from her mechanical guts, her friends were trying to find a way out of their prison cell.

Kelly was being marched by the wardrobes through dimly lit corridors. At one point the furniture had to go single file to fit through the angular passageways. She was reminded incongruously of moving into the old council flat with her dad. In the days when he was determined to be a proper dad and set up a home for them. How old had she been? Seven? Watching him wrestling with secondhand armchairs and washstands and chests of drawers. Hefting them up the cement steps to the top floor. Not letting her join in and help in case she hurt herself.

But these pieces of furniture were moving by themselves. They were brusquely shoving her along. They scraped and jostled on the glass floors and the noise echoed hollowly within them.

I could set fire to them, Kelly was thinking wildly, if I'd only kept up smoking and still had my Zippo. Or I could turn on them wildly if I'd thought to bring an axe with me. Or with a proper screwdriver I might disassemble them…

Then she started thinking about that little old woman fairy who'd hopped out of the jar. So much for the Objet D'Oom. Fancy that – all that time! Inside that paperweight meant for

Simon, there'd been a tiny old woman, talking of other worlds and all kinds of strange stuff. The jar with which Kelly had been waiting on the platform at Darlington station. All that time – that tiny Empress had been inside, waiting. Transported so far from her homeworld, and her shelf deep underneath her own palace.

Terrance had been on that planet. Terrance hadn't retired. He hadn't gone off to the wilds of Scotland or Iceland or any of the more prosaic places Kelly had imagined him sloping off for his well-earned rest.

Terrance had gone off into space. He had been on a world at the very edge of the universe. A world on the Brink of a new universe altogether. And he had stolen something very precious and dangerous and brought it home. He had caused all this fuss in the first place.

But how, and why? Kelly wanted to know. He was just a bookseller. Just Terrrance in the Exchange with the two plastic arms. Terrance who played his cards close to his chest. You never really knew much about his past, or what he was thinking or feeling. Even Kelly who had worked with him for all these years in the Exchange. She knew hardly anything about the old man.

But he had been out in Space and Time. Nicking alien Empresses and somehow smuggling them in jars across the galaxy.

Kelly wondered if she would live long enough to find out any of the answers or explanations.

The thought surprised her. Why did she think she was going to die?

Because this felt a little like being led off to an execution, didn't it? This stately procession, flanked by tall, hollow coffins. The wordlessness and the darkness were getting to her.

Why am I special? Why are they all so bothered about me?

She knew it was tied up with Terrance, somehow.

And at last they brought her into a large chamber that was open to the dark skies. Still underground, the darkness above rippled with electricity. Citric flashes of lightning spasmed like migraine above the gladiatorial arena.

The wardrobes led her to the centre of the chamber, where she saw Iris and Panda both lashed to tree trunks. There were human slaves waiting for her and they took hold of her roughly. She too was tied to one of the thick boles. The wardrobes drew back.

'I'm sorry, lovey,' Iris said.

'I don't see what you've got to apologise for,' Kelly snapped. 'It's all down to Marvelle, isn't it? It's all his fault.'

'It certainly is,' said Panda, gruffly. The bindings were so thick that his small form was just about covered up by them. His voice rose imperiously from near the sandy floor, but Kelly could hear that it was sheer bravado. He was as terrified as the two women.

'I still feel responsible for bringing you kids into this,' Iris said. 'Maybe I could have acted sooner. Got Marvelle away from Darlington somehow before you all became involved.'

'Look,' snapped Kelly. 'I don't think there's much you could have done. He's danced rings around us all, hasn't he?' She glared at Iris and, with a shock, the older woman saw that Kelly really didn't like her very much at all.

Iris fell quiet and stared into the shadowy recesses of the arena for any sign of Marvelle and his hateful poodle. Where had they gone now? She hadn't seen him since she had fallen into the wardrobe, and certainly not since she had emerged through the other side. She had woken up here, being manhandled into place by the slaves, Panda at her side.

'What did you see in the wardrobe?' Panda had asked her.

'I'm not even sure,' she had answered truthfully. 'All kinds of places, all connected somehow with this adventure of ours.'

Now she suddenly choked as she remembered a detail from her journey inside the talking wardrobe. 'Barbra! Barbra has a bomb inside her!'

'What?' cried Panda. 'How do you know that?'

'I saw… I saw inside the wardrobe… I was in her subconscious, or she was in mine… but the truth came out about what's hidden amongst her supplies…'

'Are you sure?' asked Panda.

'She knows it, too,' said Iris. 'She's suspected she's been booby-trapped for a while…'

Kelly alerted them to a new development. 'Look!'

She was staring up at the highest point they could see. The sheer walls of the cavernous room were ridged here and there with narrow shelves. On these were stationed the wardrobes themselves. They teetered and creaked menacingly.

'What are they going to do?' said Panda. 'Fall on us?'

'I don't like the look of this,' said Iris.

As they watched, several of the wardrobes were flapping open their doors like wings. The infinite darkness of their interiors appeared, disappeared. Then one took off, and another. They soared across the dark emptiness above the chamber. They swooped and dived. Then another, and another, nose-diving like tremendous, wooden birds of prey.

'We're going to be sacrificed to them…' said Kelly.

'Brace yourselves!' Iris shouted, as more and more of the things took to the air and came diving down. They plummeted playfully and turned gracefully on the air. It was almost as if they were enjoying themselves, like kestrels toying with rabbits on the soft verges of motorways. Panda was shrieking with almighty terror.

'It's all right! I've already been swallowed once!' Iris howled. 'It's a little bit confusing, but you can get used to it! Don't be scared!'

Then she saw the trim figure of Anthony Marvelle and his poodle were standing up on a ledge, watching all of this happening below. Both were laughing crazily at the spectacle.

'You!' Iris shouted. 'Where are all my diaries? How dare you go stealing my journals! Where are they?'

He hooted with mirth at this. 'You're about to be chomped into smithereens and all you really care about is the drivel you've written murmur murmur? All that miserable ninnyish stuff you've scribbled down over the years? That's all you're bothered about at the very end, Iris Wildthyme, murmur murmur?' he jeered at her.

'Yes!' she shouted. 'Where the buggery bollocks have you put my diaries?'

He shrugged. 'I don't know. I chucked them away somewhere. Clutter-free, that's me. I'm not like you murmur murmur. When I saw there was nothing of any value in the trash you'd written, I dumped the whole lot in a skip somewhere murmur murmur. Hard cheese.'

She cried out in anguish and pain, chafing at her bindings. 'I'll have you! I'll get you! I'll fettle you properly some day, Marvelle!'

'I doubt it, murmur,' he said. Then he looked at his watch. 'I suppose it's time I was off. I'll rescue the delectably peevish Kelly and go, I suppose murmur murmur.' With that, he hopped down lightly from the high shelf, and Missy came bounding after him.

'He's going to rescue you, lovey,' Iris said to Kelly. 'And leave the rest of us here to rot.'

'He needn't bother,' Kelly replied. 'I'm not going anywhere else with him.'

'Hmm,' mused Panda, watching the poet striding toward them, 'You may not have any choice about that.'

*

Through a combination of persistence and brute strength, Jenny, Simon and Barbra managed to smash their way out of their cell.

'Wow! Fancy that!' Simon gasped, as they emerged into the glass corridor. He was checking himself for cuts.

'They *let* us get out,' groaned Jenny. She was grimly checking that the Objet D'Oom was okay, tucked inside her leather coat. 'They've taken their eyes off us for the moment. They're concerned with something else just now…'

'Barbra!' Simon cried out. It seemed that in exerting herself, battering against the glass door, she had done herself some great damage. She was stooped over and her innards were making strange, clunking noises. He could hear the swish of spilled pop inside her, and all her packets of crisps had been flattened.

'Ooh, Simon,' she whispered tinnily. 'I've been such a fool. I kept quiet about it. But Iris is right. I can't keep it a secret any longer… I've put you all in very great danger…'

'What do you mean?' he asked, bending close as her voice grew fainter, and more frightened.

Jenny was over there in two impatient strides. 'What are you talking about, Barbra? What have you done?'

'I thought… I was mistaken at first. And then, I thought… well, if it turned out to be true, I might do some good, by picking my moment, you know…'

'Tell us!' thundered Jenny. 'What have you done?'

Barbra slumped against the glass wall in pain. 'While we were in that town, the first place we came to on Valcea. We stayed in that inn. And the innkeeper was telling me all about the New Gods and how he hated them. He told me about the sacrifices they demanded and how awful it was. And then he offered to stock up my insides with food and drink supplies for the journey here to the city…'

'He put a bomb inside you, didn't he?' asked Jenny. Then she swore.

Barbra looked shame-faced. 'I didn't know at the time. I should have. I should have been more alert. But, you see, I was just so pleased… to be making my first proper journey aboard Iris's bus… and to be on another world, exploring, at last…'

'How powerful is this bomb?' Simon asked.

Barbra sighed. 'Pretty bad. When I became aware of it… I tried to unhook it and have a look. But I couldn't get it. It's dug itself in, somehow. There was nothing I could do.'

Jenny was furious. 'I always knew it was a mistake letting you join MIAOW in the first place. We should have trashed you back then and cannibalised your spare parts.'

'Yes, you're probably right,' said Barbra glumly. 'But I promise, I didn't know about this till it was too late. I would never purposefully endanger any of you lot. You've been my friends…'

'Fat lot of use friendship is,' Jenny spat. 'Right. I'm off to find the others. I'm not hanging around here.'

'Jenny!' Simon yelled at her, shocked. 'Don't go! What are you doing? Barbra needs us!'

Jenny took out her black monocle in order to roll both eyes at him. 'She's going to go off with a big bloody bang, you young idiot. Get away from her! We'll all end up in flaming smithereens!'

'She's right,' Barbra sighed. 'You must get away from me.'

Simon stood in silent anguish and looked at them both. 'Is there nothing we can do to stop the bomb going off?'

'The mechanism's triggered,' said Barbra. 'It's been biding its time. But when we were pushing and shoving on the door just then – I felt it crack and give inside me. I felt the ticking intensify...'

'The clock is ticking,' said Jenny. 'I can hear it from over here. How long do we have?'

'Fifteen minutes,' Barbra said. 'I'll put the numbers on my little screen for you.'

'Oh, great,' said Jenny. 'That's really helpful. Thanks.'

'Don't be sarcastic with her!' Simon shouted. 'She's only trying to help!'

'Help!' Jenny yelled. 'What help has she ever been? She's had to be carried about and slowed down for and had everything explained to her in triplicate. She goes round offering her rubbish snacks when no one wants them, and insists on seeing things from the enemy's point of view all the time! She's a flaming liability, Simon!'

'We all are, according to you,' Simon shot back. 'Me, and Iris and Panda and Kelly. You don't really think much of any of us, do you?'

'Not really, no,' said Jenny.

'I hate to interrupt,' Barbra put in. 'But time is, erm, of the essence, kind of thing. You'd best get away.'

Simon folded his arms. 'I'm not leaving you. We're going to find a way to disarm you.'

'Yeah, well, I'm off,' said Jenny. 'I'm not hanging around a moment longer.' And then, abruptly, she was gone, taking the Objet D'Oom with her.

'I never liked her very much,' Simon said.

298

'I think she's had a lot of disappointments in life,' Barbra said. 'That's why she's like she is.' Then she eased herself up onto her castors, supporting her spine with both extended arms and looking for all the world like someone about to go into labour. 'Come on then, Simon.'

'What? Where? I thought you were about to go off with a bang…?'

'Yes, I am! But if anyone can have a go at preventing my detonation, then Iris can. You've seen how brilliant she is. She's a whiz with any kind of technology. I'd stake everything on her being able to stop this bomb going off. In fact, I'll have to.'

'Then I'm coming with you,' Simon said. 'How do we find her, though?'

'I can hear her,' said Barbra. 'Can't you?'

All he could hear was some distant, horrible cacophony, weirdly distorted inside the glass labyrinth.

'My hearing is astonishingly clear,' said Barbra. 'One of the few perks of being a vending machine is having very acute senses. And I can hear our beloved Iris yelling for all she's worth just now. Amid a whole lot of other, frankly terrifying noises. Shall we go and find her?'

Simon took her metal hand in his and glanced nervously at the red digital letters in the screen on her front. There were only a very few minutes to go.

Are we going to die? he wondered. He didn't feel scared. He felt weirdly excited. They had stuff to do. They had a rescue and an escape to accomplish. He had no time to feel scared.

Barbra did her best, perambulating as fast as she could go. She poured all of her reserves of strength into this last, rather wobbly journey through the City of Glass.

'It sounds rather like Iris and the others are being sacrificed to the New Gods,' she gasped, listening hard, and wheezing with effort. 'I can hear the most appalling sounds! Come on, Simon! Hurry!' She squeezed his hand tighter as they went.

CHAPTER THIRTY TWO

Anthony Marvelle was standing where he most loved to be. He was centre stage and shouting at everyone like a ham Shakespearean actor.

The wardrobes of the New Gods were flapping and swooping over his head. They were rather irate at the interruption, being keen to start chomping bits off their sacrificial victims.

Panda was trying his best to be brave and hoping he was small enough to escape notice. Iris was, as usual, bellowing at the top of her lungs at anyone who would listen.

'I'm telling you, Anthony Marvelle! You leave that poor girl alone! Go on, get back! Get your hands off her!'

But Marvelle was busily untying Kelly's bonds. She was torn – naturally she wanted to be free, but she didn't want to fall once again into the poet's delicate clutches. She braced herself for giving him a kicking at the first opportunity. But Missy the poodle was sitting there, bearing her fangs and growling in a way that was impossible to mistake.

'You're coming with *us* murmur murmur,' Marvelle told her.

Iris carried on shouting, 'Why don't you take me instead, eh? I can't see why you're so fixated on that girl Kelly. She's a bit of a misery anyway, that one. Look at me! I've still got plenty of life in me left. And I can still kick as high as my head, too!'

Marvelle paused and looked at her. 'What's that got to do with anything?'

'She's very agile and proud of her high kicks,' said Panda wearily.

Just then Simon and Barbra arrived in the vast arena.

'Oh, hello there!' Iris yelled at them.

The new arrivals gazed in awe at the attacking, swooping wardrobes.

'Never mind them!' Iris shouted. 'Come over here and untie us!'

Simon looked warily at the humanoid guards standing about. 'Actually, Iris, we've got another problem besides the… erm, sacrifice and stuff.'

'Yes, you have indeed, murmur murmur,' shouted Marvelle. 'I'm taking Kelly off your hands!'

'No, not just that,' said Simon. 'Barbra!'

'What's wrong with Barbra?' shouted Panda.

'Oooh dear,' gulped the vending machine, sounding thoroughly ashamed. 'I'm afraid I'm wired to explode and send this whole city sky high in… precisely eleven minutes and forty three seconds.'

Iris swore. 'Why?'

'What do you mean, *why?*' Simon yelled.

'She means, why would you want to do that?' thundered Panda.

'I don't *want* to do that,' Barbra warbled back. 'I was booby trapped by the innkeeper!'

'Simon, bring her closer over here, I'm sick of all this shouting,' cried Iris. 'Untie me at once! And Panda!'

Anthony Marvelle was narrowing his eyes. 'Explode? Blow up the whole city, murmur murmur?' He grabbed Kelly in an armlock. 'Well, never mind. Draughty, horrible old place anyway. I suggest we get on our way, Kelly dear, and Missy murmur. Where's Jenny?' He glared savagely at the others. 'What did you do with Jenny murmur *murmur?*'

'She nicked off!' shouted Simon. 'She's ran off with your precious Objet D'Oom! God knows where she's gone.'

Marvelle blanched.

'Simon, help Barbra untie me!' squawked Iris.

'Ooh, Iris, do you think you can disarm me?' Barbra cried. 'It would be wonderful if you could. I'd much rather *not* be blown to kingdom come.'

'She can do it,' said Panda gruffly. 'She can do anything, our Iris. Can't you?'

'Err, yes,' said Iris. 'Just get me untied!'

Marvelle left them to it. Time to cut his losses, he decided. He kept a firm grip on Kelly. She wriggled and cursed and he almost broke her arm. She spat at him and he laughed and murmured in her ear.

Then he looked up at the shining dome of the roof and called down the largest of the sentient wardrobes. It heard him and came flapping and creaking down rather gracefully.

It settled before him.

'Open up for me, murmur murmur.'

The doors swung apart.

'*You* are the *Dii h'anno Doors,*' Marvelle told the biggest wardrobe and all the New Gods. 'You are yourselves my shortcut across the cosmos. By stepping through you I step through the Ineffable Corridors to the very Brink and onto the sands of Hyspero. We're going there now, Kelly and Missy. We're going right now, murmur murmur, to that world on the Brink of Dark Magic murmur murmur.'

'Thank *Dog,*' said Missy, with a haughty sniff, and sunk her teeth into Kelly's arm, dragging her towards the dark open doors.

Marvelle went on, as he stepped over the threshold. 'And if you New Gods had any sense, you'd come through the *Dii h'anno Doors* after us. Get away from Valcea murmur murmur. There's no future for you here. That ludicrous vending machine's about to go off with a stupendous bang murmur murmur.'

Then he was gone. Poet, struggling girl and disgruntled poodle. They had all vanished from the face of Valcea.

The New Gods took some time to absorb this fact. They stopped their ritualistic swooping at once and turned their attention to the open doors of their leader and the pulsating darkness within.

It was a corridor, leading to the most fantastic planet in the universe. Kelly and Missy and Marvelle had already gone. They could hear the whispers and murmurs from Marvelle still hanging in the air.

'Never mind that lot!' Iris screeched, bounding free of the tree trunk and turning quickly to Barbra. 'Open up, dear – and let's see what we can do about you!'

Simon was staring at the wardrobes, flocking to cram themselves into the leader's wooden body. 'Kelly's gone...!'

Panda was pulling at the leg of his jeans. '*Pick me up!* Carry me! I think we're going to have to make a break for it at any moment...!'

Barbra was now making a much louder ticking noise. It echoed inside of all their skulls and rose above even the crashing and splintering noises of lots of wardrobes trying to fit themselves one inside another.

'Iris?' Barbra said softly. 'Can you do it?'

Iris had cleared aside the cans of pop and crisps and sundry other comestibles and was half-crawled into Barbra's interior. The whole refrigerated space was clanging with alarms and pulsating a sickly yellow greenish colour. Iris seized upon the box of eggs at the very back corner of Barbra's interior. Most of the eggs were smashed and smelly. Only one remained. Metal tentacles extended from its purple shell, fixing it firmly in place. It had grown and embedded itself into the very fabric of the vending machine.

And it was ticking fit to burst.

It looked like no device that Iris had ever seen.

'Iris?' Simon said. 'Can you do it?'

'How long have we got?' Panda asked, craning his neck to see the countdown. 'Seven minutes nine seconds! Oh no!'

Iris shuffled backwards and her face appeared, lit up by Barbra's innards. She looked devastatingly worried.

'I... *I can't do it!*'

Simon was shocked. 'Iris – you *must!* You've got to save the day... You've got to pull the plug. Come on! You've simply got to!'

She shook her head quickly. 'It's wired in too well. It's some kind of *living* bomb. An eggy thing. Something hostile, malignant and indigenous to this strange planet. It's... grown into her. It's too far gone now to disentangle. I... Barbra... I'm sorry...!'

There was a pause, filled with klaxons and mayhem.

But Barbra was very still.

'It's all right, Iris,' she said at last. 'You did your best. You *all* did your best. I can't complain. I can't complain about any of it.' The Servo-furnishing drew herself up to her full height and carefully eased her glass front closed, mustering as much dignity as she could. 'Now – you've got to run. Simon, Panda, Iris. Take my love with you. Never forget me. But please – run away! Get back aboard that bus! *Save yourselves, my darlings!*'

CHAPTER THIRTY THREE

From a certain distance it looked as if the City of Glass was melting. There were a number of brief flashes from deep within its glaucous heart. English mustard yellow, ultramarine, then a vile acidic orange. The towers lit up and seemed to shiver against the clear, Valcean skies. The sheer walls rippled and started to run…

In their mountain eerie the Glass Men – the original inhabitants of that ancient city – were struck dumb with fear. The city was to them eternal. Even though they thought they would never go back there, they were used to seeing it and knowing it was there. Now they saw the towers cracking and falling away in vast splinters into the valley below. A huge rumbling noise rolled over the mountains in waves. The Glass Men assembled and stared at the destruction.

They knew Barbra was in there. The one who had promised to come back to them.

Further away, in the village Iris and her friends had first visited, the landlord of *The Winged God* felt the shockwaves several moments after Barbra had exploded. His whole establishment was buffeted and the regulars swayed. Tankards fell to the floor and smashed. He knew at once what must have happened and he marvelled at the thought. He had done it. He had freed them all from the New Gods. His crazy plan had somehow worked.

It took some time for news of the city's demise to shudder and eddy clear across the planet. The New Gods were gone forever.

Beyond Valcea, only a few people were interested to hear of these events.

Word rippled out in various forms. News services picked it up. Tongues were wagged, legends were formed, prophecies were ticked off, tattle was tittled, statistics were added to, lists were consulted, regulations were checked, health and safety were alerted, fingers were pointed, forms were filled in minutely and history books were lavishly gone down in. But then, moments later, everything swirled gently like hot spicy tea around dissolving sugar cubes and the multiverse moved ineffably on.

On Earth the news of the Glass City's demise was picked up by one of the machines deep within the secret base under Darlington's indoor market. The city's obliteration registered as a tiny blip in the information torrenting through MIAOW's computers. Only, Magda had no idea what to make of the small blinking light that came on, somewhere near her elbow. She was too busy defending herself and her colleagues to Mida Slike, head honcho of the organisation. The end of the City of Valcea was just one more flickering blip on a console that Magda didn't know how to use.

*

On the bus: Iris at the wheel, Panda flat out on the chaise longue with his ears somewhat singed, and Simon, looking rather shocked.

All about them – the coruscating corridor of the Maelstrom, streaming violet, clementine and forest green in great waves of temporal interference.

None of them could quite believe that they had made it away from the collapsing city in time. As they regained their breath and gradually stopped shaking, they cautiously began to feel pleased at still being alive.

That final dash through the collapsing halls and passageways had been the most terrifying thing Simon had ever undergone. All around them they could hear great chunks of glass groaning and breaking free and smashing against each other. At any moment they might have been crushed or sliced or dashed to bits. All Simon could do was keep tight hold of Panda and maintain Iris within his sights as she hared into the darkness.

She knew the way to her bus. Nothing could keep her away from her means of escape.

But they had lost Jenny, the Objet D'Oom, Empress Euphemia and Anthony Marvelle, plus his nasty poodle.

They had lost Kelly to goodness knows where.

And they had lost Barbra.

In those few hideous moments of hurtling through the city, they knew that Barbra was gone. They had heard the explosion some moments ago. The city was falling down about their ears because their friend had been blown to bits and she was gone forever.

But they were able to run faster, unhampered, without her with them. Simon felt horribly guilty for even letting that thought pass through his mind as they hurtled towards safety.

But they made it. And now, here they were, flashing through the Maelstrom, away from Valcea, aboard their double decker bus.

They were quiet for perhaps thirty minutes. The reverberations settled down inside of them. A certain shell-shocked calm filled the interior of the Number 22. No one said anything. Not yet.

Then, after about three quarters of an hour, Iris popped one of her compilation tapes into the sound system. It was something horrendously inappropriate – a Seventies disco tape. Lady Marmalade came on, singing suggestively in French.

Panda picked himself up off the chaise longue and decided it was time to pull himself together. He coughed and retied his cravat. Then he tottered off to the galley kitchen. He turned back, hoping his voice would be steady, 'A nice cup of tea, everyone?' he asked gruffly. 'Or something rather stronger?'

CHAPTER THIRTY FOUR

Sometime in late November they materialised in the alley at the back of the Great Big Book Exchange.

Simon peered out of one of the windows, amazed at the frost already growing on the glass. 'We're in Darlington?'

They had taken a couple of quiet days to recover. Iris had plonked them down in a hotel that Simon had found a bit tacky, somewhere in deep space with an observation deck above something called the Golden Chasm. After a few days of availing themselves of the luxury facilities, they had landed themselves by accident in Egypt during a very nasty period and only just escaped being sealed into someone or other's tomb, having been mistaken for his servants. And now they were back in Darlington.

Simon let them into the Exchange, and found the lights still on, glowing warmly, as if he or Kelly had only just stepped out. The heating was off, however, and a pipe had burst in the flat above. It was leaking into one of the store rooms and, it turned out, it had ruined a collection of valuable pre-war comics.

'We've got to get Kelly back,' he said. 'Seeing this place only makes me feel worse.'

'We'll get her back,' Panda told him gruffly, though truth be told, he wasn't that keen on the young woman.

'We just abandoned her! Left her out there... in Space and Time!'

'Oh, don't be so melodramatic, chuck,' Iris snapped, examining one of the bookcases, and using some strange kind of device to scan the shelves. 'Aha. Particles of dust from Hyspero. It was here. This is where it was! But it's not here anymore.'

'What isn't?' asked Panda, dashing over on the polished boards and skidding slightly.

'This is where the *Aja'ib* was shelved, for many years,' said Iris. 'And now someone's taken it away. It would have been very handy for going to Hyspero.'

'That's where Marvelle has taken Kelly, isn't it?' Simon asked.

'It is,' said Iris, with a woebegone expression. 'I always said I'd never go back there. It's too... dangerous. And it's too close to the Brink. I once told myself I'd never go that close to the Brink ever again.'

'But we have to,' Simon said. 'Marvelle's still free. He's still doing what he planned to do...'

'At least he hasn't got the Objet D'Oom,' said Iris. 'If what you said is correct, Jenny still had it with her. And we don't know what became of Jenny...'

'Chances are she perished in the city as it was destroyed,' said Panda. 'There weren't very many means of escape. Just with us on the bus, and through the *Dii h'anno Doors*, with Marvelle.'

'Poor Jenny,' said Iris. 'And the Empress Euphemia, too. But...' She started pacing around, tapping her teeth with the brass and wooden instrument she'd just been using. 'If the first Empress is gone, then Marvelle is going to have a harder time of it on Hyspero. The old Empress was a crucial part of his plans to open up the Ringpull into the other universe. The Obverse.'

'So he can't do it now?' said Simon.

Iris's face fell. 'I didn't say he wouldn't be able to. Just that it'll be harder for the wily devil. He's very determined – and clever, that young man.'

312

Simon sat down at his desk at the front of the shop and glanced at the papers there. According to these, Kelly had been sitting here up until a week ago, looking after business for him.

'Oh god, I'll have to go and tell her landlady, Chelsea. She'll think Kelly's disappeared off the map.'

'That's just what she has done, lovey,' said Iris. 'But yes, you're right. We've got some loose ends to tie up here in Darlington.'

'And MIAOW too,' Panda pointed out. 'We've got to tell them about Jenny… and about poor Barbra.'

'Hmm,' said Iris. 'Quite right. There's hardly anyone left at their secret base to report to anymore…'

'And then what?' asked Simon. 'After we've tied up those loose ends? After we've informed the relevant parties about who's gone missing, who's been kidnapped and who's gone off with a flaming bang? What do we do then?'

Iris turned to him and smiled. 'Well lovey, that's when the three of us get back aboard the bus and head off again into the wide blue yonder.'

'The orange, green and purple yonder,' Panda corrected her.

CHAPTER THIRTY FIVE

Hyspero.

She was the girl who had no interest in other planets.

When Iris had seemingly offered her the chance of messing about in Space and Time, Kelly hadn't been all that fussed. It had seemed like a whole lot of danger to her. She'd rather have stayed at home and worked at the Exchange. At least you knew where you were with books.

Then Simon became involved. Then she learned just what kind of stuff had being going on under her nose in Darlington. The secret base under the indoor market, and so on. And her own boss, Terrance, was apparently mixed up in it all as well. He'd been up in space, it turned out. He'd stolen a tiny alien princess. *Twice*, someone had said. All that stuff was outrageous. Kelly was still having trouble processing it all. It was unthinkable, really.

Now Kelly felt like she had been dragged sideways into another world. A mental world all to do with the pissed-up novelist at the bar on the last night of the Writers' Festival at Darlington Arts Centre.

Ever since the night of that reading Kelly's life hadn't been her own.

And now she was here.

Roasting under a vast pink sun. Sitting on a sand dune that was almost too hot to bear. The sand was multi-coloured, like cocktail sugar.

And her only company was Anthony Marvelle, the famous poet, who was striding about the place, trying to find a dune tall enough so he could stand on top of it to see the lay of the land.

Oh, and he had that nasty poodle with him, of course. Kelly would need a tetanus for the bite Missy had given her, just before they entered the *Dii h'anno Doors*. That's if she ever got home in order to see her GP. And that's if her GP could counteract whatever kind of canine space sickness might now be swarming in her blood stream.

Blooming poodles. Flaming poets.

Oh yes, and what she hadn't yet told Simon, because she was too ashamed? She *had*, in fact, slept with Marvelle, the very night of Chelsea's party. He was a frantically successful seducer, murmur murmur and Kelly wanted to die every time she thought of her shame, that night in Marvelle's arms at the Duke's Legs hotel.

Marvelle had reeled her in. And here she was. In space with him. On the mysterious planet of Hyspero, an unimaginable distance from home.

He came trotting back to her across the multi-coloured sand, Missy at his heels.

'I've found the way murmur murmur,' he said. How could he look so neat and dapper, even here in the heat of an alien desert?

Kelly just nodded. She wasn't really speaking to him.

She trudged after him the rest of that day. Scorching her feet off, choking with thirst.

Had Simon and the others escaped from the city? It seemed like another lifetime ago, those final moments on Valcea. Perhaps they had dashed into the wardrobe too, and made their way here… down that dark and glittering corridor? But then, would Iris *really* have left her precious double decker bus behind? Kelly couldn't imagine that. The old woman would rather risk all their lives, than be separated permanently from the Number 22.

And had Barbra really exploded?

They might all be dead. They might all be dust strewn across an alien world by now.

But Kelly was far in the future, here on Hyspero. Marvelle had tersely explained that already. Millions of years into her own future. So – everyone she had ever known was just specks of dust on alien worlds by now.

They walked and walked that day.

Then came foothills and a small oasis, so they could drink fresh water and nibble some peculiar blue fruit.

'Blue fruit,' said Marvelle, trying to cheer her. 'That's when you really know you're in space, isn't it murmur murmur? When you get blue fruit?'

They walked on and the foothills became mountains. The mountains were orange and red... the colours of spices. The ground up spices that the Exchange had always somehow smelled of. She felt a great weary nostalgia for the bookshop welling up in her belly.

They came at last to a monument.

'Goodness me murmur murmur!' sighed Anthony Marvelle. '*She's* a big girl, isn't she murmur murmur?'

Kelly stared up at the massive edifice. It was carved out of the blood red rock. A face. A monstrous face. Grinning madly at the gigantic sun.

The face of Iris Wildthyme. Some twenty storeys tall.

'She's certainly left her mark on this place murmur murmur,' said Marvelle quietly. Kelly looked at him and for the first time saw him unnerved. He was out of his depth, she realised – just the same as she herself was. It was his first time on this strange, distant planet, too. And he was planning to do awful things here, wasn't he? That was what Iris had claimed. She had intended to stop him, no matter what.

Kelly found herself fiercely hoping that her friends *had* survived.

They had, of course they had.

And they'd be coming here. Surely. Sometime soon. They could never leave her in this madman's clutches.

The poodle howled. Marvelle stared up the giant nostrils of Iris Wildthyme in a wild surmise.

And all three of them wondered what might happen next.

CHAPTER THIRTY SIX

Jenny watched them go.

They were a bit hasty, she thought. Abandoning one of their friends like that.

But they had dithered and hung on for as long as they thought they could, evidently. Iris had had her head inside Barbra for some minutes, trying desperately to save her. Then Barbra had shouted at them in that high-pitched synthetic wheedling voice of hers. The voice that had grated on Jenny's nerves so often in the MIAOW base under Darlington.

So then, reluctantly, they turned and ran as fast as they could.

And Jenny watched them go.

The whole chamber was shaking and wailing with noise. The last of the living wardrobes was battering itself against the opened doors of its leader, trying to escape the Glass City in these final few precious seconds. Splinters were flying everywhere in the general panic.

Jenny clung to her hiding place in the rocks and watched Iris and her friends give up and go. They took heed of the vending machine's final, warbled words. They'd done everything they could to save her.

That was something. Jenny took note of that. They'd really tried to save her. Iris had really tried – and she looked appalled that she had failed.

The scenario was a familiar one to Jenny, in many ways. She had been present at the nerve-shredding ultimate moments of many adventures with Iris back in the old days. Somehow they had always managed to escape by the skin of their teeth.

Jenny had preferred the more orderly, regulated life of a MIAOW agent, with its form-filling, ruthless transparency and reliable pension plan. Iris's brand of racketing about was much too wayward for her.

And yet here she was – watching her friends turning to flee for the bus. She herself was clutching under her coat a glass jar containing an alien Empress and she was agonizing over what to do next.

She squinted to read the countdown on Barbra's LCD display, some thirty feet away. Three minutes now. Barbra had stopped warbling bravely after her friends. She had stopped exhorting them to save themselves and go.

They had gone.

Jenny could run after them. She knew she could easily run after her friends and join them on the bus. She could go with them and escape in the nick of time.

But for some reason she didn't.

A dry, rasping voice spoke to her above all the noise in that chamber. It was the regal voice of Euphemia, speaking from within the jar.

'Your destiny is elsewhere, my dear,' she said. 'Not for you escape on the bus. Not for you a quick return to Darlington.'

'Then what?' cried Jenny, above the wailing of klaxons and the howling of the time winds through the opened wardrobe doors. She noted with alarm that the leader of the wardrobes was trying to twist himself inside out in order to escape. He was like a great wooden pretzel, thwarted, anguished, rattling his wire coat hangers till they jangled. The noise was horrendous.

'Remember what I said about the girl Kelly,' said the Empress. She sounded quite calm and measured, as if she hadn't clocked that they had less than three minutes left. 'I told you that you weren't allowed to let her get to Hyspero. You were to use any means necessary in order to stop Anthony Marvelle taking her there.'

'Yes, but...'

'And you failed, Jenny,' Euphemia stormed at her. 'They're on their way to Hyspero even as we speak. They're probably there already, causing untold damage. And so...' Jenny could sense the tiny Empress rallying and readying herself for action. 'And so we have to get our skates on, my dear. I don't know about you, but I'm simply not waiting around here to be detonated by a vending machine called Barbra.'

Jenny was clenching her hands nervously inside her leather coat's pockets. To her astonishment one of them suddenly clasped her black monocle, which had been hidden away in the lining. She gasped and tugged it out, putting it back into her eye immediately. It was a kind of talisman and she felt her strength and moral fibre ebbing back into her at once. 'What do you want to do? Jump through that wardrobe thing after the others?'

The Empress acceded graciously. 'But we have a full two minutes first,' she pointed out. 'Take me to Barbra.'

Jenny did as she was told.

She hurried across the shaking glass floor and gave Barbra a terrible fright.

'Jenny!' the vending machine cried. 'You need to get out of here! I'm about to *go off!* Get yourself after Iris and the others...!'

Jenny shook her head. 'I can't.'

'What?' Barbra gasped. She stared in amazement as Jenny produced the Objet D'Oom from inside her coat. The gloopy contents of the jar shone stickily in the light from Barbra's overactive innards. 'But... you've got to save yourself! MIAOW needs you!'

'It needs you too,' said Jenny, twisting off the lid of the jar.

'Really?' said Barbra. 'But I thought you said I was a liability…'

'Sssh,' said Jenny, as the Empress Euphemia appeared once again, this time in an emerald frock, looking for all the world like an ancient Tinkerbell, dancing nimbly across her palm. 'Open your front up, Barbra.'

'I'm a dab hand with dismantling bombs,' said the Empress grandly. 'Royalty on Hyspero have to be, you see.'

'B-but,' said Barbra, easing open her quivering glass door. 'Iris has already tried to defuse me. Surely, if *she* can't, then no one can…'

'Ah,' said the Empress, hopping lightly from Jenny's hand into Barbra's chaotic insides. 'Well, you see, Iris hasn't got delicate, feminine, tiny, nimble fingers like mine, has she?'

As Euphemia vanished inside the vending machine, Barbra and Jenny stared into each other's faces – and the seconds ticked by.

Sweat was streaming down Jenny's face and she tried not to look at the helpful countdown.

I could have been away by now, she thought. I could have saved myself.

But instead I am here. With the green fairy and exploding Barbra. But there must be a reason for it. This must all be meant. We're needed somehow…

I used to be an existentialist, she thought. I never used to believe in stuff like this. Fate and destiny and things all happening for a flaming reason. What's happened to me in recent weeks?

'Thank you for trying, Jenny,' Barbra whispered. Jenny could hardly hear her words for all the shattering noise coming out of her. 'It's ever so good of you. But there's only about a minute left.'

322

Twelve seconds later a flushed-looking Empress emerged, holding a purple egg. It trailed bleeding, organic tendrils after it and it was still about to explode, she screeched.

'But you've managed to get it out of me!' Barbra squealed.

'I had to bite through the last few cords,' said the Empress. 'I hope I didn't hurt you?'

But Barbra didn't care. She was saved!

'Give me that,' Jenny told the Empress, and took the pulsating egg out of her arms. The Empress was shaking with the exertion of ripping the bomb out of Barbra's heart.

Now it was Jenny's turn. She took hold of the device and hurled it as hard as she could into the shadowy recesses of the City of Glass.

Barbra and the Empress whooped with joy.

'Twenty eight seconds!' added Barbra.

The Empress hurried herself back into gelid contents of the Objet D'Oom with a satisfying squelching noise. Before she submerged herself completely she instructed Jenny in her grandest voice, 'My dear, take us through the Dii h'anno Doors! Poste haste!'

Jenny didn't need telling twice. She sealed the lid on the Empress's jar, and helped Barbra close her front door properly. Then she hurriedly assisted the vending machine over to the last remaining wardrobe in the City of Glass.

He boomed at them: 'You are going to follow the others to Hyspero, are you?'

'Let us through!' demanded Jenny.

'I have let them all through,' sighed the last of the New Gods. 'I myself am the doorway to the other side of the universe. But half of me must stay here and perish. I can't save myself.'

'I-I'm sorry to hear that,' Barbra told him. 'But, er, you will let us pass, won't you?'

The wardrobe drew himself up to his full impressive height. 'I will, Barbra. And I am glad you have survived, despite everything. I think you will be needed, somehow, on the next phase of this adventure.'

Jenny swore. 'Look, do we have to have a song and dance about everything? Can we just go before this place goes sky-high?'

And so Barbra and Jenny stepped through the wooden doors.

Bang on time, as it happened.

As they sped through the bewildering corridors that would take them to Hyspero, they felt the buffeting aftershock of Valcea's destruction. There was a blast of heat and light, which illuminated for a brief instant the weird tunnel down which they were floating. The sudden flash showed that there were some pretty strange pictures on the walls, and some peculiar objects floating down the corridor with them.

'We've made it,' sang Barbra excitedly. 'We've made it!!'

*

They napped for a while and found that they carried on floating down the corridors. They streamed along quite easily, not having to exert themselves at all. Jenny felt herself relaxing for the first time in weeks.

She had no idea how long the journey lasted. They didn't see anyone else on the way, apart from a few slow-moving wardrobes. Some of them had been damaged as they had made their escape through the Dii h'anno Doors. They never said a word to Jenny and Barbra, or even acknowledged their existence. It was as if they never had been deadly adversaries back in the City of Glass.

Mostly the journey was quiet, apart from when Barbra decided to pass the time by telling Jenny a bit more about her previous adventures on space stations and robot cities, and so on. Jenny could have done with a bit less backstory, frankly. She was dead on her feet and not quite convinced yet that they hadn't been burned to a frazzle in the explosion. She needed time to come to terms with the concept of her continuing existence.

Not so the vending machine. Barbra was swimming along happily, chuntering away, unfazed by her miraculous escape. At one point she hoiked out one of her last remaining cans of pop and bags of crisps and Jenny – starving by now – had to graciously accept them.

Then, at last, there was a door at the other end.

The corridor finished abruptly. It petered out like an escalator and the two survivors nudged and bumped against the wooden door in the darkness. 'Oh!' gasped Barbra, who had been semi-closed down at that moment.

Jenny grasped the brass doorknob and twisted it firmly. 'I think... I think this is it.'

The door at the end of the corridor swung open with surprising ease.

Golden sunlight poured through it. For those first few seconds the two ladies felt drenched in light. It flooded through them like a great golden tide and they gloried in it, blinking and laughing and throwing up their hands to shield their tender eyes.

They stepped out into all that light and felt the darkness of the transdimensional corridor receding at their backs. The wooden door slammed shut and Jenny turned to see it was just an innocuous blue door set into a brick wall behind them.

'We're here,' said Barbra, stamping on the rough sandy ground. 'We've arrived...somewhere.'

Jenny nodded, still grinning like a loon. She looked up and saw that they were in an alleyway. Rough stone walls hemmed them in, rising as high as she could see. The sun was directly overhead and it lavished its light upon them. Already she felt over-warm in her leather jacket. She took out her monocle, shook it, and it turned itself obligingly into a pair of shades.

There was noise coming at them from every angle. Jangling, clattering, murmurous noise. Barbra was already shunting along and ambling down the passageway, away from the door, eager to see the source of the genial hubbub.

Beyond, there was a marketplace. A thousand covered stalls teemed and thronged with a crowd of midday shoppers. A profusion of colours and smells and sensations confronted the two bewildered travellers. They saw fish and fruit, washing machines and gramophones, servants and goblins, shark people and antelopes, porcupines, bread loaves and rotund cheeses, flagons of beer, bottles of wine, sides of beef, Christmas trees, rubber plants, crystal balls, magic carpets, sprays of dried herbs and grasses and outrageous, flaunting flowers, books of spells and atlases, jars of honey and spices, bats and frogs, chariots and writing desks, sausages, sofas and grandfather clocks, brass lamps, answerphones, ballet shoes, moonboots, puppets and dolls, sleighbells and sledges, puzzle boxes, shrieking songbirds, super computers, rolled up maps, haversacks, anoraks, jellyfish, jewels, crumpets and camisoles.

'Well, it's a bit better than Darlington market,' said Barbra.

'I think this must be Hyspero,' Jenny said, taking off her jacket and folding it carefully, in order to protect the Empress hidden within its pockets. You're home, little Empress, she thought inside her head. But the Empress Euphemia was quiet, just now. Jenny thought she could sense her quiet satisfaction, however, at having made it right back across the galaxy.

Barbra started ambling down a boulevard of silken curtains in every hue. She passed a robot or two of exotic design – one of whom was built to look something like a shopping trolley.

Something about the heady, exotic, roasting hot atmosphere made Barbra feel more buoyant. It was probably doing her coolant tubes no end of good, being here.

Just as Jenny started getting insistent and saying that they should stop wandering at will and they needed some kind of plan – the thought struck Barbra that what she needed to do was replenish her stores inside her. Here she was at the start of a new adventure and her insides had been almost completely cleared out.

They turned a corner and found a stall that – miraculously – was selling crisps and pop in industrial quantities. The turbaned man serving looked delighted to be selling his wares to one of the legendary Servo-furnishings. 'I thought you were all extinct!' he cried, slapping Barbra on the sturdy back.

'We nearly were,' Barbra told him.

Jenny rolled her eyes. She was beginning to wonder how soon before she tired of the company of this garrulous robot.

'Funny thing,' said the man at the stall. 'I've just sold several boxes of prawn cocktail crisps, and some pickled onion flavour too, and a case or two of fizzy orange pop to another party of folk going off on an adventure. Just last night it was.'

'Oh, yes?' said Barbra, sounding interested. She cast a sidelong glance at Jenny, who was rolling her eyes and clearly keen to be gone.

'Yes, we were just nattering, as you do,' said the stallholder. 'And these people – nice young man, it was, talking to me – they were stocking up for an adventure they were going on today, and they said they were pleased I stocked these rare Terran delicacies because they reminded them of a friend of theirs… a long-lost friend…'

Barbra felt a sudden leap in her tin heart and her coolant tubes gushed with sudden hope. 'What? Who? Where? Where are these people? When was this..?

The stallholder chuckled at her sudden excitement. 'Well, it was only last night. Not long at all. They can't have gone far… They were going to set off today…' He frowned and thought. 'Yes, they did say they were nearby, because they wanted the delivery made to their vehicle…' He fished around in his apron pocket and produced a scribbled note. 'Yes, yes, their temporary address… they gave me this…'

Jenny reached forward and snatched the note from his hand, rather roughly, Barbra thought. 'Are you thinking what I am?' she asked Barbra.

Barbra nodded.

And then they were running – as fast as Barbra could – down a number of those anonymous sidestreets and tunnels of rough sandstone that criss-crossed the centre of the city. They craned their necks to see street names and asked passersby how they might find the address on the crumpled paper.

Ess'chaang Street. The Alley of Ancient Volumes.

They hurried and got lost and turned corners and winded themselves in their increasingly frantic search.

'Oh, we'll never find it…' gasped Barbra.

'It's a false hope, a red herring,' said Jenny. 'We're clutching at straws. We're being silly, aren't we?'

'Even if it *was* them, they might be gone by now..!'

Then all at once they turned a corner into a shadier street. Awnings were up in front of bookshops that were dark with almost underwater gloom. Green shadows steeped the place in a refreshing calm and cool. This was it: Ess'chaang Street, the sign before them announced.

And…!

There was the double decker bus waiting for them. Dusty and beaten up and with another of its windows smashed and all of its chintzy curtains pulled. The Number 22 was waiting for them, just as they had hoped.

In two strides Jenny was over there, pounding on the concertinaed doors. 'Open up! We're here!'

A raucous voice replied from within. 'All right! All right! I'm coming! Keep your hair on, lovey! What is this? A police raid?'

The doors flew open and there she stood. Iris was in her dressing gown and slippers. A cigarette was hanging from her mouth as it dropped open at the sight of her traffic warden friend. She swore loudly. So loudly that Panda and Simon both came running, pulling on their own dressing gowns and blinking at the brightness of the street outside.

'Jenny!' Iris shouted at last. 'You're here! You escaped from Valcea! You made it all the way here, chuck!'

Jenny allowed herself to be enfolded in a bear hug by Iris, not even minding the cigarette smoke streaming into her eyes. She laughed and found herself tearing up. 'I did! I made it, Iris! We've found you!'

'Eeeh, lovey,' Iris grinned, holding hard onto her shoulders.

'I don't believe it,' Panda gasped. 'I never thought I'd be so glad to see a traffic warden!'

Jenny laughed. 'And that's not all, either,' she said. Then she drew aside to show them who was ambling across the sandy street towards them.

Simon saw her first and cried out in shock.

Then Iris and Panda did likewise.

Barbra was looking hopeful and pleased. She had even taken a moment to polish her glass front before coming over to be reunited with her friends. Now she shunted and whirred and

clicked and clunked across the alleyway into their waiting embrace.

Everyone was shouting and laughing at the same time. No one could make out for a few moments what anyone else was saying. But it didn't matter.

For now, they had plenty of time to catch up.